Dream On

Parthian, Cardigan SA43 1ED
www.parthianbooks.com
First published in 2013
This edition published 2014.
© Dai Smith 2013
ISBN 9781909844711
Cover by Marc Jennings
Typeset by Elaine Sharples
Printed and bound by Gomer
Published with the financial support of the Welsh Books Council
British Library Cataloguing in Publication Data
A cataloguing record for this book is available from the British Library.

Dream On

Dai Smith

PARTHIAN

In dreams I walk with you
In dreams I talk to you
In dreams you're mine, all of the time
We're together in dreams
In dreams

* * * * *

Only in dreams
(It only happens in dreams)
In beautiful dreams

Roy Orbison "In Dreams" 1963

Obit. Page

Obituaries had been commissioned. Some had even been written, and filed. An admirer had sent him one, updated to take account of his soon-expected death. He held it in his hands, and shrugged as he read it over again. Not for its accuracy – it was accurate enough as these things went – but for its banality, and not of the prose but of the life, his own, which it so scrupulously recorded. It even had a headline on the typescript, though doubtless the eventual newspaper would economise on that. It read: "A Life in Politics: A Politic Life".

He could feel, with an immediacy he no longer expected to hurt, the pain of the omission of the definer he would have wanted. It should have been, of course it should, "A Political Life." Two missing letters, and an epithet that damned rather than lauded. Well, that was how he felt about it. Others, accordingly, saw it differently, welcomed the judicious balance of the adjective they felt to be, even in political terms, the better one. Certainly, like his life, the more politic one.

It would make a half-page spread in the national broadsheets. Decent enough, and with a photograph, one of the early ones with his hair fashionably long, and perhaps his fist raised in mid-80s anger, one of the action shots Billy Maddox had taken during the Miners' Strike. Or perhaps that would not be politic enough. There was the usual Obit. Opening to set the scene:

> A political career that opened with much promise ended,
> if not with major practical achievements undertaken in

office, then with superlative accomplishments recorded in his chosen literary forms: the essay and the biographical study.

How easily, though, it all read like someone else's life. Anyone else's life in its inability to evoke anything more than dates and offices held and ideas proposed. Most of the barebone facts were tabulated in a detached endnote.

Born in 1944. School in the Valley and then in Birmingham from 1956 when his father gained a Headship.

Oxford, and then that surprising nomination for the Party when local squabbles and factions let a young, dark-horse but native-born, academic through a crowded field and on to election in 1970. The rest, looking back on it forty years later, was a blur. Junior office at Trade and promotion in Defence when the Party came to power and the despond years that followed that first promising decade. He considered that he had been happy despite the waiting-room feel of the politics themselves, and despite, too, being overtaken and quickly sidelined by others more ruthless than him, when a return to government eventually came. He had led a life free from Westminster's too frequent family mishaps and his books and pamphlets and biographies had been carefully chiselled and respectfully received, even in the academia he had deserted, for the insights which his political practice had brought to them. On the Obit. page they were duly listed and respectfully weighed. It was for what, he reflected, he would be best remembered.

There had been such a lot of downtime in Westminster. Time to think as well as to write. The fashion had been for hefty double-decker biographies, story-time narratives with the happy endings

2

of definitive footnotes or, at least, fulsome acknowledgements and learned bibliographies. Jenkins on Asquith. Foot on Bevan. Always the Leaders. Never the Led. History, he considered increasingly, as it was sieved not how it had been lived. Instead he listened to Voices Off. He talked to those who Also Served. He contemplated a Culture for a Society. Over the years a trilogy of studies emerged. He turned to the Obit. proof to check if it had expressed more than a titular sense of them:

His first book, *Vox Pop: A Vocal Culture* (1981), was an examination of the rhetoric and oratory of industrial South Wales – its excess, some in his Party were already concluding – through speech, accent, gesture and effect, but it slipped, intriguingly and often infuriatingly, into riffs on singing, choral and solo, onto disquisitions on humour on stage and in literature, through the roar of crowd behaviour to the antiphony of reserved silence in reading rooms and the cacophony of saloon bars. It met with a mixed reception but won a Welsh Arts Council Prize. Out of office and buffeted by the internal strife of the Foot and Kinnock years – he was a steadfast supporter of both – he wrote the biographical sketches published in book form as *Acolytes and Assassins* (1988). Here the intention, not always successfully achieved, was to throw light on major political or union careers by illuminating those who waited in the shadows, ready to assist or, as his provocative title indicated, to assassinate. So, instead of, say a portrait of that Colossus, Nye Bevan, we had a brilliant sketch of his Famulus, Bevan's fixer and confidante, the diminutive and destructive (of others) Archie Lush. The spotlight was turned, for the once powerful Communist Party, not on the ebullient and engaging Arthur Horner, President of the South Wales

3

Miners' Federation in 1936, but on the apparatchiks who always placed Party diktat before proletarian DNA. Then he swung to the right to put the egregious George Thomas, the ludicrously self-christened Viscount Tonypandy, in his sights: "of this Tartuffe, a study in sentiment and narcissism, let us say the Sunday School superintendent was always more cross bencher than cross dresser for in this, too, he had the courage of every conviction but his own." Many found the acid of such "truth-telling", if that is what it was, too scalding an element for their own political health at the hustings. Even his obituary of Will Paynter, that tough intellectualised comrade who had succeeded his own mentor, Horner, as General Secretary of the NUM in 1959, had not resisted the temptation to speculate on exactly what a CP political commissar would have done in Spain in 1937. At the fever-point pitch of the Miners' Strike this had not pleased the cheerleaders of 1984. Yet, in his final foray into this field, after Tony Blair had overlooked him for any kind of office in 1997, he wrote lightly and sunnily of those whom he had directly served for thirty years. *Epiphanies* appeared to muted acclaim in 2001, but we can now see it bears a classic status. Here, "The Terraces", as he calls them, echoing the writer Gwyn Thomas, are laid before us as a landscape, one humanly fabricated and artfully framed by and for a people who had, he claims, once created a past fit for whatever future they might inhabit. How does he do this? By a set of interlocking cameos that take us from "The Value of Allotments: The Alloting of Values" to "The Cooked Dinner: Civilisation after the Club" and "Standing not Sitting: Philosophy on the Bob Bank". All linear lines and flat planes were rejected by this prismatic writing, a form that gave a crystalline light and a receding depth to the pastimes and dreams, but ones lived and relished, of a people he clearly feared were being bypassed by a more brutalist history and that history's political helpmeets, even those from within the ranks of Labour.

He let the obituary he would not live to see in print slip from his fingers onto the duvet. Not quite what he had meant his writing to say. But close enough, and praising enough, not to be begrudged. He resolved, again, to stop being grudging. It was, none of it was, anybody's fault. Not even his own. He would, without a grudge, accept the praise and accolades it helped them to give him. Particularly the family he had nurtured, and had, he knew, despite all, neglected more than he would have wished. They didn't seem to notice; perhaps they didn't feel it. He didn't know. They didn't say.

His son, who had developed an irksome habit of patting his hand as he sat propped up in bed so that he might look out of the picture window and over the Valley, kept telling him what "A Great Life" he'd had and how he would "not be forgotten". He smiled and nodded, politic as ever, even managing a whispery "Thank you, love" when his daughter, on the other side of the bed, reminded him how much he was "Loved by Everybody". It was true, he thought, that his wife whom he'd met at Oxford had, in her own patrician way, "loved" him and he'd sorrowed over her early death in the car smash she'd had with her parents when on holiday in Italy. He'd stayed home that summer on constituency work, intending to join them later. She had never felt "At Home" in the Valley and had never hidden her disdain, her fear perhaps, of its inhabitants. Ironically, the sympathy he garnered with the death of the woman his supporters had privately called "The Duchess" strengthened his control of the local party. He steered a middle course and, by the end, this end as he might now put it, he was consulted on all sides for his political nous, his historical grip and his experienced counsel. Oh, and for the colour copy his reminiscence of the Party's greats gave to journalists. He was restored. One of them. One of us. Ours.

Yet none of this was why he had come back for selection. And stayed as the elected member. He could barely explain it to himself sometimes. Yet he knew that there had been deep inside him political idealism, and an allied will to serve. He knew this to be true of himself even then. In his father's telling, the people of the Valley, his Valley, from which he had been wrenched so young, were mythic, generation by generation, and heroic, deed by deed. If it was an absurd generalisation, it was also vividly true. It had been bred into his political bone and so vitally that he had, and did always, feel it an honour to be elected to serve. But it was not that particular igniting spark which still flickered inside, and did not die even if he was dying and she was long gone. His thoughts were a junction box of random signals. Perhaps it was the morphine. Perhaps it was a dream. He half-smiled, ruefully, remembering a train journey he'd taken across country, to the west and some political function or other, just before the cancer had struck, less than a year ago. He had looked up at the information streamed up in electronic tickertape capitals at the end of the carriage, like a miniature mobile Times Square, he'd thought, as it ticked off the station stops to come, and what precautions you needed to take on arriving and alighting. Alighting. What a pompous, no pretentious, word. He had said it to himself, almost aloud, and, bored as dusk draped the crawling train, had looked up again at the flashcard red letters of information flowing left to right in their rectangular black box. Only this last time, the electrical charges had malfunctioned, had dropped letters and left spaces, and displayed, as the train pulled into the platform, in an illuminated reiteration of desire and warning, one he knew he had to heed:

personal be   take their
longings   with you   personal be
    take   their   longings   with you

* * * * *

He had been twelve years old, sat on one of the back seats of the upstairs of a municipal double-decker bus. The bus, one of a fleet, swayed up the Valley from the grammar school, dropping pupils off at each of the straggling townships it touched. Every seat was taken. Downstairs, two or three prefects pretended to keep order, and everywhere there was noise and the deep, damp smell of sodden wool and the wet leather of satchels. Outside it rained as it seemed only to rain here. Swathes of wind-blown rain ballooning down from the mountains which hemmed them in and funnelled the rain into the streets. Rain tamping down onto the pavements. Rain bouncing off the roof of the bus and smacking against the window panes which steamed up inside, and outside turned the raindrops into never-ending rivulets which streamed drop by beaded drop into silvery snail trains. It was a cold rain. It swept in from the open platform at the back of the bus and carried its damp aftershock upstairs and into the soaked moquette seats. The caps of the boys and their black gabardine raincoats were heavy with rain and the girls, barelegged and hatless, shivered in their pixie-hooded lovat-green mackintoshes. He had looked out of the window where, even at four o'clock, the lights were on in the shop windows and the few cars there were about stared back, with their headlamps unblinking warnings, out of the gloom. He had never felt more at one with everything. This was where he was and should always be.

One of the prefects, in the casual sports coats they were allowed to wear in the Sixth Form in place of their blazered uniform, came rattling up the iron-rimmed stairs and stood at the top. At the bottom was another prefect. The one at the top said, "Right, now. One. Two. Three", and waved his arms whilst the one at the bottom began to sing. Then the whole bus, from top to bottom, began to sing, and some stood in the aisles as the bus seemed to half topple around a bend and up and over a steep hill, and some fell onto one another, satchels and caps scattering, laughing and singing and stamping all at the same time, singing, never happier, the Blues that they would never feel more, and as if this moment could be held, forever.

And he looked to the back of the bus, all singing the lyric and shouting the refrain, and he saw the girl, his age, sitting, not singing, on the long seat across the aisle, at the back of the bus, and he saw her wet, plastered, black gloss of hair cut to frame her face with its shining eyes above her wet and reddened cheeks and as he did, stopping to sing the song that still rang all around him, unsmiling she looked straight back at him.

That was why, he knew, he had come back, and why he stayed and why, never known or spoken to or seen again, she would always be there. And there she would remain, loved and unknown, so long as hearts could still tell minds that they had "never felt more".

Never Felt More

Well, I never felt more like singin' the blues
'cause I never thought that I'd ever lose
Your love, dear, why'd you do me this way?
Well, I never felt more like cryin' all night
'cause everythin's wrong, and nothin' ain't right
Without you, you got me singin' the blues.

The moon and stars no longer shine
The dream is gone I thought was mine
There's nothin' left for me to do
But cry-y-y-y over you (cry over you)
Well, I never felt more like runnin' away
But why should I go 'cause I couldn't stay
Without you, you got me singin' the blues.

In 1956 Guy Mitchell was at Number
One in the hit parade for ten
consecutive weeks with "Singin' the
Blues".

A Life of Riley

She was born in the cottage hospital within a few hours of my own birth there at the very end of the Second World War. Or World War Two, as we quickly said so matter-of-factly, as if a Third was just around the corner. Terrible as it was to have already had two in the space of four decades, or two generations, there was an odd comfort in being able to enumerate them. We were domesticating the beasts by numbering them in turn. I say "We" because that is how we referred to ourselves, whether individually or together. The last, or current war, did not, of course, encompass directly our junior part in all this as the children of the "We". Not in terms of the conflict, at least, but inescapably as the generational fall-out of wars that were fought and endured, home and abroad, by parents and grandparents. Children can be victims even if they are not killed or wounded. Perhaps we were maimed inside. Certainly hurt in ways not wholly imaginable since. And as Number Three never came along in the manner we once envisaged, we, the protected and saved ones, were also the first-in-line in all other ways. I mean that our absorption of passing life as we grew was constantly affected, in tone and perspective, by the otherness of the connected lives of all those senior and antecedent to us. By their treatment of us, sweet and threatening, private and public, turn and turnabout. By their stories. By their moods. By their scars. By their dreams. What we knew inwardly was more than what we saw. And what we saw was invariably damage. Amongst the ruins of such lives we all danced.

So what I saw, but without knowing, when I knew her in the first, and only, decade of our life together, was a life which I would come to learn was shaped by more than the local circumstances and time of her birth. I could not know that then. I was also a child, and so a victim. The mode of a victim is silence and a child's voice is prattle. The eyes are a different thing though. What I know now as I think back over that childhood is that our lives were formed less by the endlessly fresh discoveries of one thing after another which children must make, and much more by having to absorb, without apparent resistance, the dead weight of lives soaked in their own unwanted experience. Lives which had led to us. We would be spared war but not the consequences of war. That single fact permeated and tethered our lives.

* * * * *

The day Theresa Riley and I were born, our fathers were still in action across the Rhine. It was the least hazardous river crossing they had had to make since they had dog-fought on from the Normandy beachheads the previous June. Or so my father told me. They were, with the war's final outcome in sight, due for leave, but denied it, until the simultaneous event of our births and a lull in the last push of the British Army had moved them up the queue. They were both bombardiers, made up lance corporals in the Royal Artillery, enlisted in the same regiment and thereafter drawn together more by the war, and its myriad unwanted ties, into an acknowledged friendship, than by any prior fact of being near-neighbours in their terraced row houses before the war had plucked them out of the Valley. It was, in a grim paradox, the War that had made them into friends, for they had little else in common before that. Neither occupation nor religion nor politics nor pursuits nor nationality united them.

They lived where they did and they did what they did because both had married women from the Valley, and were so drawn by marriage into lives which neither might have quite envisaged or wanted, for sure. They were drawn back or into our orbit. It was our orbit without any qualification because we who were born there had no other in our early life, nor wanted any other in those cosseted post-war days. Not that this was ever entirely true of Theresa.

Our fathers had travelled together to the Valley by train from Portsmouth after shipping back from the continent they had, as those jovial newsreels put it, helped liberate. Whatever was familiar and welcoming after so long a time away, even the frequency with which pubs punctuated the main road up the Valley, would not have delayed or hindered them as they marched in step and in uniform to the hospital set in isolation, above the river and the houses and the collieries, in a wooded grove on an otherwise denuded hill. Theresa and I were to be the first home-grown fruit of their personal liberation. I was my father's first child and would be named Gareth after him, and Idwal after his father, a North Walian. I would only know my Grancha from a solitary beside-the-seaside snap of him and Jane, his equally long-dead wife. My father had met Doreen, my mother, when he'd found work in the thirties as a baker's roundsman in Wembley, and she was "in service" in West London. The war had sent them home, though my father had vowed never to work in the pits again, as he had once done in his youth. He kept his word on that, but only after the war. She waited for him through the war in the house where she'd been born, the only thing of any worth which her parents could leave to her, as they duly did.

Theresa was named after a saint, and was the third child and first daughter of Buddug Riley née Bowen. She had met Brian Riley, her Irish husband, when he turned up in the wintertime of 1935 with the travelling fair of whirling rides and hoopla stalls which pitched up in the Valleys' townships over Christmas and the New Year. Brian Riley fixed things. He painted things. He dismantled things. He moved things. He erected things and, at night, slightly built but sinewy strong he pushed and pulled the dodgem cars, everyone's favourite and squeal-guaranteed ride, in and out of line. It was the nearest we came to glamour amongst the eye-watering smart and chest-catching stench of cheap petrol fumes and the crack of air rifles or the thud of feathered darts as collier boys sought to win prizes of pink or blue chalk figurines of stalking polar bears for their cwtched-in girlfriends. One such was the nineteen-year-old Buddug Bowen, who caught the eye of dark-haired Brian Riley, and moved away from the familiar. She mistook his self-containment for some other depth, perhaps, and the wandering twenty-five-year-old fairground roustabout maybe saw a fleeting innocence of form in the girl who liked to flirt. All I can say for brute certainty is that when eighteen years later I first knew her to look at her, what had won Brian Riley over to stay was not readily apparent in the dumpy shape of the woman perpetually in the pinafore smock worn over her dress, or in the pudginess of a face permanently dented by the smouldering tube of a half-smoked cigarette from which she would light its immediate successor from her apron pocket. And yet, when she danced, and she did that in the street, alone or in the arms of one of her sons, and when she drank, as she did from flagons of beer or cider just tipped back, laughing as she sat on her front garden wall, then she was, in her motion and in her eyes, to all of us who watched, and even for those who disapproved, as undeniably vital as she was eerily enchanting. And if you looked long and hard you might have found her to be, as we secretly did, disturbing.

Disturbing, that is, even by the standards of the raucous street lives we then led. For, at that time, any excuse was made and taken for living-it-up out of the doors we never locked. Perhaps it was the sense of collective release, or a surge of individual spirits after the war, which came with the men's return to households of supportive grandmothers, aunties, sisters, mothers and children. Perhaps it was just the way we all lived then, together whether we chose to be or not, because there was no real choice. I suppose half a century on, looking back, we would appear rough even to ourselves. Our reputation at the time was not in doubt.

Fighting in the street was as much part of the street furniture as card schools and the Salvation Army band. And not just after the pubs closed. And not just between men. Cross words and imagined slights might drive women to wallop each other with the heavy squares of coconut-matting they'd been shaking, a moment before, on their doorsteps. Boys were encouraged, with the gift of birthday or Christmas boxing gloves, to match up for an impromptu scrap. Ball games, cricket wickets and goalposts chalked onto the concrete of a pine-end wall, could be played, in and out of season, by day and in the dusk, until the thud and thump brought the inhabitants out to scatter the players until the next time. Footraces, hide-and-seek in and out of people's gardens, and that Kiss-Kick-or-Torture in the bushes which grew more bizarre in its various outcomes as we grew older. Trestle tables could suddenly appear, lugged out from church halls, chapels and workingmen's clubs, to signal a street party. Special ones, for royal birthdays or the Coronation, when all political twitches were stilled by a sugary binge of jelly and trifle and iced dainties, were made grandiose amongst our drab streets by flags and bunting and balloons. After the children were fed at these parties the booze came out and with the booze came the dancers, and that would be when I first noticed Mrs. Riley jitterbugging to a gramophone record wound up to play, over and over, "American Patrol".

That particular party was for a homecoming. We'd had a few already for boys coming back from the Korean War or just their National Service. All done, and celebrated, in the lee of the bigger

War which hung over us, its end a relief, its shadow cast over our assigned futures. Only, this homecoming was neither for soldiers nor innocents. It was for James and Llewellyn Riley, Buddug's two sons by her Irish husband, Brian, now installed as a hands-on foreman in the painting and decorating firm of W.P.T. Davies, J.P. For her boys, Buddug Riley had Brian fetch his ladders and string across the narrow roadway of our street – a cul-de-sac that buckled downwards in the middle and rose at thirty-degree angles at either end – a home-made banner torn from bed-sheets, and daubed in the best red paint her husband could find. Its emblazoned capital letters said:

"WELCUM HOME JIMMIE AND LEWIE".

They were a handsome but contrasting pair. Jimmy was slender and fair with deep-set hazel-tinted eyes, whilst his younger brother, Llew, was thick-set with Brian Riley's blue-black thickly plastered hair and his pale blue far-away eyes. The boys were eighteen and sixteen years old. They'd been away a while: James Riley in Wormwood Scrubs and Llewellyn Riley in a borstal for more juvenile offenders. The offence, which they held in common, was for theft with aggravated assault. They'd broken into the vicarage, stolen petty cash and pewter plates and candlesticks, and thrown a heavy white clay pot of Keiller's marmalade at the vicar's wife when she walked through the front door as they left by the back. They missed. Or, it was assumed, at least, by the magistrate, W.P.T. Davies, instructed by his employee, Brian Riley, that the elder thief had missed. The likeable and mischievous younger sibling would have been our best guess. Either way, not everyone approved of their joint homecoming as an excuse for a party, but as I've said, a party in the street was universally irresistible whatever its ostensible reason and, as usual, the withdrawn Brian Riley was there looking on, with Theresa in the crook of his arm, as his carefree wife jigged on and on.

Brian was liked for his good manners and admired for his fortitude. He was equally pitied for his troubles and scorned for his complaisance. That last was not a word we would have commonly used at the time but we would know what it meant. You only had to look at him, and then Theresa, to know that. When Brian Riley was at home she scarcely left his side. She was a quiet, almost grave, child, who returned look for look. We stared at the difference between us as she grew more and more distinctive. Theresa stood out and soon stood apart. My father's own story, quietly told, of what Brian Riley had said to him when he first saw his acknowledged and accepted daughter had become everyone's story of that life of a Riley.

In the spring of 1945 the two soldiers had quick stepped into the maternity ward and spotted their respective wives in opposite corners of the bare and airy room. One of the nurses on duty half-clapped, half-cheered, and then stifled her welcome for the soldiers as she saw their destination. At the side of the iron-framed beds, with their council-stamped and starched linen creased into shape, were the unvarnished wooden side bars of tiny cots. Beneath heavy grey and blue woollen blankets were tiny pink heads with strands of hair and snubby pink noses and translucent pink lips. My father kissed my mother and, he said, gurgled a bit over me in all my fresh pinkness. Brian Riley had kissed his wife, who shrank back into her pillow as her soldier-husband leaned over the tiny cot, and stared at the baby girl in it. He looked back up at his wife and then over to my father who was listening close to the whispers of my mother. And then, saying nothing to anyone, Brian Riley ran from the Ward. His army boots had clattered down the disinfected corridors and out again like a manic drum roll.

My father found him in the White Hart, one pint and a large whiskey chaser already drained and another pair set up. Brian Riley, who had fought blind with him, with sand in their nostrils

21

and fear in their mouths across the deserts of North Africa, and killed murderously with him amongst the hedgerow tangle of the bocage of Normandy, only glanced at my father, and said:

"Gareth, your woman's a Darkie.
She's black. The babby is black.
Black as the hobs of hell, she is."

My father told me that after that they both got drunk, stupefied drunk, crawling home by leaning against each other on the pavement and in the gutter. My mother filled in the back story after they'd all been long gone. Buddug Bowen, she said, had always been one to go off the rails. She might, my mother had sniffed, even already been pregnant with her first son when she snaffled up the travelling Irishman, and rooted him in our spot. Llew, though, was certainly his, and the family had seemed as settled together as any other in those hard times. And then, when the war came, Brian, though a citizen of the Irish Free State as it then was, volunteered for the British Army in some species of brotherhood with those all around him, receiving call-up papers as 1939 bled into 1940. Five years away and things seen and done but not to write about, or later recount, in infrequent letters and postcards. A generation passed through a black hole of absence as empty as the gravitational pull of death itself, and came out the other side of existence. Our fathers.

Brian Riley's wife, in her mid-twenties, had brought her widowed mother into the house to look after her boys whilst she travelled by bus out of the Valley to work in the munitions factory, assembling bombs, detonators, explosives, on the coastal plain to the south. Her fingers turned yellow and her cigarette-cough worsened but she could afford endless packets of fags now, and garish make-up and cheap, bright clothes. It was, amongst all the parakeet chatter of women finding work together for the first time

22

in their lives, not enough. My mother sat with her on the bus that chugged back each day, full of bone-tired women, to the Valley. Buddug said that the money was great, but it was company she wanted. Once she asked my mother if she had the same yearnings as she had eating away at her. Needs, she'd said, and when my mother took Buddug's meaning she decided not to give her the benefit of any discussion on the subject. Some things, my mother implied, were best left alone, unsaid. What you felt was what you felt. And nothing to be done about it. And then, suddenly, in the months of 1944 before that summer of change, there was something to do about it.

The first American troops, readying for the invasion, arrived in the Valley by train to be taken by truck to their tented camps. Officers were billeted amongst the few so-called professional families we had – teachers, doctors, solicitors, clergy, shopkeepers. The G.I. Joes were under canvas on municipal playing fields and the lower mountain slopes that had a semblance of flatness. They came to us from a world we had already lived as a fantasy. Their actual physical presence was tricked out with a gift-wrapped offering of clothes, food, goodies and health. They marched, in loose and insolent formation, to the soaring enticement of brass, and they danced, louche and daring, to the swoop of swing bands assembled for the social evenings to welcome them, and all too often embrace them. My mother said that a lot of the local women, married as well as single, would take to hanging about the camp perimeters, just for a look, a smile, a contact. She said that they were like crows shuffling up together on a telephone wire, and then, one by one, flying down.

In all the camps there were, as we and they would all say then, Negro cooks and orderlies to wait and serve. But one camp, made up entirely of combat infantry, was solely for black Americans. These black GIs were never seen in the company of their white equivalents in the streets of the Valley or in its shops and when they collided in the Valley's pubs there were stand-offs, squabbles, and knives could match fists. The segregation, of course, was extended to the dances. But it could only be officially enforced for the troops. The white American G.I. was not the only overseas source of glamour for women who chose not to shun the black Yanks who had also come. When all the troops departed from the Valley there were, again, no more non-white faces to be seen, and, except for the occasional Chinese laundry worker, there would not be again for decades to come. Through the 1940s and 1950s we saw no black faces except for those glimpsed in bit parts on the screen. None at all. Except, of course, for that of Theresa Riley.

What Brian Riley learned from his wife of her wartime liaison was never revealed. He retreated into incessant work and a blow-out drinking session every Saturday night. He did not neglect Buddug materially but, it seemed, in every other way he shunned her and did nothing to halt her self-neglect. She became slovenly in bearing and her looks, though they could flash back through a memory imprinted somewhere inside her, drained from her grasp. The house, at times loud with drink and quarrel, conspired to empty itself of comfort, as if to match her. Slattern was the word that was used. Brian Riley shared neither anger nor despair nor forgiveness. He was, in all this, set apart and we, in our pitiful ignorance, allowed it to be so because we probably thought that it was the only life this Riley could now have.

The two sons had, at Brian Riley's languid insistence, attended the local Roman Catholic school and, no doubt, Theresa would have followed them when the time came if it was not for the priest who had come to the house one day to tell him, amongst other priestly things, as Brian had later told my father, that a sin should be forgiven even if the sin was there in front of him day by inescapable day. The priest had been shown the door for his lack of understanding, and Theresa went instead to the Council School, aptly named Mixed Infants. Brian Riley took her there himself and saw to it that he was free to bring her home every afternoon until she was old enough to go and return, like the rest of us, by herself. Maybe that is where the bond between them was made, and grew strong.

As for us, the silent witnesses to all this, Theresa played with and amongst us, her reserve a barrier but her presence, as one of us, not questioned, except for once when a boy told her that her skin looked dirty because she didn't wash it and was answered by a smack to his face. That brought an angry mother to the door, but a father sent her away, his own unfathomable anger fiercer than the woman's indignation. Brian and Theresa. That is what they had, separately, become. The Rileys. Father and Daughter. Outsiders, both. Insiders, too. How he treated her, and how she grew up, was to be all.

We were not, ourselves, without our common share of prejudice, and I do not excuse the unthinking depth of what we had, and the names we used to label it, if I also say that it ran mostly against the things we thought we knew as in opposition to ourselves. The familiarity of a threat, not the general absence of otherness. In that sense, Brian Riley's wayward decision to send his daughter, Theresa, to our school would have met with approval. There we had no religious observation other than a morning hymn sung raggedly to the thumped-out piano accompaniment of moustachioed Miss Bentley. Our worst prejudice was stored up for Catholics, and whether this had its origins in the tensions aroused by imported strike breakers a century before and the anti-Irish riots that had caused, or in the native distrust of the influence of priests, the chicanery of ceremonial worship and the foreignness of Romanism, there was no argument but that Catholics were, for us, a recognisable threat.

This was given a bricks-and-mortar symbolism in the squat

presence, a few terraced streets below our schoolyard, of the Roman Catholic school. Once a year, without set cause or reason, the two schools emptied from their asphalt yards in maddened swarms that rushed to meet in confrontation. Teachers were alerted too late, helpless to act as guards, swept over and around by whatever induced instinct or impulse had possessed us. And so it would happen no matter what, and we stooped to the road to gather handfuls of loose stones to shove into the bulging pockets of our short trousers. At the back of our insane child-army, the girls yelled us on and we hurled the stones, flat and pointed and egg-sized, into the air to criss-cross the rain of stones with which we were being showered. When they fell to the ground on either side they were picked up again, and the primitive battery started over. In the third year in a row when this had happened, and all before I was nine years old, a boy on their side lost an eye when a sharp-edged flint splintered into the eye socket it had cracked. We didn't know him, only his name in the paper to be read out. And, of its own accord, somehow it stopped.

Beyond these flares of anarchy in which we had revelled, back in our high-windowed Victorian classrooms, sat two by two on bench seats at our double desks, we were winnowed out as chaff and wheat, conducted towards our destined futures. The more likely candidates for success in the scholarship exam that awaited and which would ordain who was to be a clerk, of whatever kind, and who not, were sat at the back of the five rows of desks which stretched from the coal fire and teacher's table at the front of the classroom. They were in positions of attentive trust already. The least talented or wilfully unattentive were sat in the front rows of those iron-framed, sloping desks with their white china inkwells centred in the dark and pitted wood. That is where Theresa Riley, front and centre, was placed by Mr Rosser, and tormented.

Mr Rosser, balding, stocky, ancient beyond the ages to us although he can have been no more than in his mid-forties, taught through terror. He had been a prisoner of the Japanese and was spoken of by our parents in hushed tones of sympathy and respect. To us, as no doubt elsewhere to them, he told his tales of degradation and misery at the hands of that infamously evil, and "yellow", people. He had, it was understood, suffered for us, and so he made us suffer. His hands were hard. His testing of us ceaseless. He dessicated our minds with the rote learning of times tables, of numbers, the chanting of spelling words, with penmanship and shading, which is what, with chalk on a blackboard, he taught as the principles of all drawing. Reading was to be done silently: knuckles were rapped with a ruler if lips moved. The bane of his life was the essay, a task we would all have to undertake if the scholarship exam was to save some of us from the secondary modern school, a fate he could make sound like the near-death experience of a Japanese POW camp.

Mr Rosser set the range of topics to be encountered, and week-by-week he would pick one from animals to adventures to hobbies and holidays or gardens and pets. The set essay he chose for us at the end of a summer term in 1953 was: My Favourite Day Out. He gave out sheets of lined foolscap, made sure our nibs were clean and our wooden shafted pens ready to dip into the black ink-filled wells. Then he walked between the rows of desks, nodding and smiling as if we had been blessed to be with him on this afternoon. He muttered as he went: "A gift, boys and girls. A gift. A gift." He rubbed his chalk-smeared hands together: "Now. Just think. Think before you ink! A day out. Not going to be from school to home, is it? So where, eh? Where? Porthcawl and the fireworks at Coney Beach? The scenic railway and Barry Island? Cardiff Castle? Or, maybe, for you lucky ones who've been, Blackpool and the world-famous illuminations?"

We scribbled, I think, rather than thought. Mine was a bus trip over the mountain to Aberdare to visit relatives and see their magnificent, we thought, park. I used words like "odour" for flowerbeds and "splendid" for the bandstand. I wrote of "Happy Families feeding the Ducks" with leftover fish paste sandwiches. I was a tourist brochure copywriter in the making. We had twenty minutes to exhaust our imaginations before Mr Rosser would bark out, "Pens down", and the monitors would collect the wet sheets of paper. Judgement would come later. We knew it would not be benign.

Mr Rosser had long made us aware of our frailties as potential scholars. We were more froth than cream. He told us, "Gratitude is owed to the council and to the inspired generations who have secured the chance of education for boys and girls like you". We were all included by his panoramic glare around our ranks with that "You". We had to understand we were made of common clay, the muck of our ancestry, from which we had been mis-shapenly moulded. But now, for us, there were "Chances. Opportunities Your Parents Never Had." And to prove to us who these benighted and bereft people, our parents, really, in all their hopelessness, were, he would periodically humiliate us as we jumped up and down to his prompts:

"Stand on the seat anyone whose father works in the pit."

That meant three quarters of the class.

"Stand on the seat anyone whose father works with his hands."

That meant everyone else.

"Stand on the seat everyone whose father smokes."

That meant all of the class except for the three whose fathers had been killed in a pit explosion, though they'd stood for the work question anyway.

"Stand on the seat any boy or girl whose father drinks beer."

That still meant a majority.

"Stand on the seat anyone whose father bets on the horses."

For some reason this was felt as a deeply unwanted slur and even some whose fathers did indeed study form on the back pages, did not rise.

And after this, though there would be variations to his peremptory tune, would come his clanging note of doom.

"Stand on the seat any boy or girl whose mother smokes and drinks."

At which point, with relief, there would be a mass sit-down. Except for innocent and truthful Theresa Riley, who had stood after the first question and did so yet, alone and unwavering, until Mr Rosser dismissively waved her down.

Theresa had become taller than the rest of the girls, and was as tall as most of the boys. When she stood on the bench, alone at the end of the ordeal, she seemed at a higher level altogether. She stood two feet at least above Mr Rosser himself. She kept a fixed stare over his shiny head to a distant point of a far wall. So hard and long did she stare that she might have been looking through and beyond the wall itself. She stood perfectly still. Her legs were bare above her white ankle socks, her feet in the black rubber daps with which she seemed to glide over the playground and run in scores at rounders after she slammed the ball out of sight. She was ramrod straight in a red-and-white spotted cotton dress with a lace collar and three dark red buttons on its bodice. Her hair was a tangle of curls. Her skin shimmered like the translucence of a peat stream. Outside the class, when our fathers met to talk and took us along with them on mountain walks, I hoped she was becoming my friend. I wanted her to be that.

Behind the houses of our upper terraced street was an unmade back lane. It ran parallel with the street. Beyond that was a vertically running path, bounded by bushes of mayflower in season, that led to the farm which had been there before all of us. And then there was the open mountainside rolling upwards, riven by stone-bedded streams, to its plateaux of whinberry-covered uplands. But before you reached the sky, it was something quite other. The colliery, just half a mile onto the mountain and below the ascent to its tabletop, had been closed in the wake of the 1926 strike and lock-out, never to re-open. In the war it had been torn down and mangled for whatever purposes its paraphernalia of iron, steel and brick might serve, but it had not been removed. Its buildings were ruins whose rubble we inhabited throughout the summer. The pit-head wheels had been dismantled but the engine house, its long thin broken-paned windows marking out its high Victorian walls, was a recognisable space, a hall whose bolted-down turbines and boilers beckoned us to play beneath its roofless shelter. Across the blue-cobbled yards of the pit were the weigh stations, the clerks' offices, the pay office, sheer walls one brick wide across whose parapet-to-death we tightroped to safety, and outbuildings flooded with rust-brown watery pools over whose fathomless depths we swung on frayed steel hawsers that whipped back to the next waiting boy as we let go to land on the mounds of loose bricks on the other side. To the south of this wasteland left us by our forefathers was a honeycombed tumble of hillocks and hollows piled together from the rubbish spewed up by the workings. It was a landscape of ashen white and dull red shale, and it was still in places warm underfoot, smouldering and sulphurous. We knew it as the Burning Tip, and even we moved cautiously amongst its falling overhangs and crumbling bluffs. No girls ever joined us on these adult-free expeditions, and Theresa especially was guarded by her father's close instructions.

Sometimes, on Sunday mornings usually, Brian Riley would knock on our door and, pre-arranged I suppose from the previous night's drinking, my father and I would join him and Theresa to walk on the mountain before the custom-and-practice of a Sunday afternoon's sleep, when I would be kicked out to Sunday School and Theresa to their patch of garden. One time, not too many years after the war and when we were still children enough to hold hands, we trailed behind our fathers beyond the Burning Tip and the colliery ruins and its bile-green feeder dam where dogs were drowned and teenagers swam, until we reached a mountain stream that rushed a little more slowly before its helter-skelter descent from the plateau above into the dam below. Here, Theresa and I gathered smaller, flatter stones and brush as our fathers, laughing like boys, waving their cigarettes at each other, rolled up their trouser legs and, shoeless and sockless, waded up to their knees in the swirl of water. They threw their lit cigarettes into the stream from whose bottom of gravel and pebbles they heaved to the surface the largest boulders they could find, and hugged their wet mossy stones to their chests. Then, boulder by boulder, as we sat on an island of turf past which the stream flowed, they built a wall until the waters of the stream grew stiller and glassier behind its dam. It was then that Theresa and I could paddle, too, and our fathers lay on the banks of the turf island and smoked their glowing cigarettes, one after the other, until it was time to go down.

At the edge of the colliery's feeder dam, a pond about twenty yards across and another twenty to its retaining wall of quarried mountain stone, we paused. Out of his inside coat pocket my father took a tin toy boat he had bought for me in the market. It was a tug boat, black and brown and white, with a high bow and a low, broad stern on whose right hand side was a large square silver key to wind it up. For that was the joy of it. It moved, propelled mechanically and guided by a rudder that was there, in place, to make it turn, and return. We had tried it in the oval tin bath which was put before the coal fire every Sunday night for my weekly bath. But the tug boat frustrated us because the bath was too small, and so it went round the sides of the bath once we had set its clockwork in motion to cross the bathwater, and simply bumped along the sides. Now my father would show us what it could do. He smiled at me as he took out the concealed boat. He wound it up as far as its spring would go. He held the key tightly between finger and thumb. He bent down and put the boat, with its profile-painted figure of a tugboat captain in the wheelhouse, carefully into the lapping water. He looked at Theresa and me, and grinned at his friend, Brian Riley. Then, with extreme care, he let the key go and the tin tugboat bravely chugged out onto the colliery feeder dam and kept a straight line towards the wall of the dam. "Now, wait," my father said, still hunkered down at the dam's edge. "Wait. Watch. It'll turn in a minute and come back."

And as we watched it did begin to turn, its high bow rippling the water and its stern skewing to the right, until, right in the middle, the clockwork stopped dead and the tugboat began to sway gently on the water as the wind sighed down from the mountain top. It was too far out to rescue. My father, I think, hesitated. It had cost 10/6^d in its cardboard box, and I loved it most of all. There was a slight wash of water over its back. It swayed, and began silently to sink into the depths of the dam. "Oh, fuck," said my father, not turning to look at me. "Oh, sweet Jesus," said Brian Riley as he flipped his cigarette into the dam. And then Theresa took my hand in hers, and said nothing, and did not look at me, and squeezed my hand in her hand.

On the day of the essay test she had been as distantly self-absorbed as ever. She had sat alone, cross-legged, in the schoolyard bouncing a small rubber ball to and fro off a wall, catching it one-handed and then starting up again. She trooped in when the school bell rang, ready to endure another afternoon. Her school marks were never better than adequate. She gave out the sense of someone waiting rather than expecting. That afternoon when the essays telling of our fantastic days out had been placed, unread as yet, on his desk, Mr Rosser finished the day by quizzing us on the destination our essays had described. And one by one we told him of charabancs and seasides and chapel outings and steam trains and all of the setting out early and arriving back late which our valley location ensured, until we were back safe, tucked up, tired and, oh so grateful and childhood happy, we said. In the middle of all this came Theresa's turn to answer.

"Where did you go, girl?" Mr Rosser asked.

"Africa," she said.

"Africa? Africa? What on God's Earth do you mean, Africa?"

"I went to Africa."

"How for God's sake? How?"

"In an aeroplane."

"In a plane?"

"Yes. In a plane. Just for the afternoon."

"The afternoon. You stupid girl, you can't go to Africa for the afternoon, can you?"

"I did."

"No you didn't. You said you did, it seems, but you didn't because you can't, can you?"

"I did, though."

"Look Theresa Riley, an examiner would not be impressed, and I am not impressed, not after all I've taught you. See? You couldn't because no one can. See?"

"But I did."

Then Mr Rosser grabbed her by her hair and yanked her to her feet. His face was mottled, red and yellowed with righteous anger. "Get on the seat, girl," he shouted into her startled face. "Get on the seat."

"Now, for the last time, because I will not have cheek. Will not have insolence. Will not have fools and liars in this class. No matter what you wrote, you will say now, in front of everyone, that you cannot go to Africa for the afternoon, and come back. You cannot. Learn that, girl. It's called a fact, see."

Theresa looked down at him. She did not cry. She did not smile. She said, in her quiet Welsh voice:

"I did, though. I wrote it, and so I did it. I went to Africa for the afternoon."

Mr Rosser leaned towards her face from the waist. His hand appeared from behind his back like a flat pink paddle, and he slapped her as hard as he could across the back of her legs, so hard and so often on both of her legs that she did cry out, and we could almost feel the sting and smart of her flesh, and we could see the livid, puckering weals that rose to the surface of her skin and quivered there like blistered creatures. Mr Rosser began to shake. Theresa stood, also trembling but without a sound now, until her teacher pushed her down hard onto the bench.

I do not think Theresa told anyone at home, though I suppose the marks on her bare legs might have alerted her mother, if she had been aware of her child. But it was my mother who waited until she saw Brian Riley coming up the street after work and intercepted him to tell him what I had told her. He thanked her, and nodded. Nothing more than that, she said. But that is why he walked to the school with his daughter the next day and did not leave her at the gate to the schoolyard but marched with her into the classroom where Mr Rosser sat at his desk until Brian Riley hauled him to his feet by his tie and shirt-front, and hit him with a clenched fist, full in the face and not once but twice until the teacher fell to the floor, sprawled against his table. Father and daughter then left together, Theresa holding his hand tight.

Jimmy and Llew Riley were no longer living at home, the one in jail again, the other in the Army. Brian Riley gave the house and what was in it to his wife, along with what money he had in his bank book. He packed a case for himself and his daughter and, with only a handshake for my father, he took Theresa's hand in his and went away with her. It was my mother who later found in the back lane behind our house Brian Riley's discarded army blouse. The single chevron of a bombardier in the Royal Artillery had been torn off at the sleeve.

Sweets and Treats

He always wore black. A three piece black woollen suit, its waistcoat with four neat black buttons, a black knitted tie over a crisp white cambric cotton shirt with a stiff collar, black Oxford brogues and plain black lisle socks on his feet, and black leather gloves on his cuffed hands. People who didn't know him took him for an undertaker. And since he drove a new model black car, that was understandable. But he wasn't any kind of undertaker, and even a minute in his company would have convinced you otherwise. He was one of the few men you might ever meet who had two smiles, both permanently at the ready. There was the closed-lip genial smile that went with the conker-brown eyes whose depth welcomed you in, and the open-mouth-you-make-me-laugh one, accompanied by a crinkly-eyed look which radiated pinpricks of happiness to make you feel good about yourself, and of course him. He was, everybody agreed, "nice looking". By which I think they meant he was neat and tidy, aspects we admired then, and nondescript or average in general appearance, which was another virtue in a society that had banished the flamboyant to its outer edges as an undesirable and untrustworthy twitch if you just wanted to survive the troubles of the world. So he managed – neither too short nor too tall, neither too flash nor too drab, neither too gross nor too modest to seem agreeable to whoever was looking into his mirror of reflection. What you got was what you wanted to see. And around him was no disturbing aura, merely a pleasant aroma. Not of carbolic soap and shag tobacco or stale beer and the lingering whiff of urine on wool, which was the symphonic nosegay with which most men in the Valley announced themselves in those post-war years, but the scent of lavender and lemon from the hair lotion which slicked down his black patent-leather shiny and sharply parted hair, with a hint of roses on his cheeks and mint on his breath whenever he bent down to kiss me.

He had taken to doing that whenever he slipped me from my mother's loose and soft handclasp to throw me, with a short and pretend drop, up into the air above his shoulders before catching me safely, and then planting that unwanted kiss on my parted lips. "He's getting a bit big for that", my mother would say nervously. He'd laugh, and say "Bit of fun, eh, Gareth? Bit of fun, that's all." And then into his right hand trouser pocket would go a leather-gloved hand, and out would come the sweets of that week. Chocolate Rolos, warmed and gooey in the gold foil tube of their wrapper. Squared fruity Spangles. Hard tangy Midget Gums in paper screws. Home-made, hard-boiled *Losin Dant*, a taste of mints and sugar like no other, in white open paper cones, bought from the front room which Ma Stephens had used as a shop since before the war. From her, too, laid out in their shiny brown paper coffins were the friable chocolate flakes, dear at twopence each for their brief crumbly moment, but which my mother had recalled as special pre-war treats, which now came again for us, courtesy of him.

He was all about treating us. We had been punished, he implied. Now we deserved better, he insisted. Suddenly we were elevated to a difference from those around us. With him we alone went on trips, even on weekdays, to the seaside in one or other of his gleaming black cars. The Humber usually or, if he felt like it, the rather swish Alvis, chromed enough to be American. All the cars had vertically ridged and hand-sewn black leather seats with walnut trimmed dashboards and ebony driving wheels, large and imposing enough to steer a bus. My mother would sit in the single seat for two in the front, throwing anxious looks and pleading smiles back at me as I slid across the lonely expanse of the deep back seat. Before we set out I would have been loaded up with "sweets for the journey", no matter how short or how long it might be. If we ever bought such things for ourselves, in or out of the family, it was done sparingly and with the appropriate coupons carefully clipped and counted out from the ration book.

For him, nothing ever seemed restricted by ration. He would turn up with slabs of the pallid yellow "American" cheese imported from Canada, with as many as eight rashers of thick-cut gammon, not watery bacon slices, its meat raspberry pink against the grey transparency of greaseproof wrapping paper, and other cuts we rarely saw, and could not afford: rump steaks, double pork chops, legs of lamb and silverside beef. Against their bounce and juice our scrawny pieces of neck and shin were flaccid, their sour odour coming to the surface of simmering water like the beige scum flecking Barry Island beach. The after taste of thrice weekly cawls was banished for us along with the otherwise healthy diet of pre-Coronation years, shouldered aside by the sugar fest to which he invited us on mountain picnics, car rides and nights by the fire banked up with the coal he had delivered.

My world of make and mend, of wait and see, of if you're good, and maybe tomorrow, ended. It all came today. A pushbike with drop handles that was not second-hand. A panelled leather football. Comic books. A blue mottled Conway Stewart fountain pen. Oh, I was a lucky, lucky, boy. There were, set before us in sophisticated boxes, roundels of Clarnico's dark chocolate mint creams and the cocoa milk-sweetened selections of Dairy Box or Cadbury's Milk Tray. Black Magic from Rowntree's was too crisply bitter for my rotting teeth but the parcels of strawberry and orange essence would squirt and stick like paste to my sugar saturated gums. My mother, who had never smoked, would now suck and blow on Passing Clouds or Sobranies, the commonplace of Woodbines and Players left for others to drop in the gutter. At home there was, too, alcohol in the house, brought by him for when he dropped in, more and more frequently, more and more without warning. She didn't appear to mind, though I noticed she kept herself ready, or smart as he would say, for his visits. It was then that I came to recognise the off-key note of citrus and herbs that was their Gordon's Gin and Tonic in tumblers.

They had met for the first time on the day my father had died in a motorbike accident. He would usually set out, on his black and green underpowered BSA bike, at six just after first light. He would ride down the Valley to its mouth and then up the adjacent Valley branching to the left for twelve miles. He had left off working underground, no matter what it paid, as quickly as he could and found new work on the new industrial estate as an assembly-line car-parts fitter. It was one of those mechanical and mechanistic post-war jobs sent to compensate us for thirty years of misery and war. All behind us, we were told. We sucked the welfare tit with as much astonished gratitude as I would later slurp up the sugar of sweets and treats.

That morning, when he went, I would normally still have been asleep in the back upstairs bedroom. But this day he was late. I had heard him talking with my mother, laughter from both amongst their whispered words, and then his bare feet slapping out of bed onto the stone cold linoleum floor and the splashy sound his piss made into the china chamberpot they kept underneath their bed. I left the swaddled comfort of my eiderdown quilt nest and ran across the landing, bang into him. My father grabbed me and dangled me upside down over the stairs. In a terror that was feigned and a delight that was not, I screamed and wriggled for deliverance. My mother came out of the bedroom and held him around his waist, pushing his vest up over his chest and kissing his neck and tickling him under his arms. He was naked other than for that. He held me with one arm so that I screamed louder. He half-turned and cupped my mother around her neck and bent over to kiss it. I twisted to see them, two shapes, dark and fair, a moment only allowed them for this. Then he let her free, yanked me up and stood me straight. He told me to go back to bed with my mother. He kissed me on the forehead and then on the lips. I could smell my mother on his breath. "Got to go," he yelled, and ran down to the kitchen where his work clothes would have been warming on the chair in front of the kitchen range he had installed himself for her convenience and constant hot water. An indoor bathroom was to be next. Dreams. We heard him shout: "Half past seven! I'm off". And he went.

We lay under the still warm blankets and heard the bike choke in the cold and cough harshly before it stammered into life as he rode it out from the back garden, through the gate and into the unpaved lane that ran behind our street. The engine puttered before it finally purred smoothly. We lay listening, my mother and I, as its familiar noise drifted away from us.

Because he was late, my father decided that day to take a short cut over the mountain between the two valleys. That road wound steeply upwards in a whorl of bends to the plateau before it corkscrewed down to the next valley bottom. We called it the New Road because it had been built, to no real purpose of regular travel, by unemployed men on council contracts in the years before the war. It seems that as my father pushed his BSA over the top and then accelerated into the first hairpin bend of his descent, a late winter sun rose up before him like an incandescent silver disc from over the mountain's shoulder. It blinded him so abruptly that he stuttered at speed and skewed the bike to the right and into a postman's red van, which had been hidden from him by the light that had flooded the road and filled the air. The van had bulled into the bike side on, and it hurtled my father into the air for the instant of life he had left. He died in the next moment, when his head hit the road. There were no helmets worn then so his skull cracked open from the top and spilled the blood and nerves of his brains onto that rough and narrow road.

Coming up behind the red postman's van was a low slung, high fronted black Humber. The driver pulled over to the side of the road and half-straddled it on a tussocky grass and bullrush verge. He switched off the engine and got out. The van driver was already out and staring down at my father's corpse. He was dead. They told us it would have been instant on impact as if that might comfort us. As for the details my "Uncle" Jack would, meticulously and with infinite subtlety in order to play on a child's sensations, lay these out before me later. He told how he walked past the postman and bent over my father. To make sure, though he was, he said, absolutely sure – anyone would have been. Behind him he heard a hollowed-out voice in a flat monotone: "I didn't see him. Oh, Christ Jesus. I just didn't see him. I couldn't do nothing. He was just there, on my side. On my side. I couldn't do nothing." So nothing could be done, and there, as they all said over and over, it was.

When I came home from school that afternoon, the house was full of neighbours and friends. We had no relatives left alive. I was picked up and ushered into the front room with the piano. My mother was in bed. The doctor had called. And would come again. I was to be a brave boy. My father would have wanted me to be a brave boy. He would have wanted it. So he was dead. My father was dead. A stranger patted me on the head and offered me a mint to suck. It was the kindly man I would soon know as "Uncle" Jack. A brick, an absolute brick, they all said. What happened ricocheted around me and from room to room as I was hugged and pitied.

"Uncle" Jack had been driving to a job in our valley but, after the accident, and the police and ambulance calls and the waiting and witness statements, he had volunteered to go with a police sergeant to tell the relatives of the deceased what had occurred and what he'd seen. He was, as everyone quickly said of him, just that kind of chap. One in a million. Jack had even stayed after the police had left, and before the neighbours came. He made tea. He opened the door. He explained. He comforted. He made sure the doctor called. It was he who insisted my mother go to bed and it was he, when we three were left alone in the house, who took me by the hand and led me upstairs to sit with my mother on the bed I had shared with her, and my father before me, that morning. Her tears soaked my woollen school jumper to a stiff lumpiness of clots, and wet my face all over. "Uncle" Jack smiled and said, "There, there," and left us to it.

After that, and the funeral for which he made his car available, he called more and more, though never as any kind of intrusion. He made it all seem a natural progression of meeting followed by friendship. He would park one or other of his glamorously alien vehicles in the street, and wave to gawping neighbours. Soon they would talk. And why not, was what, no doubt, they were saying. My mother was not yet thirty, her wan complexion and the shadows of grief beneath her eyes giving her a faded prettiness. Like a pressed flower in a book, a flower whose live colours had not dried out. The life she had eked out with my father cannot have been easy, though I still felt the warmth of it holding us close. With him gone she would hug me closer, often without warning, and then her sighs would well up and their bubble-cries burst and spill their tears onto my hair. She worried over what next. She had worked as a pay clerk for one of the Colliery companies before the war. There were no such jobs now. Shopwork, perhaps? Friends posed unhelpful rhetorical questions but offered no solutions. And then there was "Uncle" Jack.

He owned a garage where repairs were carried out. It was one of very few in both the neighbouring valleys. He had also assembled a fleet of cars for hire. That is, if you can call three maintained and polished saloon cars a fleet. "Uncle" Jack advertised it as such and he, or one of his mechanics, doubled up as drivers. For funerals and weddings and special treats not catered for by council buses or private charabancs. Few of the men amongst us, and none of the women, could drive at all then, and there were, in any case, few cars to drive and none to afford. "Uncle" Jack was the future it seemed, a crossover into a future we could only glimpse and he already embodied. When he was behind the wheel he always wore his black leather gloves, and he never took the left one off his hand. People assumed it was a war-time injury. He chose not to disabuse them. Nor did he pretend. "Uncle" Jack had not gone to the war because of the injury to his hand. What was his left hand now was a clumpy prosthetic thing which he kept covered up. He told my mother, who told me, that he had lost the hand of flesh and bone when one of the new mechanical coal cutters that had been installed went haywire and finished his career as a collier. He congratulated himself on the escape from the dust and accompanying pneumoconiosis that would, for sure, have otherwise been his lot. With his compensation money, paltry enough, he bought the garage, essentially a lock-up with a pit in the floor, and he taught himself to drive the car he'd always wanted. When the Yanks were billeted in all the surrounding valleys his wartime services were in demand. His enterprise grew. He invested in an extension to his garage, and more cars. After the war there was to be a snub-nosed charabanc, blue with a streamlined white trim and glinting chrome wheels, for hire to drinking club and chapel outings and for as far away as Blackpool, whose illuminations were, for us, the eighth wonder of the world. Most of us only saw them on Movietone newsreels in black and white, but we craved their light as much as we did sweetness. "Uncle" Jack was one of those who hastened to meet the need.

We never went over the mountain to his house and whether or not he was married, or had been, was a question neither raised nor answered. Not so far as I knew anyway. Perhaps my mother knew, and was content. Later, it was never mentioned between us. It was "Uncle" Jack's sister who kept house for him. I met her, a woman almost her younger brother's size, when she came, now and then, to tea with my mother and him in our house. Sometimes the teatime was extended. Then my mother, "Uncle" Jack and his sister, Gillian, would expand the fun of what he called their "little get-together" with an open cupboard and the bottle of gin he left there. I would be given extra rations of sweets by "Uncle" Jack and sent out to play, and be popular with my bounty on the mountain above and behind us.

To make these visits with his sister even sweeter, "Uncle" Jack brought a wind-up gramophone player, a box of needles and a stack of brittle records. The hiss of the emerging music was removed now from both the rat-a-tat attack of brass and the moony drift of melancholy which had come with the war. "Uncle" Jack's up-to-date stuff was all soupy balladeering and the glutinous tones of crooners set to the emasculating slither of a thousand violins. The hold-and-release jerk of rock 'n' roll hadn't yet come along to break the hold-tight pitter-patter of foxtrots and the glide-together of a waltz. This was a shimmy for security's sake in that niche between the war they'd survived, and the way we were all going to be. Only not quite yet.

When they ran out of records, Gillian sat at the piano and played, her back to the bay window alcove in which the piano, otherwise silent now my father was not there, sat and waited for her touch. The piano was in the room where my father had lain in a coffin that had been closed because of his injuries, and from where he was carried away. I could not put the thought or the sight out of my mind as her fingers, nails painted as brightly red as her crimson lipsticked mouth, danced up and down the ivory keys. Gillian dressed as she entertained: loudly and colourfully in dresses of pleated jersey silk with a flower pattern. Her perfume, a cloying afternote of gardenias, mingled with the smoke of her cigarette, and stank in that room. My mother said her blonde hair owed more to a bottle than the sun or nature. I knew all this, too, though not everything, because I would ask my mother to tell me what and why everything was. But I could see for myself that her resistance to any of it was feeble, for her sighs were lost into laughter when "Uncle" Jack danced to bend her backwards in a swooping fashion, or when he whirled her into the arms of Gillian and he flopped onto the piano stool so that the music he could thump out with his still-whole right hand might continue for them.

During these months after my father's death as spring became an early summer the idea of my mother having to work at all receded. She had a pension of sorts from my father's war service, along with whatever she could claim for me, but mostly we were fed and treated by "Uncle" Jack. More than that, my mother would find a green pound note folded into four in her snap-purse and, more than once, the delicate flag of a white five pound note which we would hold to the light to marvel at the watermark coming through the curled barbed wire of its black calligraphy. Half-crown pieces or florins would materialise in my coat or trouser pockets. She would protest, seriousness conceding to a grateful half-heartedness, as he would tut-tut and put an arm around her shoulders. Soon, "Uncle" Jack spotted that she wore the same dress over and over and took to bringing new ones he'd sized and chosen himself. She would kiss him pressingly on his forehead as he sat in my father's armchair in the kitchen whilst she came and went and came again from upstairs to down in successive changes of clothing.

Through all this I felt only happy that my mother was my mother again and not some wrenched-off branch of a past life. I had no resentment of him at all and his presence in our life never extended into the night or the mornings. His takeover was far more subtle than any mere replacement. He was bigger than that, and larger than all around him through the unmistakeable power which he yielded and which made him distinct. It was, and I can say that I knew it even then, the car which underlined his power. With it he proclaimed something relative to us, yet which, at that time, was beyond us. Not wealth of a kind, but something more, a hint of a world without the boundary of limits. The car declared the change that was taking place, elsewhere in other worlds, by just being there, but it was the fact of its being there, in the here and now and not some unfolding future, which gave those such as "Uncle" Jack their temporary kingdoms over us. Leather seats and waxed paintwork and the headiness of petrol fumes made a Jack into a King as readily as if he had been a warrior set on a horse and free to survey a land without horizon.

Others my age clearly envied me as I, shy conspirator with them, waved at them left behind in the street as the car pulled off, down the Valley and beyond it. To be touched by power such as this was, in their eyes, to be blessed, and in mine too, though my father had had to die to let it come about. Did we all wish for this to be, our fathers dead? No one spoke of it. Because, of course, it was not really so. Only it left me feeling, if not cursed by the blessing, then singular. I had no wish to be so singled out, and removed. With a stubborn resentment that was not thought through and certainly not articulated, I took, piece by piece and more and more, to sensing when a visit from "Uncle" Jack was imminent so that I could avoid him. When my mother set about tidying the house and herself I would refuse to remain to say "Hello", and stay out for as long as I dared. If he turned up unexpectedly I would spot him and vanish into the garden and out over the stone-built back wall into that territory of unpaved back lanes and quarries and mountainside dens which was our domain, separate and secret from the organised world that cared for us.

One day that summer the chance came to spend a whole day apart. Courtesy of the British Legion a convoy of double-decker municipal juggernauts of pre-war vintage were to trundle out of the Valley to the seaside. Mothers, fathers, children and, by invitation to the unfortunate, the fatherless such as me whose father had been once a member of the club. No charabancs. No motor cars. The anonymity of a gathering in which, again, I could be a part, and an onlooker, not the looked-at. It would be a Saturday, leaving early and not back until well after dark. Please, please let me go. Why not? said "Uncle" Jack to my mother, and he gave me a dusty red ten bob note.

We left before nine in the morning. Rain threatened but held off. We rollicked, for there is no other word for the swaying and bumping and singing and shouting we did, on the upstairs deck of the buses where we children had been put to sit by ourselves. We ate our Shippam's fish paste sandwiches on the pale sands and washed the grit down with orangeade whilst the men filed in military formation to the pubs in the town. When they were gone the rain came, blowing in over the Channel in gusts that turned to a continuous downpour, until we huddled with others of our kind, wet and wild, under the concrete roofs of concrete shelters, our fairground pennies all spent. Fathers drifted back to sodden wives who demanded bus drivers be rooted out of cafés to take us home early. Out of the light dropping on the sea and back into the Valley, the buses juddered, and we no longer rollicked.

In familiar streets families said their goodbyes and scattered. It was not quite dark. Street gas lamps would not be lit for an hour yet and no house windows flared yellow in the half-light. I walked alone up the hill across which parallel lines of streets cut to left and right until I reached the topmost terrace which was our street below the mountain. The front door was set a few steps up from our railed and miniscule front patch of garden. I looked to the right at the curtained bay window from which piano music, slow and anticipatorily insistent, came. This room was lit. I could see a curve of light oscillating between the folds of the centre curtains. I felt inside the rectangular brass-plated letterbox for the string to which we tied an old-style black saw-toothed key. I pulled it out. It had no key attached. We had no doorbell to push so I tapped the knocker against its metal mount, and waited. The music, faster and louder, had continued. No one came to the door. I stepped down into the front garden and on tiptoe looked through the slightly parted curtain into the room before I went to tap on the windowpane.

At the piano with her back almost directly to me was the pianist, a curly-headed blonde in a loose-fitting red and yellow floral patterned dress with wide puffy sleeves that billowed down to the wrist. The pianist's hands were moving tightly, unseen to me, to the front. A glass of gin and tonic whose adult, sweet sourness I could almost inhale through the window sat on top of the piano, next to an ashtray my father had won at the fair. In the ashtray a cigarette burned unheeded, grey ash flaking off after its fire of paper and leaf. The piano stopped dead, before caterwauling off at a new pace as its player suddenly inclined to the right, to that corner of the lamplit room where the door was slightly ajar. I heard through the glass a giggle, stronger laughter, and saw the door slowly push open.

Two men came into the room. Both wore flat, black and grey checkered dai caps. On their feet were colliers' hob-nailed boots. They wore black alpaca jackets and waistcoats and dark grey moleskin trousers tied at the knees with yorks. Their collarless, striped Welsh flannel shirts were buttoned to the neck. One of them, the shorter one with the black cork smudge of a moustache sitting above a clay pipe, was my mother. The other man had a brightly lipsticked mouth and hands that came up from behind

47

to flutter onto my mother's breasts. I fell smack against the windowpane and my head stayed there as if stuck.

Gillian said, flat and with force, "Jesus Christ! Oh my God!" The piano stopped. My mother sank to her knees as if all the breath had been punched out of her. It was only then that the pianist turned to the window and raised a black-gloved hand from its keys. "Uncle" Jack swivelled fully around to see the face in the window. He picked up his cigarette and acknowledged me with it before moving it up to lips which opened imperceptibly in a face framed by the curls of a yellow wig.

I turned and ran. In a den we'd made from railway sleepers and corrugated metal on the mountain, I kept hidden beneath a stone a sheath knife, wooden handled in its leather cover, and I uncovered it to remember how my father had given it to me. He bought it for me after I had found by the side of a mountain bog a springy double-edged blade, its handle a rectangular dimpled black rubber grip. I had shown it to him only, despite my tears, to have it taken from me. It was, my father told me, a Stiletto blade. A killer's weapon. Army issue. The sheath knife replaced it for my birthday. Now I took it and ran with it to a bend in a mountain stream where the turf was deeply green and giving, and into it, crying and sobbing, I plunged the knife, into the green breast of the river turf over and over until I stopped and threw the knife away, into the stream.

That night was the last time I ever saw "Uncle" Jack in any guise, though I turned away a few times when I saw one or other of his black cars on the streets of the Valley. Quite soon there would be too many other, smaller and brighter cars to pay any such cars as his any attention anymore. Sweets came off ration. My mother married again, and with her new husband she took me away from the Valley.

Show Time

In the subdued light of the cinema foyer the woman who sat behind the glass window of the ticket booth glowed. She was herself an enticement but she was also glamorously framed by the allure of movie posters in blocky comic book colours and 3D printing, and by the faces of the stars set on the stucco-plastered walls around the booth. Amongst them, backed by the baby-pink and tawny-gold of the Greek-and-Roman pillars which profiled the walls, she still shone out. You walked towards her on the worn pile, once plush, of a blood red carpet and watched as others took their tickets and went before you past the walnut-inlay double doors with their heavy brass handles. The doors swung silently open and shut releasing and stifling as they did so, the murmur of American voices.

The woman's hair was backlit by the soft halo of a semi-circle of small electric bulbs on the board behind her. It was a Gloriana auburn colour cut in the style of a Veronica Lake peek-a-boo so that it fell in one straight drop down the left side of her face. Her right eye, an oceanic blue in its depth, glistened on its surface with splinters of artificial light. It sat on her face above a cheekbone convexed with Hollywood in mind. She was, as we would say, a real beauty, and it was only when, at the top of the queue, that you came close that you first noticed the fixed sideways and downwards twist of her mouth on the left side where her lips seemed forced into an immovable snarl. And so, if you went to the pictures often enough, you learned not to flinch, or stare too intently, when, as she issued the perforated tickets stubs from the flat grey steel dispenser in front of her, that shimmering curtain of hair moved with her movement, and you glimpsed through its cover the perpetually-held grimace of a mask. It was a mask of horror in which an eye had been dragged hideously down onto her cheek, and everything else that was beautiful about the woman was cancelled out by its presence.

Her name was Maisie. The grotesque configuration of that one plane of her face was a distortion to which she reluctantly gave voice in a slurred, grating speech, speaking only when she had to. She made herself front up to the public gaze for two double bills twice a week in the town's one remaining independent picture house, the bijou 1920s Royal Cinema. Before the war the family had run two billiard saloons, a tea room and two cinemas elsewhere, further up the Valley, but by the time I first recoiled when confronted by Maisie Robinson in the late 1950s there was only the Royal left. Her brother, Freddie, managed it and acted as projectionist. Maisie doubled up at the box office and in the dark of the auditorium where she directed her cone of light down the aisle as an usherette. Neither Freddie nor Maisie had married, but Maisie had a son, Marcus.

My mother, who had known her as a young woman, told me that Maisie had had an "unfortunate accident", and that I was not to stare. I was twelve. I peeped. It seemed more fascinating and terrible than unfortunate. The Robinsons – brother, sister and elderly parents – lived in a red-brick and bathstone Victorian villa set on one of the town's few crescent streets. It faced south, its frontage ignoring the dark cleft of the Valley to the north, and half-way up one of the clump of hills which enfolded the town. We had ourselves moved to this mouth-of-the-valley township when my mother re-married. My stepfather was a carpenter, a chippie in one of the town's large building yards and kindly enough, more enamoured of my mother than interested in me. Babies would soon follow and I drifted into teenage years and into a relative distance from family ties, all of which suited me fine. There were new friends and new perspectives to discover.

Not least the Robinsons. Not at first though, because our own Bevan-built council house – a garden, three bedrooms and inside plumbing – was on the Wheatley Estate two miles to the south of the old town's centre which the Robinsons' villa overlooked directly. I did not, as a result, meet Marcus until the second year of grammar school when the forms were more tightly streamed into "Scholars" and "Others". We were both put in the more academic class though it was quickly clear that Marcus was not exactly "Scholar" nor quite "Other", but somehow both, intriguingly and unfathomably, combined. Neither of us, in any event, was particularly sporting and in those more enlightened days if you chose not to bash others and muddy yourself, you could sit by a coal fire in a room which doubled up as a school library, and read. What you read was up to you, and not policed. Out of my satchel came Agatha Christies from the public library and the occasional Sherlock Holmes. Marcus sniffed at these, though he seemed to have consumed them at some time. Actually, everything he touched, books, food, ideas, he consumed. There was no other word for his wolfish appetite. I was to be, in my turn, consumed, too, one way or the other. From the start, I think looking back on it, he decided he could envelop me with his own tastes. From a deep canvas kitbag, more cavernous than my second-hand three-pocket satchel, came the works of authors and books whose names and titles I had never seen or heard. There were red Everyman editions of Ruskin and Morris and Butler. Walt Whitman's *Leaves of Grass* and strange things by H.P. Lovecraft, both in hardback American published volumes in blue cloth binding. Where did they come from, I'd ask? Marcus would shrug. Then the next week he might show me Edwardian editions of Arthur Machen and purple-bordered Pelican paperbacks of Tacitus's *History* and Caesar's *Gallic Wars*. He let me touch them, hold them and skim, but rarely did I ask to read or borrow anything.

It was all too peculiar. It would be many years before I finally read Norman Douglas's *South Wind* or A.J.A. Symons' *Quest for Corvo* or Fr. Rolfe's *Hadrian* or Rose Macaulay's *Towers of Trebizond*, but I first saw and heard of these exotic outriders of the mainstream when Marcus delved into his army kitbag and pulled out the treasures he had already devoured.

I think he frightened some by the crazy dimensions of what he knew. If he had not been so physically large he would have been bullied more than he was. His size protected him from other than verbal jibes about his "posh" accent, his "weirdo" diction, and his deep disinterest in anything adolescent or indeed for what passed for being adult. Schoolmasters were treated by him with polite disdain. Schoolmates were, with a rare exception such as me, simply ignored. And in the years I knew him best, up to eighteen when university took me away from him, his massive boulder of a head with its shaggy, leonine hair seemed to grow more and more sphinx-like as our several lives flitted past him.

He was never just fat for, at six foot plus at the age of fifteen, his frame held his growing expansiveness in check. But his weightiness of body and mind, hinted at an immobility of being and a settlement of purpose which the rest of us were not properly able, or perhaps privileged, to understand.

The only time, in those days, when he seemed willing to leave his home, other than for the enforced attendance at school where he studied nothing and knew enough about everything to be left alone, was to go twice a week to the Royal to see the films. He took to inviting me to go with him and lured me on by the promise, always kept, of complimentary tickets at the box office. I had, of course, seen Maisie at her workplace. Now I would call for him at the house and see her at home as well. As with her face, the first visit was scarcely a preparation for what you saw when the etched Victorian glass inner door was opened onto the entrance hall of Bryn Villa.

The hallway was still lit by gas. There was a barely audible hiss from two wall brackets and an ochre gleam was cast onto the brown varnished wood and the dun-coloured lincrusta walls. A hallstand with a plain mirror above it, and space for shoes below, was draped with overcoats and hats. And on adjacent pegs were hung four wartime gas masks. Next to the hallstand, pinned to the wall, was a fading poster, measuring about two foot by eighteen inches. Its bold black capitals stood out against the fading yellow white paper. It was an Air Raid Precaution Warning, a series of commands and instructions, a list of Dos and Don'ts, a sort of proxy transfer of powers over people to wardens from government. It was dated "23rd October, 1940". Next to the poster, on another wooden peg, was an ARP stamped helmet and a dungaree-blue cotton jacket with white insignia that looked like a handstitched and home-made badge. On a rickety bamboo table was an actual aspidistra. Something, time or desire, had stopped here.

There were two doors to rooms off the hallway on the left which at that time I never saw opened, and then carpeted stairs to the bedrooms. All life in Bryn Villa, however, happened beyond that entrance. It began where the hallway became a red-and-black lozenge-tiled passageway, with one step down to the kitchen and back scullery. There was on the facing wall of the kitchen a cream, enamelled range of ovens and hobs with a banked-up permanent coal fire in the middle grate. To the right of that was a deal table which was alternately laid with a tasselled purple cloth of a plush velvet nap or with a meal-time, white linen one. There were straight-backed wooden chairs and a dresser full of white china cups and saucers, and blue willow pattern plates. To the left as you walked through a cranberry glass door was a deep armchair with long wooden armrests and well-stuffed feather cushions. A window gave onto a back yard and in front of the window was a low divan about six feet long. It was Empire style, in a moss-green velvet. On a low wooden table in front of the divan were strewn newspapers, books and plates, some empty, some full, and invariably a bottle of lemon and barley water with a water jug and a glass. And on the divan itself, half-sitting, half-lying, like some potentate in his palace, would be Marcus.

Things, mostly food and drink, seemed to gravitate towards him, sucked into the energy force he radiated. If his mother, Maisie, was petite, his grandmother, Thelma, was tiny. Her grey, wiry hair was, in daylight hours, scrunched up into a bun as she flitted, aproned and slippered, from scullery to kitchen with endless delicacies to keep Marcus going between set mealtimes. Eggs, boiled and still in their shell but purpled with a cochineal dye, would come, three at a time, in small bowls; plates with cold cuts of home-cooked meat, beef or ham or slices of tongue, would be flanked by jars of home-made pickled onions and saucers of horseradish and mustard; on the paper doilies put on larger serving plates were iced buns, Welsh cakes and thinly sliced home-baked bread and salted butter; fruit seemed confined to black pippy grapes. There was a hanging odour of fried offal, kidneys and liver, or the sweet cloy of stuffed hearts coming from the oven, or steam ascending slowly from saucepans of neck-end of lamb and root vegetables which simmered on the hob. Marcus would receive the offerings with a flutteringly gracious wave of the free hand that was not holding a book, and then use the other hand to pop morsels and titbits into his mouth. The mouth itself, though cavernous enough for all this feeding, was framed by the softest and pinkest of lips which, when not open for feeding, seemed permanently purse-shut.

I had never seen the adoration of one human being for another before this time. Love, yes, but not worship. Marcus was unfazed, even by the occasional resentful gleam in the eye of his grandfather, William, who was usually semi-comatose in the armchair. Freddie and Maisie were more often out at the Royal than in, but when they were present they, too, soporific and beaming, hovered with Thelma over Marcus's recumbent form like the attendants-in-waiting they were. When he decided to move they edged back, smiling, as if any gesture was an act for which to be grateful. He rarely failed to reward any onlooker of this, for his bulk, heavier as the years advanced and the feeding fortified him, uncoiled with a surprising grace of movement. Then he was up and towering over them, beaming, and patting Thelma delicately on her head, acknowledging Freddie with a clap on his shoulder, kissing Maisie on both cheeks as if she was a little girl rather than his mother and, even in his imperious ignoring of grumpy William, somehow still possessing the space he was about to vacate. He addressed them all by their first names, as if they were, but not quite, his equals. He would grin conspiratorially at me and we would be off, to saunter, perhaps, to the town library for more esoteric books to borrow – he had begun his Ford Madox Ford phase and never forsook Arthur Machen – or else, in the early evening with Maisie and Freddie waiting for us at the entrance to their Dream Palace, we would go to the family's very own Royal Cinema. I'm not sure who "booked" the films that were shown and which we saw, sitting mostly on our own, from the upstairs balcony seats. The Royal was on no major circuit and few of the money-spinners came its way. So there was a diet of films other cinemas chose to ignore – John Cassavetes' *Shadows*, say, or Orson Welles' *A Touch of Evil* or Brando's *One-Eyed Jacks* – or a back catalogue that could stretch back to Bogart's *Casablanca* or Cooper's *High Noon* or Wayne's *She Wore a Yellow Ribbon* or a clutch of incomparable Astaire, Kelly, Garland musicals, or *Double Indemnity*. Did Freddie choose these? Or had Maisie? Perhaps it was Marcus. They were, anyway, always American and in the Royal no fluting upper-class English accents or cod Welsh ones or rollicking Scots were ever heard on the screen. On the balcony was another matter altogether, for there Marcus's very own voice could be heard in a distinct but sotto voce commentary, and the most peculiar thing was, especially on our industrial Welsh patch, how strained a sound it was. Nasal, yet falsetto. Rounded, yet truncated. A voice from a time and place before and distant from the films we were consuming at such a rate. When I thought of it later I thought of Ronald Colman or Leslie Howard, a clipped Thirties tone mingled with compassion and fatigue. My own adolescent thrill was for the husky breathiness of June Allyson in *The Glen Miller Story*, just the wrong side of being maternal, or the throaty rasp of Jane Russell, just the right side of not being a man in *Paleface*, or the bat squeak palpitation of Monroe in *Bus Stop*, where the voice didn't matter anymore since it came from a celluloid image just the right side of everything for an exploding adolescent boy. I sat in the dark clutching at an importunate erection rearing beneath the buttoned-up fly of my scratchy grey flannel school trousers. To my side, in a voice of no great surprise and only of friendly admonition, Marcus would murmur: "Sluts, dear boy. Sluts. Tarts and trollops all of them. Be warned."

As we grew older, we moved apart. Or rather, I moved in directions that were outward to other people and different things. Academic. Sporting. Sexual. Ambitions. Marcus remained his own centre of interest. He sat no formal examinations and left school at sixteen. He worked at the Royal, if you could call helping Freddie to move reels and Maisie to do the book-keeping any kind of work. We spoke briefly and amicably if we met in the street but the world no longer held any official sway over him and he turned his back on it. In no sense did he seem sad or even melancholy but the aura of retreat was almost palpable. When I moved completely away to live elsewhere after university the letters from home would, from time to time, drop the news of this one's death or that one's illness. And so I would learn how no one knew of Thelma and William's deaths, the one quickly after the other, until after their funerals had taken place, and how, within a decade after that, the Royal finally closed its doors.

I had, of course, long before that, cross-questioned my mother further about Maisie's "accident", and the whereabouts of Marcus's father. Once I had dared to ask him directly. He had waved the issue away with a "Best not to ask, dear boy. Absent, d'you see. Present and accounted for and all that. But decidedly in absentia, so I'm loco, but not quite 'in parentis'. Quite." When my mother considered me old enough I was told what I'd guessed, that Marcus was a war baby, one of many, some born out of wedlock. We were all war babies. My mother's story was a cracked record by now. His father had been one of the American troops who'd been billeted in the town and the Valley prior to D-Day in the early summer of 1944. My mother, who went to them, remembered him in dances as tall and willowy with a pronounced accent, southern she thought, and that he was an officer. A loo-tennant. He'd met Maisie in the Royal over a simple exchange of money for tickets that quickly became something else. Maisie, my mother confirmed, was indeed beautiful and not shy of local admirers. Americans, especially ones over six foot tall, were something else again. Maisie persuaded Thelma to take over in the Box Office some nights, and she and the American would go upstairs to the balcony. She told my mother his favourite film was the best release of 1944, Billy Wilder's *Double Indemnity*, and how they'd sit in the dark to see murderous Barbara Stanwyck's white blonde hair shine whilst Fred MacMurray's Walter Neff, her seduced patsy, and Edward G. Robinson's insurance investigator, Keyes, wisecracked to Raymond Chandler's dialogue. Her American would, after four viewings, lip synch with them to its desperate end. When embarkation time came nearer Maisie spent more time with him by day. He said he'd come back for her. That when the war ended they'd go away to America. He didn't come back from Omaha beach. Missing presumed dead. Maisie was pregnant with his child but hadn't known it when sometime after the Normandy landings a letter came from one of his fellow officers to tell her the news. It was then that she suffered a cataleptic fit, brought on by hysterical, uncontrollable grief. Marcus was born at the beginning of April 1945, just as the war ended.

Then one letter from home told me that my mother had unexpectedly come across Maisie Robinson in the town, and that she'd said her brother Freddie had died that autumn. There was no further news of Marcus. Nor more of Maisie until one day, more than forty years after we'd first met, I had a letter from Marcus himself. I had recently returned from the solicitor's practice I had long run, and my own mother was long dead by then – her funeral the last occasion I had reluctantly returned home – so he had no way of directly knowing my home address and must have counted on a squirrelled-away nugget of information – from his mother via mine? – to reach me. The letter was scarcely more than a note. It addressed me in first name terms but was more formal than friendly. Maisie had been ill for a while, and had died the previous month. He had been considering matters and wished to see me to convey his thoughts. I was to go to see him. There was a "please" appended to the statement, but it was more a politely phrased imperative than a request. You might say it was peremptory. I replied just as curtly to say it would be a few weeks before I could possibly go down, certainly not before early May. A further note, by return, said "Good, the 8th of May then. At 2 p.m., in Bryn Villa."

* * * * *

Bryn Villa, like the town, had not taken the passing of time well. It still commanded a view, but where there had been commerce and bustle below its hill there were now shops whose windows were plywood, building site gaps, like randomly missing teeth, dereliction as calling cards and decay: cracked windowpanes, peeling paintwork, chipped masonry and a mockery of shoe shops and estate agents. Where the Royal had been was a Hold All Sell Cheap Mart, stuffed with plastic household goods and gimcrack ornaments for every model home. I winced. And Bryn Villa itself seemed both reduced in size and dingier than I remembered. I knocked loudly, more than once, and from behind the etched glass door, further down the passageway I heard the splutter of coughing and the shuffle of feet until both stopped and Marcus opened the door.

I half-expected to see the hallstand in its customary place. The ARP warning. The wardens' helmets and coats. The aspidistra. But there was no room for them. All that had changed. Down the hall and stretching as far as the eye could see on either side of the wall and up to the ceiling on wooden planked shelving which sagged in places under the accumulated weight were – books. Hardback books. Paperback books. Books with torn covers and no covers. Books on their side. Books stacked on top of each other. Books overspilling onto the floor and into corners. Outsize books and pocket size books. They crept up the stairs, and under the low wattage light bulbs could be seen as both shelved and floor clutter on the upstairs landing. I sensed, more than immediately saw, that they would be everywhere now, in every room, up and down, in every corner and every cupboard, on every chair and table, in boxes and suitcases, in the attic and in the coal cellar. Marcus's mind had filled the house with itself manifested as a material thing.

He stood before me, larger in all ways, from his baggy pullover and loosely belted trousers to his head on which his halo of hair seemed to have slipped to his face and inverted itself as a beard. As before, he was not straightforwardly fat although his whole body was somehow now all one thing. It was more that he seemed swollen, about to burst before he grew, perhaps, even bigger. He ignored the hand I held out and instead turned with that familiar fluidity of his, almost pirouetting off his right leg, to clasp me on the shoulder, guide me inwards and mutter, "Dear boy. Pleasure, dear boy. Pleasure."

We walked down the towering funnel of books to the back kitchen where he scooped volumes off William's old chair and flung himself onto the divan, scattering half-opened books to the floor as he did. There was no cooking aroma now. On the table, amongst the books, were cans, opened and unopened, of baked beans, tinned fruit, processed meats and half-cut loaves of bread. He saw my glance and gave me one of his beatific smiles. "No time, dear boy. No time. One does what one can. I could make you tea? Though the milk may be a little off. Imparts a pleasant tartness I find. Will you? Or perhaps not?" I said I was fine and how was he? He didn't answer the question but just said he had a story to tell me. One, he thought, only I might understand. Or believe.

"My name," he said, "is Marcus Robinson. As you know, Gareth. Yet, as you may have surmised, dear boy, it is not. Or not exactly. Which is to say my given name is Marcus, after my father it appears, whereas my assumed name – rather too Swiss Family or Lemon Barley wouldn't you say – of Robinson, derives from placement rather than conception. I'm sure you follow. Around the time we parted – you to stay, me to go, so to speak, or vice versa, eh? – Maisie decided to lay before me the evidence of that which I had, silently, hitherto half-guessed and of which I did not enquire. When I say 'evidence', I mean only her memories because there were no letters, diaries, keepsakes whatsoever. Other than the U.S. Army kitbag which I had inherited with, as you'll recall, its cornucopia of books, the start of my lifelong obsession I suppose, or should I say pre-life, I wonder? I had, of course, noticed that most of the books were inscribed with 'Marcus James Ambrose' and some with 'M.J.A., the Third' which makes me the 4th, wouldn't you say? After some signatures was the place name 'Miledgeveille, Ga.' and others had 'Georgia State College', and dates of course, from the late 1930s to 1944, the year, as Maisie told me, he was killed. She wrote to the Army later and had letters sent on to what she believed to be his parents. No replies ever. Letters returned unopened. She had me by then. She gave up. Understandable, I feel. There were no photographs either. Maisie said she'd begged him, just as a keepsake until he returned, but he'd said it was bad luck, and besides, unnecessary when their images of each other were so bright. Romantic stuff, dear boy."

He paused and took in some air through a mouth far too small for his face.

"They never found a body they could identify. Missing Presumed Dead, and all that. She had, as you saw, all of you saw, gone into shock. She had not known she was pregnant. She came out of it apparently when I arrived. Lovely for her, eh? Though she was no longer lovely herself, of course. Except in the dim light of her box, eh? I think I started to speak in this particular, shall we say, absurdly refined manner, because she willed me to be a gentleman. I know that makes no sense but it was what happened, and I acquired my precocious vocabulary from the books. I was, you see, not meant to be a child. I was, shall we say, a substitute. I was, shall we say, him."

He paused, again, and looked hard at me with an intensity which lacked all his usual, informal geniality.

"Let me go further, dear boy. I was a receptacle. I was a simulacrum. I was a mirror. I was a recording device. I was meant to stop time ticking. And I did. She insisted, you know, that I watch all those American films with you. She loved the thought of that, of the two of us, up there on the balcony, in the dark, absorbing all that, that American-ness, and those accents you loved and I professed to hate. I grew, shall we agree, more exaggeratedly *not* American. But she knew better, and so, despite myself, did I. Listen."

And then he stood up and as if a button had been pushed he began, verbatim, to spout reams and reams of disconnected dialogue and monologue in which, with startling precision, his voice moved up and down a register of tone and was pitch perfect across a galaxy of actors. He was Bogart, a low tremolo made sinister by an almost indefinable lisp, duelling with Ingrid Bergman and Claude Rains – who loved him the more? – and, seamlessly, he was hurt and bewildered yet stubborn and defiant Gary Cooper in *High Noon* in a bespoke Western accent of hesitant, drawling authenticity. One-liners, challenges and whole, packaged speeches came from within him, and all without a let-up. This was not memory, it was a transubstantiation of Marcus James Ambrose the Third. He managed the manly gurgle of Clark Gable, never quite crossing the line into falsetto, in *It Happened One Night* and his bereft and bereaved John Wayne, Captain Nathan Brittles in *She Wore a Yellow Ribbon* or in *The Searchers* as the implacable Ethan in quest of the hopeless cause of a reunited family was more than imitation, it was a homage to what that great, befuddled personification of American power and pity had managed to stumble through in a lifetime of acting parts that were more real than he was himself. And how had Wayne done that? Marcus showed me by misplacing the emphasis on every proper noun and end-lining, which he now repeated. The Duke had needed to plonk his furrow-browed recall of the words so woodenly in order to get to the end of them. And, by so doing, he no longer acted them. They acted him out.

When the bravura performance stopped after ten minutes I would have been inclined to applaud, to join in the joy of his performance, if it had not been for the tears that had run and stained his face all the time. He sat down abruptly. He did not bother to wipe the tears away. They ran into his greying beard and bedraggled it into wet strands of ashen string. He saw my concern for him etched on my own wrinkled and sagging face, and Marcus smiled. His tone changed again, back to the warm comforting voice that expressed confidence in its own all-seeing knowledge:

"One more speech, I fear, dear boy, to round things off you see. A shortish one, I promise. No two-dollar words in it. Do you remember that one? We thought it good at the time, didn't we? To puncture the pompous who thought they could teach what they didn't know, eh?"

I nodded. They were the words the dying Fred MacMurray speaks to Keyes in the final confession and retribution scene of *Double Indemnity*. I said:

"Walter Neff pleading to Keyes for brevity. And Keyes saying 'You're all washed up Walter,' and Neff says 'Thanks, Keyes. That was short any way.'"

Marcus gave me one of his grins of wolfish pleasure. I had been taught by one who knew.

"Exactly, dear boy. Wonderful ending, don't you think?

Though not the one James M. Cain put in the 1936 book, did you know? And in that masterwork of noir, Walter is Huff, not Neff and his inamorata, though still Phyllis, is Nirdlinger not Dietrickson. D'you think that last is Viennese Billy Wilder's jibe at the full-on Kraut, Marlene? No matter. The point is, in the book, Walter and Phyllis, Huff and Nirdlinger, not yet 1944 MacMurray and Stanwyck, get away with their crime. The murder of her husband. The insurance claim. Double indemnity paid for railway accidents. The one they faked. The company man, Keyes, lets them go because it's better than the bad marketing reputation they will get otherwise from one of their own agents, Huff, being the killer. Beautiful, isn't it? Greed wins out all the way round. Not quite, of course, since Cain will, moralising even in the maw of the Great Depression, have us infer that our two star-crossed assassins are so psychologically damaged by their evil that they will make a suicide pact, and will go over the side of the cruiser to Mexico, and into the forgiving sea. Mmm. Where's the life to come there, eh? None.

Yet consider the film, dear boy. Neff has repented his sex-crazed madness. He has killed Phyllis, though it seems at the end she loves him, and, mortally wounded himself, he confesses all to Keyes on recording cylinders via a dictaphone in the early hours of a morning that will never end for him. A different kind of justice for the mid-1940s. And an unforgiving Keyes. And yet, do you remember dear boy…"

And here Marcus rose and swivelled above me on one foot, and out came another voice, the wannabee tipped-trilby smart arse, yet irredeemably small town and suburban, back-of-the-throat voice of Fred MacMurray and the answering, tight-lipped riposte, as warm as a sun-drenched sidewalk and as hard as its paving stone, of Edward G. Robinson. Marcus looked straight into me.

"'You know why you didn't figure this one, Keyes? Let me tell you. The guy you were looking for was too close. He was right across the desk from you."
    "Closer than that Walter."
    "I love you too."'

Marcus slumped back onto his divan. I thought it had all ended, but nothing ever ends with movie dialogue. I should have known that. It echoes. Into so-called real lives. It seeps and it drips and it shapes. Marcus James Ambrose the Third now propped himself up on the reclining arm of his divan. There were no tears left, and the final voice was deep, southern and, in places, slurred into an accent that cared little if it was understood, or not.

"Yus suh, Aaah knocked that pretty lil Welsh girl up as good as Aaah possibley could. Mah folks wuz all daid and Aaah had noah intenshuns of bein' the laast of mah kind. *Double Indemnity*, thet silly-ole movie, was mah own ideah. A kinda life-after-daith insurance, yuh see. Aftah all, a daid man is hard to find. Aaah came back, is all. Aaah went, so that I'd be heah to come back. Aaah came back, cos Aaah was heah. And heah Aaa've bin evah since. Nevah pre-sume nuthin' 'bout the daid, not even when they've gawn missin'. Ain't nuthin' goes missin' forevah, d'yuh see? Except for sou-uls, a-course, yuh can indeed lose them. It's jest them ole bahdies of ours, which won't die. They jest change into somethin' else, into someone else, into some place else."

65

Marcus closed his eyes. I sat and waited, but it was finally over. He said no more. He slept, and yet he was not sleeping. He asked me neither to stay nor to leave. He had finished. I stood and walked back down the passageway to the hall and on through to the front door. I stood quite still before I opened it. Back in the kitchen, I heard a man from Georgia talking to himself and to someone else. He sounded animated, in a dialogue, sure of what he was saying in both voices. I opened the door and let myself out into the world which our fathers had left for us to die in.

Who Whom

"A gang of irresponsible hooligans posing as followers of Lenin and Trotsky ... had distributed unauthorised tickets to the unemployed, allowing admission at half-price."

Western Mail, February 1921

Crowd disorder at the turnstiles at the Wales v. Scotland Rugby International, at St. Helen's Swansea. The crowd capacity was 35,000. The Attendance was 60,000.

* * * * *

"If the South Wales Miners' Federation has decided ... to affiliate to the Communist Third International ... perhaps it is the beginning of a new era. How many miners are there in South Wales? 25,000?"

Lenin, August 1921, a misplaced hope, a misplaced guess.

The number of miners in South Wales was 250,000. The resolution to affiliate was overturned.

* * * * *

"Who whom?"

Lenin, October 1921, his definition of power and relationships.

All Frittered Away

It was the immediacy of things that always got to him. The heat, first, as it bounced off the shoe-black tarmac to the fish-white underbelly of the plane as he tottered down the too-narrow aircraft steps. And then the unfiltered intensity of the light which gave the shabby and tawdry buildings an enamelled sheen so far removed from the damp, concrete-crazed greyness he'd left behind only two hours ago. He sniffed the air, a redolent mix of pine and jet fuel shimmering and distorting the couple of hundred yards he had to cross to be first through passport control. He sucked in his sixteen stone plus gut and moved at a calculated speed from his pole position as front-runner to guarantee he would hit the car rental desk before anyone else. He glanced over his shoulder at the pack of men half his age who were rapidly closing in on him. No chance, he thought. Not bloody likely with the start he'd had, not with her blocking the aisle so that he could pull down the overhead bags and swing them, just sufficiently, into the backs of whatever geriatric or family or backpacker might be reaching up to do the same. There was an art to it, he reflected. And it required practice. And, at sixty five, Richie Davies was still agile enough and forceful enough to move past foreign bodies and through foreign parts like the wing forward of imminent destruction he had once been, forty years and a lost lifetime away.

Only, passport ingratiatingly given and listlessly returned, then with only a glass partition to circumvent, there the annoyance that she did go on, and on, just a bit. Bringing him to the mark, so to speak, all too like a hard-driven mid-week training session before a big Saturday match day.

"Make sure now, Richard, you've got the voucher. Identification number. Driving licence. Don't take the excess insurance again. Waste of money. And check it's not an automatic this time."

These words shouted as a final binder. They'd ricocheted down the tube of the fuselage as he had set about the first of what he knew would be a continuous list of tasks, readied in her mind for what he had grimly come to call his "working holidays".

The trouble – the word he reached for all too often to label these twice-yearly, lengthy forays to the Sud, or Pseud as he glossed it when he was back safe in the Club – had begun four years previously when Geoffrey, her bloody cousin he muttered to himself whenever his name was invoked by her with gratitude, had died suddenly and left them his *petite* bloody *maison de campagne*. It seemed, just a couple of years into full retirement, a gift. Some gift, some horse, some mouth, was what he had quickly decided. And petite, he concluded, it was bloody not. She, though, could see only charm and the faintly exotic, "Our little bolthole in the *Midi*. Not grand, mind you," was the phrase she shared with their friends, letting it trail away in their imagination.

He did not need to imagine it. After four years of ownership he knew it and its surroundings only too well. It sat at the top end of a narrow, dry gulch valley, rock-strewn brush-covered hills on either side for a mile down to the main road, and a five minute drive down the stony single track to the red-and-ochre roofed village complete with church, tower and shaded handkerchief-sized square. It was a village from which every native inhabitant aged less than fifty had long moved to the mod con villas with air-con, pool and lawn, which sprawled across the countryside like a rash contracted from California to be downsized in France.

He had every sympathy with this low-cost, low-maintenance decision making and secretly applauded the alacrity with which the locals had abandoned their past.

The vacuum, to the sound of euros exchanged *sous la table* to avoid tax, had been filled by younger people. Incomers. There were some Dutch and German, he'd noticed, but mostly it was indeed the professional, romantic English who now nested in the low-beamed, uneven-floored, tiny-windowed, overlapping clusters of village houses which morphed one into the other to keep out the sun, retain the heat and ward off all those outside their walls. He often thought of them as cave dwellings dug out of one continuous face, or better still like the undulating terraced housing of the Valleys. But if they had been the actual terraces in their actual place then, he was sure, they would have been shunned, avoided, like they did the Welsh from his own *Sud*, too prickly, too damp and too close to home. People and houses both. He, anyway, had never felt more Welsh, something he had rarely had to contemplate in the past, than when he sat in the village square on the swing seat placed outside the one-room bar, sipping a thimbleful of their pasteurised lager, and having to listen, for you could not avoid the nasal decibel level, to the Saxon herd who popped in and out of the caves they had paid local builders to re-model to fit the pics in the glossy mags which she pored over. He hid behind his Ray-Bans and noted how – absurdly he thought – they kept kissing each other three times on alternate cheeks as the locals did – only they weren't, were they? – whilst ignoring (what a gift of being unselfconscious, they had) their ill-behaved, bilingual children racing in and around the cars which were stuffed into the square as if in a scruffy municipal car park.

Cars, that was another thing which burrowed as an irritant under his skin. The residents, incomers or not – and some of those he had learned to his amazement actually commuted by air to well-paid City jobs from Monday to Friday – all had their ramshackle run-arounds to hand, but he had to hire every time, and it cost a fortune. That and the supercilious desk attendants at the car rental who always set him off into a grumbling mood.

It was happening again as he fumbled with the documents he'd slipped into a transparent plastic folder, until he found his licence in an inside jacket pocket. Behind him in the queue his rivals, he sensed, were simmering. He handed over his torn and folded green paper licence which he had not yet bothered to replace with the new laminated card. It was taken gingerly by a woman in her thirties, he guessed, appraising her quickly, with that peculiar colour of dyed hair which reminded him of bilberries strained and sugared over the meringue of her head. He noticed the eyebrow raised behind the canary-yellow plastic frames of her round glasses. That's what in the lingo it meant, she'd told him, that supercilious. Just that. A cocked eyebrow raised to indicate a superior position. A desk. Authority. Being French. He braced himself for what he knew was coming – and where was she, when her sixth-form French, not his phrase-book 'O' Level, was required – the message from afar that would come to him up close and personal from those purple painted lips in an impenetrable *Midi* accent which actually enunciated all words ending with "Ts", and elongated end-stopping "As", like an Italian tenor intent on slathering the backrow of the upper circle. He had no doubt it was deliberately intended to confuse and humiliate. Him anyway.

So he had a strategy prepared. He would regard these close, enforced encounters with the waiting disdain with which he had once viewed opposing fly halves of the twinkle-toed or swivel-hipped variety. Dancing dicks, fancy-arsed crowd-pleasers who would, he guaranteed it to himself, get their full come-uppance at some point in the game when, the ref conveniently unsighted, he himself would come, just a trifle prematurely, off the back of a wheeling scrum to crunch whichever type of his tormentors was about to receive the ball and, either the side-stepping or gliding kind momentarily transfixed, smash fourteen stone of bone and muscle, hardened by working on the building and construction sites her father owned, into their shocked fragility. Few had survived those particular close encounters intact. None ever forgot them. He ensured that by delivering some tasty "afters". It was his trademark, a calculated ferocity which had led to his nickname in the Press – "The Gravedigger", affectionately shortened by those on the Bob Bank to just "Digger" – and to the lasting awe in which his playing days were still recalled by the favoured fans lucky enough to have been there to witness the mayhem, see the bodies separated, hear the protestation of innocence, note the shaky legs with which he'd left the No. 10s for the rest of the game. It was all, he'd argue, within the laws, wasn't it? After he'd barrelled into the playmakers he'd underline his destructive intent with an elbow rammed into the ribs, a finger pushed into flesh or tissue, a knee dug deep into a groin, a hand imprinted onto a chest or a throat. He sometimes, even as he physically marked the bodies prostrate beneath him, wondered to himself if this was all somehow in retaliation for a week of sweating and fetching and carrying. The work, her old man had said, which he had to put in before the partnership – Braithwaite and Davies – would materialise. He had been given the promissory wealth, as a wedding present, on the day he'd stopped shagging Myra without the benefit – that was a laugh, too – of a marriage licence.

Over forty years ago now, with an imperceptible shake of his head to acknowledge it, and here, before this day-glo desk attendant, he was still sweating and fetching and carrying, with only the memory of "Digger Davies", best openside flanker the Club had ever had, and who should, in the opinion of the cognoscenti, have had more than that one cap, and that off the bench, against the All Blacks to show for it. His body had the scars and the breakages to prove it for sure, but it was the scarring of his mind and the damage to his spirit which truly haunted his memory. How much of that unrepeatable star-tapping, that glimpse of glory, had he himself allowed to fritter away? For others, even then, it was just rugby football, only a game, something to grow up from and go beyond, but, and even then, he knew better.

He sighed audibly at the desk, waiting for the high-speed drivel of question and information to end. His strategy was to cause annoyance by muttering, in his best Welsh, "Uhh?" at the rising of any plucked eyebrow and then punctuating the end with the full stop of *"Mais oui"* when he sensed the time for a thrice-scrawled signature had finally arrived. A bit like gobbling up some passing fly half but then, inevitably, like the blindsided referee suddenly restored to vision, at that precise moment Myra would appear at his shoulder, joining him at the front of the queue and about to prolong matters, as pre-planned, by fishing out her own plastic laminated licence embossed with the passport photo she had had taken professionally, four times, until satisfied that she "looked her best". Digger Davies grimaced and shifted to one side for Myra to inform his inquisitor in the impeccably accented French of a Parisienne:

"Moi aussi. Je suis un conducteur, s'il vous plaît."

The point was, as she never failed to point out, that he had to be first in the queue, and so exposed to Gallic superciliousness for a time, if they were to implement her planning instructions. They had to come together at the closure of the plan. Or rather, if they were together at the start, they would be last at the end whereas if he hurried, a trifle illicitly, and so started the action, why then, by the time he came to the end she could be with him, as she had to be in person, if she was to be put down as the alternative driver.

Simple. He could see that, couldn't he? Well, yes, since she put it like that, he could, but, as he once put it in rebuttal, she never bloody well drove anyway so what exactly was the point of it? That's not the point at all, was the conclusive rejoinder.

Digger looked down at her as she held up proceedings further by asking for precise directions to the *location de voitures*, though they'd been there regularly, and the number, *en français s'il vous plaît*, as if that mattered, which you had to punch in to get out, though it was invariably 1789 he seemed to remember and never 1940, which was bloody typical, and all this to lubricate and demonstrate her grammatically correct and colloquially hapless French in a mincing accent she'd acquired, he was sure, from Leslie Caron in *Gigi*. Still, he had to admit that even in her early sixties his own re-incarnation of Gigi looked eye-catchingly enticing in a loose cotton blouse of a red-and-green abstract pattern – gypsy was it? – and the blue-grey poplin trousers, cut away at the calf and fitting appropriately around what the boys in the club would have said – to his inward satisfaction – was an "arse that hadn't dropped". She was still what they had all said she was forty years earlier: "the complete package".

He first saw her at the club's Christmas party. She was back from her second year in teacher training college. He was making a name for himself amidst the mud and rain of Valleys' rugby pitches. A future International was what he heard whispered around him as pints were pressed on him and squat committee men squeezed his formidable elbow. That particular night the booze had worked sufficiently for him to lose a natural shyness and not enough to make the collective oblivion of male camaraderie more enticing than conversation. He told her his name was Richie and asked for hers. She had her wheat-coloured hair cut in a severe bob. Her eyes, more green than grey and yet neither, were set boldly in an oval face. Her mouth, generous to the point of insolence, was a vivid glossy red. She was, he could,

79

see, a looker but, more, that there was an air of proprietorial command about her which he couldn't quite fathom from her accent, which was local, or her interest, which was decidedly casual, in him. In those days, Digger was raw-boned and big-chested but with surprisingly liquid brown eyes fringed by unexpectedly long lashes beneath a mane of fashionably long, black hair. It would soon have been exhausted, that conversation hook-up at the bar, if Bobby Braithwaite had not come up on his blindside, gripped his elbow and pirouetted past to take Myra around the waist of her short and spangly party dress.

"Met my daughter, then, 'ave you, Digger. Mind you watch your Ps and Qs then, eh?" he said, and waltzed off.

Bobby was a key sponsor. He had coughed up for the free bar for players and committee for the Christmas do, with the club proudly topping the unofficial league of those amateur days. And it was Bobby, the town's principal builders' merchant, who mostly stuffed the brown paper envelopes with the fivers, in varying multiples, which the 1st XV picked up from the club's treasurer at the end of every game. Her father's warning was what seemed to ignite a spark for Myra. He had fretted over her incessantly, suffocatingly, since her mother, Tegwen, had died when she was still just a toddler. By the end of the evening Digger and Bobby's daughter were, everyone could see, "an item" and, the boys muttered, the kind of package they'd all like to open. Almost casually, whatever lives they might have had in mind, separately, ended that night. "Richard" would be the name by which Myra would choose to call him, not the familiar "Richie" and certainly not the crudity of "Digger". She had plans for him.

He'd left the grammar school with a clutch of indifferent 'O' Levels and been steered by his collier father and doting mother away from the pits and into the Tax Office – "Security for life, see, boy," his father had intoned – where a lifetime of columns and figures and mechanical calculations awaited him. He still lived at home, and the 1960s passed him by, at least in their subsequent alleged and clichéd manner, in a blur of commuting to work by train, pocket money for beer and fags, the occasional piss-up, back lane fumbles where he "scored" more and more often with more and more willing girls and, of course, the rugby. That grew in intensity with a move from the school team as fullback to centre for the town's second string and, aged 18, his first appearance for the real deal, the town's XV. By the time he had, in the parlance of the Bob Bank supporters, properly "filled out" – steaks, Guinness, Easter Tours of Cornwall and skin band, or bare bum, performances that saw the entire Pack once held on bail in Gloucester – he had graduated to the back row. Every Monday his father, home for early morning bed after the night shift, would run his coal-pocked fingers down the column of Saturday match reports and read out loud the sporting encomia which garlanded his big, gentle, daft, lethal lump of a son:

"Early in the second half the tide of the game – which Llanelli had dominated with astute kicking-out-of-hand and two calmly struck drop goals by their young will o' the wisp Bennett at fly half – changed when Richie Davies, possibly offside, caught the Scarlet Number Ten hesitating whether to run or kick in midfield and clattered him to the ground with a flying tackle to the midriff. It took Bennett a full five minutes to recover as the flanker seemed, almost literally, to bury his opponent after bringing him down and, quite properly, this particular gravedigger received a severe reprimand from Mr Leyshon the referee, which was accompanied by a caterwaul of booing from the home crowd, who seemed to think their promising wing forward guilty of no more than robust play. Either way, Bennett played on shakily until he was replaced, and the Away side lost all their earlier fluency. And indeed the game by 13 unanswered second period points (3 penalties and an unconverted try by Davies in the corner from a disintegrating scrum) to six (the two first half drop goals). Surely the unfortunate Bennett will be a Welsh star for the decade to come and one probably protected, in the red of Wales, by the man who creased him this Saturday for shining, briefly, in scarlet?"

Old timers, and good judges, saw his style of play as a welcome throwback to the 1950s and predicted great things. Yet he seemed, maybe because it was an unfashionable club and he refused all blandishments to move to the grander coastal clubs, to hover on the brink of a breakthrough that never quite happened. In the early 1970s he was, in his mid-twenties, at his peak, honed to a physical edge by training nights and working days for Braithwaites, mixing cement, wheelbarrowing bricks and swinging a sledge. His wages had been trebled at a stroke and Myra, no snob in such matters, had made it plain both to her Richard and to her father that she regarded the graft as an apprenticeship which would end with their eventual marriage. She didn't quite say, though her disdain was clear, that she expected the extra rugby graft needed for International recognition – its sweating, fetching and carrying for no purpose she could see other than some absurd and passing back-patting – to end at the same time.

What naturally decided it for him was the unwillingness of the national selectors to make him first choice, even when illness or injury or retirement had removed those deigned to be above him in their pecking order. He was named in squad after squad. He trained and he trained. He could accept that in an era so star-strewn, even amongst the back row contingent, as the 1970s were, he might graciously have to concede to Dai and Tommy and John and Terry, but to be put on the bench behind others he knew he could eat for dinner, breakfast and tea was a hurt he nurtured. He sat on the bench, Home and Away, and he never played until it was made worse when he finally came on in the second half to shore up a well-beaten Welsh XV against an All Blacks side made maraudingly vengeful by their own uncharacteristic blips of a few years previously. Inevitably, perhaps, he had a stinker of a game: missed tackles and dropped passes accumulating like the lies of a schoolboy who hadn't done his homework. But he had, and that was the problem. He had served his time, learned his trade and was ready to serve his country, and here it was, at last in forty minutes of spotlight, and all to no avail. For the next home International he was dropped. Not even in the squad. Or on the bench. Dropped after one game. The hurt, he felt, was too severe to bear. His decision was instantaneous and, he told the press, savouring the word he'd looked up, irrevocable. He had retired from international rugby. Myra was delighted and hastened to book a wedding date. Her father gifted them a newly built four-bedroom detached in an estate of similar "executive dwellings" on disused colliery land, promoted Digger to the Board (of three, joining Bobby and Myra) and added his/their name to the company's signage: Braithwaite and Davies. Bobby gave him all the time off he needed to play for the club and, under his ferocious leadership, they won the unofficial championship for the first time and then three years running and took the Challenge Cup at the fourth attempt. Then Digger, honour satisfied and the town sated, hung up his boots. He was, his old man told him shortly before his pneumoconiotic lungs packed in after the second successful national strike that decade, "made". A made man.

So why, it would be Digger's fate to wonder on into the next century, did he feel the opposite of that? Somehow not made at all, but un-made. Like the whole bloody world, was his increasingly assertive conclusion with advancing age. He found it difficult to explain precisely what he meant. It was as if the rhythm of lives once held in common had become a jangle where every part could still be heard and recognised but not now in concert the one with the other. The way he figured it was that his parents' lives dovetailed into, echoed you might say, their own parents' and back beyond that, yet it no longer held true in any identical way. He became crotchety when all that he had himself lived through, intimately felt even, was reduced by the turn of the new century to documentary films which, neat and tidy and removed, could have been referring to the Romans or South Sea Islanders as much as the native inhabitants of the Valleys. Always there was some perfunctory journalistic nod to the upheavals of the mid-1980s, making central the Miners' Strike – rebellion more like, he'd insist – when, he'd tell them, it was all over by then, the last kick of a dying horse. The sentimental and the defeated easily took offence.

He worked more out of the office, on site, than at a desk, all of which suited Bobby Braithwaite and didn't seem to bother Myra, who taught effectively but dispassionately in a primary school until an early retirement taken to coincide with her father's last illness. Their marriage had been another of those passages through the limbo of a comfort to which Digger had settled. There were no children. They didn't worry about why not, and neither was inclined to adopt. Present time, their time, just passed. Then it was Digger who ran the business. He moved into the office, and off site. The business expanded in the housing boom after 2000. Myra cared for her father. She took yoga lessons, went to language classes, Welsh as well as French, and visited Geoffrey. The more time passed the more she talked of the time to come. Digger, puzzled, would just shrug.

His own projected delight after her father died was first to sell the business at a solid profit and then to take their ease. By which he meant punctuating the routine of the season, and the seasons, with well-timed – outside the International fixtures – trips abroad. Really abroad, he'd stress, not bloody France. Thailand. New Zealand. Singapore. America, of course. Plans for Japan. India maybe. China for sure. Digger liked all that. Business class flights. Taxis. Four and five star Hotels. Pools. Room service. Bars to discover and sit in whilst she shopped. Restaurants out of the guidebooks. Sightseeing without any hassle. Perfect. And then, only a few years into this, bloody Geoffrey died. Trust him, and trust him to spell his name like that, too, thought Digger, for whom it all stopped again or, rather, with the house inherited by Myra, it all began again.

Now, although they could afford better, it was all cheap flights with bare-boned carriers, and all rolled in with everyone else, because they were the airlines that flew to the local airport, itself a Toytown strip carved between sea and plain with, worryingly enough, two tiny red fire engines forever sat on display on the apron outside the cafeteria-sized Arrivals Hall. They had tried driving all the way down but the time it took to get back made it seem uphill all the way, so flying and renting had become the pattern. A lifetime of sweating and fetching and carrying was about to be reprised. A lifetime in which the things to which he had related early, to which he belonged because they expressed who and why he was, had been taken away too early, leaving only where he was physically rooted and where the only stuff that now moved them all along was the impetus of Who Whom. That was the phrase he'd picked up from his rugby coach, who'd heard it more than once when the Valley was still littered with the useless dicta of its political past, and re-applied it to the mechanics of back row play. All, considered Digger without being in any manner forensic about the sentiment yet from experience certain of its damnable accuracy, all just frittered away.

* * * * *

The *location de voitures* was without shade. A frying pan of numbered sections. Theirs was Number 88 and in it was a *"clair gris"* Audi, an upgrade from the Compact he'd booked. Digger walked around it three times with the contract in his large and callused hand, checking, as instructed, that there were indeed no bumps, dents or scratches. The sun turned his sparsely covered scalp a blushing pink as he completed his tour of duty. He nodded as much to his wife who had already opened the car and had sat in the driving seat to give the air conditioning a chance to kick in. Digger put the bags in the boot and walked to the driver's door. He motioned for her to come out and move over. To his surprise Myra made a pretty mouth and mimed through the closed window a clear "*Non*". Digger asked again, and again was denied. She even buckled up and began adjusting the mirrors. It wasn't that he wasn't used to her mouthing negatives. It was the positive reason for the negative which puzzled him.

She never drove from the airport, and if she did at all after that it was only to HyperU or a garden nursery and back to the house waiting at the end of its stony single track road into the cul-de-sac where the hillside *garrigue* began to rise above them. The back of the house was not a problem for Digger, *garrigue* or no bloody *garrigue*, because it could and must grow as it pleased. It was the other wildness that concerned him. Geoffrey's cultivated and tended wildness, the famous Wild Garden. That, or the English Garden, was what the locals called it. That, and *pittoresque*. They said so every time Myra invited them to leave their new build villas, their manicured lawns and easily maintained swimming pools, to have an aperitif – usually more than the one – amidst the scramble of box hedge and umbrella pine and black bamboo and cypress and juniper and oleander bushes and pomegranate trees and mimosa and roses and herbs and, he thought, God knows what else bloody Geoffrey had planted, in bloody "rooms" for God's sake, to create in Languedoc his idea of a Gertrude Jekyll paradise. More like the hell of bloody Mister Hyde, was Digger's silent rejoinder. The resident English assured the resident locals that it was all truly English, and used a lexicon of French words to prove it. Myra who, Digger would point out after several aperitifs of Gin Tonique, was bloody Welsh, smiled and glowed.

Digger thought it was all bonkers. He preferred the silvery-grey and gnarled olive trees which dotted the stepped and abandoned vine terraces above the garden. He thought them forlorn because they had never fruited. Something to do, he was told, with not having male and female trees in the correct proximity. All down to Geoffrey, was Digger's view. He never fruited either. But then neither had Myra and he, so he let the analogy, too accurate all round by half he could see, wither along with the olive trees. Still, that meant they didn't have to be tended, pruned and watered, and as such they stayed in Digger's good books, for that was decidedly not the case for the rest of the place, whose lavender and sage and wall-climbing plumbago and hibiscus in pots and hollyhocks and geraniums, and on and on, ever needed watering by hose and can. And the pool, an odd aubergine shape – Geoffrey again – had its own blue glint and sun sparkle garlanded around the cream-stoned irregular patio by a Mediterranean mélange of flowers and foliage which only needed daily sweating and fetching and carrying to keep up their appearance, as Myra had once observed, and now required.

And now, apparently, she required to drive. When, sat belted beside her, he asked why, it was to be mysteriously told that the car had just felt right to her. It was asking to be driven. It was an Audi, for a change, not one of those squat Opels or grotesque Méganes which, appropriately enough in her view, advertised themselves in animated TV adverts by sashaying their rear ends in imitation of the bottom wiggling tarts they so resembled. Digger held his breath. So she wanted to sit behind its well proportioned leather clad wheel for the forty minute drive to Chez Elle. He decided to make no further objection. That, he guessed as they pulled smoothly out of the parking lot, would have been as pointless as the old Pontypool three-quarter line's total for the entire season. He liked this grin-making conclusion so much he almost shared it with her: no tries, see? A back line who couldn't score tries, see? All the points, from tries anyway see, from the Pack, see? He thought better of it, and stopped smiling.

He did not, unlike most men he knew, actually mind her driving at all. Myra was a capable, unhurried driver, not as fast as he was maybe, but not as impatient or reckless either. He could relax. No need to be a human satnav. She knew the way, and once they'd negotiated their passage across the middle intersection of a treacherous dual carriageway and turned into the far, slow right-hand lane – why oh why, she'd say automatically, couldn't they put up two sets of traffic lights, and he'd agree, though normally he was doing the stop-start-accelerate negotiation – and then straight on for eight kilometres to the Péage and the Autoroute. He fumbled in his pocket in readiness for the five euros he knew would be needed and placed it in the side pocket. They crossed over the dual carriageway with an ease that caused Myra to smirk with satisfaction. He closed his eyes, supernumerary to her effortless superiority, and settled back for the ride.

Digger's mind always drifted when it was not directly engaged with the task he'd been set. Time to take stock was how he put it, a kind of where-was-I pick-up, a personalised inventory. Nowadays, where he was most of the time was in the past. Lights came on and off like in the old fashioned pinball machines with the bottom-push flippers to make the balls collide with the nubby targets. Digger was content to let whichever random hit was ready to light up. It depended where he placed himself. In a seldom-used and chilly front room it was the respectability of the smell and feel of polish on the furniture and Brasso rubbed bright onto the candlesticks, or in a back kitchen the sulphurous splutter of a banked coal fire and the sweet vaporous fumes from a *cawl* of glutinous shin beef and root vegetables. Outside, wherever, on the street or at the pictures and certainly in pubs, the tobacco of dozens of brands of cigarettes swirled into curlicues of blue smoke that stung the eye, caught the throat and filled nostrils with the power of a shared addiction. Digger had given up smoking a few years into his marriage except for the rare cigar he accepted at Christmastime, and sucked rather than smoked in the club. Men, he remembered, would bring their single Christmas cigars in their silver aluminium tubes, and a mutual sharing and appreciation would occur. A round of drinks, too, was a ritual when money was not so fluid a commodity. You neither refused nor baulked nor missed your turn to pay, unless you wanted to be known and labelled for as long as others would remember, and they all had long memories in a world where you were known, street by street and generation by generation, by whose boy or girl you were, what you did now as much as where you came from, and even, though mysteriously, how you lived your life. Digger wondered how that could be known. But it was. How reputations could be handed out like good or bad conduct medals. How could they be? But they were.

Digger brought to mind faces. They all came with tags. Unwritten and unspoken but tags all the same. A gallery of mug shots. Most of them, Digger ruefully noted, in the ranks of the departed. And not all, by any means, regretted. Not by him at least. Not, for instance, her late father, Bobby Braithwaite. Digger could never quite work out why the old bastard, as he not so fondly referred to him, ever considered himself a cut above those all around him because, as he had stressed, he was not really from "around here" originally, but from Oxford. Which, Digger would stress for the benefit of everyone around him, and who were indeed from "around here", he bloody was not. Or, at least, being born there wasn't the same as coming from there, was it? It was Bobby's father, who'd met Bobby's mother when she was "in service" in a "Big House" at Witney outside the city of spires, who came from Oxford and who was a scout in one of the colleges, the university connection at which Bobby airily waved.

The prat, said Digger. They'd met on her day off and, with the maid quite rapidly no maiden anymore but pregnant with Bobby, went back together to marry in chapel and see what work an Oxford man might find in the Valleys. The rest of that indigent and indigenous population were moving in the opposite direction. Bobby's father got the message and joined the exodus. Alone.

"Mind you," the opening gambit of numerous conversations in saloon bars and workingmens' clubs, and, "Say what you like," the consensus invariably advanced was that Bobby Braithwaite was an "'ard man", "a tough old bugger", "a right bastard" and "you wouldn't want to cross 'im". Tales would be told and heads would nod at the saga of bare-knuckle fights and one-punch knock-down and kickings and head-butting at which Bobby had specialised before graduating to sealed envelopes, veiled threats and generous hospitality. The path by which the local boy, the Oxford man, had risen to rooted fame and reasonable fortune.

He felt Myra slow down as the first warning sign for the Péage instructed her to do so. He blinked into the sun, and reached into his pocket for his Ray-Bans. Very Big O, he thought. Digger looked out of the darkened car window at the regimented and scrupulously tended vines in the passing fields of the lowland plain and up to the meticulously maintained dry-stone walls of the near-distant terraced hillsides and sighed at how soon he would himself be accumulating, stacking and sorting the ancient fallen stones of their own extensive, and higher, terraces.

He closed his eyes again. But he was firmly back in the present now. Or the future that was set in stone. Bloody great honey-coloured slabs of limestone which had weathered and slipped from their artful setting or been knocked away by scrambling goats to lie in heaps on the orange-crumble earth. It would be for Digger to rescue them and re-build the ingenious ramparts which generations of toiling peasants had erected to shore up their wedge cuts into the otherwise unyielding slopes. That was what he was, then, was it? In her eyes as in her father's before. A toiling peasant.

Of course he did have the building skills for the job. Hard learned and well taught. And, with a hint of pride, the strength yet to do the back-breaking job. There was, too, the praise to be lapped up: her guests gazing up at the fruit of all his early morning work done before the sun could rise and sear his bare back and sizzle his hatless head. Then, it was, from locals and incomers alike, and all not within a personal generation of the construction of a dry-stone wall, "*Superbe*" and "*Magnifique*" and "*Extra … Extra!*"

Bloody extra it was all right in Digger's roving thoughts. The only thing he didn't have to do to keep bloody Geoffrey's bloody albatross ready for its destined entry in the bloody *Maisons et Décors* spread which Myra had in mind, was to prepare, clean and maintain the bloody Aubergine. He couldn't, thank God, be trusted with that. Not with the delicately correct amounts of chlorination, the Ph. factor or some such calculation in pink in a test tube, and the timing of the filtration system and the exact pulse to the skimmers and the suction and the lights for midnight swims – as if, he thought – and the throbbing pump itself. Thank God, he intoned, that for all that she had employed a "pool man". Digger had privately, and childishly she said, christened him Pedro. His real name was Philippe, a hulking, taciturn, pig-tailed misery guts – Digger's alternative appellation – who turned up in cut-off jeans, a torn T-shirt and ripped trainers and never accepted Digger's weekly offer of a cold beer. Digger never stopped offering, though his look now was cloak to the "Suit yourself, Froggie, you twat" variety which he reserved for cover-all usage when annoyed. Nonetheless, he took care to veil his dislike, just in case he found himself made available from the bench as first substitute. Sod that, he figured, as the Audi glided expertly into the middle lane towards the tollbooths of the Péage, when he had more than enough to do as it was.

They seemed, or so it felt to his arms and in his shoulder muscles, to spend as much time here as they did back at what he called "proper" home. Especially since the cheapo flights now went all year round. Myra never stopped either. Planning and organising. She had had him to strip all the flaky green paint off the wooden shutters and windows, up and down, back and front, doors and windows, inside and outside, to putty and prime and paint her *volets*, as she referred to them, a light blue that she had seen, in all the glossy magazines which she bought and piled up, designated as "*typique*" and "*lavande, presque gris, un peu foncé*". The walls had cracks. They had to be filled in. They became a curdled cream colour that was, deliberately, the off-white side of yellow. Or so she told him. There were tiles to be replaced. For the roof, old ones, sourced for their lichen and atmosphere-touched rusty terracotta red, slotted to blend in, and for the floors smoother caramel oblongs to complement the originals which Geoffrey and Wilfrid had, so cleverly she pointed out, bought dirt-cheap in Spain. The kitchen and bathroom, suitable enough for bachelors, was re-plumbed and re-appointed with new fixtures by the all-purpose handyman she kept for his uses. Digger was resigned not bitter. Yet he gnawed on the bone of what exactly the purpose was, beyond the outcome of a handsome, restored and refurbished square-set stone house in an exotic and replenished garden. The worry nagged away at him. His worth. His utility. His value. His purpose.

Myra had stopped the car on the footbrake. Digger handed over the five euro note to his wife, who reached her hand up and flashed her full smile at the scowling female face high above her in the glass-sided cabin. She accepted the twenty-five centimes in change with a gracious "Merci, madame" and flung them into Digger's lap before purring through the upthrust barrier. Digger experienced a sudden surge of melancholy. Perhaps it was the sex. Or relative lack of it. He looked over at Myra and inexplicably felt a twitch and a liveliness he had not expected. Expectation was another thing altogether. That had been dismissed long ago. There were moments, of course, and he could conjure those up, including the time on the pine dinner table after the opera and the Prosecco reception, when her slinky Donna Karan wraparound had somehow slithered with one tug to the parquet floor, but many possibilities had been deferred with a brisk admonition not to be silly, their age, and later, maybe.

Digger picked over such a prospect for the weeks to come. He stole a prolonged look at the potential donor of such a prospect and noted his stirring had not yet deserted him. Promising, he decided, as Myra switched from the right into the left exit lane in order to head for the Autoroute entrance signposted above for the city to the east, their direction, rather than the other one to the bifurcating west. She moved into fourth gear and she guided the Audi dexterously around one of those interminable French curves to the left at a steady and instructed fifty kilometres an hour. Then she screamed. Digger jumped. He turned his head to look in front of them. He was staring at an oncoming Renault Clio. Out loud, but in a strangely calm tone, he heard his voice say above her scream, "Fuck it, Myra, we're going to crash." An in an instant, they had. Head on.

The noise had been a muffled crump. Both drivers had instinctively stamped on their brakes. It had been to no avail in avoiding the collision, but it had made the impact happen in slower motion than it would have otherwise. Fast and hard enough for all that to cause Myra to be pulled forward onto the steering wheel and bruise her breastbone and for Digger to bang his hard head against the windscreen. Their airbags, thankfully or not, had not deployed. Later, they told one another that their lives had not passed before their eyes though they both thought, in an icicle of a moment, that they were going to die. They had not. They clutched hands and asked each other if they were all right. They were. They had survived.

The other car had skewed to their right as they hit each other. The sole occupant sat as still and silent in his vehicle as they did in their own. Digger felt nothing but relief that Myra, though trembling and giving out tiny indeterminate cries, seemed to be unhurt. He felt equally thankful when a young man opened the door of his Clio and stood looking first at his car and then directly at them. He seemed more bemused than anything else and definitely, assessed Digger, not hurt, the silly bugger. The man turned full circle and went to the back of the Renault. He opened the boot. When he closed it, Digger could see, he was wearing the compulsory yellow slip-on waistcoat. He began walking towards the Audi. Digger unbuckled his belt and got out, thinking what's-the-French-for-you-silly-sod,   wrong-side-of-the-road. Maybe Myra would know in a minute.

Digger managed a woeful grin and a wave of his arms at the sight of two write-offs. Insurance job for sure. The Frenchman pre-empted his own attempt at explaining they were foreigners with a solicitous: "*Ça va? Tous les deux?*" Digger nodded. His pronunciation would announce he wasn't French anyway so he began, magnanimously in his view, what was going to be a difficult conversation with the young idiot, with a generously returned, "*Et vous, monsieur?*" In reply there was a curt nod and a shake of the head to indicate all was much clearer now. His spoken reply to Digger's concerned query was lengthier, colder and angrier in tone than Digger had anticipated. Nor had he understood most of it. Digger muttered sharply: "*Un moment, s'il vous plaît.*" He beckoned Myra to join them. She sat motionless. Maybe in shock. Shaking, he could see. Surely the police or somebody would be here soon to sort out this arrogant bastard.

For the first time since the accident Digger became aware of what was happening around them. There was noise again. There was traffic moving. Somewhere a siren was wailing its imminent arrival. Digger looked at the traffic, moving slowly to gawp at the wrecked cars. More to his astonishment than any initial consternation, it registered with him that the cars and lorries crawling past were in the right-hand lane going away from them, moving on, and that the only discernible traffic in the left lane, the one Myra had pulled into, was backing up and honking their horns behind the bashed-in Clio which was unseen beyond the bend, and was blocking their own progress. "Oh, no. Oh, fuck me gentle," whispered Digger, and looked behind him at the empty road back around the bend the other way to the Péage, and then at the raised yellow-and-white lengths of rubber studs that divided the two lanes.

He put an arm around his wife, who had stumbled from the car to his side. The same sickening realisation of what had happened now flitted between them. Digger had been dreaming of Myra when she went through the toll booth barrier. Both would have assumed that, as always when you left the Péage, it was one-way traffic, the mad scrambling re-positioning, and then, just as they had done many times before, into the left lane marked for Montpellier with the right shearing off to Toulouse. She was still sure there were no signs, no warnings, no indicators, to tell you different. Except, and now that she re-ran it in her mind, all the exiting cars had funnelled into the right where she originally was, all westward bound she'd thought, as she crossed those funny central markings to the left, to the east, alone. There had been re-routing, a temporary Déviation, that had sent her into oncoming, exiting off the motorway traffic. She began to quiver uncontrollably from the roots of her dyed blonde hair to the tips of her hot-pink painted toes. Digger held her up and then gently sat her down, her head in her hands, at the side of the road.

Their French victim was pointing a jabbing finger at Myra. His voice was harsh. Digger heard him say, "*Votre femme ... stupide ... pas de jugement ... votre femme ... imbécilique ... votre femme ... votre femme. Votre. Femme. Votre. Femme,*" like a jackhammer out of control. He was getting louder and repetitive. Digger looked at Myra, rocking back and fro, head to knees and back again, making no sound, not a whimper, covering her face with her hands, her tears seeping through the gaps between her fingers.

"*Alors, votre femme,*" the accusation began again, accompanied by more furious stabbing gestures, "Votre femme, Monsieur ...," until Digger said, in a reactive heartbeat, "Precisely, sunshine! My bloody *femme*, not yours, so shut the fuck up!" There was a pause, a hesitation when the tormentor becomes the tormented, which Digger knew well. He acted. He yanked off his sunglasses with his left hand. He took two strides forward and wrapped his own right hand around a wagging French finger. He squeezed hard. There was surprise and then alarm and silence at last. It was Digger who spoke now, bending down right into his opponent's face, to deliver some verbal "afters", a dialogue with only one outcome.

"Now listen, butt. *Écoute, eh? Je suis le conducteur. Pas* my bloody *femme*, right? Bloody moi, see. *Pour vous pas de problème.* OK? *Le* whiplash? *Hôpital?* OK. Insurance? *Monnaie?* OK. *Pas de problème. Je suis le conducteur.*"

"*Mais ... c'est votre femme qui ...*".

"*Pas de* bloody '*mais*', you clown. Jesus Thomas! Me, see? *Comprendez? Vite! Pas de* bloody witnesses, see? *Je suis le* only *conducteur. Ma faute*, OK?"

The Frenchman gingerly extracted his finger from Digger's grasp. Bruised, not broken. Not yet anyway. He ran a sweaty hand down the front of his freshly ironed, short-sleeved, monogrammed shirt. He looked up at Digger and said,

"OK. I follow. I understand. We do. Liked you sayed."

Richie "Digger" Davies nodded and sighed and walked away. He bent low on the driver's side of the open Audi and moved the seat backwards. He got in and adjusted the mirrors. He leaned over and found the lever to pull the front passenger seat forward. He took the key from the ignition and pocketed it. He went to comfort his wife.

A navy blue police car and a blue-and-white ambulance screeched to a halt behind them. Digger hunkered down and waited. The Frenchman he'd fingered did all the talking. Explanations seemed to be about the fools from *Angleterre*. The male cop seemed amused. He probably amused himself often by the looks of him, Digger speculated, a bigger and butcher version of that Johnny Hallyday he'd seen on her CDs. Only with a gun strapped on and in combat boots. His female sidekick was just as gimlet-eyed but smaller and less butch. She did the organising whilst Johnny postured for the passing traffic. Myra and Digger were ushered off the road and into the obligatory fluorescent jackets. Documents were checked. All in order. Reports were written up and passed over for comment. It was clear who was to blame, and why. The French whiplash sufferer was to be taken to hospital. Digger insisted that he and his wife were not physically harmed in any way. It still took a further three hours to sign everything, to have the cars and themselves carted off to a nearby garage where such collisions seemed to be a regular occurrence, to sign more forms of claim, and no counter-claim, to speak to the hire company's Paris number and arrange to pick up a replacement car that was a taxi-ride away across the nearest large town.

When Digger was finally sat behind the wheel of the new car – a Mégane, maroon in colour and sassy in the rear – which he was driving carefully along minor roads to their village, he allowed himself a slow smile. He talked. Myra listened and nodded. He found different ways of saying it, over and over. They were lucky. They should be grateful. Think of how, despite all the bollocking he'd had to take from those *flics*, the tossers, and how they'd dished out their severe reprimands, that they hadn't even bothered to breathalyse him. Not that the double G & T he'd sipped on the plane would have counted. Well, probably not. Still, you'd have thought they'd do their job properly, better than that, wouldn't you? All Johnny Bloody Hallyday could do was ponce around, strutting his stuff, rubbing his fingers through his punk blonde hair. Bloody rubbish, he was. There was more about her, the woman, wasn't there?

"Yes, love," Myra agreed, and then, "Thank you, love. For taking the strain … the blame. Thank you. You were great."

Digger's strong, thick fingers pinched into the leather of the wheel.

"No probs, love," he said. "No probs at all. All for you. Anything for you."

It took less than an hour after it all ended to reach the house. In the late afternoon the sun was still high above the waving cypress trees and the temperature not yet below 80° fahrenheit. Digger invariably translated from centigrade to take what he called the true reading from the thermometer nailed to the side door of the house. He opened the lavender-grey double-doors and put the bags inside. He felt almost at home. He had a sense of well-being that was only partly caused by the familiar, dark coolness of the interior.

"I'll unpack later, love," Myra said. "Why don't you go and cool down? Have a nice swim. Looks nice."

"Aye, OK, then. Think I will," said Digger and, winking, "In the buff, mind. Trunks are in the case. But nobody to see, eh?"

After the plunge into the crystalline pool – fair dos to Philippe – he lay back, dripping wet, on the blue-and-white striped cushion cover of the wooden lounger. He put his broad hands behind his head and dozed. Water globules glistened and wobbled on the barrel of his hairy stomach and burst on the thickness of his thighs. All around the cicadas were keeping up their end-of-the-day one-note-in-concert, a plastic squeaky toy sound, made incessant as if being held in the mouth of a dog who would not give it up. His triumph, if that was what it was, seemed insignificant and momentary but still satisfying. Digger drifted, as usual, into the past that had once seemed so open. Was it the same for everyone? He couldn't answer that. He only knew that closure was not what he had had in prospect once, and yet that prospect was the thing for which he had compromised the moment. His head felt heavy. He would never manage to be clear on any of this, would he? It wasn't the rugby, or Bobby and the business, and certainly not Myra. Was it resentment, then, against the whole manner of a changed time and place, something he couldn't really shape or resist? Not that either. It was Who Whom. That was the revelation. Who Bloody Whom. Something about once knowing who the who was who did it to others until, somehow, the who was us doing it to us. And not understanding it.

He didn't look up when she lifted the latch of the pool's wooden gate – fenced all around by legal decree and by virtue of his sweating, fetching and carrying – because he was still in a reverie, muddled but crucial to the underlying thought, about the connection between fly halves and flankers, a chain as much as a broken link maybe. He snapped out of it when he heard the latch click shut and her footsteps click-clicking across the patio towards him where he lay at the side of the pool. He half-raised himself to see Myra standing over him. She had put on a black one-piece swimming costume – but she never swam! – that was cut flatteringly low over her rounded breasts and high on her legs. She was wearing matt black open toe and ankle-strappy high heels – the ones he sometimes persuaded her to wear just for him – and her hair, freshly washed and brushed, was bunched up in the back and held there by a comb – the way she knew he liked to see it done – and her mouth, her glorious mouth, was a bright scarlet gash.

"Christ! Myra," he said.

"Shhh. You can close your mouth now, Richie. And I'll open mine. If you're ready that is …," she said.

And, since he was, his *femme*, Bobby Braithwaite's only and lovely daughter, Myra, bent over him slowly, and slipped her poised and carmine lips over the offering of love which had risen up to meet her, and which she held helpfully and firmly at its base as she began to bob slowly up and down with the assurance of a once habitual and now returning, and customary act.

"Christ!" Digger thought he'd tell the boys. "Maybe not all frittered away after all, eh? Bet not many sixty-five-year-old fly halves get such good treatment. Who Whom be buggered!"

And with that he fatally raised his head to get a better look at himself, and promptly groaned.

Filthy, Gone

And then she said:

"I've never seen the crem so packed. It was jam-packed. Overflowing. Into the yard outside. People were standing there for ages. In the rain, mind. Soaked to the skin, they were. And inside, all squished up on those wooden benches, cold and hard under your bum, you know, or standing, dripping, in the back. So, I gotta say, I was glad Trev had nagged me to be ready, said we'd have to be early, by the door, in the porch, hanging about for half an hour, mind, if we were to get a seat. I mean, you had to wait outside, didn't you, couldn't go in, like, till the family had come. There was a big silence when the hearse pulled up, people shuffling, respect shown isn't it, all to the one side, but then coming together quick in a crowd, so we had to scoot in straight behind and sit down, as it turned out, just a few pews behind the family while the whole place, like I say, just filled up so quick with people. I had to keep turning my head, slowly, you know, respectfully, to see who was there. Altogether, like.

And I'll give her that. She looked great. In the circumstances, like. Made an effort. You could tell. Always lovely to look at, Myra, mind, even if she is a bit of a stuck-up-cow. Not 'oity-toity, cos she will speak to you, but thinks she's a cut above, don't she? Always did. Mind you, fair play. She never said nothing out of place to me – she'd have the back of my tongue if she had! –

others, yes, but not me. Ever. Even if she thought she might have had cause, years ago, of course.

And another thing was, she didn't overdo the black. Easy for the widow to do that but it can drain the colour awful if you're not careful, so I'd have to say her pallor was just right. Pale, mind, wan even, but offset by a swanky-looking brooch, diamonds I'd say, knowing her, and a little ribbed-silk red scarf round her neck. Club colours, see. Well, the Order of Service said it was to be a celebration of Digger's life. They used that, the name, on the leaflet. Nice touch, I thought. He'd've liked that.

Richard "Digger" Davies, and his dates, sixty-five he was. Who'd have thought. But not "Richie", see. She never called him that, mind. I know that for a fact, don't I? You remember.

Anyways, I'd have to say she was looking nice for him on the day. She'd had her hair done, more blonde than it ever was, if you know what I mean, and her lips were a post-box red. Stood out. She wasn't on nobody's arm, of course. Well, no one particularly close now, is there? No children, as you know. He didn't have no brothers or sisters, same as her, and all the old ones gone. Couple of cousins on his side, and their kids, scruffy buggers in black leather jackets, drainpipes, no ties. Typical. That was all. So she walked in, quite dramatic mind, behind Richie's coffin. Plain black dress, a little jacket, black court shoes and tights. They must've held an umbrella over her from the car cos she didn't have a coat or mac with her, and, oh ay, she held a single red rose in her hand. Almost like being at the pictures. They'd been in France, where it'd happened. Always going there, on holiday. I expect Richie, as I always called him anyway, was as tanned inside that box as she was outside it. They went regular, to that place she'd inherited from that pooffy cousin of hers, you remember, Jeffrey Whatsisname, 'came an actor. Went on the box. He's dead, too, years gone now.

And all the time, I have to say, as it all went on, I found I couldn't get my mind off Richie's big old body, all squashed into that bloody coffin. Shame. I didn't feel tearful, well not then, at least. Just what a shame. Of course my thoughts were straying, I admit. A bit naughty, I know. Still I kept thinking of that body of his as I'd once known it. Couldn't help it, and I may have swallowed a bit hard because Trev asked if I was all right and I wondered, oh God, he can't know, can he? Usually slow on the uptake on things like that, Trev, but then again there was Myra, sitting just in front where I could've touched her and she must've seen me when she walked past, though she didn't let on.

For certain she knew I'd been going out with him when she first picked up with him, didn't she? Don't you think? Don't know what Richie told her, mind, but she'd've been as slow as old Trev if she hadn't known it, because, see, it didn't exactly stop between Richie and me, for quite a time after that I can tell you, and there was that other time, later. He was a bugger for all that, mind. I thought to myself if there's any tap-tapping coming from that coffin it won't be his hands he'll be using, I can tell you!

It took six of the rugby boys from the club to carry him in on their shoulders. Two of his old pals in the middle and the other four at either end, from today's team. Quite tasty-looking, they were. The young ones, I mean! I think I recognised one of the older ones, but I wasn't sure. It might have been that Tiny Thomas he went drinking with after the games back then, before meeting up with me later in the Memo. Only, if it was, he was not only huge, as he was then, but fat and bald, so who knows, but I think it was, because he caught my eye and winked, the cheeky sod. Tried it on with me, only the once mind, when Richie was paralatic with drink. I let him try, to punish Richie, but can't say I ever fancied him, even back then.

Lots of old faces to clock all round, really, so I found myself giving little smiles quite a lot, not really knowing who the hell they were, or are I should say, though I kept, you know, respectful, sad, not wanting to give the impression I was enjoying it or anything. People get funny ideas, don't they? Still, I'd decided not to go in black myself. I wore that silk-and-linen jacket-and-skirt in deep pink I got, you know, that white blouse with the stitching round the collar, and, to hell with it I thought, my cream-and-tan skyscraper heels. My legs are OK, love, even if the rest is starting to sag a bit! Not that Trev seems to notice one way or the other. Or, at least, not until lately he hadn't. Seems to have got his second wind from somewhere, and I know where!

It went on a bit, the service. One of those modern affairs, you know the ones where the minister is more like a master of ceremonies, or even a bloody bingo caller, than an actual vicar. This one called out the hymns by numbers, eyes down and page eight and all that, and off they went, between the tributes and the prayers, with "Guide me, O Thou Great Jehovah", naturally, and that other one they always sing, in Welsh, "Arglwydd Dyma something or other" and ending up with the anthem, all of the rugby boys bursting out of their blazers, all puce-faced and bellowing *"Gwlad! Gwlad!"*, exactly like as if they were at some international or other.

Trev was as pop-eyed as the rest of them. The M.C., minister so-called, though he did, to be fair, say a few religiousy kind of things now and then, was bobbing up and down, cueing in this one and that one, usually from the club, to say all about Richie. Or Digger, as they all referred to him. Calling him that in front of Myra, so she must've given permission, because she never called him that either. It was him told me that. She'd told him, and no messing, that he was to be Richard from the off for her. So she was the one who must have decided to allow this familiarity from others. A bit late in the day. Every time they called him "Digger" I could see, well not actually see but, you know, sense, that tight little smile on her chops, and yes, I do admit, I always envied her those cheekbones.

And then it was all about how he should've played for Wales more than just the once. One of them forgot himself in the pulpit and said it was "a bloody disgrace", then said "sorry", but there was a snigger all round and everyone was muttering approval. Of course I never saw him play, myself, well only the once, bored out of my mind and freezing to boot I was, but I could tell they were over-egging the hard-but-fair and never-a-dirty-player bit. That's not what he told me; he positively relished being a thug, from what I remember, and his endless dirty remarks about how really, really hard he could be with me if I'd let him. Cheeky sod! They all said he was a team player and a one-club-man – not so far as the ladies was concerned, he wasn't – and that we'd none of us ever see the likes of him again. I suppose that's right if they meant we were all getting on a bit, but, no, they were building him up bigger than that, I can tell you.

People started crying. Men and all. Can you believe? I

sneaked a look at Trev and he had tears squeezing out of his eyes and trickling down his cheeks. He saw me looking before I could turn away, and squeezed my hand and whispered "A great man, Rita. A great man." I was, I can tell you, more than a bit gobsmacked by that and I must've rolled my eyes, unintentionally, without meaning to look like anything was going on, but he gave me a very funny look, and I think maybe that's what started off what came later, over these last few weeks. At the end the coffin sort of slid back on rollers, like it does and those heavy blue velvet curtains with the gold trim closed across it, and he was gone. It felt a bit like going to the pictures, like I said, only in reverse. You know, the end was the only bit we'd really come for.

Everybody filed out, in turn, row by row, after Myra and her so-called family and the music they played was that cheesy Sinatra thing "My Way" when, if she'd've asked me, I'd've told her something by the Supremes was more his thing. "Baby Love", he liked. He drooled over that Diana Ross so much the one time, he really annoyed me. The rain had stopped outside and Myra was there, real Lady Muck now, shaking hands and kissing people on the cheek. I kept away, in the back, let Trev do all that, and we'd filled the card in so she'd know who'd been there. I wanted us to go home after that, but Trev insisted we had to go back to the club.

There were hundreds there too, most probably everyone who'd been outside as well as inside the crem. And, fair play, it was a proper buffet she'd laid on. More like a wedding party than a funeral wake. None of those turdy sausage rolls and curled-up sarnies and pukey cocktail sausages on toothpicks. Plates and knives and forks, and not plastic and paper neither, and proper slices of beef and ham cut off the joint by proper catering staff, and poached salmon and bowls and bowls of minted new potatoes and dressed salads, and rice with sweetcorn and red peppers. It was a proper spread. Caterers were from Cardiff, too, not up the Valleys, thank God. As much wine as you liked, oh and desserts, not that I had one of those, and a free bar until five o'clock. They had to wheel some of 'em home, no doubt. So, hats off to her, she pulled the stops out, though I suppose money's no object for her, still, fair dos, it was a proper send-off, done proper.

We had to bump into each other, didn't we? She was polite enough and I said how sorry I was, which was true. Only, where we were standing, near the bar, and that was packed at the time, was, funny enough, made me shiver, almost exactly where he was standing when he first met her. I bloody well remember that because I'd gone to the toilet and when I came back he was chatting to her, chatting her up I could see, and I was *not* best pleased I can tell you. Turned on my heel. Plenty more where he came from, I thought. Only there wasn't, not really.

She went home with her father, old Bobby Braithwaite, that night, so he came looking for me in the other bar afterwards. I played it cool, of course, and then when he kept at it I was angry with him. Couldn't help showing it, could I? But his line was that it was all about getting a job, he was fed up in the tax office, better wages to be had, and so on. Well, I wasn't green but what was I to do? We kept seeing each other and I sort of pretended I didn't know he was stringing both of us along for a bit after that. Well, when I say stringing, I mean her, not me, me he was shagging the arse off! Wasn't exactly a secret was it, when we'd disappear from the club or a dance after he'd had his hands practically all over me, down the nearest, darkest back lane. He even had a favourite back gate, set slightly deeper into the wall. He was my first, you know. Honest!

And I did think, him loving shagging me so much, that he'd choose me in the end, above her, because, let's face it, she was always a cold bitch and I know for a fact it was ages before he got into *her* knickers. And then it was all precautions, rubber johnnies, which I never ever liked, made you sore they did, and fumbling about. Whereas, it was, between me and him, "sweet and luscious", his words not mine and, to be honest, I didn't want to let him go, cos he was, let's face it, bloody gorgeous.

All this, going through my mind, well you can't help it, can you, as I was standing there looking at Myra and nodding, and wondering why they hadn't had any kids whilst Trev, who was all right in bed early on, nothing adventurous mind, had given me three without hardly trying. Perhaps it was Richie after all, not her, because he banged me often enough, when I was only seventeen and eighteen, and oh, that once or twice I told you about later on, without me ever missing.

I didn't linger. Not much to be said that could be said, was there? She just said it was very sudden – the heat and a bit of bother on the motorway or something, and she'd found him at the pool. The pool. Had to get that one in, I suppose. The pool. We had an Indian after all that: me, Trev, and some of the boys and their wives, from the old days. She didn't come. I couldn't eat much. When it came down to it, I was more upset than I thought. But, I have to be honest, was it for him or for me? All that time gone. He was a couple of years older than me but we were both so young, weren't we? Couldn't get enough of each other, really. It was mutual. God! That time I told you about in his mother's front room. He'd taken all my clothes off, he loved doing that, and licking me all over, and telling me it was all right, because I was shy, believe it or not, and then slipping his cock, no plunging more like, into me, his big arse whacking it in, and God it was lovely, and his mother rat-a-tat-tat-ing on the door, asking why it was locked when it was never supposed to be locked, and me wriggling to get free from under him, but he wouldn't let me, oh God, till he was finished. And then I had to put my hand over his mouth. He was always a groaner. Even years later, must be twenty years ago now, when I'd met him by chance in Marks and Spencer's, not looking my best I can tell you, and my knees were wobbling to see him and, well, you know, I told you, we had a drink and he drove us to Cardiff, to the Angel, and we just fucked all afternoon. I can't say it was as good as back then but it was the thrill, the risk, of being found out I liked, and he was still, you know, appreciative.

He didn't talk too much about him and Myra, though he did say, perhaps he was making it up for me, that they didn't make love too often anymore, and that was years ago, mind. He'd say things like that, Richie, "making love" rather than a cruder word, though he liked me to be naughty, as he'd say. We just stopped again after that, after a few times. He'd seemed interested in my kids – names and whatever – but I didn't detect any regrets of his own not having any. You know what, I think he actually did go after her with a job in his mind. And, you've got to say, he did well enough out of it. No struggling on a primary teacher's wage like Trev, and even when I started back in the tax office again, that didn't make a big difference. We're OK now, house paid and some money after Trev's old man, and that bachelor uncle in Swansea, so no complaints, but I wouldn't have minded a few bob when I was younger. So I can see where Richie was coming from.

But what I couldn't see, then or now, was all this hero worship of him. I read the notices in the papers, Cardiff as well as local, and name of God, you'd think he was a superstar, or something. He was, they said, "the embodiment of the gutsy spirit of the valleys" and that he played "like a man possessed for his own people". What the hell did that mean? The best one was that "Richie 'Digger' Davies came off the terraces onto the field of dreams straight out of the people, and when he hung up his boots he re-joined his butties". Trev cut that out, and his photo, and pinned them to the board by the phone. He was obsessed with him, talking about him all the time, how he'd always say "Shwmae" and have a pint, and how he was "the best of his generation", to look up to, as Trev, my age not Richie's, did whenever he saw him playing or walking down the street, usually with a girl on his arm in those days, everybody gawping. Before me, and Myra.

Our memories of Richie were stirring, alive as we were to him in our different ways, and maybe it was all that which set Trev off the way it did. He was leafing through the team photographs in some old club history over breakfast and he suddenly looked up at me and he said, "Rita", he said, "You went out a bit with Digger, didn't you?"

"Oh", I said, "You know that, Trev, couple of years before we met. You know, dances and discos, and that. Casual." And he gave me a very strange look and he said, "Richie Digger Davies didn't do anything casual, Rita. If he went out with you it's because he wanted to."

So I said, well what else could I say, "Yeah. I s'pose so."

Only he didn't leave it there. We were lying in bed, reading, when he propped himself up and he said: "Rita, I want to know, and I won't mind, honest, I want to know, if, you know, you ever slept with Digger." I bloody well started then, I can tell you. But he went on, "I mean, I know you went with that Johnny Williams and got engaged, and you told me, fair play, you weren't a virgin or anything, when we met, and I said, fair enough, and neither was I, though there was only that English girl in training college as I told you, and that we'd never mention the past again. And I haven't, have I? But I need to know, now, Rita. I can't explain it, but I can't help it either. You see, Digger, stands for so much. Means so much. To me. To all of us."

I'm telling you straight, I thought he'd flipped his lid. But not a bit of it. He made this long speech about how special Digger had been, and how special that made any bond between him and us, and I thought what d'you mean "us", it was me he was shagging, not you? He just wouldn't stop – Trev, I mean. Had I? Ever? More than once? He didn't mind. It made me, in his eyes, even more special, too. All a bit crackers. And bloody persistent. So, after he'd gone on and on at this, one day I'd had it up to there and I told him, it was all in the past, none of his business really, what I did before we met, and, just to shut him up I thought, I said, yes, there were a few times. With Richie. Christ! It was that "few" which did it. Set him off again. How few did few mean? How many did few mean? Funny thing is, I wasn't, you know, worried. More surprised. I didn't want to hurt him, and I didn't want to rake over what was long riddled through. And that was my mistake again, because when I fed him a few details, to authenticate it, so to speak, how he'd been a bit forceful the first time, didn't believe I was a virgin, and I'd cried, and how he'd made it up to me and I thought we'd get married, I let him again, a few times, well, Trev, was like a dog with a bone. He wanted more, not less! What was I wearing? Was it in the kitchen? Were we standing up in the lane? Did we do it in Digger's van? What was he like? And he meant his cock, I'm telling you, not his personality. I made it a bit romantic and lovey-dovey rather that what it actually was, you know, and he was on that like a flash. "No. The real thing, Rita. I only want true stories." True stories? True stories? Right, you bastard, I thought. I'll tell you. Or some of it anyway. So I did. And, thing is, when I looked at him a bit sheepish, he was more aroused than I'd seen him in years. You know, playing with himself. So I laughed and I said, "Oi, you don't want to waste that!", but he said, "No, keep going. We'll do it, together, later. Now, for now, tell me about you and Digger doing it, holding your arse and fucking you." After that there was no end to it. Not so far anyway. He doesn't seem to care, so long as it's about Digger and me. I tell you, I'm running out of stories and he spots any made-up bits and makes me tell him the ones he's already heard over and over. Mind, our sex life, not just his wanking, is better than it's been for years. He makes me dress up for him, and all, and sometimes I have to call out Digger's name, only I say "Richie, Richie", which somehow excites and upsets him more. I don't know where, or when, this is going to end. Sometimes I think about whether I'll tell him about later on with Richie, or maybe not, or about that lush Italian I met with you in Corsica when we went away from the

men for a week, or perhaps not, eh? But since the funeral,
I'm telling you, who'd have thought it, eh? my Trev is just
filthy, gone."

A Talking Point

It was strange, now that he was gone, finally gone and reduced to speckled ash in a bronze urn and plonked on her mantelpiece, that she could only think of him as "Digger". It was the nickname she had avoided, with some distaste, when he was alive. Yet it was everywhere now he was dead. It was literally unavoidable. In the press. On the radio and television, even. On the lips and in the letters of friends, his not hers, and acquaintances, mostly hers, expressing sympathy with cards and phone calls. It was used in all the formal tributes and underneath all the photographs in the papers. She heard it whispered, sotto voce, as she pushed a trolley down the aisle of a supermarket. She was "Digger's Widow". That was how she was seen and talked about, and the perception sat on her shoulders as squarely as his ashes sat above the empty fireplace in the house he'd knocked through for her. In reply to enquiries she found herself using the nickname as if it were the most natural thing to do, and, worse, it was how she began to think of him in her own mind. Not her Richard anymore. Certainly not someone else's Richie. Digger. There it was. He had become again what in his prime he had been, a talking point. And the reference was undeniably to the one and only "Digger" Davies, her late husband and the town's last, true working-class hero.

She wasn't so sure about that last bit. Marriage to her had brought him the security of working for her father and eventual ownership, with her, of Braithwaite and Davies: Building Contractors, and, after its sale, the comfort of a well-upholstered retirement. The detached Victorian house that scowled down on the town from the common across the river from the terraces where he was born and brought up, and the *maison de campagne* in the *Midi*, which, she conceded, he did not like as much but which was, as he also admitted, better than a caravan in Saundersfoot. Yet, nothing that had happened to him, materially, after his glory days on the rugby field seemed to diminish the aura with which his life had then been, briefly and lastingly, touched. Myra had puzzled over all this long before. Her conclusions were generally the same. They were sentimental, nostalgic, immature, unrealistic, and fools. This "They" was her catch-all pejorative for those who had not noticed, or did not seem to mind, his thickening body, his barrel of a belly, his grey and skimpy-thin hair and his veined nose. Digger liked a drink and They liked to have one with him, in the institute where her father had made him a member, or in the club where his face, topped by that one tasselled International cap, adorned the wall, or in one of the many pubs where his name was still, as They would say, legend, and his presence ever welcome.

In this sense They owned him because They had created him, and his physical alteration, even his social and economic distance from Them, could affect nothing of what was a cultural bond she could not, even if she had wished it, share. Not that she wished it. Nor was this only about sport, though Myra could see that was its catalyst. No, this was something to do with a coming together, in crowds and across generations, in which she had no desire to participate and which her father, though dismissive of its inner purpose, exploited for its business potential. What had made Digger special was not only his origins in the town and his working-class antecedents, not only his loyalty to the club when well-placed others tried to entice him away, not only his physique and his genuine skill at the game, but, above all else, the style of his playing. He was, like Them, unfashionable. He was, like

Them, shunned. He was, like Them, confrontational in everything. He was, like Them, rewarded but discarded. He was, like Them, not going to change for anybody. He was, like Them, root and branch, a part of something bigger together than They could ever be separately. He was, They said, A Team Player, A One Club Man, One of Us. He was Their Digger, and nobody else's.

Myra saw all this, over again, as she'd half-smiled and fully acknowledged the faces that swam in and out of view at the crematorium. The fact was – as she had recognised on her return with the body when she was greeted, almost like royalty, by a welcoming party, a delegation as it turned out to be, from the club – it was to be Their funeral more than hers. Digger had finally been elevated to the pantheon of untouchables where They had long wanted him to be. They had gathered around her in the days before all the arrangements were made. They whispered at her like a Greek chorus in one of the plays in which Geoffrey had once appeared as some blind, demented king. "There will never be another like him." "Would have been a giant in the professional game." Her loss was the town's loss, was Wales's loss, was rugby's loss. "Greatest player the club ever had." "A servant of the game." "A role model for all wing forwards, never mind so-called modern bloody flankers." This, and much else, was arcane praise Myra neither sought nor understood, no more than she required the help They offered. Yet it came in such waves that it was easier to agree than resist. There would be a selected cohort of players, old and new, to carry him in. There would be tributes from the club president and the town's Member of Parliament. There would be, if it was all right with her, no invitation extended to the Welsh Rugby Union and no official WRU Representative. "Because of the snub, see, love," one explained, and she nodded. There would be short eulogies from three of the survivors of the championship winning teams of his heyday, his old pals "Spike" Jones, "Moxie" Moxon and "Spider" Webb. The three would be under strict instructions to keep it clean, They assured her, and again she nodded.

Finally, when everything from hymns to running order to the post-match reception had been mutually settled, the committee's delegation sat on Myra's red-and-gold Egyptian motif settee – "Like a bloody barge", Digger had often complained – and came to the point. They appreciated how much Myra had not let "family grief" prevent "club celebration", out of deep respect, for one of Their stalwarts. Very grateful indeed, for all that, They were. And They intended to name a new lounge under the stand. It would be, when funds were ready, built next year and called "Digger's". But in the meantime, They would be honoured if Myra would allow a special ceremony to be held at the end of the season, in front of specially invited people and open to all, when They would scatter Digger's ashes beneath the posts at the Red Cow end of the ground. What did she think?

They went away pleased with Themselves, and not forgetting to remark how she was still "a smart piece even if she was a bit frosty". Digger, They muttered, had "done well there". And now They would do him proud. Which, Myra had to admit as she thanked Them all in a pretty little speech after the funeral at the club, They had indeed done. One of Them escorted her to the designated posts for the ceremony to come before she went home, glad to be alone at last, to sink into her Egyptian-motif cushions, and think.

What she mostly thought, in a roundabout, where-was-I way that had no discernible pattern, was how sudden it had all been. His death, of course, but all that hastened after it. The difficulties, immediate and prolonged, in France. The unexpected gush that met her, on all sides, when she went back home. The game plan, as They had put it, which she felt constrained to follow – "Don't worry, love, we won't let you drop the ball" – and the day itself.

Even so, it was more than that. She looked at the framed photographs on the nest of side tables, ones of her mother and father, of her in cap and gown, of Geoffrey in costume and mufti with, and mostly without, Wilfrid, and of Digger. Digger, big and beaming in a wedding suit complete with its Valleys' customary silver-foil wrapped white rose which she'd tried, in vain, to remove from his lapel. Digger in a red rugby jersey with the Prince of Wales feathers, his one cap lying across his thick-fingered hands. Digger, with her, on holiday in Venice. Digger in the garden in France. Digger to the life in photo after photo and in location after location. Digger over and over again. Not her Richard. Their Digger. As he always was, perhaps. Then. And certainly now. And as for in-between, the years with her, it was the suddenness with which all that, her control of his destiny, had been superseded which was nagging away at her. In fact, that was it, wasn't it? The suddenness of change. The suddenness of life itself. Not at the moment of going, but the whole of the living that had been the life. Not the cliché of where has it all gone, because she knew where it had gone, all right. That wasn't it at all. It was the shuttered closure of the lens of that actual process of living that had happened. She held the thought for a second before it blurred. So abrupt, so unwanted, so unexpected, the click of a beat upon which her husband had died. In an instant. The part clouding the whole. But it was a partial memory she would always keep to herself. Myra shuddered at the remotest chance of anyone knowing. God, how They'd all love to know. It would be the Digger story to top all Digger stories. Legend. And, Myra shivered, imagine that tart of his, Anita or Rita or something, no Lolita any more judging by the way she'd turned up at the funeral, imagine her knowing. Telling people. She closed her eyes to banish it all. But the scenario, played out and ongoing, would not disappear.

What a thing to happen, she thought. What a way to go, was

what she knew Digger's vulgarity would have added. One minute she was concentrating on Digger rampant and the next, in an instant, with a groan which she'd thought was a cry of pleasure, he'd shuddered all over and twitched, rather unexpectedly, to one side, so that she almost toppled sideways. Then, and she was proud of this, she neither panicked nor screamed. She bent over him and she blew as hard as she could into his mouth, and she crossed her hands on his chest and thumped as hard as she could and she spoke and urged him back. But she knew he was gone. She had known it at once. She took off her shoes, held them in her hand and ran to the house and phoned the local medical centre, five minutes away in the village. They answered on the third French buzz. She hurried upstairs to put on a towelling robe. She threw some water onto her face. She ran back to the pool, and tried again. The doctor, who knew the garden well, was driving up the path as fast as he safely could. She ran to meet him. He examined Digger. Gravely, he stood up and put his arms on Myra's shoulders: "*Madame Davees, je regrette de vous dire que votre mari est mort. Je vais faire un appel et l'ambulance arrivera bientôt. Est-ce-que vous voulez rentrer dans la maison avant que l'ambulance arrive?*" Myra had shaken her head so the doctor, the young M. Paul Gonzalez, not his retired father the older M. Henri Gonzalez, covered Digger discreetly with a towel and they both sat and waited.

After that most matters seemed to be handled with the meticulousness and the sluggishness which the French reserved for all matters, even private ones, that strayed into the public domain. Digger was taken to the city hospital one hour away. Myra would follow the next day, driven by Doctor Henri Gonzalez, who had taken a call from his son and visited Myra in the early evening. She mentioned, in passing, the accident on the Autoroute and Digger's agitation. M. Gonzalez had waved his hands expressively in a gesture of sympathy. Myra remembered both him and his wife had attended, with the English expats resident in the village, one of her own late summer garden parties two years previously. She did not ask about his wife whom she knew had since succumbed to the cancer that had already been at its work then. When he touched her hand now she felt there was an extra understanding of such marital loss – his drawn-out, hers instantaneous. Others, her village friends, volunteered their services but she'd accepted the offer of a lift from this slight, bearded man, casually but elegantly dressed, who was, she guessed, a year or so younger but not so much so that she didn't think, the following day, to dress at her own demurely but sharply tailored best.

It was Henri who shepherded her through all the formalities of identification, of triplicate signatures and the release-of-body forms, before she could organise air-transport home for Digger, and a ticket for herself. It was Henri who drove her to the airport and returned her hired car for her. Before his son came to pick him up he waited with Myra until departure time and then kissed her, twice not three times – was that significant because it was different, she wondered – and said *"Souviens-toi, Myra; ici, c'est chez toi toujours maintenant. Au revoir, ma chère Myra,"* before almost pirouetting away, as if any next move, next time, would be up to her. Myra flew home as bewildered as she was flattered. She had nothing with which to reproach herself, she reflected. No guilt to feel. Once back, the pace of things gave her no time to brood. Only now, with just the special ceremony to come and Digger waiting in his urn to be scattered, did Myra allow herself to drift back to France.

It had been almost five years since her cousin Geoffrey's death, and with it the gift of his house to her. Even Digger had liked it or the thought of it, at least when he went out there with her at the start. Myra had known the house for ten years before that when Geoffrey left London to settle there with his partner Wilfrid. Myra had always been extremely fond of her cousin Geoffrey. He was the only son of her mother's sister, Eluned, as she was the only daughter of Bobby Braithwaite and Tegwen Hughes, her quiet and quite forgotten mother, whose central place in her father's world she had first been given, and later assumed. Geoffrey was eighteen months older than her and so they grew up together as childhood intimates and teenage co-conspirators. Eluned, Aunty Lyn, had married the manager of a gents' outfitter who, as a professional, measured inside legs with care and, as an amateur, played a front-room piano with verve. Myra preferred the tinkling liveliness of that room to the empty echoing former coalowner's mansion, become council property, which her father had snapped up at auction, if not for a song then for no more than a monetary consideration and a favour to the leader of the council. Aunty Lyn was to be her daytime and weekend mother. Geoffrey was her guide in play and in life. Like his father, Ron, he was a performer, and unlike Ron he would find his own way. He shared his dreams with Myra. In some senses, they became one. Or two halves. "Peas in a pod" and "Thick as thieves", Lyn would say to Bobby as Myra and Geoffrey played at doctors and nurses, their uniforms, only the best, supplied by her father. Geoffrey, of course, was the doctor. Except when the children were left alone and roles might interchange, especially because Geoffrey liked wearing Myra's outfits. Later, her clothes. This closeness ended when Bobby, running upstairs to fetch her one afternoon, stumbled upon a particular cross-dressing charade. Myra was thirteen, Geoffrey almost fifteen. Stern warnings were issued. They were confronted by their futures, terrible to contemplate they were told, if such nonsense continued. They had lives to lead, or so they were told.

Not necessarily, of course, the lives they would have wished to lead. Myra succumbed, surprisingly more quickly than her cousin, and withdrew into herself, admired for her pert good looks but never touched by anyone into an opening burst of life.

The same could not be said of her cousin, who discovered there was a discreet way of really being himself in the Valley and, more flamboyantly, a short train ride away from it. At eighteen, Myra left the private school to which Bobby had sent her as a day girl, and went to a training college for teachers in an English spa town. For a while she envisaged it as a passport out. It was not. It was more of a rubber-stamped visa in a cross-border exchange that boomeranged. Exactly why, the young Myra could not explain. The older woman looked back and resented what appeared to her to be a stage on which she had, by upbringing and expectation, to perform a role. The one Bobby had envisaged for her. At home. His money would buy the entry into that thin sliver of professional and rooted middle-class life with which the town re-dressed its shambling presence and its eruptive past. Her rebellion, when it finally came, turned out to be Digger. She made a trophy out of the town's very own favourite creation, and he introduced her to its topography of back lanes and mountain tops. Her father railed, at first, at the waste of it all, and with such a worthless, penniless sod, until he reined her in again with the offer of a flat they could live in on an estate the firm was building. A job, marriage and a partnership did the rest.

Geoffrey, on the other hand, had only exits to take. After the College of Music and Drama – where Jeffrey had first become Geoffrey – he picked up secondary roles in provincial theatres and, with his background and accent, began to secure occasional, meatier parts on television, playing militant union firebrands or working-class victims of pit disasters. Ludicrous but lucrative was how he put it to his friends. He met Wilfrid, a landscape watercolourist of charm and reputation, and a society portrait painter for commission and cash. He was in his mid-thirties, and his lover some two decades older. The law, just about, had become more accepting but there were, as yet, more insidious barriers, still more so in England than abroad. They moved, permanently as it accidentally happened, to the South of France. Myra visited, once or twice a year and always alone. When Wilfrid died, the phone calls grew more frequent between the cousins, and the length of her stays increased, though Geoffrey never came back. Digger suffered her gushing raptures about the house but was glad he had never been asked to go, never had been, and never would. He was wrong about that, too.

Through all of Myra's daydreaming, sudden reveries in which the sun seemed to disperse the clouds that smothered the Valley's summer and the remembered sound of cicadas overwhelmed the traffic's drone, two obstacles to any real exit for her would not go away. The one was the urn with his full name and dates on it which her guests commented on in the hushed tones with which they might have praised a Chinese vase of the Ming dynasty, and the other was the letter from the club which, periodically, she took out to read. It was embossed with the club's shield and motto: Play Fair, Play Hard. She read the letter again:

"Dear Mrs. Davies,
On behalf of the Committee and the Club I write to express again our deepest condolences on the Passing Away of your Late Husband, Mr Richie Davies. As you know, Digger was one of the Club's Great Servants and a fabulous Player who'll never be forgotten. Thank you for the Presentation of the various Memorabilia with which you have gifted the Club House Lounge to be opened in his name next Season, which we hope you will attend.

In the meantime for the Opening of this Season on Saturday September 10 we would be pleased to confirm that unprecedentedly and unanimously the Committee has agreed that your late husband's ashes will be scattered by this year's Captain in a Special Ceremony under the Posts where Digger scored so many memorable Tries and where, we all agree, he truly belongs.

We would be glad to hear when you feel able to transfer the magnificent Urn we have all admired to our safe keeping in advance of this proposed Happy Occasion which I'm sure will inspire a great deal of Press and Media interest.

Yours sincerely,

W. E. Williams (Hon. Sec.)

Myra was in no doubt as to the importance of the letter, and its implications for her. She was giving Digger back to those to whom he belonged. It was appropriate. It was fitting. It was deeply symbolic. It was what They all wanted. And, she thought, folding the letter tightly into a square, it was what They will not have. It was wrong. He was hers more than he was theirs, and whether he liked it or not he was going with her. The more she pondered the more certain she became. She would sell the Victorian gothic pile and leave the town. She would live, permanently, in Geoffrey's house and find someone to tend the garden. Perhaps Henri Gonzalez would know someone to recommend. She was sure he would.

And she knew, too, where she would scatter Digger's ashes. He would rest beneath the male olive tree in touching distance of the female olive tree which had never fruited. Who knew, perhaps it would at last, with a little loving care and some constant attention, fruit after all. In any case it would be a talking point. She looked forward to that.

No Photographs
Of
Crazy Horse

"If life seems a succession of dreams, yet poetic justice is done in dreams also. The visions of good men are good ...

When we break the laws, we lose our hold on the central reality. Like sick men in hospitals, we change only from bed to bed, from one folly to another; ... lifted from bed to bed, from the nothing of life to the nothing of death."

Ralph Waldo Emerson

"Illusions" in *The Conduct of Life* (1860)

First light. Slow and insinuating. Taking texture from its passage through the linen blinds. Splintering. Faster now. Refracted across varnished pine boards. Stirring shimmers of particles pooling into corner recesses. A noise. Muted and electronic, but abrupt, repetitive, insistent. He used his fists to bunch the pillow around his head. To stifle the burr of the bedside phone. And the prickly headache buzz of last night's red wine, and Scotch. But the light, picking up speed from the day breaking over the Narrows, flooded in and veined his eyelids pink until they blinked open, swollen eyes contracting, gummily closed again, for mercy, then half-open, finally shuttered, like the blinds, against the light they had, nonetheless with no mercy, to let in.

"Hello?"

His voice thickly muffled with the mucus of sleep and the emery board rasp of booze. Again, stronger this time, with a rising note to his cautious early morning drawl. At the other end, somewhere, a hesitant, but audible, dry swallow. Silence. He sat up.

"Hello? Who is this?"

Uncertain. More silence. Annoyed. Do they know what time this is? What the hell? Put it down. Then a young woman's sibilance. His hesitancy matched, and countered.

"Billy? I ... I want you to find me. Please?"

"Who ...?"

"It's Haf. Branwen's daughter. You know ... Please. Please come soon. I'm sending you something. You'll see. You'll understand. Then. Please help. Come. Please. Come and get me back, help me, please ... Daddy."

The connection broke. He had sat up. Swallowing hard. The Welsh voice lingering, insistent in his ears, even after it had stopped. The accent had trailed memories. Conjured up bygone dreams. He looked at the alarm clock, black on white, the hands bumping its tick around the dial. It was nearly six in the morning in New York City. Just gone noon at home. He turned over. Restless now. Maybe a dream would come.

One

Shadow Play

WEDNESDAY

It did not feel like going home. Not even partly so. But it did feel like going back. It was not a comfortable feeling. I drove west into a late afternoon sun that slipped further down the horizon as I let the boxy diesel hatchback I'd hired at the airport scuttle and drone its way down the M4. I fought the mild jet lag of a transatlantic crossing more than I did the lane-switching traffic. Slow lane was fine by me. I needed some contemplation time before the city's lights guided me straight to my hotel bed, and sleep.

You know how it is sometimes, when, because you must, you play a part, but for real I mean, because you don't have any original lines to say or fresh ways to enact them. Too many life scenarios already seen and done, whether originally for real, or not. Journeys. Quests. Homecomings that were nothing of the kind. Umbilical cords that were never quite cut, and so could still strangle. And it's as if you always have the clothes for the part, ready to put on. Where do they come from? You have the words queuing up to be said. How could that be? You even have the end in sight, but it's one stumble at a time to get to it. And what is this ending anyway? Going back was like letting time that was past suck me back in, and I was ready for it. I had the stuff, all of it, that I'd need for the trip. None of it meant that I wanted to make it. Going home was going to a place which was no longer there for me. It was with me all the time, though. More ready for me than I could ever wish it to be. Intimacy. That was unavoidable. Knowledge. Now that was a category I truly despised. Something known already. So generally imitative of something else. My old man had never pretended to have knowledge. What he did have was wisdom, and his brand of wisdom was as cold and dark as a gun barrel and as cold and unforgiving as the air through which I had been funnelled home.

It wasn't any kind of wisdom, though, that had brought me home. Worse, it was a lack of knowledge. Of certain knowledge that is, and certain came with two meanings, both of which I had to nail. For what was uncertain I could blame the postcard Gwilym had sent around five years before, and for what currently passed muster as certain there was Bran's written reply to my enquiry. It was "No", as I remembered. I had left no daughter behind, and so I had no daughter now. Yet that voice on my phone had coupled her own with mine and mine, it had said, was Daddy. So, yes, I knew what had taken me home, and, wise or foolish, what I needed to do. But first I'd need to see her mother again. There were things, it seemed, to find out. There were things, unbidden but undeniable, to remember. So, I remembered them. Even if all I had wanted to do for a very long time was to forget.

THURSDAY

I slept heavily and woke late. I cleaned myself up, and avoided the hotel breakfast. I'd kept the car overnight. I needed it for a quick burst of re-acquaintance, or rather a fresh acquaintance with the new city and all its novel markers. A proper capital city, I'd been told, at last.

I drove the hired car directly north out of the city centre. It was mid-morning and traffic was stop-start rather than snarling. The day was overcast for late March, but with an opaque white light behind the low cloud cover. Dishwater grey through the glare. It suited my mood, and my meander past familiar sights which some twenty years plus had done little to change. Not in this part of town anyway. The Edwardian wedding cake civic centre buildings still swelled with early twentieth-century pride. But in the interest of a future promise to be cashed in one day. Natch. And then almost straightaway, because this was a town that had been laid out cheek-to-cheek in its Victorian days of origin, the strings of red-bricked terraces like entrails pulled out and de-kinked. Student lets now, judging from the bicycles piled up in their tiny low-walled fronts and the oblivious helmetless riders weaving in and out of the stuttering line of cars. The dockers and railwaymen and steelworkers, who had once marked these streets with a confident workaday presence and crowded the brassy mahogany pubs, were long gone. I remembered them as men who, amongst themselves, acted as hard men even when they were not, all baring their lips to let go with an accent, peculiarly their own, which could slice through the thick tobacco blued smoke of saloon bars like wire through cheese. Something else gone from that rich pungency of the old centre was the sweet fug of mashed hops brewed up for the city's very own beer, cloying the senses and swaddling early morning streets. Liveners being readied for the thick heads of the previous night and the deep thirsts of overnight workers. Once, and no longer.

It had been too early for a pint when I picked up the car from the hotel's garage. I began to think I'd need a livener myself, and sooner rather than later. Maybe I'd need to find the brewery before I could locate that light and dry, cream and golden beer which my mouth could still taste. Maybe after two decades away there was no brewery, and none of that beer left as it was.

The thought curdled in the churn of my stomach as I left the centre behind and steered past batteries of traffic lights on every intersection of the four lane two-way avenue that tramlined me out of the plain. The city had grown, or rather spawned, in spreading concentric rings of housing from its docks and commercial heyday to the commuter and professional housing of the suburbs through which I was now crawling. Tree-lined avenues of brick-and-stucco semis built for the artisan and the salaried, even in the 1930s, a decade which had pissed over most people here with the freewheeling grace of a drunk in a urinal. The interwar houses had weathered better, despite the ceaseless rumble of cars and trucks, than their 1960s counterparts: flat-roofed boxes for housing, schools and hospitals. The one style fits all school of architecture from the decade that had misplaced its brain.

I'd bought a new map. I'd keep for later the grim dual carriageway that I knew from almost twenty years ago as a corridor through the hills and into the valleys I'd once escaped. It looked on the new map as if there were livelier arteries shooting off a pulsing interchange. On the actual ground it was more engineering circuitry than roundabout. I circled it twice before I picked the right lane, and took the slip road signposted for the west and the motorway. I had an appointment at noon back in the city. I took the scenic route. First exit off and flat out down the link road towards the bay.

I was on a highway belt that cinched in the older and flabbier bits as it bypassed them. An ersatz new world to anyone who had seen the real deal of any small American city. Deep cuts isolated the tough council-house estates where I had once roamed, camera at the ready. There were glimpses of skeletal iron frames cranked up out of building-site mud and the apple-green and white cladding of the retail sheds that were the winking outliers of a neon-lit twenty-four-hour world. They didn't convince; more end of the line no choice than any kind of centre.

I slowed down as the road curved upwards on a stilted flyover that was just high enough to offer flashes of the former industrial core of the city to the south. It was gutted, rusty and leaking. Its roadside heralds were apartment blocks whose roofs curved and dipped like skateboard runs. The surfaces were weather-boarded in strips which had already turned from honey to flaked grey in the salt winds blowing in over the mud flats from the sea. Miniscule iron-railed balconies decorated their chunky bulk like bracelets on a bruiser. This was the sense of the place I had guessed from hearsay and the occasional letter but I had not been able to feel for myself: its broken rhythm, its re-drawn boundaries, its pretence of itself. I decided to save the full-blown, street-level version of the bay for when I was more attuned to the whole transformation. Perhaps the woeful tackiness had been avoided there. Perhaps. There would be hope in pretending so. Perhaps not. I followed the signs for the centre.

At least the jail was still stone-stolid and unrelenting in its midtown location. It greeted me as I re-discovered the city streets and ended the joyride. I returned the car to the parking lot of the hire company and walked back to the hotel – another former office warren now decked out as a travel destination – ideal as neutral ground rather than the location of her doubtless ritzy apartment for a meeting that was as nerve-wracking as a French kiss on a first date. And I had reason to recall that encounter with a shudder of dread pleasure as I waited over a tepid filter coffee for my first sight of Branwen since the winter of 1985.

Even after more than twenty years she didn't disappoint. I'd like to say she never had but I was too old to lie anymore, to myself or anyone else. Still, whatever she was doing to herself, she was doing it well. On the surface at least. There had always been murky depths with Bran even if it had taken me some time to come up for air. I stood up as she scanned the room to see which booth I was in. The smile was tentative but the way she cocked her head slightly to one side was no less coquettish than when she had posed for me with a lot less on than the blue striped seersucker suit, sharp jacket and skirt to the dimpled knee, which she was expensively wearing. I had time for the quick once-over before she crossed the coffee-room floor. She imperceptibly slowed down as if she knew it. Of course she knew it. This was Bran after all. Some things wouldn't ever change.

Her eyes were the colour of anthracite, and just as slow-burning. Her hair, glossy, thick and black, framed the oval of a face which was almost Mediterranean in complexion. She used to say it was the Iberian heritage of the Celt. I'd countered it was the legacy of randy Spanish sailors shipwrecked from the Armada in west Wales. No make-up, just an *amuse-bouche* of a mouth and, I knew, a personality darker and harder than any mineral. At a modest 5' 10" I seemed to dwarf her compact 5' 2" even with the kitten heels she was wearing. A kiss, for which we both positioned awkwardly, drifted away in unease. She held out her hand. I touched it and the platinum wedding band on it.

"You're looking great," I said.

She shrugged out a thank you. I forced out a smile.

She sat opposite me, ordered a herbal tea, more coffee for me and we stared a necessary while longer. Then, as from long habit, we got down to it.

"Why did you come?"

"I told you on the phone. She … Haf … asked me to help her."

"You don't take that seriously, do you?"

"I don't know. I did. Something in her voice. Shouldn't I? Do you know where she is? What she wants?"

Bran fiddled with her granulated sugar packet, shifting the contents around in its unopened paper envelope like a blind fortune teller looking for a lucky grain of truth.

"She can be difficult. She's … a silly bugger when she wants to be."

"Meaning?"

Her one revelatory weakness, slight and momentary but intense through the translucent skin around her neck, was a flush that wrapped her like a scarf. Or a signal as I recalled and reminded her.

"Oh, you know it means nothing. I just can't help it."

"That's why it says something, isn't it?"

"You're not listening, Billy. I've told you. I really don't know where she went. Honest, as they say. She's been gone for over two months."

"The college?"

"Nothing. She hasn't turned up for lectures. And no messages for any friends."

"The police?"

"Why? She's telephoned me … you … other people. You, less than a week ago. She's not lost, Billy.

"She called me daddy, Bran. Why did she do that?"

"For God's sake, she's still a kid."

"She's almost twenty-one, isn't she? I wasn't there, remember."

"Messing about. That's all. I'd have told you, wouldn't I?"

"Would you?"

"She isn't."

"She could be, though, couldn't she?"

"No! It's just a game. Hero worship."

143

"Hero worship?"

"Of you. Of your work anyway. She's got everything – the books, posters, photographs, clippings. She plastered them over her bedroom walls before she walked out."

"Why? Did you tell her about us?"

"She knows. Not from me. Mal said something one night when he'd had a bit. After that documentary programme about you on television. She cottoned on. Worked it out, that 'friends' was a catch-all word."

"How old was she then?"

"About sixteen. Later she heard us quarrelling. Things were said. Not by me. Look, I've never been close with her, this mother-and-daughter thing and such, and it just got worse after that. She practically moved out then. In spirit if not in body. And this disappearing stuff, that isn't the first time either."

I tried to think it through but all I could see was the deceit by which we had all lived. I didn't know what to believe. It was what had sent me away. It was what had pulled me back. I tried again.

"You were clear she wasn't mine. I asked no more. I'm asking now. Again."

This time the smile was more pitying than playful.

"You're still a fool, Billy, you know that."

She puffed her cheeks. Like an adder, I thought. And blew softly at me a breath that was at once sweet and rank.

"That summer after the strike you got more and more, I dunno, miserable … melancholy. Even before that you were down about everything and everyone. Worrying. Down. And for me it was still what I'd felt, something alive and different, as if that bloody history your old man went on about had come to life, and with me in it. Christ! I was even a star supporter! You and me were coming to an end anyway. You didn't quite see it, did you, but then there were lots of things you didn't see, or didn't want to see."

144

She paused, and calculated.

"I wasn't wild and I wasn't calculating. Not then. Maybe later. But at the time I just slept with the people I wanted to fuck or who wanted to fuck me, or neither but anyway! And you were around, too, when you weren't off photographing and documenting and revelling in the whole mess, in your own sad way. So, like I said, I don't know. Take that for a no, from me. And yes, maybe she thinks so."

"Why did you marry Mal?"

"A marriage of convenience."

"That all?"

"We'd been lovers. I was pregnant. Strictly, in case you're still wondering, just after you'd gone, and I told him it was his. Later, we just became a partnership. And after that, four, five years ago, we split. Still married."

I could have wondered about a lot. And worried, too, but all I was thinking was whether to tell her now what I knew of that convenient partnership and its convenient continuation and how all that I knew was only because of the papers which had arrived without further explanation the day after the telephone call. Instead I gave her my mobile number and asked her to call if Haf did get in touch, that I was going to look around to see if anything of the made-over old patch might stir my professional interest, and that, maybe, we could have dinner before I flew out.

She looked quizzical.

"Seems a long way to come after such a long time for such casual reasons."

"Well, I would like to meet her. Perhaps we'll agree about something or other."

"The only thing you'll have in common with her is a mutual distrust – dislike? – of yours truly."

I didn't demur, just deflected the crack.

"DNA?", I asked.

"For Chrissake! What for?"

"Sentiment."

"Sentimentality is more your bag."

"Do they measure that in DNA?"

"You'd have bucketfuls, you always did," she said.

We seemed depleted, and I was once more, somehow, dispossessed.

* * * * *

I walked out of the foyer minutes after she'd gone, leaving me with her mobile phone number and memories I kept batting away. I held tight to the manila folder I hadn't opened to show her. I turned left and straight on, which were the only directions, my old man had said, that were ever worth taking. The city centre's layout was an easy recall: a pedestrian grid lay on top of its nineteenth-century right angles and a few defiant statues of socialist politicians and Irish boxers had been more recently erected to match up to its capitalist and liberal founding fathers. No role models for women in bronze or marble yet. The girls were missing a trick there. No doubt it'd come. The only female equivalents were in stone, flanking the steps of the Old Library that stood kitty corner from the Victorian indoor market. They were still draped in Grecian finery and clutching books, and they were still called Study and Rhetoric, the monikers by which I fondly remembered them, but they weren't ushering me in to find Power and Knowledge, their more worldly sisters any more; it was the milk of Lethe, strictly of the alcoholic variety, they had on offer nowadays. The library had become a pub, and not of the kind I favoured. It took a while to find one I did.

If the library was a theme pub, then its satellite hostelries seemed to have become just as thematic. On every other corner there was a piece of Erin that should never have left the fantasy factory or an iron-grilled and Cajun-manufactured homage to New Orleans. The wine bars were like gentlemen's dens with crazed brown leather club chairs and newspaper racks or decked out with splashing fountains, crushed velvet drapes and shameless stone nymphs last seen in a Naples brothel in 1944. Or so I imagined my old man, who'd been there then, might have got round to telling me. At this rate, the breweries would end up making replicas of the old pubs that were actually old, but on the same site. I found one that seemed reluctant to change and sat at its bar in front of its ornate mirror. There was a God after all, and He was still serving up the metallic, brassy and frothy beer I could taste on faraway nights in my close-up dreams.

I found the new replacement library amongst a wall of designer shops and stores. Glass wallfronts soaring high. Berlin, Boston, Basingstoke. The new one had neither the sumptuous wall tiles or echoing terrazzo floors of the old one, and all yesterday's newspapers were no longer preserved intact and bound into a giant's commonplace book, but shrunk onto the pinprick palimpsest of the page-by-page screen. I whizzed as well as the next bozo of my deprived generation, slowly and irritated, blessing my having grown up without all this non-tactile blur of gadgetry. The electronic future had not just arrived, it had hit us on the blindside, uncaring of the way we had once groped with pen or paint or camera to shine some kind of light. What was once unknown or untraceable could be collated now or hyperbolically enhanced to give the impression of holding the water that still inexorably ran on. But my own hard-won vision had been no less fuzzy over time, and had left me sightless, a click or two away from the lies I had stopped peddling.

Haf's papers – copies of letters, of e-mails, of bank statements, of notes on hotel pads, figures and dates on envelopes, on everything except the back of the proverbial cigarette pack only punters and smokers still used – guided me haphazardly to the daily pages of record I needed to see. The story was sometimes half-hidden in an inside paragraph, occasionally hailed as another brilliant success for inward investment and, latterly, brought into the frame of the new government under the rubric of "Regeneration", a concept which had struck me as a cross between the hopeful mythology of resurrection and the hopeless metamorphosis effected by the mortician. Why didn't they just try to generate something instead? The past and its places were never quite the organic thing a notion like *re*-generation so smugly implied. Whatever the case in hand, and there seemed dozens as I read on – from building works to art centres to tip clearances to adult education classes in aromatherapy and IT training – money, large and small packages of subsidy and grant aid, did not seem to be a problem. It was more a question of how do they get it out of the door in sufficient bulk and with the speed that didn't allow bureaucratic windows in Europe to shut. In a de-industrialised region of such classic proportions as this one had been, the fit was perfect even if the outcome was debatable. The longer timescale raised the cynical thought that the actual recipients, if not the potential beneficiaries, would be, one way or the other, long gone before the final reckoning.

I whizzed on for a few hours. My notes grew fuller as I honed in on Haf's direction finder. The penny-ante stuff was all about worthy efforts, statistically measured by lame targets and grandiose objectives, to "up-skill" and "re-train" for the "knowledge economy" that had passed a generation by and was, allegedly, still held back by the low aspirations entrenched in a stubborn work culture, one long dead in practice and suffused, as it resisted the social mortuary, with the undesirable luddite and gender attributes of a leftover underclass. The jargon fed by sociology to journalism came easy. But my confusion over what was being regenerated by whom for whom for why, grew incrementally. There seemed precious little that had come to fulfilment outside the cities of the plain. It seemed we were still looking to the hills in vain. I began to pucker up for an inner Biblical trumpet of warning. Still, capital projects, with big outlays and vague embracing ambitions, were more realisable, less measurable in their ultimate outcome, and very big bucks indeed. The one thing, it seems, we had going for us, benighted denizens of a blasted past in those hills and valleys, was land. It was filthy, useless, contaminated land, soil and acres where you couldn't grow vegetables or re-create a pre-industrial haven, but it was land that was available, cheap to buy and, both subsequently and consequentially, expensive to purchase even if the purpose was only re-generative, the gain a social one and the project uplifting.

Gradually certain names began to re-appear. A single speech. A stellar proposal. A projected consortium. A political desire. A community need. An educational enterprise. A PR exercise. A feasibility study. A government decision. Names I knew and some faces I recalled. Bran, Gwilym, Ceri and Maldwyn amongst them. I turned off the screen. An escalator took me down to street level. The streets looked greasy in a watery sunlight. People drifted along in a city adrift. I drifted amongst them. A stranger amongst strangers. One of them. Not of them. I began to stare. No kids this time of day, women, alone if young, in twos if not, married couples, yellow-jacketed building labourers in groups of five and six, and all clutching paper bags full of smeared baguettes, and the more than occasional street dweller even more adrift than the rest of us. What I didn't sense, as a taste, or see, in an instant, was the feel of poor people in the way that was all around us a quarter of a century ago. I guessed that it was an advance, but at whose expense I couldn't be sure. Poverty came in all manner of guises, as my old man drummed into his adult classes. Maybe that had been the other problem. The drumming as opposed to the learning. The observing as opposed to the living. I had long felt separated from both. The escaping as opposed to the staying. Coming back was not my idea, I told myself. But I had and now I had to swallow my mistake and leave, or chew it so that I could spit it out and move on.

I headed for the train station and a train north but first I called ahead to find out when Gwilym could see me. There was no "if" about it. Gwilym, I knew, would want to see me. I might even be an "opportunity", and he would not have ceased his love affair with one of those, animate or inanimate. Late afternoon, lunch unfortunately "not-doable", then wall-to-wall meetings, in his office, say 4.30, chirped a secretary who, if I knew him as I had indeed once known him would have the attributes to go with the breathless little-girl-lost voice.

The approach to the railway station had had a facelift all right. The designer who had worked on it could have made Ava Gardner look like Bela Lugosi. He wouldn't have spotted the reference as an insult. You could still, with a squint, detect the creamy ceramic tiles and wooden 1920s fretwork behind the monumental planed stone with chewing-gummed bench surround which he must have picked up in a Moscow 1950s catalogue of late Stalinist gesturalism. More street people, combining the hippie scruff look with beggarly homelessness, sat or lay in shop doorways wearing their obligatory dogs on leashes as filthy and braided as the owners' hair. I glared back until they looked away. The dogs I mean. The street people kept their own eyes in touch with the infinite.

The platform was crowded. A mix of shoppers, a glitter of mothers who outsmarted their gawky teenagers, older couples in beige and grey and wool, clutching their bags and each other against intrusion, and a swirl of students seemingly intent only on what their touch screens were telling them. I'd been prepared for the rash of bilingual signage in the streets and even for the Welsh-language announcements for "*y trên nesaf*" and, in Welsh, the correctly pronounced valley townships that followed, but what came after a posh and male Welsh accent, even to those whose grasp of Welsh foundered after the first few lines of the national anthem, was more alien yet. The train information given in English was impeccably English, with the syllables of every place name I had ever known or grown up with, separated out into a speak-your-weight tone that managed to locate every wrong inflection and stress possible in the brave new world of desperanto. Most of us on that platform were being addressed in two languages we did not speak. I felt more speechless than I had for two decades. I left the city and let the view between the hills open up. We seemed to stop every five minutes. In a bowl beneath the final mountain, an hour later, nestled my final destination.

There was a new halt for the Research and Development Park just after the town itself. Gwilym would be at lunch, and allegedly meetings, for a few hours yet, so I got off the train early. The town's river still ran through it. No one seemed to have honed in yet on the one natural asset, apart from the shrug of clumpy hills, which might have given it a focus to replace its vanished industries and lost trade. No change there, or in the boarded-up shops of a shopping precinct constructed like a pebbledash concrete box with a flap entrance and a soaked-in stink of urine. It had taken me no more than ten minutes to walk from the station, another glory lost to boy scout design, past the rash of estate agents, shoe shops, bread shops, junk jewellers and the flashing tumblelights of slot-machine joints spitting the crackle of their noise, endlessly, onto the streets. One or two Italian-owned and run cafés gave "generation" a good name and the cobbled square off the main and winding street whispered possibilities. But the indoor market was more shoddy goods and plastic utilities than the piled-high stalls of fruit and vegetables and locally slaughtered meat and home-cooked hams and pies it had once been. People must be eating something, though. There seemed more bulk on the pavements, more waddle in the shop doorways and more roll in the gait. I didn't see any obvious students in the town. They must stay on the train and leave by train for the city when lectures ended. Familiarity was not cheering me up. I needed a drink, and The Lamb was nearby so I went there, and entered the past.

A narrow, low frontage with a door and boxed-in entrance. Two bars to either side, divided by the central run of beer pumps and shelves of bottles, both long and hemmed in like railway carriages from a Western movie. The one to the right was slightly smaller, to accommodate a Ladies at the end and had an embossed and floral wallpaper pattern to support its claim to be the lounge. No one went there in the day. Some things would stay the same, wouldn't they? I turned left into the bar proper where a rotund, sawn-off and silent, landlord had once patrolled behind his counter. His name was Idris. So he was known as Id. And one night an autodidact from my old man's class had decided that made Id's voluble wife, Mavis, Ego. Both Id and Ego were shades now, as shadowy as the black-and-white poses of half-naked men, some clutching enamel medallioned belts, which were framed and scattered over the spit-yellow, tobacco-stained walls. These were the champions, of the world some of them, from a time even before mine. Their shadow dancing in the ring had been as explosive in the mind as on the canvas. I took them in at a glance. Freddie, Tom, Frank and Glen, Tommy and Jimmy, Dai and Howard. All still there. Behind the bar a woman in her late sixties was adjusting a curly black wig in a cracked mirror. She glimpsed me in it and without turning, said "Waddya want, love?" I asked for a bitter. Her fire-engine red lips had been cut out from a pin-up of Marilyn, the effect only spoiled by the paint going up under her nose and almost down to her chin, and the ravines of powder-caked wrinkles that surrounded them. They scarcely moved as she said "Pint or glass, love?"

From a corner at the far end of the bar where the light from the scrolled front window did not reach, a voice which didn't need a bellows to fan fire rumbled.

"He don't drink no glasses, Doreen. Give him a pint of Whoosh."

I moved down the bar towards the voice, and left my tenner on the bar.

"Shwmae, Billo," Tommy said, and stuck out a hand that was no bigger than a shovel.

"Long time no see," said Lionel.

"Siddown, butt," said Tommy, slowly letting my own hand limp free from his calluses and pincer fingers.

I sat at the round wooden-topped table that was held up and steady by buxom iron Brittanias bearing their shields. Either side of me, as in the Town XV's second team front row of my youthful athletic prime, were Tommy "Coch" Harris and his fellow prop, in work and sport and drink, Lionel "Blondie" Pemberton, a surname that hinted less of vanished gentry and more of West Country farm labourers turned late-Victorian colliers. By the time I'd met them, colliers both, in the murk of the Second XV's scrum, they'd already forged a veteran reputation as players who were as dirty as they were slow. Stalwarts by then, protecting a young hooker on rain-lashed nights on muddy fields from opposing sods no rougher or gentler than themselves. Their nicknames were for the ginger crew cut of the one and the tow-haired straw thatch of the other. Their short schooldays had ended with NCB apprenticeships as faceworkers, in the 1950s, and a succession of pits as they followed the few seams that remained stubbornly open as collieries closed as rapidly as flies' eyes in the '60s. Closures and forced redundancies finally drove them out, and into work as labourers and brickies. I had seen no better or tougher sight since I'd been home.

"Aye, long time no see," echoed Tommy.

"Aye, s'right," echoed Lionel back.

"Pints?" I asked.

These boys knew a rhetorical question when it was posed. About drink, anyway. They drained the fullish ones in front of them and Tommy tapped his empty on the table to alert the Marilyn lookalike, who had just pulled one for me, to keep going. Lionel got up to fetch them and set my change and three fresh pints before us.

"Cheers," he said and began drinking as Tommy, without bothering to ask, did what I wanted and gave me a *Whitaker's Almanack* tour of the town in the years I'd been gone. I listened to the lament of decline and deterioration.

"Aye. Same old same-o," agreed Lionel, when Tommy finally drew breath.

Tommy wiped the froth of his grey straggle of a moustache after this reflective and biting bottom-up comment on the panorama of the recent past. Living it had aged them. Neither "Coch" nor "Blondie" quite did it any more as accurate descriptions of the now salt-and-pepper and bare-patched heads nodding and drinking on either side of me. I said as much. "Aye," said Tommy. "That's what a life on the buildings, humping bricks and mixing in the freezing fucking cold will do to you. You should see my bollocks!"

"S'right," Lionel added, and went for three more pints.

Tommy was in full spate by now, a great circular flow of fact and opinion, all revolving around the life and times of artisan builder and bullshitter supreme, T. Harris, Esq. It all came back to buildings. They held us and defined us. So what was wrong was, in his opinion, that what lay behind them had changed. They were cheaper to construct, dearer to buy, quicker to deteriorate. The wood was not seasoned. The foundations were not settled. The exteriors were all cladding and the interiors all slotted together from a kit. So where was the pride in that, he wondered, and offered an answer by widening his viewfinder to people. The town had gone all to hell. Big City incomers, toffee-nosed, hippie, English, Welshy Welsh. The rugby club had gone all to hell, betrayed by Judases of various stripes and flavours. And now there was talk after the demise of Id and Ego of a makeover for The Lamb, to give it a more "authentic feel", with stone-flagged floors and wooden beams and a re-faced bar to replace the truly authentic leatherette, plastic and formica it had worn in over forty years. All a disaster. Still, in The Lamb maybe, some work out of this for a pair of jobbing builders in semi-retirement, and a few pints on the job thrown in.

"S'right," said Lionel.

"Pints again?" This time from Tommy.

I was tempted. Another and I'd have settled in for the afternoon. That would be no trouble for them, but I had more calls to make before I could slip into forgetfulness with them. I left them swilling away the grime and dust they had absorbed all morning, and across a lifetime every morning since they had left secondary modern entrapment at fifteen with bruised knuckles and a dislike of authority and its preachiness which had sustained them into the righteous anger of their mid-sixties.

I waited at the lights to cross the two lanes of busying traffic and looked up at the platforms and retaining wall of what had once been one of Europe's busiest rail interchanges. A funnel to the world for coal out and people in which filled and emptied day and night for half a century. It had shrunk inside itself like a terminally ill patient in a baggy suit. What was tacked on to the original façade had the unwelcome effect of loose-fitting false teeth sitting on shrivelled gums. There was nowhere to buy a ticket, and I rode free for the ten minutes or so it took for the diesel to grind its way up an incline beyond the town to the halt.

* * * * *

After the frayed edginess of the town, spread out beneath the mountain escarpment, there was a surreal feel to the Development Park. At least from a distance there was. Up close you could still see the railway cutting, now concreted over and the tunnel now bricked up, through which an exodus of coal had once rattled to the sea. Most of the site was a car park. I crossed it, as instructed, until at almost its far end I came to a red-brick wall which sectioned off a lawned area that you entered through open iron gates. The gates were fancy. Their railings were painted silver and had gold spears to top off the effect. You were welcomed in by a slate plaque that was six feet long and four feet high. It was mounted on a granite plinth and stood ten feet up from the lawn. The grass was so green it sparkled. The grass did not quiver even for a synthetic nano second. The deeply cut grey lettering on the plaque said: ADEILAD ALFRED WALLACE BUILDING. Another twenty yards down a yellow-brick path took me to the frontage of a very new, low slung two storey building. The oval windows which studded its riveted white cladding were framed in steel and glowed blue. It took me less than a nano second to admire it. I went through a series of automatic doors that swished open and closed, into a reception area where I had to state my business at a desk which could have issued airline tickets. I was sent to another series of glass doors, all electronically locked, where I was acknowledged over the intercom and buzzed through to the inner sanctum. I'd been told to ask for The Directorate, and here it was. The last time that one had been up in lights was in the 1790s, just before Napoleon doused them, dissolved the collective and crowned himself, literally I recalled, Emperor. The only thing Gwilym had in common with Bonaparte was an ineffable self-regard and the short-arsed cockiness that often accompanied it.

A door to an outer office opened and Gwilym's PA stood framed in it. I seemed to remember the little guy asked Josephine not to wash until after he'd come home. Maybe Gwil had a different olfactory arousal. This Josephine had definitely washed. And sprayed. And perked and painted. She was to natural fragrance what chemical is to organic. She was to natural blonde what chicory is to espresso. Her jersey silk dress had had its pink and red geometric pattern imprinted big on a size that was a tad too small and too short, and just right. Her voice, when it came, was more doll than baby and excitingly formal, as in "The Director is expecting you, Mr Maddox. Do go right in. Coffee?" And she half-turned on her teeteringly high pink suede stilettos and gave me a smile as sweet as a sucked sherbet lemon as she adjusted her made-for-the-job horn-rimmed glasses. Perhaps she was really efficient, too.

I said, "Yes" and "Please", and did as I was told. Gwilym was sat, head bowed over neatly stacked papers, behind a veneer-inlaid desk that could have done duty as a stage prop for *Il Duce*. It was cleared of any clutter. As pristine as the paperwork looked virginal. Only a mounted and gold-plated rollerball pen broke the gleaming expanse of its surface. *Il Duce* looked up as if he was due for a surprise instead of an announced visitor. He cracked a smile that went all the way from who'd've believed it to whaddya know, well well. He opened up his arms to receive me even before he rose slowly from the desk and advanced around it towards where I stood with Josephine hovering just behind me. She might have seen the move before, because I sensed her sliding out of the room – discretion and valour and all that. I stood my ground as Gwilym thrust his arms up as high as he could reach to pat my shoulders. He was staring lovingly up into my face, a technique Josephine's high heels might have helped him perfect, and saying quietly, but with feeling, "Bill. Bill. Bill. Well. Well. That's just great. Bill."

What could I say back? I thought about a speech, but just said "Gwil. Gwilym. Eh, Gwil!" and wrapped my arms around the back of a dark grey, pure wool suit. We clutched each other a while longer, until he gradually let go with what seemed like the reluctance of velcro to detach itself. He gestured to a corner of the room where two blue cloth tub chairs squatted either side of a lower splay-legged table. We sat. Josephine returned with a silvery tray on which she'd positioned a white bone china coffee pot with matching cups, except for the gold trim around the lip, a milk jug and a little bowl of white and brown sugar lumps. The spoons rattled as she put it down. Gwilym smiled at her. He called Josephine Morwenna, and thanked her. We poured our own coffee and, as before, discreetly and with valour she turned and retreated. I guessed that from the back she would look even better. So I looked. And she did. I turned my wayward head as Gwilym began to speak. It sounded rehearsed. That would be about right for Gwilym who had always been as instantaneous as freeze-dried coffee without the boiling water.

"Fantastic to see you again. All these years. Older," he snickered, "but aren't we all? And looking good, kiddo. Looking good. Are you home for long? Any special reason? Great to see you, whatever."

Kiddo, I thought? Maybe the outmoded slang went with the inquisitional probe. A sort of Welcome Home that was as sincere as a Commercial Christmas. Was there any other kind anymore, kiddo? He slurped a little coffee and sat back, waiting. I studied the dots on his shot-silk tie and the cufflinks in his off-white cotton shirt with its shiny pearly grey buttons, and I contemplated his journey from railway signalman's son to the *Duce* of the Directorate. I didn't feel I was intruding on any secret thought process. He probably contemplated the same route with some satisfaction at least twice a day. He was just a year older than me, and we'd been at university, almost overlapping, in the late 1970s. I'd dropped out. He hadn't. A doctorate had arrived for Gwil via a "comparative sociological study" of the coalfields of Durham, Appalachia and South Wales. He'd met Bran in her undergraduate years after I'd already left to become the next Robert Frank. Another dream. I was surfing on the first waves of published glamour when Gwil had gloatingly introduced me to her. Maybe he thought the fact they were size compatible was sufficient security. Mistake. She dropped him, and we began. I didn't detect resentment at the time. We'd told ourselves it was a freewheeling world and included ourselves in the spin. There seemed less envy of the relationship and more envy of the career, mine, one that was soon worlds apart from graduate fellowships and junior lectureships and monthly pittances. Yet he'd clung onto the educational ladder and occasional letters told me of two marriages, twice divorced, and no kids behind him, and finally a view from almost the top of his particular pole to compensate for all the effort. It worked for him, this viewpoint, gloating being good downwards, envy being pointless upwards. Besides, any other emotion would have taken him too long and too far away from thinking about himself, and his own needs for power and privilege. It was the relative not the absolute nature of these commodities that mattered to him, so I directed the past freight we both carried back to his favourite topic, one so precious he rarely shared it openly with others. Himself. I didn't answer about me, I signalled the comforting topic of Him, and looked around at the framed certificates, at the dusty tomes gathering sightless motes behind glass, and the painting that filled an entire wall with its incongruous rebuke of his inward vision.

"You've done well. I can see. Congratulations."

There was a disconcerting but characteristic giggle in return. He stroked a small razor trimmed beard, one that gave neat, circumscribed length to his small-featured, cutely handsome face. Gwilym had unnaturally round deep brown eyes, almost glassy, beneath his plucked and arched eyebrows. The eyes glistened now in a self-deprecating way that, if you knew him as I did, was anything but. Christ, I thought for a moment he was going to flutter his feathery lashes at me. And then, in a trained instant, almost uncannily quickly, the look tightened and hit-switched to a more attentive, focussed mode. It was as if the whole thing was there, just in that look. The passage from junior lecturer to dean via the journeyman authorship of a couple of convoluted and densely footnoted academic articles, with a bland textbook survey thrown in along the way, to the heights, and salary, of administrative grandeur. And now this, Director of an independent unit for research and development, for business growth and social regeneration. It was the link that was missing which interested me more than the outward show of success and the inner conviction of merit. Gwilym still believed, in his innermost sanctuary, that the latter was a deserved compound of IQ and effort. He never got satire. Not if it was directed against his own deserved needs. Just deserts was a different thing altogether. Not that he would appreciate the distinction.

"It's a terrific opportunity, Bill. Even in these challenging times. Especialy in these times. We're bringing you know, together here, the private and the public. Pulling in the best ideas, and the most go-ahead people. Graduates on short-term contracts. Start-up pods. Peppercorn rents. All the latest kit. Spin offs for commercial ventures. Creative industries. Links into business and government. Able to form partnerships across the piste. Not tied down. Fleet of foot. University connections that do not hamstring us with the caution of academic regulation. Innovative to the core. Mal's idea originally, of course, and he worked his socks off to secure the funding. A dream come true. So when they asked me, the Board, you know, to leave the University, where, did you know? I was the Pro Vice Chancellor, well, I didn't, despite everything, hesitate. What a chance, eh, to put into practice all I'd studied and researched. What else could I do?"

I tried looking impressed. At his bravery. At the opportunity. At the personal sacrifice. And I must have succeeded.

"I can see you're wondering a bit if I've gone mad. Solid career, and all that, thrown away on a, let's be honest, gamble. Now, Bill, I won't lie to you, salary is on a par for a guaranteed five year contract, so I won't exactly starve, and, as you can see, there are the perks and trappings of power, which are enjoyable, and at my, our, advanced age, why not? Eh, Bill. But the bottom line is, the real thing is, this is a once in a lifetime chance to give a lead. To be, and Christ we need it here don't we, a leader. That's the reward, and that's the responsibility I've taken on."

A smile to dazzle a whole plank of Board members followed the soliloquy, topped off with that cherry of self-sacrificial selflessness.

"So very, satisfyingly, rewarding."

"Rewards, like charity, begin at home," I said as blandly as I could manage. It puzzled him momentarily. I couldn't be that vulgar, could I? Try me, I thought. This time the smile came *sans* teeth.

"It's well paid, as I said. You'd expect it to be. For the responsibility. I don't deny that. Though senior colleagues elsewhere in Academe proper …"

The voice trailed off in a wistful sigh for appointment in faraway universities whose "catchment areas" were not so compromised as those more locally situated, and whose "culture" was more aspirational than needy. The same look came to both our faces. Unbidden and, for him, unwanted. Who'd employ him in such Groves of Academe? He was forgetting his guest and the feel-good factor he liked to create in all possible circumstances. He hurried on:

"Anyway, anyway. What about you, Bill? Really really great to see you, by the way. Great. Exhibitions. Retrospectives. Books.

Newspaper articles – I've read them all. And wasn't there a documentary film you made, quite recently? Got shown on BBC4 over here? About Mexican immigrants to Los Angeles who'd made good, as they say? Great title: Wetbacks to Greenbacks?"

I nodded. He changed tack. Opportunities for both of us had just flitted across his radar screen. A better future.

"I just thought," he said thoughtfully. And he probably had. "I just thought … would you consider some, temporary of course, to suit you, part-time, appointment here? A research fellowship perhaps? And we could help, you know, with any, er, archiving, or whatever. A permanent home, perhaps? A depository of your lifetime's achievement under your own name? I don't know about you, but that'd excite *me*. We could get external funding for that, I'm sure. The William Maddox Photographic Centre. Nice ring to it.And, hey, talking of names, what d'you think of ours ?"

I smiled. He smiled. I waited. He settled into accustomed pedagogic mode.

"No? Don't blame you. I've had to inform quite a few. Well, he was Welsh of course. And nowadays, things have changed quite a lot in that department, Billy boy, we have to stress that connection. Born in 1823 was old Alfred Wallace. Just as everything in our part of the world was beginning to take off big time. He was from Monmouthshire. Gwent as they say now. Clothes on a poodle but still a dog underneath. Our dog though. And he died in 1913, just as our madcap growth, our boom and bust, iron and coal, and people swarming in, was about to end. Perfect timing. And here's the thing. He was the boy who first came up with the notion of the natural selection of the species, the key concept to understand the evolution of everything. Not Charles Darwin, Bill, but his correspondent and co-worker, our own Alfred Wallace. No one really denies this anymore. Wallace was the originator and the catalyst to Darwin's work. Fantastic, eh? And the thing is, it gets even better. For us to use his name, I mean. Because, you see, Charlie's emphasis was all on competition, between individual units in the same species, so to speak, for there to be any survival of the fittest. But old Alfred, our pal, more in keeping with us, showed that wider environmental pressures were what actually forced adaptation, change, to survive as a whole, in any given local world or environment. So any survival of the fittest, and that was Herbert Spencer's spin on Darwin's biological theories when applied to economy and society, has to place individual life within the frame of culture and society. Which is, after all, what we need to hear in this benighted part of the globe, isn't it? Moving on together. Sorry about the lecture, you know me, but I thought you'd like the idea."

I dutifully nodded. Gwilym took that as a good sign. He waved his hand in the air. Modest and self-deprecating.

"I'm getting ahead of myself. As usual. You know me. Always the doer! And I still haven't found out why you're home. Bran? Have you seen her?"

I nodded again. I should have been sitting on the back-shelf of a car.

"Yes, I have. That's partly why I'm here."

"Partly?"

"Yes. And for Haf. Why don't you tell me about Haf, Gwil?"

He poured himself another coffee. I waited. He put his cup down, a little too heavily. The coffee spilled from the saucer onto his inlaid and varnished coffee table. He ignored the puddle. He was considering my request. Its innocence. Or not. He began slowly.

"You remember I wrote to you. Perhaps I shouldn't have. Wasn't my place. But, you know, everything had gone – went – so lopsided, for a while, after you left, after you and Bran split. All so uncertain."

He paused and looked up. He switched effortlessly from the

academic to the demotic. Just to show he could. Just to show we were still blood brothers. He was wasting his time with that one, and had done years since. I didn't bother to alert him to it. Not yet. He leaned, like a buddy, towards me. Go ahead, kiddo, I thought. And he did, effortlessly.

"Look. I started. We started. That autumn. To see each other again. Just after you'd gone. Casually, of course. Not like you two had been, of course. Then, it ended. Again. Only, as you know now, she was pregnant. Quite soon. The girl, Haf, was born. End of June or July '86, I forget. Bran married Mal after that. Maybe. No, certainly, they'd seen each other around the time I split … she stopped … with me, I mean – around the same time, so I just assumed it was Mal. I didn't, you know, enquire. Well, not for years anyway. Maybe I shouldn't have sent a card. I confess I was out to hurt. Her not you. I'd met her at a party. She wasn't with Mal, and he'd spoken, bitterly, to me, about his bitch of a wife. And, he said, her, from the off he said, lies. I was between marriages myself, and pissed. I tried it on, to be honest. She made it plain, brutally plain, I wasn't a runner, let alone a rider anymore. I certainly wasn't on her radar screen by then and, for Bran, it was all TV reporting and small-screen stardom those days – not PR and networking yet – so, a bit narked, I asked out loud, pissed, who the fucking father was then, and if not me now, then maybe me then, and how she'd be the one to know it. And she just stood. Icy and looking at me, and said "No chance", that I was a tosser then and a shit now and she always knew how to protect herself from any unwanted, 'dribble'."

He swallowed. I think he expected me to feel a twinge of sympathy. I felt a pain elsewhere. Gwilym hadn't noticed. He wanted it all to come out now. He'd stared in the mirror so long that monologue was the sound of sweet reason to him.

"So, naturally, Bill I thought of you. You hadn't come back when your old man died that Christmastime. No one blamed you, I mean. You were away. But, I thought, years later, and, yeah, I was angry, that maybe you needed to know. In case you didn't, I mean. So I just sent the card to the newspaper's address. You never replied, so I let it drop. I assumed you'd ask Bran. You know, I mean, if it was yours, or not."

He let his thoughts trail off. I wanted an end to this. I told him I had written and that she'd sent an even briefer card back, but one that just said, "No." I told him I hadn't known about him. Or anyone else. And she had married Mal after all. So QED, and all that. Gwilym seemed to think this made us some kind of blood brothers because his face lit up again. He said that then it must indeed be Mal that was Haf's father but that, for reasons beyond him, neither Mal, nor apparently Haf, now thought so. "Unless ..." he began to say, looking sly and even more conspiratorial. I shook my head and half-turned in the bottom-scrunching bucket that called itself a chair to take in the room again. It was an oval office no less, with high ship-like portals for windows and, as well as the permanently closed books, an array of glass cabinets full of the kitsch and wonky macquettes and shields and framed certificates that academic dignitaries from all over the globe gave each other now, objects as pompous and self-proclaiming as those which former trade union leaders from the self-declared Socialist Republics had once carted over by the suitcase in order to show eternal fraternity and everlasting solidarity. But on the single biggest wall space was an enormous painting in oil and chalk. It would be vivid anywhere. In this room it was positively life-giving. I breathed it in as relief.

"I didn't know you collected art, Gwil," I said.

It was his turn to swivel slightly to take in his exceptional picture.

"Not me. Not really. It's part of the university collection. Hanging in here on loan, for safe keeping, I'm told. Valleys boy. Dead now. I'm told it's good. Is it, do you think?"

It was better than good. It was amazing.

On an overall background of night-falling blue, chalky ribbons of roads, lit by blindly groping yellow car headlights and the electric fuzz of stalked street lamps, switchbacked, and the outline of a black river curled down the canvas like an indolent tape worm. It was a map, a flattened-out cartography where hills and stars and the horizon of a sea were boundary markers. At the centre of the painting the artist had placed the open stage set of his house, the stairs, up and down which the same male figure serially, endlessly and repetitiously ran, and doorways in which the figure was framed as in a coffin, windows with the figure poised before a miniature representation of the whole. Exploding cones of orange and spurts of red scattered a scintilla of seeds to the horizon, and beyond.

"There seem to be collections of his work, private and public, but I'm told he's not to everyone's taste."

"Not for the palate of those who are without taste," I said.

Gwil let this one lie and returned to the bone I did not wish to pick. Not yet anyway. I told him, but without her equivocation, what Bran had told me that morning in person. I wasn't in the paternity picture. That seemed to satisfy him, but to leave him with other niggling thoughts.

"That really puts Mal right back in the frame, then," he mused.

"Is he around?" I asked.

"Still lives in town. We see each other frequently, of course. Officially, I mean. You know he's my chair. Chairs the board."

I nodded again. My neck was getting used to it. He gave me one of his helpless, not-what-you-think, grins.

"He appointed me, of course. But the thing is, William, we both saw that what this place needed, to take it forward, without losing its mission, its natural constituency if you like, was a leader who … who had the local in his – or her of course, though that was never likely here! – in his inner being, but had risen above, or rather beyond, it. Maldwyn knew my track record in admin and saw my ability to spearhead, well, a new way forward, tying the community and its civic leaders together more."

"Tightening the bonds, so to speak," I supplied.

"Exactly. Well, not exactly like that, but, yes, in a closer intimacy."

I had my moment, like a gap in the field of play. I went for it.

"That's what Haf has been telling me."

"Have you seen her? I don't follow. You're losing me here, Billy boy."

I didn't want to do that, so I passed the folder across the desk. He opened it with the quivering annoyance of a man being told the revenue was making a random check of his self-assessment returns. As he read rapidly through the file, I began to think they should.

"Some of this, er, material is private. Confidential. You have no right to this. Not that there's anything amiss, of course, but, what exactly are you doing, going to do, with it? Haf is behind this, isn't she? She's got her own agenda, you know ... Green, anarchist, personal. Whatever."

"Whatever you say," was all I said in return, and held my ground.

The Director sighed the sigh of the weary and put-upon for whom all explanations were tasks to perform for the ignorant or unknowing. I interpreted his look for him. "Try me," I said.

"It's quite simple. We are part, or will be part, of a wider consortium putting an entrepreneurial park with equipped office space and conference facilities at the heart of what remains one of Europe's most materially, and socially, deprived areas. We are engaged with our partners to match-fund, mostly in kind – time, salaries, facilities and so on – to secure the European grant, and the private funding, we will therefore attract. These ... documents ..." he waved an airy arm over them, "are records, open to

167

misinterpretation, of necessary, and frank, private communications to make it all happen for the good in this part of the world in which you no longer live." He snarled the last bit. "Incidentally, I'm the one out of touch, aren't I? What *have* you been doing, Billy boy?"

"Small wars and bigger famines, Gwil. You remember Nye Bevan's late-career crack about sitting on our arses watching the world starve on our television sets? I'm positioned at some useless end of that spectrum. Or I have been. As for private communication as you call it, don't we have a Freedom of Information Act nowadays?"

"Not for all private and corporate issues, you'll find."

"Public interest, Gwil."

There was a different kind of sigh, now, not of resignation but for the reconciliation of understanding he hoped would come. He prefaced it with the interchange of my given name, a trick which he had always considered cute. About as cute as a cat with the chicken roasted and ready on the table.

"Bill, Bill-o. *William*! This is still me. This is you. These are our friends. We, together, all of us are still getting things done. We can't always go around declaring the detail for bureaucrats, can we, or nothing would happen. Again, only good things will come of all this. Believe me."

"Good things?"

"For the people. For our future. For up-skilling and our global profile. For …"

I cut him short.

"Spare me the Rotary speech."

I retrieved the folder. I reassured him.

"This wouldn't convict anyone of anything. Just make a few scribes enquire into the nature of good friends and good things, that's all."

"Then, what d'you want with any of it?"

"I told you. I want to talk to Haf. I want to know why she sent me this stuff."

"Because she's a troublesome little cow, that's why."

"Meaning?"

"Meaning she fucks up her 'A' levels, and just about everything else, and I arranged for her to be admitted to the university and she, I don't know! Spies, is that the word, and steals? Spies on Mal ... on her own father? ... and me ... and her mother and, now even Ceri. God knows how, and makes it seem as if we're a _"

"Conspiracy? Cabal?"

"Oh, fuck off, Billy. That's stupid and you know it. This is all personal with her."

"Is it?"

He suddenly stopped. Polite formalities were to be the order of the day. Back onto safe ground. I felt we were at an end again. He threw me the scraps he felt would take me off his territory. I could be someone else's headache not his. He told me that he had no current address for Haf. She had been living in Mal's house, he thought, in town. He gave me the address. He was sure Mal would explain it all better, and sort out any difficulties I might be misconstrueing. He might even know where his daughter was, if she was his daughter. He couldn't resist that one. Meanwhile, he was sure I'd understand, he was very busy and, if I didn't mind, he had to move on. I didn't mind. I'd had my memory of him confirmed. Whoever was hurt, it wouldn't be Gwilym. He played the cards he held in front of him at any one time. Back then they had been those of a political activist with showy zeal in place of any kind of a conscience, and upbringing for social camouflage even as he distanced himself from it. But the hand he played was always solo. The tricks were all for him. He showed me to the door and asked Josephine to guide me back to the outer world. The look on her face told me she had heard enough to disapprove of me, and seen enough of me to wish me out of her sight quicker than she could flounce. How clever of Gwilym to keep Temptation in his outer office. I didn't let her in on the speculation but I wondered if she was about to enter the inner sanctum as compensation for the bad smell I'd brought into it to spoil her boss's day.

* * * * *

This time, the train took me back to the city centre in under an hour. I kept looking at my watch and not the blurry scenery of my childhood – down the valley, through the market town where rivers met, trading estate, viaduct, castle, weir, human sprawl of back gardens and back lanes in a back catalogue whose pages I had no wish to re-visit. I drifted aimlessly away from the station, moving against the crowds going home. I needed to eat something, but pizza joints with cardboard discs covered in tomato gloop and spaghetti with a thousand meat sauces that all tasted the same held no appeal. A billboard said The Italian Restaurant as if it was the only one possible. I didn't believe, but I walked into the connecting side street to take a closer look. Closer, it was called Casanova's. Perhaps they were serving oysters on the half-shell and viagra in sweetie wrappings. It was an unassuming shopfront, discreetly shrinking away from the spaceship strut of the nearby rugby stadium that was the nation's new Millennium mecca. It was a human apology in a monumental universe. I'd take priapic Casanova over phallic Mussolini anytime, and its modesty, as to décor and menu at least, sold it to me. I'd take a chance. Again. I could put up with pictures of Naples and coloured maps of The Boot if they really cooked their own food. They did. It wouldn't have been out of place in Brooklyn. I mopped up the juices of a Roman beef stew with bread that tasted of bread, and considered the day that had been and the deeds to be done, and my only sour thought as I drained the bottle of Montepulciano was, if it was this good, how would it survive in this city of food brands and restaurant chains? A crowd came in as I paid the bill. Maybe I'd been given an answer.

It had been a drinking day and a drinking evening. I decided to give the night a chance to join us. I went back to the air-conditioned whirr of my tenth-floor room in the hotel tower block. I hit the button to stop the noise and drew the curtains to cut out the outside sodium-lit night. I located the minibar beneath the TV set. They had Famous Grouse, but Bushmills too. And Welsh water for the Irish I preferred. After that, if I needed it, there was some Welsh whisky to let my palate consider. Penderyn, it said on the tiny bottle. I thought they'd hung Dic, the village's namesake, in 1831 and just two minutes walk from where I was now. The idea was to end rioting and riots forever. He'd come back though, it seemed, as a spirit. Like me. With that distilled Celtic trio to snuggle up to the beer and wine already inside me I calculated sleep would come when I wanted. I didn't want. Not yet.

Instead I opened the folder. I spread the papers on the bed. Photocopies, faxes, handwritten scrawls, official letters, tables of figures, newspaper articles, photographs, bank statements, and a postcard with a Welsh Dragon on it that said, "Look, please. Then help. Love, Haf." I looked, again. Helping and loving seemed a tall order. And, as Gwilym had told me, there was nothing to startle an old maid in any of it. Not unless she was an old maid who knew a kettle of fish from a posy of flowers. They were traces, indicators, connections, negatives that needed developing, and an investigative journalist to make them stick. I didn't have the time or inclination for any of that. What I did have was a voice on a telephone and a signature on a postcard, both of which worried me in a way I didn't want to think about too closely. That feeling then, and a hunch. I re-shuffled the evidence, some of it keepsakes that had been purloined, and picked up a small white sheet torn from a hotel notepad, somewhere boutique and bijou, by the look of it. Somewhere in London. It looked as if it had been left on the dressing table of a room, waiting for the return and attention of another occupant of the room. It had no date on it, just the message which read: "Ceri love, the Eurocrats' meeting went well. All almost in place. Now Gwil to sort the board next week, with Mal in the Chair! A no brainer then! So, a proposition for you. Light shopping now. Meet me in the bar at 6: will be wearing new purchases but you won't be able to see them … until later. Love, Bran." Oh, and a large X in lipstick in case he was slower on the uptake than a cog-and-ratchet funicular railway on the upward slope. On the downward side, I grimly assumed the proposition had escalated into the position which explained the congregation of partners. My old friends. My dear friends. My friends with faces and parts, real and acted, crowding in on me. I swept all the stuff off the counterpane and reached for the Penderyn that might bring sleep, if not the noose-tightened slumber that had once done for Dic.

Friday

This medicine always worked. But in reverse. First you felt better, then oblivious, then distraught. I must have slumbered like a mutt. A drugged one. Curled up and fully clothed. I woke with a growl even before I tried opening my eyes. I tried harder. I blinked to peel the eyelids back. They felt as if they were sellotaped shut, only on the inside of the shutters. I scanned the room until its blur came into focus. There was the untidy mess I'd made and left, and then there was the tidy ease, kitsch Cymru, from woollen-covered chairs in a Welsh blanket pattern to artfully placed wooden love spoons as wall decor, which they could re-assemble daily at will. Any dream would do, except for the one I was in.

The growl turned to a groan as the booze hammered away behind my dilated pupils. But I was master of those pupils and a lifelong student of these pulsating moments. Water. Aspirin. A shower. A sharp shave and vigorous toothbrushing. A naked foray into the corridor to retrieve the local newspaper they delivered daily for free. I guess they had to find readers where they could nowadays. A lingering shit in the company of said newspaper. These two faecal tasks accomplished in one sedentary motion, given the state of my bowels and the standard of the journalism. Another shower followed, and then into my visiting clothes. Old-fashioned jockey Y-fronts. Mismatching socks, but both dark. A button-down Gant shirt, blue-checked in a mix of cotton and poplin. Navy chinos pressed in-house the night before and cinched around my expanding, but still respectable, waist by a broad black leather belt with a rectangular Mexican silver buckle. The boots, bought in Tucson, Arizona after a trip to see the university's photography archive, were squared off in front and slightly heeled, their blackness relieved by a tooled-in climbing vine pattern and a dull metal sheen where they were topped and toed. The jacket was a soft black cashmere, single-breasted and short-lapelled with big patch pockets by Hugo Boss, the burly man's friend. Red capillaries were retreating in fleeing veins from the blue of my eyes, and my sour breath, coming up the airways from a stomach too turbulent for breakfast, was being held off by the toothpaste mint-fresh cavern that was my mouth. I looked and smelled as good as I could manage. After all, I was about to call on a millionaire, wasn't I? That, at least, was how Maldwyn Evans was listed. He had got himself into the IT game early on and used that expertise, unusual in this place at that time, to make property deals which tied together entrepreneurial bullshit about the "knowledge economy" with a low level of kitting out. All the buzzwords – regeneration, media, hi-tech, computer literacy, low skills to high skills, Silicon Valley in the Valleys – of the late 1980s, and of course a hotline to public grants. Buildings and land were the more old-fashioned, and more profitable, accompanying attributes. Not bad for the foul-mouthed and resentful Applied Science student we'd all patronised, and put up with and, clearly, underestimated. In the Miners' Strike he had been good for spreadsheets, maps and plans and electronic jiggery-pokery with funds. The things we had all seen as incidental, and maybe he'd already known was the only manageable future in prospect. I checked the mirror. I called down for a taxi. Just hoped the cracks in the veneer wouldn't show.

The taxi driver didn't seem to notice, anyway. He began talking the second I stepped into his rattle-trap and sat on his shiny black and vinyl-coated seats. At least I blended right in. If I was sick I didn't think anyone would notice the difference. His cab had certainly seen action in the line of fire. By the way he gunned the engine, so had he. We headed out of the city to the gap in the hills where the city dwellers thought the Valleys began. And he delivered his diatribe about all those beer-swilling, fare-dodging, vomit-flecked, rude and swearing, underdressed Valley girls and their worse, because violent, male paramours. In the end I told him I'd written the script, acted in the play and paid my dues in the audience so why didn't he pull down the curtain and give me a break. I thought he was going to sulk but he just shit-grinned in his rear-view mirror and said "Got you goin' there, mate, didn't I?" And carried on.

There was a time the traffic would have thinned and eased as the road arrowed north of the motorway. Those days seemed to have gone. I clung to the suit strap-handle with my left paw and watched trucks cut in, boom past, get overtaken by midget cars and open-backed council lorries, and road spray kick up and slime windscreens. An unremitting ribbon of rushing vehicles ignored the constant warnings of speed cameras and the electronic boards flashing updates on hazardous conditions. The rain came down more heavily as we entered the driver's fabled Indian territory, and he said, amiably enough, "Always the same up here, mate, innit?"

After fifty sphincter-exercising minutes we pulled off the dual carriageway onto a slip road that entered the southern end of the town, where the green lung of the park wheezed in the damp under a pall of petrol and diesel fumes. It was a smell that brought to mind the once-a-year pungency of the open-air travelling fairgrounds of my youth: leaf mould, crunched gravel, whirring fuel-induced rides, cheap perfume and the tongue-smarting tang of vinegar-sodden chip paper. All in the mind of course, and about as Proustian a moment as the returning bile in my mouth. I was no more a romantic than my driver, just a tad more resentful. I made him stop at the park's iron gates. The rain had eased. I would walk through the park to Mal's house set above the town. My head told me it wouldn't clear, whatever I did. My heart told my head to shut the fuck up. My guts told them both not to bother.

In the rain the park looked green, almost hopefully so. Hope was relative, neglected and recurring. I heard fat raindrops splatting onto the broken-up concrete at the bottom of the empty swimming pool hidden away behind its faux 1920s hacienda walls, with their red-tiled roofs, terracotta-wet today, and now sheltering only the memory of the echoes of revellers who'd usually been as cold as they were half-naked, and definitely eager to end both states. This was a town of bridges, though only one was worth a second glance. The footbridge crossing the pent-up river which was angrily spitting gobs of white foam over its stone and shopping trolley strewn bed, was decidedly not, but it had its uses. It led straight into the town. I paused at a curve in the High Street and looked up to where bands of terraced housing girdled the town's encircling hills. In the half-light of a grey, cloud-mopped morning they could almost have been designed. Destined anyway, with the colliers' rows in locally hewn stone highest up the ascent, leaching down onto the artisan dwellings of colliery officials and clerks and small shopkeepers, all above the necklace of two grander streets, Victorian chokers of dressed stone villas, embellished with red and yellow brick tracings around confident bay windows. The church below them was a cold mid-Victorian exercise in domination. Inside, I remembered, it was a confection of black tiles with scarlet trim and the penny-lantern dazzle of catalogue-ordered stained glass. It still stuck its spire up like a chiding finger above the surrounding pack of chapels barking at it like irrepressible dachshunds. But all that nonconformity, in religion and behaviour which had once energised the town, meant that such Anglican hauteur could never dominate let alone supress. Even its symbolic presence had been pushed aside by a glum and tiered car park which out-muscled and overshadowed the once Established Church as surely as the original workers' terraced houses were now overlooked from the plateau below the mountain by random patterns of housing that had nothing local about them other than their location. Let it go, I thought. A rash is a rash and you shouldn't scratch it. But the splurge made me itch. If no one had thought any of this out, well, no surprise there, any more than the blue-black bruise of a Stasi-type police station. New public symbols, beyond any thoughtful purpose, and the official mind was invariably blank. Blank enough usually for someone else to profit. And no one would have been quicker to do that than Maldwyn, whose house, larger than the rest, turreted and screened by monkey puzzle trees, I thought I could glimpse on the lower slopes.

You entered the house via the back entrance. A few steps down off the street and a solid wood-panelled door. New. With a brass knocker, one that was both shiny and new. It doubled as an electric bell push. I pushed. The sound of the National Anthem – the '*Gwlad! Gwlad!*' bit – jangled electronically from my finger. I let go. The straining choristers were choked off from a reprise, and I heard a dog bark in compensation, or maybe better judgement, in their place. Then a loud chesty coughing. Footsteps and chains being released behind the door. It opened. I expected to see Mal Evans, entrepreneur supreme and my replacement at Bran's side. Instead I found myself looking down at a very small man, just five foot tall, around sixty, with a puffy red face set on a body whose dimensions, and solidity, resembled a Tate & Lyle sugar cube. He didn't say a word. From inside the house, past the entrance porch, down a freshly painted passage, a voice reached us.

"Oi! Wheelie, who the fuck is it?"

Wheelie, with me sagely assuming his duties went beyond opening doors to driving the Lexus I had seen parked outside, said nothing. Just looked. I helped out.

"Tell him it's Billy," I said.

"Billy who?"

I pretended alarm, as if after this length of acquaintance I didn't expect speech. Not on our first date. Wheelie wasn't into mockery, whether mine or home-made. He shuffled powerful shoulders and teetered on the balls of his feet. A boxer, then. Certainly a fighter. Wheelie glared. I supplied the cue.

"Just tell him."

Wheelie reluctantly turned his back to me and snarled down the hall in a voice soaked in paraffin rags and squeezed out to dry. "He says to tell you it's just Billy."

There was a moment, a beat, before, on cue too and on time as he would have instinctively felt it, how he always felt it. The voice returned to us.

"Billy, boy. Come on in. Bring him down Wheelie, you daft twat."

The fresh paint smell was like an inappropriate but expensive perfume. The age was originally Victorian. The makeover was garish art deco. Below the dado rail was a deep turquoise shade on original heavy Lincrusta embossed with roses and trellis; above it was a matt black finish on plastered walls hung with three oval and gilt mirrors on one side and three rectangular silver ones on the other. The floor was carpeted in a beige weave with crimson zigzags, which presumably covered the original quarry-floor tiles, too authentic for the glamour in which Mal had invested. Pine doors led off to the right and left, and there was a turned oak staircase at a right angle just before the final and open door at which the faithful Wheelie stopped and shuffled to the side to let me pass. I smiled as unctuously as my hangover allowed. It must have come out as a grimace.

A dog, a hazelnut-brown Boxer with a white mug, worked me over first. The sniff and slobber were harmless; the bared teeth were all show and no delivery. He moved off. I knew Maldwyn

Evans, however, for the real thing. He was sitting on a burgundy red leather brass-studded swivel chair in front of a knee-hole desk. He was staring at the glaring square of a laptop. I stood and waited as the screen faded. He didn't turn. He just said to sit down wherever I wanted. I stood and looked at his back, at his pink short-sleeved sweater over a red-striped shirt, at his designer jeans and silver and blue trainers. They all bore names. None of them were his. I guessed that's why he liked them.

Beyond the desk were French windows almost the length of the wall. The other three walls were all tendrilled up in hammered gold and leafy green, with spiky cadmium yellow whorls. There was another mirror, gold leaf on the surround this time, above a black marble fireplace in which plastic fronds of red and green foliage stretched out to their superior wallpaper friends. There was no real friendship between me and Mal. Never had been, even when we'd been friendly. The dislike was more cooperative than mutual. We helped each other out by despising one another.He swivelled his chair around on a dark blue and cream silk Persian rug that filled the room and looked like the only genuine thing in it. "Kosher" would have been Mal's vernacular. Right and wrong simultaneously, as always. He saw me surveying the surrounding, the porcelain knick-knacks, or figurines, the discreetly lit and extravagantly framed oils of fishing smacks, river banks and jagged mountains, the deep blood-red leather wing chairs and the dimpled sofa. Dimpled and studded, to keep up with the matching decor. He waved. I sat. He gestured proprietorially at all his domestic splendour.

"All right, hey?"

I nodded as obediently as a nodding dog. I'd got into the habit. It beat lying outright. The boxer seemed to approve. Of my nod anyway. The dog sprang up from his spot in front of the fireplace and loped over to an outstretched hand and I caught sight of a shadow fluttering in a pane of the French doors. The driver had not left us entirely alone. I put on my quizzical face. You could always tell when I did that. It was followed by a question and a thumb jerked over my shoulder.

"You going out for a spin with Wheelie soon, Mal?" I asked.

He frowned back and then laughed like the happy shoulder-clapping best friend he made everyone want to like. At first.

"A spin? You mean him? He's not a driver, Bill, he used to work on the bins, mun. Wheelie bins. Wheelie, see. Hear that, Wheelie? Billy boy, by here, thinks you're fucking Stirling Moss! I wouldn't trust Wheelie in a Robin Reliant, leave alone my Lexus. Mind you, he's quite useful in other ways. Handy, like, aren't you, Wheelie? Oi, go and close that door and fuck off, me and Billy here got some catching up to do."

The old retainer phlegmed a grumble to himself and the door was shut. I began to wonder about a drink. There were bottles and silver-chased ice buckets in a glass-fronted cabinet, and a gin and tonic might have rung a cerebral bell or two. But I mistook Maldwyn yet again. I always had. He just came to the point. "I didn't expect to see you here. Ever, if you know what I mean. Bran told me you'd want to see me and why. About that. But there's nothing I can do for you. Nothing."

I waited.

"And, yeah, Gwilym rang too. Not happy. Not happy at all. So I know all about that too, and the crap you're putting around about papers and deals. Which comes from her, and I don't have to tell you fuck all. But I will. To get it over with, see. And you out of my life. Again. Permanent, and I mean permanent, this time."

"So, tell me," I said.

"Tell you what, exactly, so we're crystal?"

"Tell me how and why a charitable trust, Tir Werin, is acquiring acres and acres of land above the Valleys. Tip spoil, iron and coal tumps, useless until decontaminated, I guess. But expensive, it seems. Twenty million pounds expensive, it seems."

"Gwil already told you. A state-of-the-art facility. For conferences. For research. For regeneration for fuck's sake. And tourism."

"Tourism?"

"Yeah! Get your head round it, right. What else d'you think can happen round here? Industry? Forget it. Have you seen the empty sheds – hangars more like – we got everywhere? And have you seen the buggers walking the streets, the ones that are left now? The smart ones have either gone, or work south of the motorway. Hi-tech here? Californian monkeys would do better. Tourism means using the only thing left once you've got through the streets and the shit to the mountains – a landscape! We can build beyond the valleys and let people come and stay in luxury. And provide jobs for those not too idle to do them."

"As what? To serve your made-over world?"

"Yes. To bloody well serve. As security, as waitresses, as cleaners, as gardeners, as cooks, as … what-the-fuck-ever. What's wrong with that? You tell me."

"Where's the money coming from, Mal?"

"You know, so don't give me that. It's all in the open. European money. Private money. Now or never. And it's got to be now."

"Direct to the trust?"

"Yes."

"Of which Ceri is the leading trustee and public face, and which Gwilym serves as Secretary, when he's not running his research outfit which fronts up, intellectual credibility and all that, for the trust. The same research park whose board you chair with Gwilym as your chief executive, so to speak."

"Yeah. So what?"

"And the money from Europe and elswhere goes to Tir Werin, so that the trust can buy this otherwise useless land. And the seller is Valleyscorp, isn't it Mal?"

"I'm no longer a director."

"I bet you aren't."

"Watch your mouth, Billy."

"Why? There's nothing wrong, is there? Nothing wrong with the bank statements that show you were buying this land, and more, for Valleyscorp over fifteen years ago. For tuppence, or less. That you made it over to Bran and Haf when the IT bubble burst and your holdings crashed and you needed to cash in your nest egg, I'd guess, one way or the other."

He was listening now. The silence was somehow more disruptive than intervention. I was running out of rope, and he knew it.

"You haven't got a clue, have you, pal. Not a fucking clue."

It was time to wait again.

"It's completely set to one side. I have no connections. Not with Valleyscorp,that was doing people a favour anyway, and not with Tir Werin, which is Gwilym and Ceri's vehicle to get some fucking thing done around here. And I don't even live with Bran anymore. As you know. I don't touch no money, see. Get it?"

He knew I didn't. Not yet, anyway. Besides, he didn't get what I really wanted. Maybe because I wasn't too sure about that myself. Not yet anyway. Suddenly, Maldwyn did emollient. He stood up. Six feet plus up with the same broad-shouldered, big-chested flat-stomached look and only a hint of a concession to flesh around his clean-shaven chin. Rugged, I think they call it.

"Come and see my garden. You'll like it."

And his eyes, as hazel and flecked as the boxer's, signalled an exit through the French doors. He didn't wait for an answering signal. The handle turned and he stepped out onto a flagstoned patio below which steps led to the garden. The dog was out and down first. Mal beckoned me on.

The rain had stopped, leaving that peculiar hillside tumble of slotted slate roofscape at its best. Its age glistened back to an early promise and the sun was not too weak to hide the wrinkles, and strong enough to promise better. Fat chance, I thought, but then the unexpectedness of the garden swallowed me whole. From the first stone steps down from the patio's platform where the whole town lay before you, you stepped onto a lawn, springy, green and turfy, that cushioned you better than any carpet, and was longer and wider than most of the terraced houses. It was held in on three sides by shrubbery mature enough to make me feel frisky, and which at the far end gave way to a screen of trees, a copse almost, that hid the town and all its ways completely. You could sit on that lawn anytime for over a century and not see the labour that had secured its cultivation or hear, except as a murmur, the friction of any human traffic. You could play croquet on that square.

Mal could tell I was moved. He thought I was impressed.

"Nice, huh." he said. It was a statement more than a question. I gave him one back.

"Whose was it?"

I knew the identikit ilk of the social group if not the singular identity of any previous owners. Coal mine managers. Town clerks. Solicitors. Publicans even. Provision merchants, wholesale and retail, for sure. Butchers. Bakers. Candlestick makers wouldn't give me a full set, but I had always been a spectator at that particular species of card game.

"Beynons," he said. And it was enough said. Suppliers of bread to a ravenous workaday town and its feeder villages, from handcarts up and down a valley that had burned its Victorian breeches quicker than a liberated Frankenstein, then buttoned them up tight with Edwardian respectability. The bread was moved from carts to vans, and then to shops. The bakehouses were very local and quite profitable before they were sold on to retail moguls who were more profitable than local in every way. The people who had sat on this lawn and smoked Craven A through ivory cigarette holders, with a whisky soda in the other hand, in the tinkling 1920s or the jarring '30s, knew London as Town, and school as somewhere away. They had better taste than Maldwyn, too, or, maybe they just interfered less and let what came naturally just naturally come.

We took a stroll through the copse. Me silent, him talking. This idyllic Eden on a dungheap did not end at the lawn's edge. More terraces of stone and grass, low walls and moss-pocked grey statuary, the usual simpering boys with flutes and attendant dogs, a white-limbed nymph, her marble pudendum discreetly draped. How many wistful adolescent glances had she had, I wondered? The live-in maids, yesteryear teenage girls from the terraced streets, would have been warmer, and dutifully accommodating. The garden fell away in a deceptive arrangement of formal shapes and undulating curves to a high wall, a wooden door and an embankment above the railway cutting. The town was back in sight and to the right lay the rugby ground's stand and field on the site of another one of the town's former collieries, a shaft more than a pit where my mother's father had worked. I had played on that field, above the seams in which he had clogged up his lungs with dust. Sentiment didn't even scratch it. I remembered him.

I had to turn Mal away from the trance of his own reverie. Prices. Bargains. Fools. Costs. Where he'd come from. His. Not anyone else's now. Where he was going. But the only dialogue he would understand would have to be confrontational.

"You'll need the transfers to be regular, then. Does she make them out to you, or one of your set-aside accounts?" I asked.

"You what?" he replied.

"As far as I can see the money goes into Tir Werin, then out via Gwilym as Secretary, with Ceri's approval and fixing of the patsies he's corralled, to Valleyscorp, aka Bran, and then, in dribs and drabs, somehow to you. Only Haf would now have to sign the cheques, too, wouldn't she? So why shouldn't she? Or, put in another way, why should Bran pass it on to you if the great divide is as divisive as you suggested?"

"Fuck off" was his not unexpected explanation. I tried another route.

"I've come to meet Haf; she wants to see me. But no one seems to know exactly where she is and she's not on anyone's call list. I only know about all this other stuff because she provided a paper trail. It's no big deal to me to see where that leads. Only her."

"Why?"

I knew he could answer that himself. I waited again.

"You think she may be your fuckin' daughter, don't you? Well, maybe she's mine, eh?"

"Right," I said.

"And wrong, butty. D'you think you and me were the only ones dipping the wick in that honey pot?"

I bridled. He noticed.

"Oh, OK, you were in residence – sort of, as I recall. But there's other possibilities beyond you and me."

"Such as?"

"All I'm saying is that when Bran and I split, or were going to split cos it wasn't getting any better, she told *me* it was you and she told Haf it wasn't me. And you know what, I don't fucking know, or care."

Mal stopped and stood right in my path, right in front of my face. His voice was dry and contemptuous. He said,

"That's why I threw Bran over. Know what I mean? That's why Haf stayed here. See? And what's it to you anyway? You left, remember?"

Mal turned. My time was over it seemed. Again. I put my hand on his shoulder. Heavily. I pulled him back. He made no move to take my hand away. Mal had controlled things, all things in his path, for too long. I took the hand away. Mal said what Mal thought.

185

"Don't be stupid. You've pissed me off enough."

I said that enough was nowhere near enough and that I would hurt him before I was finished. I said he was one of life's jerry-builders, and a bastard with it, and that I would pull him down. Mal grinned.

He said, "A bastard," and, liking the sound of it, repeated it in a whisper to himself. I saw Wheelie at the top of the steps, clutching what may once have been a pit mandrel but was now only a baseball bat.

"I'll see myself out," I said and walked to the bottom garden gate, hoping an unlocked door would save me any grief. Probably very personalised grief. I lifted the iron latch and turned an iron hoop and went out onto the cinder embankment path. I followed it to the railway bridge, then left the path, crossed above the line and headed back into the town. It was time for that drink Mal hadn't given me.

* * * * *

Once upon a time there were more pubs in this town than the buttons on a collier's *coppish*; that's a fly to anyone born before 1960 and a zip to the rest of the world. Me and the dead respected the fashion of fumble. But the buttons had gone from trousers as sure as the pubs from every street, whether main, high, back or back of beyond. The Full Moon had waned and The Rising Sun no longer brightened anyone's day. I noticed the council office had abandoned their stand-out 1930s modernity in favour of a re-fit as a cavernous ocean liner's bar-lounge, all shiny tables and chairs and brass-railed mini decks, one which had no doubt sailed into every small town. That was one voyage I would avoid then. But I did need a settling drink.

My head no longer throbbed like a cold diesel engine so my stomach had assumed the role of chief victim. I decided to punish it some more. The rugby ground had once been the pulse, heart and, yes, the strained bowels of the place. I went there. A few cars in front of the clubhouse. The only faces I knew were on the walls, in black and white rows. I was amongst them. So were Tommy and Lionel. The bar had fizzy lager and frothy beer. I had a pint of Guinness and took it outside to the field. A steep concrete stand with plastic flip-up seats on one side, an open-sided shed over the stepped terraces opposite, two posts and a field. A visual cliché, of course. But what turned the truism into its own heart-stopping truth was the setting. From the stand you could take it all in at once, and behind the shed were the street-lined slopes of a town with more guts than sense and more passion in its life than almost anywhere else I'd ever been. Urbane it was not. But it summed up urban as a smack in the mouth to any country boy. Directly to the north the hills opened up to the higher mountains courtesy of a gap so narrow they almost folded over, one into the other. And every few minutes a train measured the distances in-between consecutive townships with that regularity of unstoppable motion which such places had once assumed as their rightful destiny. Only, the motivation to match the punctuality had been mislaid. It was all wound down.

On the field I saw ghosts. On the terraces I glimpsed shadows. My ears boomed with the bass rumble of crowd noise, the smack of boots on ball, the slap or even crack of hands and fists on faces and legs. The stout I was sipping was as black and icy-cold as my soul felt. I didn't have a matching heart anymore. Mal was right: what the hell did I care? What the hell did I want, coming back like this? Or maybe just what the hell? I needed another pint. My stomach stopped complaining so we went together in search of another afternoon of induced quiescence.

I did the damage in a quiet corner of the upstairs bar of a workingmen's club that had somehow survived into the new century. There was no one to bother me as I read the newspapers accumulated on the speckled yellow, blue and red formica tables. Formica had been posh, the latest trend when I was growing up. That and green leatherette banquettes. They still had those too, and they still had the Ronettes on the jukebox. Nobody tried to talk to me. Perhaps I wasn't looking too nice and tidy. All these "ettes" had not extended here to baguettes. I ate a ham roll to see if the bread was still like pap and the meat like a rolled-out slick of piggy plastic. Tasted good to me. I had another to try to fool the alcohol. No fooling. I walked to where the river had once encircled the town's early ironworks and the covered-in canal had once sent the barges to the sea.

At the old Iron Bridge I took in, as if for the first time, that unity of hills and river which the makers of this town had managed to disassemble with every unplanned decision they had ever taken. The late afternoon light was being pin- pricked by car headlamps. Spring was not yet sprung. Me, I was springy as a newborn lamb to the slaughter. I hoped my last intended watering hole would not have been dried up by the dessication of fashion and youth. I needn't have worried. The squat stone drinking den was intact and, though spotlessly clean and daily swabbed, its interior was as it had looked for half a century. No music. No distractions, and an outside urinal whose basic floor and lime-washed walls would have made a Frenchman blush.

I sat on a wooden chair at a polished wood-and-iron rectangular table which was set beneath a mirror proclaiming Dewar's whisky, and with the insignia VR. I don't think the old girl had ever made it here. It had been a second home to my old man. I stayed as the lights went on against the fading afternoon, and silent drinkers drifted in and out. The rain was spattering against the windows again. It was drumming inside me, too, a persistent beat of melancholy and uncertainty which the booze had only helped dig deeper. When the barmaid began to give me a wondering glance just once too often for me to be misguided enough to consider it as admiration, I decided to move.

I saw them at the pub's corner, idling in the gloom, as I walked past them, but I only sensed their threat an instant before I felt the first blow to the head. Something wooden and weighty had opened up my skull. Baseball bats were far too universal these days. I went down into a loose slurry of small stones and gravel besides a row of empty steel barrels. I reached for the lip of one of them to get to my knees, but I never made it. A steel-capped boot to my arse took me down hard and another pain of sorts drove into my ribs and beat a tattoo on either side with a drum roll follow-up to the head. I was being worked over by boys who knew an established routine and didn't deviate from it and didn't care about leaving a mark and the occasional fracture or broken bone. I vomited the day's pleasure onto a boot and was rewarded for my thoughtfulness with another kicking. The drink had been a temporary anaesthetic but the pain that surged through me was like shards of bone splintering and tearing into flesh. Those were my bones. That was my flesh. My eyes felt as if they were popping inside out and burning up like funeral pyres. Only my ears still seemed attuned to whatever my body was about to leave behind. And they heard a different kind of noise to the rhythm of boots. A shout. A voice. One I knew. Insistent and quiet as it delivered its own message to Maldwyn's messengers:

"That's enough. Leave him be. Fuck off. Go on. Now, I said."

Tommy.

* * * * *

Two

His Old Man Said

His old man said that "Sweet Dreams" was a lie fed to children. So he was brought up on memories. Sometimes the old man would call them history. Most of it wasn't in any book. Daydreams, he would say, were the narcolepsy of those who drifted through lives too feeble for roots. He taught all this, sourly and as best he could, in and out of classrooms. It was his wisdom, from his experience. Only it didn't connect. And when it did, when a generation appeared to come awake, and finally act, then he was curtly dismissive, in ways that could be both incomprehensible and hurtful.

* * * * *

His old man understood the eager impulse to act. To understand was not to approve. He said it was self-indulgence. He called it social gratification. He thought it was a political wank. He'd say that ignominy was seeking refuge in ignorance. He talked like that. It made it all the harder to pay him any attention any longer. When he was not angry he seemed almost sorry for it all, that it had come to this thrashing about, the lies of rhetoric fuelling the necessary expression of bravery. The way he talked was the way he thought.

* * * * *

His old man would nonetheless turn out of bed with him in the murk of a wintry dawn as the strike's buzzsaw activity lengthened. They would join small nodes of men gathering into guerrilla squads to trudge over mountain roads into other valleys to bypass police blockades, and swoop to picket and push and shove. The old man would begin to argue that to compromise was not to surrender, only to be told to shut the fuck up. Billy would move away from him, using his camera as an excuse, using its viewfinder to find faces, locate gestures, swim amongst the sea of expectation that swirled around platforms of oratory where Scargill eerily referred to himself in the third person, and to them as if their individual lives had been melded together with his. Perhaps, finally, they had. Images began to define events. But not, ever, for the old man.

* * * * *

His old man cadged a lift to Paynter's funeral in Golders Green just before the bone chilling cold Christmas of that year. Billy walked with him. At seventy, the old man was stooping a bit now. They walked through a dank late-morning gloom, past incongruous evergreens and dripping shrubbery, towards the crematorium. The old man had nodded to those he knew, acquaintances and former students, comrades he would have said once, all come to acknowledge the deceased eighty-year-old who had once had his teeth smashed out in police cells, couriered Russian gold through Nazi Germany, served as a political commissar in Spain, saw people killed there by decree, maybe even approved of it, and later through various modes of compromise led his union tightly and well. Billy had seen him once, in his retirement, shoulder to shoulder with the old man. Same height, short, and his breadth wide, and his temperament stubborn. Billy had photographed them, never seeing hero-worship in the old man's eyes before. The camera failed to capture it.

* * * * *

His old man had winced and drifted when Billy stood off the path to snap the bareheaded, dark-suited men who walked up in clusters. Some old timers. Officials, of a later time and ilk. Like a family that was cold shouldering itself. Scargill at the centre of a bristling group. Greeted and shunned. Billy clicked. The old man was one of those to be called to speak. The president would have to listen, standing at the back. The old man had been measured about the life, but icy as to its meaning. When the old man mentioned 1926 it was not a banner to be waved but a shiver to be suffered. Resilience was always limited, he said. A union was not to be tested to destruction, he said. There was never one last punch to deliver. The president was grim and scornful but the family quarrel was open from then on.

* * * * *

His old man had predicted the way sense would finally be seen. He refused to give Ceri any credit for seeing it. For him that particular recanting had come too late and was as calculated, if self-interest allied to emotion was any kind of forethought, as the earlier embrace of madcap confrontation. For Ceri, he felt, this was yet another tack towards a career of contrariness, of the forthright that was a masquerade, of a transparency that was draped in shrouds of meaninglessness. It was an emptiness, a vacuum, filled only by an estimation of himself in which his own time had betrayed him despite his own best efforts. The old man said this was not, strictly speaking, the opportunism of a careerist; it was more the retreat of an integrity that could not be sustained in individuals when collective aspirations dwindled. There was less and less to be representative about more and more of the time.

* * * * *

His old man was big on generations. Billy's was to be forgiven for its callowness. No choice there. But despised for its parasitical identification with others who would be made mere ciphers in the subsequent drive to harvest their experience. Utilisation masked as youthful altruism. The patterns could be seen even then. Gwilym, the railwayman's boy, a PhD underway, one envious eye on Bran, already lecturing, available for blithe comment on TV and radio on "Our People's History". The old man spat at that. Maldwyn, electronics and engineering a genetic inheritance from a colliery electrician father, convinced and convincing that communications technology could democratise everything. Advising Ceri on the logistics of maps, communications and picketing raids. Bran already subbing for newspapers, readily welcomed into inner circles for her evident sympathy as much as her good looks, soon receiving exclusives and scoops and contacts denied others, and parlayed into TV pieces to camera. Billy, with his camera never out of his hand now, exhausted by the pace of things and the unrelenting tirades of his old man.

* * * * *

His old man had never liked cameras. Or so he said. He certainly never owned one, or borrowed one, or used one. He bought one for Billy when the boy was sixteen, out of an act of misplaced generosity, as he wrote on the card. Not so much a card, more a page torn from his sketch pad with a contrite fatherly face drawn in by the same hand which had endlessly drawn Billy's mother. The sketches lay in a drawer, not forgotten but not looked at either. Billy preferred the few snapshots and the couple of studio portraits taken of her as a schoolgirl, looking demure and solemn. She smiled in the curling, fading snaps. At a desk, mussing up her pigtails, in a ruched costume by the sea, a face at the back in a garden, at the front on a protest march. His old man was in that one too. But his old man never took any photographs of the woman who had died giving birth to his son.

* * * * *

His old man said photographs were false prompts. They made the memory stutter out one instant which blocked all others. These were the fixed images which surfaced to hint at but not reveal the depth of a life. His son hated him for claiming to know all that. For Billy there were only such images of her, and they were few. They kept no family albums, no shrunken memorials. The old man pointed out that those keepsakes only captured what was meant to be happy or celebratory so, in their want of the ineffable melancholy of life, they betrayed twice over. For being what they were and for only showing the need of the perpetrator. The soul of the captured was never made captive. It only lived on in the mind. In memory.

* * * * *

His old man favoured painting when it probed the relationship of culture to nature. The camera could document and catalogue but its transposition always threatened to be the residual sentiment of nostalgia. When Billy grew old enough to argue he would counter with the works of the great mid-century masters. Magazines and books yielded their fruit to the boy and the old man had to agree that their cut-outs of wars and streets and industrial grind and resistance to it evaded the glib and the condescending. But he still insisted it was the subject that gave the work its substance, not what they had done with it. It was, he'd say, as if only the emotional spasm Bevan had once ridiculed had been revealed, but not the intellectual star-tapping which the Tredegar dreamer had wanted for us.

* * * * *

His old man said that the nouns "artist" and "poseur" were synonyms. Both paradoxically concerned with removing the self in the very act of observation only to show how self-consciously it had been done. For him the vantage and the viewed were inseparable. His riff was that all life was memory even as it was experienced, there and instantly gone, so that we forever lived in the past, even as it left us. We lived on by imagining that past which was the future we yearned to remember. The dream of life was aspiration. Its nightmare was memorialisation. We trapped ourselves in the techno-present by the cloying memento mori that was the falsification that photography bought. Memory, which was History, was a jumble of relationships to be savoured, not a grid of relatives to be connected.

* * * * *

His old man fed the boy scraps about his past as if he was a hungry and insistent dog. Bit by bit. A piece at a time. His mother's grandparents built up the picture of their daughter for him, but it came as coloured shards of a sacred window, so that he glimpsed the child and schoolgirl and trainee teacher only through their blinded eyes. "Good people," his old man would say when Billy came back from visits there, to his own more pared-down home life, set amidst the old man's canvases, brushes, easels and the lingering smell of gooey oils. They had died, young, in their sixties, the one after the other as if arranged. Billy grieved, just like a dog. And asked more about what he didn't know, his teenager feistiness setting up confrontations which the old man diverted with trivia whenever he could.

* * * * *

His old man explained his own being alone in this way. He said his mother had tied him to a high chair when he was barely three years old and fed him, and then walked away. He was in a scullery kitchen. It must have been evening because it was next day that he had been found, his wrists chafed red, tear-streaked and piss-smelly with shit squashed beneath him on the chair seat. He had been given to a relative, his mother's older sister, to bring up and never saw his mother again. His given name was David. Maddox had been her maiden name. She had been a maid, the old man said. In a big house. It was just after the first Great War. She was unmarried. The old man said he didn't know, for certain, who his father was and that, anyway, at the time of his abandonment the man was dead.

* * * * *

His old man said you could divide life by decades or by smells and tastes. That these vanished along with fashion in clothes or music or speech, but that they were ever loitering, ready to call up a whole time. He said the '20s, for him, smelled of damp and decaying plaster as water seeped through a tiny back bedroom and the lumpy bed he shared with his "Aunty's" three sons. It tasted of cold dripping and sweet, mashed-over tea. The '30s was the acrid smell of cigarettes and the bitter-sweet taste of Fry's Five Boys chocolate bars, and the mingled smell and taste of underground workings in deep collieries where horse manure and fetid air penetrated mouth and nostrils. The '40s was the taste of fear in the mouth and the smell of burned flesh filtered into human acceptance by the numb of alcohol, and indifference once horror was made routine. The '50s, he said, was the last time he knew these things distinctly, and the smell then was of newness and happiness, and the taste was of my mother's lips.

* * * * *

His old man was constantly against the grain in all things. He loved to smoke. Usually untipped Players or Capstan Full Strength which came in weirdly effete, mauve-tinted packets. If he had lived beyond the mid-1980s he would have scorned the huddle of fellow conspirators in the fug of a den for their designated dirty habit. For him the addiction, for such it was, was also a ceremony, for such he made it. The old push-up packs with their frisson of silver foil just covering up the plump white paper rolls of tobacco. The spurt and flare from a struck match. The rich field tang of burning leaf. The wispy curlicues of blue metal smoke. And sharing. Billy had been with him once in a crowded bar full of colliers at the start of Miners' fortnight, two weeks of caravans and sand and beer to come, with cigarettes flung the one to the other as individual packets were opened up for all. There were men, the old man told him, who brought the habit home from what was then not a distant war. Then they more often than not shared a match and a fag passed on from one battle-dressed baby-faced veteran to another. If it was the warmth of glamour, no less was it the attitude of bravado.

* * * * *

His old man claimed to have met Burt Lancaster. The actor, he said, was not then either a star or indeed an actor. He was a circus performer enlisted into the US Army to divert and entertain the raw troops, mud-soaked and bombarded to a standstill outside Monte Cassino in 1944. Everyone "knew" Burt Lancaster by the time the old man asserted his own former friendship. He told his adult students how *The Crimson Pirate*, in 1952, was a deliberate riposte to McCarthyite witch-hunts, with the Red Flag waved in the philistine face of Middle America. And what else was *The*

Flame and the Arrow in 1954 if not an assertion of the New Deal which had sustained the young Burton Lancaster in the '30s? The old man met scepticism head-on with an account of getting smashed on rough red vino with the tumbler and hand-springer from East Harlem who'd got a mental and physical education in a settlement home no different from the miners' institutes that had once added intellectual juice and social cohesion to the Valleys. No one quite believed the old man on this.

* * * * *

His old man thought the War might change everything and for a time he thought that it felt as if it had, or would yet. He had returned, on a late demob via Austria after North Africa and the slog up through Italy, to work in the pits again. Nationalised if not socialised, he'd say. It was another front line. Welfare was to be the first step, not the last, neither public ownership nor social care only marking time, but signalling what was to be next. He lived in the front room of an overcrowded house and paid rent to the family. Everything was limited. Beds were shared as readily as scarce pint glasses were fought over, to be filled as they were emptied. For a few, brief years before the 1950s the sense of unfulfilment and possibility irked and sustained them. Underground, men wore army berets instead of the new safety helmets. Nights, if he worked days, were indiscriminately passed between pubs and pictures and political wrangling. If he worked nights he slept days. He grew weary. He was single and coiled with anger. A chance remark made underground took him to a WEA session and to the opening of things up by, at least, an ordering of their otherwise confusion. He was never sure that was progress. But he met the boy's mother, Mona, in Coronation year and she decided self-improvement in order to help others was to be his lot. He could never release his memory of her into any forgiving of himself for her dying.

* * * * *

His old man had been to Spain before package holidays. He said he'd gone as a fellow traveller, and grinned, with the alibi of art-history research as excuse for the stuffed money belt he'd worn for the Party. It was always the only Party, even when he stopped working and voting for it. Mona had fretted but gone with him. Was it there, Billy would wonder, that he was conceived in 1957? Bill Paynter himself, now the president in South Wales, had gripped the old man's hand and asked him to go. The old man said you could never forget Paynter's handshake nor his unrelenting eyes. No forgiveness in them. Not for himself anyway. His own first wife had died in childbirth, in 1940, leaving the young revolutionary with twins to raise.

* * * * *

His old man had thought of Ceri as a son until he considered him to be yet another prodigal. Early on, joining the old man's class he was soon, by calculated choice, attached to an older generation, and so perfectly positioned to link, though cannily dismissive of his own contemporaries when it mattered, into his own generation, as a leader. Even as the working-class hero he would fashion himself into, both for himself and the needs of others, in the 1970s. By then the leather jacket and rolled brylceemed quiff had given way to a more class-universal garb, one that was more suburban Rolling Stones than subterranean rock 'n' roll. Either way, whether on his home patch or further afield, Ceri, with his easy, self-assured manner and gentle, yet chiding, malice, offered himself as knowable and serious and exotic and welcoming, open to a future that embraced change, not as tribal as the more common ingrowing political follicle. One like the old man soon seemed to be. Ceri would hug you close and clap you to his confidence. He was difficult to resist. The act was no act, the authenticity was sincere, and not to believe in him was to show a lack of faith in the purpose. And in the old man's weekend schools Ceri gathered others to him like a cultural pilotfish guiding a shoal. In his prime Ceri, now with a craggy face more hewn than sculpted, more planed by intent than moulded by experience, became, in the unofficial guerilla strikes that lit up his special sky, almost the physical embodiment of the Idea others had configured. Men, at this time, admired him and wanted his friendship, and women generally just wanted to fuck him. He generally just obliged.

* * * * *

His old man could hold harsh opinions. He would say that his protégé, Ceri, was a music hall act who came to believe in the propaganda of applause. His old man had been a connoisseur of variety acts and a regular to the variety theatre in its last golden post-war flush. He'd sit through the trick unicyclist, the songbird imitator, the Irish tenor, the check-suited northern comics, the exotic fan dancer, the Hungarian acrobats from Glasgow, the sopranos, crooners and dancers and the dress-suited compères. He claimed to love to read the safety curtain, a kind of commercial Mondrian he'd say, marked out from right to left and top to bottom with squares and rectangles of colour within which haberdashers and hairdressers and animal feed and furnishings and ladies' corsets and liver salts and linoleum and hire purchase and soap and newspapers, all declared their worth and wares. The finale would inevitably be a double act to follow the saccharine warble of Ruby Murray or Joan Regan or the buck-toothed hoofing of Billy Dainty. The old man loved the banter, Socratic dialectic he'd say, between Jewell and Warris or the young Morecambe and Wise. The last two names Billy recognised from television. He doubted the old man had seen them live on stage any more than he'd met Nick Cravat or Burt Lancaster in a mess tent in the drear of an Italian wartime winter. His old man, he thought by the mid-1970s, was full of bullshit.

* * * * *

His old man was not yet sixty when the coal strikes of 1972 and then 1974 derailed any lingering complacency about industrial accommodation. He thought the NUM's own double act of Gormley and Daley had schemed and organised to a tactical perfection and with a moral beatitude that knew its own origins. After those deceiving moments had passed he increasingly railed, and despaired. Nobody heeded. He told Billy, whenever he came home these days, that somehow, somewhere along the line, we'd become a cultural *nomenklatura* parasitic on our own half-dazed working-out of our past or else, like Tommy, just endlessly turned and turned around, with the change or aim of self-direction lost or repressed. Easy meat for the *nomenklatura*. The old man liked Tommy, so the despair worked in deeper and deeper when Ceri led the charge into 1984, and Billy's generation jumped to offer its support. To be inside, really inside Tommy's head, he'd rage, you'd need a blowtorch, a chisel, a pair of tweezers and an advanced degree in Victim Studies.

* * * * *

His old man told him we'd swallowed our own shit and mistaken it for nutrient. He was good at upsetting people. He told Ceri at Paynter's funeral that the strike had become an orgasmic shudder orchestrated by the pimps of history, himself included. A generation of wannabes actually wanted this release from stasis into an oblivion that would eventually engulf not them but the

Tommys and the Lionels who'd tasted the saltiness of being, again, in the collective frame. Except that it was only the glycerine slick of temporary notoriety for them, the stage army. And for Billy, Bran, Maldwyn and Gwilym there was, at last, the longed-for generational credibility and, of course, whatever happened, having for themselves the bonus of not being personally doomed thereafter. On the contrary, his old man said, the dreamers would perish and the doers would profit. And it was clear who he meant and why. He railed but did not convince.

* * * * *

His old man shocked them all – Billy, Bran, Gwilym and Mal – one day by telling them he did not believe in any of it, any more, especially not in their activity in the strike, and even in any struggle that was defined as they defined it. He told them that the moment had passed. He told them, again, of what Bevan had said in 1951, when the moment was still there to seize: that even in the '30s, with three million out of work and ingrained poverty everywhere, they couldn't guarantee majorities for Labour even in the worst hit areas, that building socialism was not about pressing buttons. They argued. The old man was silent. Then he said that, once, when he was eleven years old, in the lockout of 1926, he followed a group of boys down a back lane where, it was said, they would all see something, but only if they had a halfpenny or two farthings or a cigarette butt. At the back garden gate of a terraced house whose steep garden ran up to the steps that led up again to the home itself, there was a queue and an older boy who was taking the coins and dropping them into a tin. The old man said the boy's name was Byron Keys and that his father had been imprisoned for riotous assembly. Stoning blacklegs. That the Keys family were ardent and active members of the Party. That the payees lined up and went in up the garden

path, past the wilting rhubarb and the scruffy blackcurrant bushes
to the paint-flaked wooden door of an outside lavatory. Each one,
in their turn, had to lift the latch and go inside and look and turn
and come out. For a halfpenny you could look at Byron's ten-
year-old sister, Ginny, sitting on the seat with her knickers round
her ankles. His old man said that if they didn't get the point, his
own point was well made.

* * * * *

His old man said they acted like participants but were, in reality,
avid consumers. He made it worse when he called them parasites.
He broadened the definition to include himself, to make the insult
seem lighter. It didn't. He tried to explain that he, too, had gone
from being inside it all to being – he searched for the correct
instance – like Sam Spade in *The Maltese Falcon* when his partner,
whose wife he was banging as well, stumbled around in the dark
looking, not for clues as he pretended to think, but for excuses
for his behaviour, an *Übermensch* of consciousness, with the world
he inhabited slipping away without him, which was what, here
was the most terrible thing, the very thing he wanted. See? the
old man would exclaim. See? More as if it was a statement than
a question. All they saw was an old man in delirium and all they
heard was a rant against the seriousness which they needed to
invest the fun they were having with the ballast of other people's
gravity.

* * * * *

His old man didn't live long enough afterwards to witness the
successive falls from grace. He had stood on the embankment
when the last stand-out colliery workers walked back in behind
the thump of a drum and the dirge of a plaintive brass band

before dawn on a March day. He watched a more circumspect Billy move in and out and around and from the back of the straggled line, taking pictures. He knew there would be no easy routes mapped out from now on. They'd run off the maps of a known and once cherished world. The dynamics of action had been replaced by the melancholia of that loss. The pits were morphing into mausoleums. Billy looked closer at the assumptions behind his own feverish images and found any traces of the real had gone, or else were just lingering as accusatory, shadowy presences. That last march had been one final act of public exposure before the shades of anonymity closed in.

* * * * *

His old man spent his last autumn and winter in reflection. He wondered how that history which had now left us could be properly remembered. He decided that lists and structured narratives were another species of lie. That the simultaneity of any actual life was what gave it value and so any flattening or compartmentalisation was as much of a subsequent denial of the humanness of living as, in life, was the denial of the interconnectedness of desire. He said that the art of self-perception, in our common life, had been smothered by the perception of ourselves by others, and to which embrace we had too readily succumbed. You would need new forms, fresh categories, a deliberate breaking of the neck of convention wherever it sought to inhibit full expressiveness. Just as the history had been lived. You couldn't do the tragedy bit without it seeping, or even racing headlong, into melodrama. You'd need comedy, black and ironic, to keep it sane, and the surreal to prevent the historic and the epic being registered as romance. Increasingly, he was sure that painting alone, or other types of fine art, provided a field of vision that allowed the otherwise ungraspability of the world to be confronted. At its best, painting was intellect suffused with emotion, working colour and form, beyond the shamanism of music, the pretence of words, the smash and grab in the jewellery window that was the best photography. The old man wrote to Billy to tell him that the adage "show" not "tell" was for adolescents, and that we had all grown up. He said how could you "show" anymore, other than in the gabble of a nursery class seeing everything new for the first time, if what was truly there to be shown now necessarily resided in the act of telling. That the one big thing to hold onto in our ruins was the consciousness of ourselves, not just what had been experienced but how it had been perceived, imagined not only felt. His son had left by then and he was dead when Billy had the last letter.

* * * * *

His old man had once told him that there were no photographs of Crazy Horse. The Oglala Sioux war chief had been assassinated in 1877 one year after the Plains Wars had ended with the pyrrhic victory over Custer at the Little Big Horn. A former ally, the Sioux warrior Little Big Man, had pinned his arms back and a soldier had bayoneted him in a guard house. It was predestined but it was also planned. The other chiefs, the wily Red Cloud, his enemy, and the indomitable Sitting Bull, his friend, posed for and were captured by the lens, and the names of all of them had been stolen and corrupted into English, even that of Tashunca-Uitco, which properly means His Horse is Crazy. But the face, the body, and therefore mostly the spirit, of course, of Crazy Horse were never taken by whites. Only an Indian pictograph shows us Crazy Horse. He made sure that what was to tell about him would remain simple, true and ultimately unknowable. His friends wrapped his body in a red blanket and took it with them out onto the prairie, and carried it about with them as they travelled, until they buried the body of Crazy Horse weeks later, in secret and with no traceable marker. They called themselves not Sioux but Lakota, an alliance of comrades.

* * * * *

His old man submitted to one last photograph. It was of his clasped hands. The veins were bunched and somehow pulsing, even in their stillness. There were black, raised blobs of oil paint flecking his knuckles and staining his nails. The fingers were twined, suggesting a prayer. He never said prayers. They were, for all that, the hands of a maker, and of one who had dreamed. Billy would use the photograph as the centrepiece of an exhibition. It came as a shock, since no one had seen the images on which he had begun to concentrate in the dog days of the strike and its sour aftermath. He had no appetite to home in on grief and misery, or even despair and anger. The earlier photographs which had suddenly brought professional recognition and fleeting fame, those faces featuring defiance, rage, bravery, resolution, unity, exultation, the gestures of speaking and listening through all the true joyfulness of what was, in the end, a false and fake scenario, none of those could suffice now, even as negatives. The old man had warned of the vacuous drudgery and drift that was to be the fate of those with no boltholes left to find. Billy surveyed those inhabiting the ruins and instead picked up the bits and pieces left, the segments that told of their fracture. He shot backs. He blew up fists. He took away the support of arms and legs and just left the torsos. He cast down at feet. He pinpointed an eye or two. He showed mouths shut. He closed off the things and cropped the people that had whispered and shouted, and let the ears remain deaf to further entreaty. Photographs were a piled-up detritus of humanity. A tangle of hair. A sullen neck. An arthritic knee. A discarded banner. A child's extended arm. An empty seat. A wiped brow. And hands, hands, hands. Fluttering, open-palmed and waiting, held together and praying. Something had fled. Had drained away. Something had been beheaded. Something had been killed. He called the exhibition and the book of it he made "No Photographs of Crazy Horse". And when it was finished, he said goodbye to the old man and left. He never saw him again. He carried him inside himself, and would now forever.

Three

Double Negative

Monday

Tommy told me I'd slept. On and off. For almost three days. That Lionel had remembered how he'd once been a St John's Ambulanceman – a uniform, a peak cap and International tickets – and had strapped up my ribs. Only thing to do for them, apparently. They'd used Dettol to clean out the cuts. All they had in the house. I'd screamed. And cotton bud tips to swab out my broken nose. They used a lot of those. Tommy didn't like to have wax in his ears. They stayed cleaned. The nose had to stay broken. But that wasn't the first time it had been flattened, they laughed. Then they'd washed me, stuffed me into pyjamas. Old-fashioned wincyette. The jacket had big white buttons and the trousers a drawstring like a small rope. Blue convict stripes all over. Baggy but comfy, said Lionel. They had rammed aspirin down me and later, Tommy said, with a wink, what he called "specials". Painkillers. I told Tommy killers weren't what they used to be. Tommy told me to shut up and be grateful. Then they left for work.

I lay back on an ivory-coloured leather couch with wrinkles as big and rifted as the elephant hide it resembled. They said that after they found and rescued me they'd carried me here. Tommy's house. They told me it wasn't far and they were strong. So not to worry. I hadn't. I didn't. It was now mid-morning, according to the alarm clock ticking away with no respect for its surroundings. It sat on a shiny mahogany-laminate mantelpiece above a stone-façade fireplace, all dimpled surface and in coloured pastels, baby blue to blusher pink with a predominantly woozy pearl grey. Or maybe it was just me that was woozy. The room was a knock-through from front door and white PVC window to artexed walls and ceiling and Goldilocks pine table and chairs, and a scullery that had grown into a kitchenette. It was functionally modernised with dishwasher, humming fridge and ceramic sink in white with chrome mixer taps. The framed pictures on the wall were photographs of rugby players – team photographs season by season, the rows stood behind one another, with the front tier sat on a bench as the club's whole squad assembled pre- or post-season. I was in one or two of those, a sliver between the two behemoths who were my minders. I was duly grateful. Then and now. Above the clock and the mantelpiece was an enlarged portrait, tinted and soft-focussed head and shoulders of a woman with big, frizzy chestnut brown hair, a scatter of freckles, a shy smile made warmer by eyes that looked right at you, and the neckline of a 1970s cheesecloth peasant blouse with teasing drawstring. Norma. Nice Norma. Dead Norma. Tommy's wife.

I swung my feet off the elephant hide onto a wall-to-wall, off-white shagpile that had seen better action, and more days than it should have. From a sitting position I could see the fronts of houses above their stepped gardens. When I stood up I could see the pavement, road and river which ran past the house set in its terraced row. I knew where I was. A few hundred yards down from the car park where I'd been smashed up. If I squinted I could see the blackened plates and rivets of the iron footbridge over the river, and the adjacent modern road crossing. Modern being only a century and more away. I sat down again with a necessary suddenness. My head was expanding and contracting like a Tango player's bandoneón. A concertina would have been acceptable. I felt my face, all bristle and grunge. They hadn't bothered to shave me. Understandable. I fingered the broad part of my nose between index and thumb. Yeah, broader than I remembered it. And sorer too. My mouth tasted of fur and bile, clogged up and clingy at the same time. I decided to go back to sleep. It was an easy decision to make.

When I woke next it was to the chimes of 'Ghost Riders in the Sky'. The yippee-ay-yey bit. Only electronic and insistent, so I knew I wasn't dreaming. I could see a small shape on the other side of the frosted glass of the front door. The bell stopped but the image still shimmered through the double-glazed distortion. I was in no mood for apparitions. Particularly not bell-pushing ones. I stumbled across the shagpile towards the door and fiddled with the lock and catch before wrenching it open into the shimmer of a drizzly afternoon. The figure in the doorway tilted her head in a mock-quizzical way. She asked if she could come in. To see how I was. As if she couldn't see that already. I held the door ajar and she stepped inside in front of me. I staggered back to the elephant's graveyard and slumped back down. Bran smiled as I looked up at her.

She had had her hair done so that it framed and softened her face and belled out in a thickly-cut sway above her neck. She didn't sit down so I looked up from her feet, in black and red peep-toe court shoes with a higher heel than you'd expect, to her knees – one bigger than the other I knew – just on show below a short, wheaten-white, belted wool coat that looked, from its sheen to the detail of collars and cuffs, expensive.

"D'you still like what you see?"

I tried not to grunt and not to think of the strawberry birthmark on the left cheek of her arse. She loosened the belt and took the coat off, folded it on a chair. I shuffled a bit on the Babar couch, partly to ease my pain. I sighed. Not this, I thought. Yes, this, I hoped.

"How'd you know I was here?"

"Chance. Or, sort of chance. I needed some work doing. I rang Tommy. Usually do. He told me you were here. What had happened. I'm sorry."

"Me too."

"You look terrible."

"Feel it."

"Can I do something? Shave? Wash? Toothpaste? Coffee?"

"Can't think of a thing I need," I said.

"Oh?"

I employed the silent trick technique I had perfected in the days when I had once been as intent on pleasuring as on being pleasured. To avoid Rise, Decline, and inevitable Fall, I closed my eyes and Conjugated.

Amo. And meant it.

Amas. And once you did.

Amat. He may still.

Amamus. We were once anyway.

Amatis. Anyone you wanted.

Amant. Our present. From a Past. Without a Future.

And then the whole imperfect, perfect, and pluperfect knowledge.

Amabam, amabas, amabat, amabamus, amabatis, amabant.

Amavi, amavisti, amavit, amavimus, amavistis and *amaverunt.*

Amaveram, amaveras, amaverat, amaveramus, amaveratis, until *amaverant.*

I opened my eyes. She was still there. I knew she knew no Latin but, as ever, Bran was in no hurry. She decided we needed coffee and she needed a visit to the bathroom while the kettle boiled. She could see the kettle and the coffee in the kitchen and walked in to switch it on, but she didn't need to ask where the bathroom was. She went straight upstairs on the internal wooden staircase to my left. I watched her come back down in a cloud of certainty. I would not be hers to use again. The coffee came in white porcelain mugs covered with the blue of a forget-me-not pattern courtesy of the National Trust. Or so it said on the bottom. That Tommy never failed to surprise.

"Instant OK?" she asked.

Too late now, I thought, as I sipped the scalding hot gravy mix spooned from the industrial size instant coffee tin that was more in keeping with Tommy the builder than the mugs someone had bought for him, but I said:

"Yeah – fine. So, tell me again, what brings you here?"

She gave me a smile so coy she must have employed it last in nursery school.

"I'd have thought that it was obvious. No?"

"No," I whispered back.

"No" sounded a bit ungrateful, but I was compensating for broken ribs with my new monosyllabic personality. She sucked on her lower lip. That was awful pretty to see. I stirred again but this time, fat chance anyway, refused to be shaken. And my faithless companion was much reduced, and nubby anyway. Age, I guessed.

"What did Tommy tell you?" was my only follow-up now.

"What I told you … that he … and Lionel … found you. Being kicked. Rescued you. Brought you here to get better."

"How'd he know where I'd be?"

"Sorry?"

"No. I am. Tommy's OK. He's just not smart, is he?"

Bran crossed and uncrossed her legs. It wasn't meant to be distracting; it was just a reflex. I tried not to be distracted. My reflexes failed. Old nubby uncoiled a little but I needed to stay coiled. And to remember.

"Bran," I wheedled, uncertain what the dictionary said "to wheedle" meant, but effortlessly capable of it. "Look, whatever mess you're in with Mal, let him bounce, not you. Haf may …"

The name of her daughter altered the rules of engagement. She broke them off, let's say.

"Haf? What's that bitch been telling you? Leave her to her own devices, Billy. Leave her be."

It was my turn to let steel pendulums swing and splice.

"Leave her be? You let her go. Not me. You didn't even tell me about her. When she was born. That she might be mine. Or, yet, how to find her. Why not, Bran? Why the fuck not?"

Bran leaned forward. Her voice was the whiplash itself now. I heard it cut me before I felt it.

"You want to know. You want to know. OK, you sappy bastard. You can know. I front, work for, I *am*!, ECA – EuroCymruAssociates – and we, I, lead on institutional bids for Euro initiatives – cash and projects, schemes and funding outcomes. Consultancy. Expertise. Advice. OK? Because the money has to be channelled. From Brussels. They don't just give it away. Well not quite. There's an audit, business plans, bids, and, crucially, match funding. So, that means finessing the time of an organisation's staff – at premium rates – and its established assets, everything from buildings to porters to electricity and IT and onto the notepaper and biros – to ratchet up what can be turned into those particular lines in business plans that say "in kind". Then, if we can, matched in cash from other sources. From government. From business. Keeping up? A trust, one with a worked out agenda in economic regeneration and social well-being like Tir Werin, and connected to movers and shakers, is not just ideally placed. It *is* the place, the virtual place."

She paused. None of this was exactly news. Nor was what she was presumably going to say next about to indicate any suit for possible malfeasance. Check out my legal know-how, I wanted to crow. But this was leading somewhere else so I stayed quiet. And continued to ache as her sweetness disappeared and she poured the old Bran vinegar into the wound she could always open.

"Yeah, OK. I see you can guess all the moves, but, believe me, the outcome is one to leave alone. The moves ... well, you know those; Mal had made a pile, dot com and all that. And he diversified. But not enough, as it happened. So he took out insurance, buying up land across the heads of the valleys. Cheap. Useless land. No good for local homes or for commuters to travel to work elsewhere, or for factory sheds and inward investors. Good for schemes, though. He persuaded the powers-that-be to establish a Research Park. He invested in it. Of course he made himself the chairman of the board, and had Gwil, dear, sweet, shitty Gwil, appointed as Director. With my contacts and Ceri's profile, we promoted Tir Werin in Europe as a practical vehicle to make real the ideas and schemes dreamed up in the Alfred Wallace Building. Neat name, huh? Mal geared Gwilym up to write the business plan for a major regeneration centre, with social benefits and visitor offshoots. Feasibility studies. Project money. Grant aid and start-up money, to purchase the necessary land. Now, soon, take-off money. Follow?"

I nodded. Bran said nothing. So I did the follow on myself.

"Only the stuff I've seen kind of suggests the money went round and round, so to speak. From Brussels to the government to Tir Werin, to Valleyscorp, so to you, and Mal? and I'd guess to Ceri. Our old friend and comrade, Sir Ceri Evans."

Bran flicked me a smile. I threw another stick on the fire dying between us.

"Suggest, you say. Doesn't prove anything, does it?" she countered.

"Not yet, no. I'll want to talk to Haf, won't I?" Was that a threat? She seemed to take it as such. She was right to do so. But then she surprised again.

Bran stood. She picked up a soft leather handbag that didn't gleam and was studded with dull bronze metal clasps and non-functional straps. She opened the clasp that was like an antique key and reached inside the bag for a shiny, black fountain pen with a snow cone on top. Nothing cheap for Bran. She unscrewed it, found a scrap of paper and scribbled quickly. She stood directly above me and crumpled it into a ball. She dropped it in my lap. An address, of a kind, for Haf. She said:

"I was hoping you wouldn't go on. I don't like what happened to you, Billy. I wanted to make it up to you. No-go, it seems. Contacting her will do you no good either. But if you insist, go ahead. Maybe you can talk some sense into her after all. Remember she'll lose out, too. Think of that, eh?"

She turned, and then she turned back. I knew it was never going to be that easy.

"You said you wanted to know, didn't you? So, I'll tell you. She thought you were – that you ought to be – her daddy, so when I told her you weren't, she went with Mal. Her stepfather. And ruined our marriage, for what it was worth. Ended it anyway. Since then she's just gone on making trouble and the latest is to have revenge – on him and on me – by spreading these lies. Which will only re-bound on her, the idiot. Or half-lies, if you like. Where the fuck does she think the money for her comes from? It'll do no good. Mal is having her legally removed from Valleyscorp – incompetence, drugs, whatever it takes. Unless you can persuade her not to hold things up, to get in the way of things she doesn't understand. Oh, and one more thing … you're really not the daddy. Honest. Cross my heart. Hope to die."

And she let herself out. She left behind the smell of musk and a citric aftershock. And I felt, as I always did with Bran, that none of this should have been this way. And that I was not a fool to want it different, only one to think it had ever been possible.

* * * * *

I skipped the shower because of the bandages, and settled for a shave and a shampoo. I cleaned my teeth with my fingers and a pink-striped toothpaste. I found a T-shirt with the least naff print transfer in the quietest colour – army drab – some jeans and deck shoes and a pair of matching white socks and a red and yellow pullover that looked like a dog had revisited his dinner. Apart from my jacket, thoughtfully brushed but still stained with blood and dirt, my own clothes were nowhere to be seen, either torn and useless or washed. I guessed the former. My wallet was on the kitchen table and money and cards were still inside. I expected nothing less. These boys might have been rough, but they weren't muggers. I didn't bother with the thank-you note. I left by the door I assumed I had entered a few days before.

A small rain was falling. Not enough to soak you unless you walked through it for hours. That wasn't my intention as I winced over some broken paving stones back into the town, but enough for its prickly damp to blur the vista. Moving forward somehow eased the pain in my ribs, though I still had to stop to lean on a garden wall or two. My breathing was all of the outward kind, a desperate wheeze followed by a short hissing intake. I was beginning to sound like my old man. Probably looking like him too. The whole effect attracted a few glances. Not admiring ones. And not especially friendly or even concerned ones. Maybe they thought I carried a threat. From the outside. They'd be familiar with that. The more I saw on the streets, I was starting to think, the less I knew. If I wasn't who I looked and sounded like, then who was? I heaved myself up off a low wall and left the side street. Public transport was fine by me, for all those other people. I needed a taxi. I stopped at a bus shelter to ask where I could find one. Right across the road, they said and pointed.

A waiting driver flipped his lit cigarette out of his window, gently oscillating as he did the "Dim Ysmygu" sign hanging from his rear mirror.

"Where to, butty?"

The name on the scrap of paper which Bran had tossed me said Heritage Centre so I said it, too, and we took off. It took less than ten minutes to navigate out of the circular road system, hit the old road east, sweep past the long straggle of what the guidebooks and estate agents so emphatically called "Miners' Cottages", and through the main gates of what had once been a working colliery. I paid. The taxi left, its socially considerate driver only lighting up as he pulled away. I stood in a tarmac-laid car park that was neatly marked out in bays, and looked at the glass front they had erected as a curtain across the dressed quarry stone in order to mark out a modern entrance to the winding house. Inside was a shop area littered with furry red dragons, giant glitter pencils, and tiny coal maquette sculptures of colliers, their wives and street ragamuffins. The entrance opened up further into a mock-up of shops, a coal-lit kitchen with Mam, her wire hair in a bun, larger than life and deader than the flanking models of the mufflered collier and the leaping-into-his-arms child. I averted my sensitive eyes. The only thing that was welcoming was the Croeso sign and the silence that truly meant No Visitors. The assistant at the shop's counter hadn't looked up from the receipts she was checking from all the profits the Centre was making in glinting paraphernalia. Everything else appeared to be free.

I walked up the open metal staircase to the first floor. Tables, chairs, coffee, Welsh cakes. And, unexpected by me, a pitch-roofed gallery space. More sentiment I guessed, and so only half-glanced at the walls. That stopped all the assumptions I was making right there and then. I opened my eyes and began to look. Maybe that's when my heart opened again, too. Or maybe that was later. Either way it wasn't shutting down now.

There were five or six canvases and a few drawings from each of the five painters on show. The work was certainly singular in each individual style but it hung together, more like a collective emotion than a group. I felt the need of the old man's guidance for detail but its overall glow washed over me in any case at the fag end of a sodden afternoon, with only the unforgiving glare of the overhead panels of electric light to pick out colour that was insistent but mostly muted. There were no eyeball-teasing globs of colour erupting off board and canvas in great tears of flaking pigment. And though there were entrancing and painterly marriages of acid green and frothy underskirt pink and gritty ochre to quiz comic book blues and reds, this work, as a totality, was not about sensing delight, it was a structure. It was a scaffolding, one erected to climb towards an idea. The work was a counterclaim against what had been stolen, what had been hidden away, or mislaid, or forgotten, or neglected and abused. They had painted the structure of lives. How it felt. How it was. How it should have been understood. How it could be. How, whatever the contrary outcome, it still mattered.

It had been seen, then. The structure of that culture which I, too, had once had inside me, and held and let fall. It had been seen, here, variously, and transfigured into something it was not other than as a vision that was as unmistakeably real as it had once been actual. This was, I could see, what, and maybe only this of it, could be taken forward. In all this work there was not a trace of the identikit Valleys, stereotyped and drooled over in words and images by force of their once eccentric particulars and through a vestige of falsely heroic narratives. In these native hands these places and people had been disassembled, and put back together.

The last section of one wall of work held me longest. It seemed attuned to a future. The painting technique was looser in execution, enormous canvases filled with brushstrokes that owed their liquidity to the reckless arm more than the dab of a controlling hand. The customary framework of a familiar landscape was intact. A look down from the mountain plateau back into the rash of buildings below. Homes slotted in clumps, and rearing public houses on perpendicularly set street corners. The legacy was there still to view, and to live in, albeit unusually caught, as if in sun traps. But it was the bodies that were so different. They did not stand or sit as if defined. They jumped and raced and swung each other around and somersaulted on trampolines in a riot of upside-down mobility. Limbs were muscle taut beneath short-sleeved shirts. Or calves and legs, brown and liquescent, were running free of flying skirts. The painter moved in and through his mobile subject-matter, refusing the viewer the luxury of seeing anything as settled. If the past was a place that made the present a prison for the mind then this blotchy capture of living was a signal for release. In the light of the exhibition I sensed all my old man's early courage more than his late resignation.

* * * * *

It was dark, a crepuscular enfolding light, when I finally left that gallery. I asked downstairs when Haf would be coming into work since there was no sign of her anywhere there that afternoon. No one had even heard of her. But they were helpful. The senior manager was called. She was young, pretty and smiled a lot. She was helpful, too. I smiled to help her helpfulness along. I wasn't young though, and a second glance hadn't impressed her. She frowned and asked to see my scrap of paper. Just Haf and Heritage Centre was what it said, scrawled in Bran's near illegible sloping hand in black ink. Mont Blanc ink. And pen to match, I'd noticed. The manager now came all over dismissive. She tapped the paper with a false plum-coloured nail. Maybe, she said, it wasn't the museum and gallery but the hotel just up the road. I was duly dismissed.

The hotel was an unexpected take, in red colonial brick and white stone pediments, on an American cross between a motel-lodge and a small hotel. Its automatic doors slid open to let in the passing, weary commercial traveller, or more likely wedding guests as I sleuthily surmised by the reception rooms and banquetry suites on offer, their insides a glimpse of silver and gilt carved chairs, with green or purple crush seats, all set before long white-linen-draped tables. I asked for Haf at the main reception desk and was, without a query though maybe a once-over of my drawn face and downmarket clothes, courtesy of Lionel, told she was working her shift behind the bar.

The bar room was more wood: upright struts as in a cowboy movie to partition sections, and the black beams of a false plasterboard ceiling as in a Pickwickian tavern. The bar had brass rails at its foot and ran across the entire length of the room. The muzak was treacly Kenny Rogers or entreatingly twangy Tammy Wynette. The girl behind the bar was pressing a nozzle to deliver flat-topped pints of urine-coloured liquid. Four silent customers sat together, waiting at a centre table which was covered with paperwork and by four mobile phones that the group had ejaculated in front of them in premature expectation of a call to bring them to life. No chance of that, I thought. I stepped a few paces further into the room. I looked across the patterned expanse of swirling brown and orange carpet at the young woman who had called me daddy from across the Atlantic. I stared. It took me a while. She was busy serving and washing glasses. She didn't look up in my direction. From the tables on the outer rim of the room, and a step up behind the railing of uprights, there was the beginning of the buzz of early evening, post-work drinkers. Local government officers, some business people, the newly retired, a collar-and-tie brigade that would have discouraged your Tommys and Lionels from entering as much as the chemical sniff coming off pints of filtered and resurrected lager would have disgusted them. An aftersmell of lunchtime's industrial vinegar combined with the dead pasteurised beer to hang over the atmosphere as a formaldehyde gag. I could have done with the devil-may-care rapture of tobacco smoke to remind me that death usually came after life. The cigarette smokers were in the purgatory for exiled puffers outside the main lobby. I chose a table at the back near the door and further from the bar. There was waitress service if you waited long enough. I was happy to wait. I inhaled the forlorn cinema-goer's memory of Jeyes cleaning fluid that came my way every time the toilet door opened and closed. I was beaten-up, tired, emotional, and sober for once. What more could you want? I was beginning to wonder. A wine list, perhaps.

When my turn came I asked for a glass of red wine, anything I said that had never been in contact with Antipodean soil or been inside the staves of an oak barrel. I made myself understood by simplifying it to "Nothing from Australia". Customer service was delivered – to an extent. The wine came in a glass that could have doubled as a small bucket. I tasted more pampas than eucalyptus. A malbec to put a twist in a gaucho's boleros. I decided sipping would be an effete pastime with this drink, so I just drank. I ordered another, with peanuts on the side. The waitress seemed to approve of this as a gesture to the normality of the local culture. An hour or so passed. The bar was fuller, but still appeared empty as if it was waiting for the Cattlemen's Convention to roll up. I kept the bar and its attendant in my sight. It was early evening when Haf was relieved. She checked out her till. I checked her out as she said her goodbyes and exited via the servants' quarters. At least I presumed that's what the door at the side of the bar was. I followed as discreetly as I could, and into the car park behind the hotel. She walked over to a dented Renault with red trim and the puckered look of a veteran boxer, and the name of a Muse. I moved a hundred yards behind her as she searched in her pocket. The rain was back but softer now. It made water droplets glisten in her black hair. The hair was jagged, off her neck, and spiky on top, fuller on the side, an ugly frame that still couldn't spoil her face, though one that seemed more fatigued than her age deserved. She wore jeans and a shapeless red puffa jacket and she cursed as she scrabbled for the car keys. I moved closer. She turned the keys in the lock and opened the door and looked up to see me at the passenger side. I was afraid I might startle her but she said "Hello" even before I did, and told me to get in. So I did the same. She ran her fingers briskly through her hair to shake out the drops that had clung to the thick, short strands. She gave me a long enquiring look. I seemed to be attracting a lot of those lately. She saw my bruised face and my puffy eyes, and said nothing But I was not being dismissed. What I saw was how lovely she was. More Bran than me. I stayed silent. Her mouth was turned down at its corners. More me than Bran. I wanted to hold her, to kiss that pursed mouth's hurt away and tell her I was sorry. She could see that anyway, and I was no longer being thoughtfully silent, just struck dumb. She fired up the damp cold car at the third attempt and we jerked out of the car park onto the empty road to the south.

I asked where we were going. She said, "Home", as if she meant it. I was all for that belief. Besides it wasn't far, a few miles back and on through the town, then a backstreet tour of brick-trimmed homes which were evidently, from the rubbish outside and the old bangers parked up on the kerbs, student accommodation. Owned by Maldwyn no doubt. There was no number on the house. There was a white cheap wood-panel partitioned door with peeling varnish and a flaking gold-coloured knocker. The curtains of the one ground-floor window were thin and brown and floral, and pulled together like a geriatric's stained lips. The passageway was littered with unopened bills, flyers for takeaways and free newspapers. We walked past the doors to all the downstairs rooms, and up the stairs past a kitchen area which was sending a reek of cooking oil through the house. There was a landing to the right, and at its far end the locked door of what had once been the front bedroom of three-up three-down working-class respectability. There was a Yale lock which Haf snapped open with another key on her car ring. And we were in.

It was not what I had expected. There was a colour scheme – deep blue walls, a stripped and waxed pine floor, a rug with a geometric red and black zigzag pattern within a cream border, a dark grey woolly sofa with Scandinavian rectilinear understatement in front of the two sash windows. The wood was painted white, the floor-length curtains heavy calico and lined, but somehow light bearing even before she turned on the two yellow floor lamps, and the one on a cubbyhole desk in the left corner. A simple bed, white coverlet and blood-orange scatter cushions in a knobbly silk material, was butted up against the same back wall. She took my coat and draped it on the bed alongside her own. She took a black angora sweater out of a wall cupboard and put it on over her white linen shirt. There was no chair so she waved to the low Swedish sofa. I sat and she stood, quizzically in front of me, the third wall behind her. There were no books. No television. No racks of CDs, DVDs or whatever other disc storage system had come to pass. A laptop and printer and all the gubbins was the exception to the rule on the desk. On the wall were photographs. Some copied. Some blown up. Some from magazines and newspapers. Some small and original. All of them mine. She saw me looking at them, taking it all in. Or some of it.

When she finally spoke the voice was low. Quiet. Every Welsh-accented syllable like the ding of an alarm clock's bell. "Well, what did you expect?" she said. "I've been living with you, for years, one way or the other, haven't I? And now you're here. At last. I knew you would be, you know."

I retreated into small talk. How long had she been living here? A year or so. Was the kitchen shared? Yes. Two boys downstairs. Bathroom and lavatory. One up, one down. It was OK. Did I want coffee? She wouldn't be long. I stood up and looked at the pictures. That one with a Leica. That with a Rolleiflex 2¼ inch that had survived a dunking in a south-east Asian river. That one in a bright sunlight which had made the shadows elongate like dark accusers. This one worked and cropped from years before. These done as quickly as they had had to be. My eyeballing life laid out and reduced to a wall-poster display. I looked away.

The coffee arrived in thick, plain white china mugs. No sugar as requested. We stood, awkwardly, my back turned as hers had been to the wall of memories. I was waiting for her to begin. It was unfair, but whatever had brought me here was her doing and only Haf could make this happen now. So she did.

"You were good," she said.

And I laughed: "Was, is right!"

"Time to be good again, maybe," she said.

"Time has to come with a chance to be good," I said.

"But that's what's brought you here, isn't it?", she said.

"I don't know yet, Haf. I don't know what you think can be done or should be done."

"You said my name," she said.

She sat down. I sat beside her. And Haf told me her story. She already knew mine. Or thought she did. When she finished talking the coffee was cold and my heart was colder. She picked up the two mugs and stood above me as I muttered something that had words about me and sorrow stitched into their hopeless apology. I had learned some things I'd be better off not knowing and some I couldn't forget. She was more stone than flower. It was all over and not finished. Not by any means.

She looked at me as if she meant it and spoke the sentence that I knew I had to hear.

"Do you want to fuck me, too?"

Tuesday

The signs to the nearest railway station had encouraged me to walk. A quarter of a mile felt like a marathon. The train encouraged me to sleep. I resisted until I made my way back to the city centre hotel, showered and slept with a Do Not Disturb card attached to a doorknob that the cleaner still insisted on rattling the next day. Twice. At noon and then at one. My deep fellow feelings for those on minimum wage, or less, dwindled, then vanished. I opened the door. I enquired "Yes?" She looked. I was scowling. She smiled. She left. I was sorry. I closed the door. I took my battered and naked body back to bed and slept some more. A lot more.

In dreams, maybe, I had made up my mind.

I made a few calls to old journalist friends, still suppurating away on columns that were always going to be more Wurlitzer than Pulitzer, strictly regional papers whose declining circulation was a constant reproof to their national pretensions. That's what I had to listen to on the phone anyway, from one veteran hack after another until one finally yielded up the extra-directory and private mobile number of Sir Ceri Evans, of whom, once, well more than once, and long ago, my old man had sourly said, "His cock will find him out". He'd been wrong about that, too. So far.

I wasn't exactly surprised to find that Ceri – even after 20 years – wasn't fazed to find me on the other end of a phone. He'd come straight to it after the perfunctory, gushing but patently disinterested, greetings. He said that the others had been a bit put out and were hoping I'd ring so that, with all that had been close between us once, or at least with him and the old man, he could put me straight, clear up any misunderstandings. Relax over a drink. Lunch perhaps, or dinner if I preferred. He mentioned a brasserie on the waterfront. Oysters, ice cold chablis and a sidelong view of the hot new government building, if you really must, he laughed, or the mercy of nightfall. I opted for dinner and the dark. He was in Brussels, negotiating for Wales he said, but a small plane was bringing the Big Man home the next day. We arranged for dinner around eight o'clock the following night, Wednesday. He told me that on Thursday he had to first finish and then make the speech which he was to give at the conference on a New Valleys Dawn to be held that same morning. Good, I told him. I'll be there. He thought I meant only at the dinner. Good, I thought. And that gave me the Tuesday to rest, and the time before I met Ceri to be a tidy boy.

The rest of the day passed in a haze of occasional room service and frequent painkillers. When I surfaced from a stupor every now and then I attended to bits of business. I booked an airport hotel room at Heathrow for Friday night and an early Saturday morning flight back to JFK. I read the file Haf had given me one more time, checking dates and facts and figures. Then I slept some more. When the dreamtime ended I got up and showered myself awake. I dressed, ordered coffee, stared out at the usual mixed bag of weather, and then I picked up one of the lined yellow pads which always travelled with me and began to write.

What I wrote was a conventional putting together of quotes from private notes and letters and bank accounts. Conventional and, if read the way I intended it to be read, lethal. And what my friend the hack would make of it was a storyline that had 'A' (or Mal) linked to successive sales of low-grade or contaminated land over a period of years since the mid-1990s. Councillors and council decisions were drawn into this web and innocently so on a separate basis, but more intriguingly not when they and the land parcels were totted up altogether. Then there was the grouping of these heads of the valleys plots under the holding company, Valleyscorp, which had been put in trust in Haf's name but directed by 'B' or Bran until her daughter was eighteen. That date had been reached three years ago. Less formal documentation placed 'C', or Ceri, in the frame as a key player in regeneration policies from Poland to Penrhiwceiber and back. Perhaps they hadn't felt the need for discretion. Why should they? Loans and gifts were not directly connected to any of this, were they? Not until, maybe, the payment details grew more frequent and larger as the scheme unfolded. Which is where 'D', or Gwilym, came into play, as the respected deviser for Tir Werin, adjunct to the Research Park, of an ambitious regeneration project which required both funding – from Europe – and land – available, at a seemingly reasonable price from Valleyscorp. Our 'A' had, by this time, long resigned as a director of Valleyscorp but as chair of the board based in the adapt-or-die Wallace building encouraged, and you might say, led our 'D' to the fruition of his scheme. Or, at least, to parts one and two of it. Money and land. Construction and delivery would be later. With Ceri and Gwilym as principal trustees of Tir Werin, lines of profitable communication would be kept open. What I had was a prospectus for growth that bore all the hallmarks of idealism and was, in its outline, all in the public domain. But I had little doubt that the career of Ceri would be, at the very least, tarnished by the detail of transactions; that the reputation of Gwilym would not be enhanced as he planned for his birthday honours; that Bran could present herself, at best, as a virginal third party with her daughter's interests at heart; and that Maldwyn could be legitimately accused of chicanery, underhand dealings and collusion with others to subvert the use of public funding. Maybe even be convicted. Underneath all this laying of explosives though, was the fuse that had been lit to set it off as dynamite. And the fuse was Haf.

I wrote that story, too. It isn't too pretty but this is how it went.

She'd been born in the summer of 1986. Maldwyn was to be her father figure since Bran and he first lived together then, and married a year later. Both, with the adventure of the strike behind them, had more to do with "getting on" in careers floated by the wider public recognition they had cashed in on, than they did with the daughter who lived with them, and a nanny, until she went to the school from which she could have come home every day but didn't. Haf was a boarder with a home, or homes, as property moved them upmarket, but still just a few miles away. Holidays were periods of tension, not release. As she grew older the rifts and the rows between Mal and Bran first upset her as she tried to pull them together in a child's fantasy way, and then they drove her down into herself.

Then, when she was sixteen, she refused to be a boarder any more. Refusal and resistance could not be overturned by an irate Bran. Haf paid lip-service to 'A' level study at a local FE college. Haf tried to shelter from constant recrimination by being closer to Mal. Indifference was her best reward until Mal walked out after a quarrel with his wife that was more explicit and even violent in its threat than before. It was after that splitting up that Bran, cruel or vindictive or just Bran maybe, told Haf that Mal was not her father anyway. That she'd been pregnant before they had come together. Then who? And she said me. Billy Maddox. That I'd left in the winter of '85, and never came back. That my father had died suddenly before the Christmas of that year, when I was on an assignment in the Far East, and uncontactable. There were no other ties for me here after that, and she hadn't told me of the one there was. End of story.

Only, for Haf, it was a beginning. She researched my life, my work, my pictures. Her bedroom filled with the grainy images of photojournalism and the edgy, tricked-out and edited compositions of the dark room. If that was the retreat inside herself, the outer journey was uninhibited by any baggage. She did what the abandoned young do, and on the streets there was booze and pills and sex, and then Mal again. He'd moved by now, and without Bran, back home to his mansion on the hill. Haf moved in with him. To hurt Bran? Not a chance. To infuriate? Every time. She fucked her "father". He seduced his "daughter". Who knows (she certainly didn't) the sequence of these moves? It wasn't a crime, was it? It wasn't, she said, as if they were related.

It was a crime, nonetheless, so far as I was concerned. Mal's crime. For Haf the crime that concerned her was happening elsewhere. When she hit eighteen and Mal talked of university she also found that she was required to be a co-signatory on all kinds of transactions in which there was no common denominator other than Tir Werin. She asked. Bran came into the picture again. She and Mal, it seemed, had interests in common that could elide other divisions. Gwilym spoke to Haf. A career was in prospect for her. He could see to it that she was, despite poor exam results, admitted into a Media Studies course at the university. It was her duty to help the Tir Werin scheme to fruition. She asked what it meant. She was told about Sir Ceri's deep interests in its welfare. What a great man he was. Mal was blunter. If she didn't sign there was no money. What the fuck was wrong with her? What indeed. Bran was less inquisitive. She told it to Haf as directly as Mal, only in language made more personal than maternal by a vicious anger. Mistake. Haf kept signing but she started digging, and enquiring, and collecting, and photocopying. Her silence was interpreted as complaisance at last. It was a cloak for snooping – in drawers, in briefcases, in handbags, in office files. Finally she stopped signing papers. She moved out.

Wednesday

I spent the next morning re-writing and clarifying before putting it into my laptop. I was a laborious typer. It took me past an in-room sandwich lunch before I was ready. When I finally finished I found a printer and had copies made. I put them into envelopes marked by name for Haf, Ceri, and Maldwyn. I stamped and addressed envelopes to Gwilym and Bran, and a final one to my old friend the hack. I put the first three in the pocket of the navy peacoat I would wear over a pullover and jeans. The others would go into a postbox. The hack would only use his if I didn't have my way another way, and either way it would keep others honest if I ever had to ignite it. On my way to the city centre railway station I found a DIY store. Inside I found a lump hammer, hard and squat and with a comfortable heft to it in my hand, and wrapped it inside a newspaper and dropped it inside a hessian bag. It swung reassuringly to my side as I walked. The rain fell all over the city again, and I used its incessant wetness to wipe clean a face that had seen too much to like anything much any more. What I was to do was maybe for Haf, perhaps for me, but mostly for my old man. He would have told me I was another Sam Spade, half a century and more too late. That I was still role-playing and knee-jerk reacting. And I whispered back into the rain that he was right, and that there was nothing else for it in the trap of image and imitation into which we had all long fallen. I didn't wait long for a train. This time the scenery, through the windows, dissolved in the rain.

Haf was waiting for me in the bar. She was bundled up in her Puffa jacket, her jeans tucked into her ankle boots, and only her much too pale face on show. It was a pretty face. It was a good show. I gave her the envelope and drank a bottle of Italian beer whilst she read it. She didn't smile. She did sigh, and look at me as if she hadn't wanted me to know even if she had had to tell me. She asked what next. So I told her. Or some of it. I missed out the very next bit, and skipped to where I was going to meet Ceri that night. I told her the plan, and why, and she nodded. I kissed her on the cheek. I looked at my watch. It was time to leave. It was long past the time to make things right. There was time, though, to tidy a few things up before another tomorrow came unwanted upon us. I left her with the promise of a different tomorrow, one still to come.

I got to the heritage centre, five minutes away, about an hour earlier than I'd arranged and just in time for the first tour of all somebody else's yesterdays. I took it. They certainly weren't my yesterdays. They were set at a convenient distance, filtered through a haze of nostalgia which blurred any recovery of any real time. The pretend real selves here were bigger than life-size dummies – cloth-capped colliers, aproned Mams and rosy-cheeked urchins with the occasional top-hatted coalowner and moustachioed engineer – all in static cameos with booming stereophonic voiceovers. It took an hour to shuffle from one engine house to another – I skipped the underground simulation – and the only time I felt a twitch of recognition was, irony of ironies of course, when I sat in front of the slide show of old photographs and saw the innocence of all those there captured and exposed, again, for all time. It was because they didn't know, taker or taken, what they were doing that I felt, at last, undone in face of the enormity of it all.

I waited at the tour's end on the wet cobblestoned yard of the former colliery. I was sheltered against the rain by an out-of-time and out-of-service red double-decker bus that was parked side on to the main building. I had left the voice message for Maldwyn to come to meet me in the yard after four. It was now 4.15 and the fine rain was blowing from the hills, overlapping in parabolas against the rain-beaded windows of the bus. One solitary drop would be momentarily still and then start to run, a tail following behind. I peered through the smearing dropping lines on the glass, back towards the enclosed entrance way and its swishy automatic doors. They purred and two figures stood, not moving, just looking out, not seeing me on the other side of the bus. I put my right hand inside the hessian bag to feel that the short shaft was lying the right way. I called Mal's name out into the rain and then I moved, holding the bag's handles in my left, to the back of the bus. And waited some more.

Through the shadow fall of a rain becoming more and more insistent I saw one of the two move back into the entrance hall where the papier-mâché butcher and baker guarded their heritage shop windows and a collier flung his raggedy son into a flight that would never come down. Then from behind these grotesque mannequins a third man moved and clutched one of the others around the shoulders until he broke abruptly away and moved back to the doors, which whispered open and shut as their sensors invited a response. The glass panels gaped as two men stood on the line, then closed tight as they crossed it and out into the yard. Wheelie was just a step in front and to the left of Lionel. They looked at the bulk of a loaded coal dram to one side of the bus and at the recesses of the engine house wall beyond the bus, and they split, with Wheelie going the longer way around its front and Lionel more directly across the visible side to the back end where I crouched, and waited.

The rain had filled the fissures between the cobbles with small jewelled puddles. The stage props, real enough in the colliery yard, seemed ridiculously familiar. The gold lettering on the bus, the thick rubber tread of tyres that had once jolted paying passengers, the wet cloth smell of the damp moquette seats which I could see inside, their chromium grip bars dulled by the dank. It was seconds in reality. The doors hissed and opened once more, and in their light I saw a third man coming around the front and the side to the back. Lionel was already there, past the conductor's pole and platform. He stopped when he saw me, hesitating for the instant in which he looked for his back-up support. The bag dropped to the floor of the yard as my right hand appeared with the lump hammer in it. It was a foot away from Lionel when I swung it up, short and heavy, into his balls with all the force I could. His hands had fluttered down as useless as a couple of butterfly wings and were swatted aside. He grunted and dropped to his knees, from where he felt the hammer, now switched to the horizontal, smash into the bridge of his nose and spit blood, bone and cartilage onto the cobbles. He lay slumped, head down and silent and I turned to threaten Wheelie with more of the same, but his days of dealing with anything that was not already prostrate had gone. He stood stock-still. Then there was the third figure. I swivelled to face him. Of course, Tommy. He pushed me aside to check I hadn't killed his lifetime prop. I hadn't. But I had hurt him bad and the emergency ward would soon see him, a trifle less intact than when he'd woken up in the morning. Like me, he'd live, with a few painkillers, a bandage or two, and a caring friend. The same one.

That friend stood up and said: "You bastard. You fucking bastard." I nodded and held the hammer ready.

"Tommy," I said. It was an acknowledgement, just that.

"He'll fucking kill you," was a reply more than a threat.

"Maybe. He half-tried already, didn't he?" A gambit, but it worked.

"Christ, Billy. That was, you know, business. And in any case I stopped it going too far. Christ, we took care of you, you ungrateful bastard."

An apology? I didn't think so.

Tommy bunched his fists.

"I won't wait for Lionel. I'll do you now. And *I* won't stop. Not this time."

I showed him the easy swing of the hammer as his body tensed to rush me but I really wanted words to stop him. Words to direct him elsewhere.

"D'you know about Haf, Tommy? Really know?"

What I knew was already enough, I gambled, to ease Tommy into the violence that had always mirrored his sentimentality. But I didn't know everything yet. Maybe that was just as well. For all of us.

"What're you fuckin' getting at?"

"You're fond of her, aren't you? Seen her growing up. After Norma died. You with no kids. Maybe Bran even encouraged you to think … well, she's good at that, isn't she? But then she'd have told you 'No', as well, because she wouldn't want you too close, not with Mal and her, making the nest, so to speak. And that's what I want to tell you about your boss, see Tommy."

He wanted to shut me up. I could feel that, like a current whipping back and fro between us. And he could have done it, too. Hammer or no hammer. But he wanted to hear it, too. So much that I was no longer sure I should say it. But then I did, say it outright, because I wanted the dirt to sting and maim. Not him, of course, just Mal.

"You know when Bran and Mal split up. And he'd have told you that, amongst other things, like maybe she was fucking elsewhere when she wanted, maybe even you, for old times' sake, eh Tommy? That she'd told him, her husband of course, that Haf was not his after all and she'd told Haf, her troublesome, meddlesome daughter that it was me all along, her Daddy-in-exile, so there was the row of all rows and Mal left, and later, soon, Haf followed. And you didn't know, did you Tommy, that Mal, your boss, was soon fucking her. His maybe daughter. Haf."

He said I was a fucking liar, but he flinched and whispered when he said it. I told him to ask Bran. Or better still Maldwyn. He looked over my shoulder to where the automatic doors had opened again. Mal was standing where the yard and the rain and the truth began. He shouted – "Tommy, what the fuck's going on?" – and moved further into the rain. I dropped the hammer. Tommy pushed past me and gathered Lionel up.

"Give me a hand," he yelled at Wheelie and he gave me the look that told me even as I walked away that he believed me, and there would be consequences. Because with Tommy there always would be. I dropped the envelope for Mal at Tommy's feet and said, "Read it before you give it to him. Then give it to him."

* * * * *

I walked away from the yard and back out onto the road. I bent into the rain, as naggingly penetrating as ever, and walked up the road. It was a hundred yards or so, but I broke no records getting to the hotel. In the rain, on that road, the hotel looked more incongruous than the first time. Maybe it was me that just wasn't congruent anymore. Out of step. Out of time. Out of place, and yet inside from outside. It was beginning to sound like the soapy wisdom of a moody song. I told it to stop. I had them order me a cab and waited in the dry.

* * * * *

Sir Ceri Evans was running late. There had been no further messages. It was probably the common assumption of what had become an uncommon life. That he could be late with no apology. I was at ease with that. I was even more at ease with the large G & T that was nursing me. The brasserie was at the back of a grooved wooden deck two flights up from the pavement of the washed and scrubbed waterfront. The marble-topped table had been booked and I had been sat at it on a spindly bentwood chair for over half an hour. The view was of a flat viscous lagoon that struggled to reflect back the light of its ambient Venusberg café-bars and restaurants. That, too, was OK by me. I needed a matt finish to soothe the prickly gloss of the day. It was more soothing anyway than the signature buildings near which the taxi had dropped me for my short promenade to the brasserie.

The buildings were new to me. I struggled not to sum them up too quickly. There seemed around the parliamentary one to be a skirt of slate that lapped up the steps and into the building as if to bring to a darker ground the plate glass which promised transparent government. Its pine roof had a funnel of wood which looked like a wheatsheaf ready for harvesting. It felt more sauna than smoke-filled room. I wondered if this county council Cymru had really stripped itself down so soon to such an indecent basic openness. Indecent in comparison with all its past traditions, that is. I was encouraged. And, as a traditionalist, relieved to see that somebody must have commissioned a lot of slate from a grateful constituency. Next door was an architectural Leviathan. A gargantuan sheepfold, in slate again, topped off by a riveted brass-gold biker's helmet with a stencilled message in a bottle about horizons and stones that was in cut-out lettering in English and Welsh. It glowed in the dark like the jagged mouth and eye-holes of a pumpkin. I had walked through the strip and huddle of eateries, bars and cafés to the restaurant where I sat and waited.

I let my mind, what was left of it to match the battered body where it had found almost fifty years of house room, wander. Back, of course. To Ceri eventually. I had followed his career as it soared from union office to county council eminence and serial chairmanhood as he moved – who didn't? – from left to right and was then rewarded with a knighthood. It had served to transmute him into an elder statesman stance. Non-executive positions on the boards of public utilities and not-for-profit organisations were added to his portfolio. He was rewarded, appropriately of course, as a consultant on public affairs. Pro-bono, he polished his CV by chairing Task and Finish groups and gave his weighty name to their shelved reports. He graced conferences and sat in on seminars. He became revered, honoured and trusted, the more he grew independent of his, and our, past lives. It was, I suppose, a familiar trajectory. Certainly one which would not have surprised my old man. But would he really have predicted it? Would I have really believed that kind of outcome for that Ceri from that time?

That Ceri. That time. My old man's Ceri had been twenty-five or so when I was first made aware of him. He had, the old man said, just wandered into one of his WEA classes, on Art and Literature in the Industrial Age, or some such stirring title, and sat, apparently transfixed, at the back. He was, in the early 1960s, considerably younger than the dwindling band of educational veterans which my father's grizzled application of social history to culture usually attracted. Ceri was an orphan and an apprentice collier who had married Olwen at eighteen. Lady Olwen now. Ceri never threw anything away that might prove useful, and a lifetime of philandering – early and late – had not broken the utility of his marriage to Olwen, who ran his home and raised his children to be teachers and solicitors, all in his absence. The marriage was no fiction, it was just a side story within the space of his personal, always personal, narrative. He had been recommended to go to the old man's class by the kind of union official who, in those days, acted as recruiting agent for educational uplift. He had been told to broaden his horizons if he was to make a mark in the union. He was already a Young Communist of course. But then that was like saying, for his youth and ardour in that place at that time, that he went to chapel or liked the movies or shagged girls or chainsmoked. He didn't do the first and the last, as a matter of fact. But he did believe. And he did see how that helped him to be seen, to be noticed. In the Good Cause, of course.

He became an assiduous attender. Assiduity would become his hallmark. It was funny, so I said ha-ha to myself, how you had to wait to the end, of a life, as of a book, to see how it all turned out. And that it could have been different. Maybe. Choices. Pathways, and all that. Only I didn't go in for "all that" anymore. For some people in some places at some times it was fixed. Our time had been made for Ceri and he always seemed to know it better, quicker, than any of the rest of us. Maldwyn had just seen ways to make money, but he'd do that any place any time. Bran was a chancer who needed to escape what her good looks had made easy and mundane for her as she looked in the mirrors which were other people's eyes, and for her the exit routes to success were never dependent on the satnav of exile. Gwilym flew high inside cages erected by others, and never understood the difference between fluttering his flashy wings and flying to any purpose. Tommy was collateral damage in a society that had devalued the power that thousands of Tommys together had once shown. Me, I had mistaken my despair for insight and my contempt for courage, and I'd used my small gifts only to direct my retreat. Haf was what was left, hurt and hopeful. If I owed anything to anyone in the ruins of this time and place it was, I thought, to her. It would depend on the price I could exact for damages. It would depend on how bad the damage had been. I was counting on Ceri to tell me.

* * * * *

The voice entered the room first. Greeting the waiter with a "Phillipe!" and a bear hug, and a smile that let his eyes wander over the faint blush from "Nadine, lovely," more quietly said, as a petite blonde bobbed into view and took his coat from his back. A thicker back than I'd remembered but still proportionate to his height, just six feet, and his wide shoulders. His eyes made a quick inventory of the room, three or four couples who clocked him even as he ticked them off on his highly tuned radar screen, and me. He grinned, opening up an abyss of a welcome on his handsome crag of a face. His hair was still shaggy and lustrous on top and greying in all the right distinguished places elsewhere. He was in no hurry to cross the room. This was a piece of theatre for Ceri. He patted the lapels of his well-cut bespoke dark-blue single-breasted suit, fiddled with a black-polka-dot-on-light-grey tie as if he was Oliver Hardy, and let the voice take over again. Out it rumbled from some warm, deep, irresistible cavern. "Well, well, well. Little Billy Maddox. How are you, butt? How are you? Bloody well come 'ere."

He was with me before I could even rise from the table. He had made it a lifetime's practice to invite warmth but to make sure he gave it out first. I was grabbed and pulled in towards him, held almost as if I was a child. Size, as they say, had nothing to do with it. This was all about technique. In anybody else the body cinch, the handshaking wonderment, the brown eyes lit up with an irrepressible delight at being, just the two of us, any old us, together, would have been a giveaway. Politician. Kisses baby. Congratulates Mother. Envies Father. And all that. But Ceri had somehow made natural to himself what in others were lame gestures. What you felt was what you got. Or so it appeared. What you saw was what you truly saw, and what was not to like? Everyone liked Sir Ceri Evans.

He finally let me go, still cracking a smile, and sat down with a thump. As always, he went straight to it, by whatever back road he felt safe on.

"Surprised about the knighthood, were you? Can't imagine what your old man would have said. Well. I can, actually! But hey, Lady Olwen loves it, and she bloody well deserves it, doesn't she? More than me, anyway!"

He laughed so all-embracingly that the other diners looked over, happy for him, and so now for themselves. He waved a little self-deprecatingly, as if to say "Enjoy" – me, this hour, your being here, with me. He had lots of ingratiating habits. He deployed the next one. A shy hesitancy, signalled by the repetition of inconsequential words, as if he was readying himself, gearing up for the task, this Ceri, for whom there had never been any hesitation in reaching out and taking what he wanted, the biggest-beaked fledgling in the nest yet with the modesty to tip his head away as he simultaneously swallowed the worm whole. All for him.

"It's, it's … er … a case of recognition," he began. "Recognition, see. Not, uh, not, for me. For what I tried to, we, in the old days, your old man even, represented. See. Oh shit. Fuck the title. That's not important. Though, mind, the Lords was mentioned, too. Aye. But. See. I have to keep active. Working. Mostly in Europe now. For Wales. So there it is, see."

And he spread his hands on the table and looked imploringly at me. I told him it was OK by me. That I couldn't speak for the old man. But he was dead, after all. Ceri said, "Yes," and looked mournful, as if it was yesterday, not years ago, and he wasn't exactly asking the old man's opinion or permission even in those days. We airbrushed the history we'd filed away. We decided to order. Proper decisions. Ceri was no fine diner. So far as food, his "grub" as he called it out of some further gesture of solidarity with people who had actually eaten it as fuel for work, he liked it large, quick and showy. The blonde waitress drifted to the table like a fish drawn to a hook. He must have tipped well before.

"Shall we have the usual, Billy? My usual, I mean, of course. Sorry, butt. Oysters. Chablis. Fillet steak. Chips, natch. No bloody veg, and a bottle or two of Costières de Nîmes. OK? Rare or medium rare? "À pointe" as I've learned to say, eh, Nadine?"

Nadine hovered, and glowed a little. I'd like to think she was indulging the customer as an old fool. Unfortunately, I could see she was enjoying the exchange. He hadn't missed a beat. Still had the rhythm at his fingertips. The steaks would be rare but not too blue. Wrong colour. Even for an Independent, he said. We agreed, and laughed. That led us to more political banter and reminiscence over the Boys' Own meal we were scoffing. Two bottles of the deep southern red took us into a shared cheese plate. I broached nothing, waiting for him to make a move. He finally came to it over coffee and cognac.

"Anyway, this has been great, Billy. Just great. I'll pay, mind! God! Makes me feel young again, seeing you. D'you fancy that, do you? I think, I think, she's up for it! I know I would be!

"But, anyway, what, what're you bothered about, bothering with, this, er, this regeneration scheme? Bran tells me her daughter, daft kid, is causing, making, waves, trouble 'bout it. Can't see why. It'll do a lot of good, see, for a lot of people up there. Dependent on me, it is, getting all the pieces together, in place. Nothing wrong with that, is there?"

He leaned back. He swirled his spoon in the sugary grit of his double espresso. He made a face of genuine puzzlement. I reached down and opened the folder in which I'd put all the papers Haf had sent me. I scattered them on the table. He scarcely glanced at them beyond a peremptory flick of a few pages.

"Oh that," he said. "Gwilym told me about those. So what, Billy? You don't think we're stupid, do you? Do you? S'all on the level. Derelict land. Deprived communities. *Our* people, Billy. All for *their* aspirations. A portal to the outside world. Valleys on the map again, eh? European money. Welsh welcome. Know-how imported. Knowledge grown and exported."

I rifled through the emails in front of him which confirmed the payments from Bran, or rather from Bran's piddling little PR outfit, into his bank. Thousands that totted up to hundreds of thousands of pounds. I showed him the newspaper cuttings and the committee transcripts that detailed his enthusiasm as he lobbied with all the considerable skill he'd acquired for ear-marked grants. Millions of euros. I read out the letters from the commission in Brussels and the civil service in Cardiff nominating Tir Werin to take a central role in the proposed scheme and to act as recipient of the disbursed money. Then there were more confidential notes about Tir Werin, the plans and drawings of what were, acres and acres of, iron and coal wasted tips and hillocks and plateaux, and what exactly could be cleaned up, and how, and at what cost it could be built upon. Homes as well as the primary project. Retail units as well as research centres. High-end leisure as well as conference facilities. And most of the grant moneys conducted discreetly by Gwilym as secretary into the accounts of the owners of the land. And that was Valleyscorp, the company trust in Haf's name, with Maldwyn nowhere in sight. Valleyscorp was Mal's sleeper. It was a frog which Tir Werin, as princess, would kiss to wake it up into a terrible new kind of beauty.

There was more, of course, but that seemed to me, as it had since I'd first seen it, more than enough for questions to be asked. I asked him to justify how the public good he was espousing worked out as such personal good fortune.

Quite reasonable, I thought. But Ceri, as ever, was not disturbed. He told me that none of it would stand up, that all of it could be explained away, and that, besides, the payments to him were fees, registered for consultancy and advice. It would have been impossible to move those mountains of cash without a general political will and inside a common framework of policy far beyond any feeble effort he could individually offer. Also, I should grow up. Also, I should wake up. Also, I had no idea any more, if I ever had, of how the lives of ordinary people – I loved that ordinary – were settled now, or fucked up, by the dealings of what he airily called envoys to power, committees of notables, and entrepreneurs directed, by such as him whenever and wherever he could, to do social good. Not just to ensure their own gain. Though, of course, and be reasonable, don't be stupid, there was, inevitably, and why not, that too. A little bit of greed, he'd learned, was good. The wheels had to turn. Needed oiling.

He seemed to like the industrial metaphor. His own conversational wheels ran more smoothly from that point, with no grinding of the gears as the Ceri who had only ever used conflict if it served his ultimate, personal purpose came back into view. He'd never gone away of course. It was always, beginning and end, about Ceri. That was his abiding purpose. And it wasn't really the incentive of greed that drove his wheels on. It was what he wanted to see in the light of other people's regard of him, and hear in the warm gurgle of his own voice. He leaned across and held my arm down onto the table amongst the relics of our meal.

"Look, I know you're hurt. But you're making it too personal, butt. See, things have changed. You can see that, can't you?"

His thick, strong fingers pressed gently on my forearm. Reassuring. Just like Sir Ceri.

"What I'm saying is, is that, that, there's nothing else, see. To do, mind. What are our natural advantages? What's left? More to the point boy, how can we help? And it is about that, see, Billy, helping, I mean. Because they can't help themselves, see, any more. Perhaps they never could, eh!"

He swallowed. He pressed. He gave me his friendliest shrug that went from smile to body language to actual words.

"Hey, I know your old man would've laughed at all this, eh? You and me having a debate like this, after a bloody bourgeois spread as he'd've put it, eh. But, look, he was great, he was great. Then, see. You have to see that, Billy. It was all then. Only now you can't be romantic like he was. And, you know, he turned from that at the end, too. Too cynical then, he was. You said it yourself at the time. Remember?"

He paused. He took his fingers from my forearm.

"Got to stop beating yourself up, Billy. Difference between me and your old man is that I went and did it, didn't I? And it had to be different. Not saying he didn't teach me a lot, but he couldn't teach me that, could he? And you can only lead what's willing to be led, see. Best thing now is to help. And this, er, scheme, project, is only that. Another way. Look back and you'll see there were always, various, different, ways like this. Find a way to make things happen, is all. Get real, like they say, eh, Billy, go with the flow? You come from a long line of helpers, butt. You could help now."

When I saw he was finished, silent and smiling, I smiled back and gathered up the papers and returned them to their folder. I told him I agreed with him. That that was, indeed, the way it was now. That he had always known, for a purpose perhaps, how to dance between the cogwheels and neither stop the machinery nor get mangled by the machine. I told him, too, what I still expected him to do, and where the papers would otherwise go. He waved this away like splatting a bothersome fly from a waiting sweetmeat, and snarled, disdainful of my stubborn behaviour, that it'd be a news story for a day, a flash in the pan for a week, a dead duck in a fortnight. I said,

"Sure. And you, Ceri? But you Ceri? Land speculation? Second phase, of course, after the regeneration project is built. But then an infrastructure ready for construction and sale. Well, dirty but OK, I guess. A largely public enterprise expanding, a little too close to some benefactors perhaps, but ultimately benefitting others. Houses and shops and retail outlets and a new road grid. Profits for the prophets. A bit messy. But OK. And then again. A senior public figure. Of some influence. In places of crucial decision-making. Still an idealist. A rebel, even. But one with hundreds of thousands in the bank, directly from a source attached to the whole scheme. You'll be crucified."

I added a "butt" to show there were no hard feelings. Then I told him what I wanted him to do. He looked more amused than bemused. More dismissive than compliant. I reached inside my jacket and took out the envelope marked with his name. I gave it to him. I walked away, leaving Sir Ceri Evans to pick up the bill.

Thursday

I woke late the next morning, around ten, to the flash and blink of the red light of the bedside table's telephone. I had a message from reception. A Branwen Williams had called at eight thirty-five. She'd meet me in the lobby at eleven fifteen. I blinked back, my eyes as red as the pulsing light. Ceri's booze doing its trick. The one I always fall for. I cleaned up and put on a black T-shirt over black chinos and stuffed my bare feet into a pair of black tasselled loafers. I grimaced into the mirror. Colour co-ordination. Not exactly my game, unless minimalism is to your taste.

I was downstairs at eleven and sat in the far corner of a wannabee atrium. I hid behind a newspaper I wasn't reading. One I couldn't have read even if I'd wanted to try. My eyes wouldn't allow for the close attention needed. If there had been a potted fern I'd have hidden myself in its fronds. I could have watered it by crying occasionally. Twenty minutes later, she was late, and at eleven thirty later still. I could feel the blurred newsprint starting to come back into focus. I scrunched my eyes to prevent that. I waited some more. I was good at that. I had long experience, and currently a deeply felt lack of mobility.

I clocked her entrance, in both senses, at eleven forty five. She smiled at the East European behind the desk and gave him my name. She turned at his reply, in the direction where I'd told Pavel I'd be when requested. The one doing the asking was, for Bran, definitely dressed down. She had on flat dove-grey suede shoes with an understated silver buckle. The look was not quite, and yet not not, casual. Perfectly judged, unlike my own sombre ensemble, from the light grey cotton, flecked and knife-edged creased, trousers to the open-necked pink shirt worn beneath the darker steel-grey of a wraparound cardigan with a loose belt. It left her elegant wrists on display. And on the left one she wore – nice touch this I thought – a silver and turquoise Navajo bangle, late 1940s I'd been told, which I'd once bought for her in Arizona before all the skies of our lives had clouded over. There was no discernible make-up this morning, and her full hair looked tousled. I'd tousled her a few times myself. She was a fine tousler, all right.

And a mind-reader, too. Now she smiled at me. I could see we were going to get along fine. She sat down opposite me in the matching armchair. Its charcoal fabric framed the pretty and complementary picture she made as if it had been designed for it. Somewhere, maybe, it had. She crossed her legs at the ankles. I kept mine straight. She said, "You're all in black," as if colour coordination was her constant and actual game. Maybe it was.

"Thank you for seeing me. Again. You know …", she said.

I did, and told her that was fine and that we had unfinished business anyway, didn't we? She raised one carefully under-plucked eyebrow, and said nothing. So, I told her I'd seen Ceri the night before and had made him a proposition that might affect all other current propositions, if she knew what I meant. She did. She told me he'd told her. Ah, I thought, with a twinge of discomfort at my all-round slowness, that explains the tousled look and the uncharacteristic lateness then.

I had said nothing about the small suitcase she had been carrying and which sat, shabbily out of place, by the side of her chair. It was clearly not like any overnight bag she might use even if, which I doubted, she'd use one. It wasn't even colour coordinated. Either with her, the atrium or the present day. It was too defiantly retrogressive for the faux retro of the lobby and too rectangular and brown to play off the black-and-white steel-framed pics of Manhattan and Paris and Milan with which this transient space moored its uncertain identity. The last time I'd seen the suitcase was on top of my old man's post-war utility furniture wardrobe. I tuned back in to Bran's insistent murmuring.

"... I understand ... I really do, Billy ... what you're saying. To Ceri. To me. And maybe, because you know how well I know you, Billy – so much unforgotten between us, isn't there? – I understand your motives. But I still want to get you to see, things have moved on, you know, to see that it would be, well, not sensible, just sentimental if I can say, to let yourself be blinded by them, and you would, really, spoil so much that is good. And necessary even. Good, certainly. We're all convinced of that. If you pursue them."

I pursed my lips. Not in a discouraging way, I hoped. I wanted to give the impression of hidden and unforgettable things. Things that were indeed between us still. Things I could release if I wanted, with the right persuasion. I wanted her to continue, to be persuasive. And I wanted to know what she was doing with my father's suitcase, and what was in it.

The speech I had coming was a good one. Prepared, rehearsed maybe, certainly drafted by Ceri for shape and punch, but clear and committed in its message. It was a speech about bringing hope to the hopeless. How could anyone possibly object? Some things were as undeniable as they were familiar. We'd been too young to appreciate the obstacles to our idealism. We'd imagined a moment when things would be possible because of all that had gone before. We could re-root, re-investigate, fertilise the lives and institutions of ordinary people – like her mentor, Ceri, she fought fashionably shy of that old calling card, the working class – with fresh energy, new ideas and determination. We hadn't been wrong, but we had mistaken what we had really had to play with to make the change possible. OK, maybe we were too excited, even too enjoying of the world turning upside down but, come on, what was the alternative? And it isn't as if the daily existence of ordinary people was adequate, was it? Even for them. She knew why I'd left. Caught between the icy dismissiveness of my old man and the despair at our generational failure. Which is where, she said, Ceri came in, couldn't I see? It had taken him some time, too, but he had been amongst the first to recognise that the fight was not ended, only re-located. He was our bridge. It wasn't, then, that we had to settle for less, only for something different, because needs and opportunities were no longer the same. The politics had atrophied because the whole way of once being had disappeared or shrivelled beyond use or recognition. Aspiration didn't have to begin at Basingstoke, did it? Community was just a romantic notion. Individuals deserved better, didn't they? What was wrong with that? Wasn't that what we were, really, all about, then and now? You didn't pull the ladder up after you like an Indian rope trick, you helped others up, you encouraged others to climb and you did what you could for those who wouldn't or couldn't.

And I had to see how radically altered people were, hadn't I? They voted unthinkingly in the past and now hardly bothered to vote at all. The past was, OK, often glorious to read about but romanticised like hell and probably shit to live through. Especially if you were a woman. She gave me that from down-under look that told me she knew this instinctively, of course. I nodded her on. Which was why, she confided, they needed not support nor comfort nor flattery but the kind of civic and cultural leadership that could ensure social and structural change. Ceri had given up on the petty squabbling of the remnants of his own political past to embrace the wider vision that a new coalition of interests offered and for which he, and some others with both roots and networks, could serve as a conduit. These channels had to be dug and lubricated by people with the same local knowledge and soaring ambition. But these people – a modest, implicit acknowledgement of herself, Gwilym and Maldwyn this time – were not somehow cheating or conniving to exclude ordinary people. No, they had an extraordinary desire to help people who, in these serially neglected and benighted valleys, could no longer help themselves. As a group, she said. As individuals, she said. It had to change, didn't it?

Bran then led me by the hand through the plans they had devised together to provide an exemplar which would be the envy of regeneration projects across Europe, and wider still. It met all the current needs of its surrounding dependants – economic and social – and, what was wonderfully more, it would bring the sharpest brains and the deepest wallets into a cultural symbiosis. She liked that word. She liked it so much she used it twice. I could see the symbiotic connection she was eager to make. Money and minds, together. Wow. What a sweet combo. When she saw the light bulb was on she expanded on the fruits of this treasure trove and gently explained how such deals were always complex, fraught with bureaucracy, be-devilled by rivalry, hamstrung by low expectation and clouded vision. There had to be leaders, big and bold enough to translate their individual ambition into the passion for progressive action that had always inspired them. It still did. That was the point. To create a mini storm by false accusation that would, nonetheless, take time and trouble to refute, with all the collateral, possibly fatal, damage the project would suffer, well, to do that, would be to make the mistake, but in reverse, we'd all made two decades ago. This was now. It was great I was back but I had to be back, if not for good, then, at least, in the interest of the good. And the people of course. Of course.

Hats off, I thought. She was good. Really good, PR taken to the nth degree, and presented with flair. Reasoned intelligence without too heavy a sell could be a winner every time. Not this time though. What a crock of shit, I thought. We are for them despite themselves. They are finished otherwise. They don't understand anyway. Their usefulness is dependent on how they are used. Their history is cut off from any future they might have. Their remaining purpose is to stand aside or be led to higher ground they don't even glimpse anymore. QED.

I pursed my lips again. She seemed to think this signalled how bowled over I was. Yeah, that and some. I readied myself for the bullet to the brain still to come. She tapped the suitcase with an unvarnished fingernail. Did I recognise it? I said it seemed familiar. She told me the old man had asked her to take it away when he sensed he was dying and to give it to me if I ever came back. That it was full of notes and papers and a few books and magazines he seemed to have researched and culled. Some writing by him and a few letters, she said. She thought, and Ceri had agreed it seems, that it was all revelatory. In an uncanny way, she conjectured, it might be said to connect up me and the old man, and lots of other things which had seemed too large scale to be personal. Yet, here it was, up close and personal. I'd understand.

She stood and formally shook my hand before thinking better of it and leaning down to kiss my cheek.

"I'll leave the case," she said. "It's interesting, I promise. Please look at it. You might say it'll clear your mind. No doubts, eh? Love you, Billy. Really do. Sorry it didn't work out. But life never stays still, does it?"

I watched her leave, smiling at Pavel as she did, making the air around her fragrant by her passage. Funny how deceptive things like that can be. I looked at the case. I sighed for a time long past. I picked it up as I got to my feet, and carried it to the lift and my room. I had some reading to do. It was lucky my eyes were starting to feel up for it.

* * * * *

I placed it bottom-down on the bed and contemplated it for a while. Whatever was inside would do me no good. Bran would not have brought it to do me good. It was what effect it was meant to have which alone concerned her. I went for a walk. Just to the window. I looked out from six floors down through the screen of treeleaf to the wall of the mock castle beneath. That wall was equipped to snarl back. The wall ran alongside the main road which roared past. The wall was topped with stone animals – a whole Victorian menagerie of them – pouncing and crawling and leaping over the battlements that would hold them in still flight forever. A whole city had sprung up around their sculpting, one paid for like them in the same mineral coin that had made it, for a time, the world's Coalopolis.

I crossed the royal-blue carpeted floor back to the foot of the low divan bed and stared at my nemesis. I leaned forward on impulse and released the two rusting metal catches which sprung up and back with an emphatic snap. I paused. I knelt down. I opened the lid of the cheap cardboard and leatherette case as slowly as inevitability would allow. I had no curiosity, only anxiety. If I knew the shallows of Bran all too well, I knew the depths of the old man even better. To be wary of one was to fear the other. A scent of curling brown paper and a whiff of dead days uncurled to meet me.

There were three hardback volumes, dating from the 1920s and '30s. Some magazines, a few maps of the coalfield before 1914, a book of statistics, a red-covered Edwardian railway timetable for coal freight traffic, loosely strewn papers, some typed on old-fashioned 'flimsy' but most scrawled over in my old man's blocky hand. I shuffled through them. Notes, extracts, disconnected paragraphs of continuous prose and questions, a list of things to do and read, and titles or perhaps headings. At the very bottom of this pile were twenty or so pen-and-ink drawings on 6" by 4" white paper, bundled together in a folder and each initialled with the old man's D.M. in the left hand corner. They were of ruins, bombed and blasted, of armoured cars and upturned vehicles, of black-limbed trees and shuffling men. They were of Monte Cassino and 1944. A final buff folder just said *Letters* on its front, and was marked *Personal*. It was obvious, from the books alone, that the material he'd assembled was a foray into the life and times of David Alfred Thomas. The old man had read into the history of the coalfield, and its various makers. But nothing as intensely gathered together as this, so far as I knew. It took me a quick trawl to establish who exactly the object of all this was. The subject had died in 1918 and when he died he did so as Viscount Rhondda. He'd been cremated in Golders Green. The old man must have known that on the day we were there together when Paynter followed Rhondda to the final fire in 1984, because none of the papers seemed to have been worked on, from the few dates he'd added to pages, since 1958. Lord Rhondda's ashes were later buried in Llanwern, his country seat in Monmouthshire, as Gwent was then known.

I resisted pulling everything apart too rapidly for one swift explanation. I wanted to see why this person had caught my old man's attention for this much effort. The cornerstones of the life were no great help. He'd been born in 1856 into the large family of a hustling, bustling mid-Victorian coal speculator, Samuel Thomas, who'd branched out from the Aberdare valley to hit pay dirt with the opening up of rich seams in the mid-Rhondda from the 1870s. Enough to pay for a public school education and then a Cambridge degree for his bookish son who, in turn, inherited what became the Cambrian Combine agglomeration of pits. I could see why that might be of interest to the old man. It was around aggressive managerial demands that the Tonypandy riots of 1910, along with the year-long Cambrian Combine strike, occurred. But this was clearly no historian's quest. No spinning enquiry either into the political detail that festooned the days of a Liberal MP in Imperial Britain until Thomas gave it up to concentrate on a dedicated career as coal capitalist. And more than that, one who longed to control destinies, shape lives, fulfil them through his own power and will. He had spelled it all out in chilling detail in essays and speeches of overweening ambition.

I skimmed a book of memorial essays by his devoted daughter and other contemporaries, along with a hagiographic biography, picking out the salient factual points: that he had been a fortunate survivor when the Germans torpedoed the *Lusitania* on its return transatlantic voyage from New York in May 1915, and that his chief contemporary and one-time political rival, Lloyd George, Minister of Munitions in that year and made the Prime Minister of the British Empire in December 1916, had been quick to use Thomas's negotiating skills in America to ensure consistency of supply in the wartime crisis over munitions, and then placed him in his wartime cabinet, from 1917 as Food Controller, from where supreme administrative and imaginative genius allowed besieged Britain to live on rations rather than borrowed time. That won Thomas his Viscountcy, and probably hastened his early death at sixty-three. How large their lives were. How central was their Wales. How significant was coal itself. How it all still lingered.

* * * * *

The old man had begun yet another something he had never finished. It would have been called: 'The American Prince of Wales'. He had left me shards. Perhaps they had illuminated enough for him, and if you read carefully enough you could still cut yourself on their splinters. I read slowly, as if both subject and author were whole again, then smashed into pieces, glinting, coalescing, but all beyond the reach of my understanding:

> *His was a concept as much as it was a reality. He ached to make of the reality he had been given something inconceivably greater*

than its material form. But it was, he knew, that which was merely material which was the matter he must dynamite – but how? – into the future that lay still and inert in deep fissures. Of coal. Of that mineral which, alone, vitalised the blood and iron of conflicting Empires and for which he had more beneficent dreams.

It was said of him that he knew Jevons' 1865 tome, The Coal Question: an Inquiry concerning the Progress of the Nation and the Probable Exhaustion of our Coal-Mines, *nearly by heart and could and would cite chunks of it out loud, as if it was an amusing party piece. For him it was Nirvana and Apocalypse both. In drawing room and office, at the dinner table or the theatre, he would bore and impress, rant and reason, to the effect that to be born into a coalfield such as South Wales, more, to be charged with its destiny, was to bear a gift incomparable to birth by lineage or politics by choice. The world itself, he would say, could thereby, by this vast reserve of coal, be secured, for a time, for ourselves. Time bought to grow and develop. Elsewhere if need be. He was, this Welshman, in the phrasing of the day, no "little Englander"; but nor was he, this modern Prince, to be defined by the happenstance of being Welsh.*

In spate, his clipped conversation raced into speech, and his speech roared into exhortatory impatience. In 1896, when Lloyd George, his Liberal parliamentary colleague, and fellow radical, sought a different future, a Cymru Fydd, *around a sense of a distinct Liberal Wales, it was D.A. Thomas who urged wider horizons beyond this, as he saw it, cultural myopia. That year, in counterblast, he wrote a paean to his dream, a world spinning on the axis of his locus:*

"… there is no part in the United Kingdom which has so many national and artificial advantages as Cardiff; and these must tell in the near future. In a geographic sense the Welsh

capital is admirably situated for the North and South American, West Indian, African, Pacific, East Indian, Australian, Mediterranean, Black Sea, and South and West Continental trades. As a loading port she is unrivalled; numerous vessels having to come to her from London, Liverpool, and Continental ports for outward cargo. Coal is the heaviest of all our exports, and the coalfield of South Wales is the most valuable in the Kingdom for export of cargo and for bunkering steamers.

"... The time has fully arrived when Cardiff should seek to form a large Atlantic trade, both in goods and passengers ... Cardiff is first for minimum distance New York to Birmingham, and second to London ... In all these phases of trade and convenience for commerce there is a distinct advantage on the side of Cardiff ... It is true the principal item [of deadweight tonnage] is that of coal. But it must be borne in mind that coal forms the staple at present for the outward cargoes of all outward bound ships. It is something like three fourths of the whole deadweight of cargoes in our overseas trade. Cardiff has an unlimited supply of the best bunker coal in the world behind her. The coal of the South Welsh basin, as yet unworked, is estimated by the Royal Coal Commission at about 34,000 million tons. Just conceive it!"

His ambition was not to be confined. Neither by the conventional limits of a commercial life set by others nor by the root of the place where he was born. He intended, on the contrary, to use that rooted vigour to reach out beyond the circumstances of birth and upbringing, and to use his own given time and allotted space to make a great social experiment. In essence this is what America meant for him. And in this was he so very different from those who opposed him?

He made it plain that, although he made a great deal of it through his extensive business dealings, he was not ever merely seeking to make money. It was more that wealth and an assured fortune were his means to make the success he desired follow on. His definition of success was not a narrow one: it would be broad enough to encompass all manner of social and cultural growth. Seeded, tended and controlled by him. His people, as he never ceased to think of those amongst whom he'd lived and who now toiled for him, were, in literal fact, his end. The end purpose of his means. They, he often explained to those who asked, whether in the Press or in Parliament, thrashed about, in a welter of strikes and riots and grumbling, because they, by the nature of things, did not, and could not, possess the means to attain the impossible Nirvana held up before them by Idealists who, in every other sense than for their foolishness, earned his respect. Indeed, he was, he averred, one such himself. The difference was that he had both a finite goal and the practical means to achieve it. He was with his people in this, neither for impractical Socialism nor for the sticking-plaster Welfarism of Lloyd George. He had imagined how a novel collectivity, educated and disciplined and led, could come to a similar understanding of both the benevolence of such a system on this earth and the absolute necessity of the kind of leadership he could ensure in and beyond his time. And the key to this was the happenstance of Coal, its supreme importance. He would invoke his admired Jevons to the effect that coal "is the mainspring of modern material civilisation ... not beside but entirely above all other commodities ... the material source of the energy of the country, the universal aid, the factor in everything we do, without which we are thrown back into the laborious poverty of early times." Given this faith, this responsibility, he knew how to conceive of his duty. Being humble was not part of it.

His was a Faustian impulse, to build in despite of the frailty of Humanity and the febrile vitality of the Valleys. He recognised both these tendencies in the pre-War fever for Syndicalism, or workers' control, where all leadership, of owners or by union bosses, would be eschewed in favour of direct democracy and decision-making. Again made feasible in this place as in no other by the concentration here of power and people through coal.

'Welsh syndicalism' echoed the advance nature of coal capitalism, expressed here in the words of its foremost theorist, the miners' leader, Noah Ablett: "where the tendency to place the whole industry into the hands of one firm is proceeding at a phenomenal rate, scarcely a month passes [in 1917], but that there is news of two large companies amalgamating, or steps taken to form a large combine." So the answer for Ablett and his followers was to be "an industrial union – on a revolutionary basis for the abolition of capitalism", since "we shall never attain freedom by looking backward. We must go on with the times." But that was where D.A. Thomas already felt himself to be and he understood Ablett's insight into the fearful plasticity of their world because he shared it. In their self-created landscape the spirit abroad was that of an absolute social being – Capitalist or Socialist – which haunted the mind.

Ablett's ideas would resound for a short time, then dwindle to survivalism and welfarism in the devastated industrial backwater of the 1920s. D.A. Thomas would not live to see this, and by the end of his own days in 1918 had come to personify the mining valleys as a cutting edge for the entire modern world. His vaulting ambition, only thwarted afterwards and only for those who came after, would require of his biographer the ironic perspective that Conrad focussed on Gould, the silver-mine owner of Costaguana in his 1904 masterpiece Nostromo, *to bring the meaning of the life to any kind of remotely satisfactory analysis. A conclusion would remain perpetually in abeyance. He died before his realm crumbled. But it was never, for him, a mere industrial concern and therein lies his fascination for those of us who have indeed come after him.*

All of the missionary zeal that fired him – "The wise thing for democracy to do is to give every child in the land an equal opportunity for making the best use of its talents, so that where there are now hundreds of industrial organisers there may one day be thousands" – as he saw it, to create wealth to increase happiness was founded on the inheritance in coal he had received from his grandfather and father in the Mid Glamorgan hills. Did he think of this inheritance as such an "equal opportunity"? Talent as an industrial organiser was nonetheless certainly his. He turned the Cambrian Combine in mid-Rhondda into one of the largest integrated coal concerns in the world. Nor did he stop there: agencies in the sale of coal, companies to import pitwood from France, distributive organisations in shipowning, companies to establish coal depots, insurance, stocks and shares, and ever more collieries, all were engrossed in his maw. He operated in France, Spain, North Africa, and North America – and all on the basis of steam coal from the Valleys. How his world was to be perceived was also within his remit, for he had financial control of numerous journals and newspapers in Wales, and planned for an influential journal of opinion in London.

In effect when he stepped aboard the Lusitania *in 1915, ostensibly to further his North American interests but, I am convinced, to begin the secret negotiations for munitions with which Lloyd George would openly charge him later – he had risen above any diurnal politicking. He was, he knew, a colossus beyond all that, one centrally placed at the core point of his age. It was what Joseph Conrad had recognised in* Victory, *the novel he published that year:*

"There is, as every schoolboy knows in this scientific age, a very close relation between coal and diamonds. It is the reason, I believe, why some people allude to coal as "black diamonds." Both these commodities represent wealth; but coal is a much less

portable form of property. There is, from that point of view, a deplorable lack of concentration in coal. Now, if a coal-mine could be put into one's waistcoat pocket – but it can't! At the same time, there is a fascination in coal, the supreme commodity of the age in which we are camped like bewildered travellers in a garish, unrestful hotel."

We know from his secretary's account that in his luggage was indeed Joseph Conrad's just published novel, and we can safely speculate on the wry smile with which he would have read Conrad's Jevons-inspired encomium to coal. Accurate in all its particulars, other than that D.A. Thomas had, in fact, such a "concentration of coal" that he did carry coalmines just as if they were diamonds in his "waistcoat pocket." If he and his entourage, his daughter Margaret, his Secretary and the maidservant, had perished on their return journey the story, remarkable enough for its Tycoon lineaments in the age of the Industrial Titan, would still hold interest. But there is, of course, more: the emergence in wartime of a dedicated Public Servant of enormous capability and, at the Ministry for Food, the boss of Sir William Beveridge, whose later imprint on Welfare Britain would be so immense. As a Minister D.A. Thomas was confronted officially for the first time – since he must surely have known the average rate in his own Rhondda of almost 200 deaths per thousand live births in the decade to 1910 – by the appalling nationwide statistics for infant mortality. He now dreamed, as his legacy, of a nationwide Department of Health, one whose creation he demanded immediately. What emotion had ignited this principled ambition? What lives crossed and ended and led out from here to the world he would never see? Why did Lloyd George exclaim that an "interest in the health of infants is rather an unexpected passion for Rhondda?"

There were other such pages, complete in themselves but all terminating abruptly when the old man had plumbed the necessary, to him, depth and then shied away from any onerous, unnecessary to him, further tabulation. So many hares started and let go, as if he was content with the print of a hare's foot as being more alive with the subject's once-and-vanished vitality than with any hunted-down, stuffed and mounted variety. Some notes were stark, and others enigmatic, as if what secrets there were lay here, in revelations that were to be unpacked later:

- *His daughter said he preferred women to men as house guests though his professional life was entirely in the world of men.*

- *His daughter said that every servant they had was devoted to him. He would have no male servants around him or even in the house. It was, she said, the parlourmaid who tended to his comfort and well-being, even serving as his valet.*

- *His daughter said he always took the best of what was put before him, irrespective of others, once ate twelve oranges at a go and went from a bottle of port a night to being a virtual teetotaller at the end.*

- *His daughter said he took regular sun baths and that on warm days at Llanwern he would warn all but a servant away from that part of the roof where he would sit naked beneath the rays of the sun he adored.*

- *His daughter said that when the* Lusitania *was going down she went to his State Room to find him but neither her father nor the ship's regulation life belts were there. He, elsewhere, pushed a woman into a lifeboat and followed her.*

- *His daughter said she was washed overboard and, in the water for hours, was near death before rescue. Father and daughter were reunited on the Irish shore off which the great liner had been sunk by the German U-boat.*

- *His daughter said that as he was dying he had wished, though it was a rare precedent he invoked, that the Viscountcy he had been given in June 1918 be remaindered to her for life after his death. Because of his "great services to the State" the King had agreed to Lloyd George's request.*

- *There was no one to replace him in her life. When his ashes were interred she had a choir sing "Now the Labourer's Task is O'er" at the graveside, and when the music and the voices stopped, she had descended into his grave to say her own private farewell to her father. She kissed his urn and placed her mother's bridal handkerchief upon it.*

The old man had scrawled in his own hand, in ink across this last typed page of notes – "You couldn't make it up, could you. Just conceive it! All aboard the *Lusitania*?"

* * * * * *

It was late afternoon by the time I read, and re-read, everything. I had been hungry for nothing else through these hours. I put the overhead light on as rush-hour traffic began to back up alongside the city's castle walls. I had saved the "Personal" folder to the last. It was the least of all the papers in bulk. I had already read the four letters inside, however, several times over. One more time, then. I fetched a cold bottle of Mexican beer from the room's fridge, uncapped it and drank from the bottle without the benefit of a salt rim, a glass or a segment of lime. The letters were zest enough, and my blood pressure had every reason to avoid a saline solution. I had more problems than solutions. But I did have questions, and maybe as echoes, a few answers. The first letter was in black ink on headed paper. From Llanwern Park, and dated 16 December 1915.

"My darling Gwennie,
I send this with Blackmore to deliver to you by hand. He will bring me your reply if you will. Do not be afraid, for I will not abandon you. I know your time is near and when it has come you will return here, with the infant, and there will be no questioning of you, or of his presence, in my house.

What you have given me is not forgotten either and my joy in that gift of love and ecstacy sustains me in my labours. These, as you know, will increasingly confine me to London and Whitehall but, when you are ready, we will find time to be together again, and, I hope, find happiness in our meetings, so unexpected and vital for me, again.

Your David
Or, as you call me in memory of my place of youth,
Your Dai"

The second letter was on lined paper. It was written in blue ink and in a more child-like hand. The date was the same. It was just marked as from "Cheltenham". It read:

"My Dai,
For that is how I do always think of you now even if it is not the proper way to call you, and I will use David if you do prefer, though you do not, do you, as I know all too well. Well, I am near to the time now and they all

take care of me here, with no questions or evil looks which some can give you. I long to see you again and to meet like you say and am so happy you came back safe from America this time. What a fright we had in May and I will never forget it nor the way you saved my life, or I could say now, can't I, both of our lives. What I will do or say when I come back to Llanwern I worry, but I will be discreet and with your help pass it off, though I do think Miss Margaret, Lady Mackworth I should say, has her own thoughts which, what can I say, are true as you know my dear, and very, very naughty boy! Dai. Until we "meet"

Your very own Gwennie
X for a promise!"

The third letter was dated 3 July 1958 and the address was in Piccadilly. It was more formal.

"My dear Mr Maddox,
You will wonder, perhaps, that I only write now to acknowledge your note, of the 24th of September, 1953. Please be assured no discourtesy was intended and I had my reasons for not replying then, which are, indeed, different now.

I would be glad to see you if you care to come to the above address in the afternoon of the 3rd of July after two o'clock, when I will be pleased to explain to you what I can of the circumstances of my family's connections to you and to which your earlier note, and its enclosures which I have kept safe to return to you, alluded.

Yours sincerely,
Margaret, Rhondda."

The final, and fourth, letter was not dated. It was from my old man to me. I'm not sure it explained what he thought he was explaining at the time of writing, probably the mid-1960s since he had not dated it, but it would have to serve me half a century later as a settlement and a legacy. It did.

"Dear Billy,
I've often toyed with the idea of writing you a letter when you're too young – not quite ten yet – to understand it and yet when, with a life to come, I can speak more openly and fully to you here than, perhaps, when you are older and, believe me, face to face is often less than transparent.

But then it seems so artificial and I would not wish to write like some latter-day on-high purveyor of advice. So this is not, wherever this finds you and whatever you will have done by this time of reading, any advice at all. We will, no doubt, exhaust that, wastefully I suspect, as you grow up and away from me. No, this is information. Of a sort. Information I include here with the notes and passages for a work I began and will not now finish.

That I started at all is down to your mother. Shortly after we married in 1953 – amidst the ballyhoo of a Coronation year and the stupid bastards with their flag-bedecked street parties. Here, of all places, but I do go on, don't I, so I'll stop Here! – I showed the two love letters to her. Gwennie was my mother. I had had nothing to do with her and no contact with her until the letters came through the post in late 1952. They'd been sent to the address of my cousin Jimmy's mother, her sister, long deceased, and so then passed onto me by him. It seems I had a half-brother and he wrote, at her "dying request" he

said, from Birmingham to give me the correspondence.
Nothing else. No message. No explanation. Frankly, I did
nothing. Not even a reply.

Your own mother's curiosity was something else. She
worked out Llanwern to be, possibly, the country house,
ironically enough demolished in 1952, and "David" or
"Dai" to be D.A. Thomas, the coalowner of ill repute, so
far as I'm concerned, who became Lord Rhondda in
1915. Well, well, I hear you say. If true, the capitalist
bastard was shagging my proletarian mam. Joke here, eh
Billy? And, bigger joke yet, I was the bastard she was
carrying, to be born on 28 December, Holy Innocents'
Day, 1915. Or not so wholly innocent, as it turned out.

Margaret, his daughter, was still alive. I sent her a
polite note, asking for information and hopefully a
meeting. I'd copied the letters and – foolishly, maybe –
sent her the originals. I heard nothing back. But, egged
on by your mother, I did some research, became hooked
and even after she died, leaving you bereft and me a mess,
and both of us alone, I tinkered until I thought I might
write something about him. You have the fragments in
the suitcase. So you'll see I got so far and trailed away.
With no regrets, I must say. I'd seen what I needed to see.

There's just one more capstone. The letter inviting me
to meet Margaret came after your mother had died. I
hesitated to go and, truthfully, in the end did it because I
could feel Mona, your lovely and wonderful mother,
urging me to square the circle. Well, I guess I did and I
didn't.

Oh, Lady Rhondda was pleasant enough. And very
grand, her flat more intimidating, with knick-knacks and
occasional tables and paintings, than any home I'd ever
been in. Also there were photographs of him, and her,

separately and together in chased-silver frames. I'd seen photos of him in the books. No resemblance there I could see. Can you?

Anyway, she told me that my mother had been "rather a forward young woman." "Pretty", she'd grant, "but decidedly forward." It was possible, "likely but regrettably" she said, that her father, under some strain and relaxed by the sun he sought, "took advantage" or "was possibly seduced" by the dark-haired seventeen-year-old from Pontypool who'd been in service with them for over a year. Margaret added that she thought it "most unlikely" that my mother, at that age and coming from where she came, was "altogether innocent in such things".

That much was conceded but no more. In her opinion my mother was as likely to be pregnant with the child of the chauffeur, Blackmore, or maybe someone from the village, as she was with the offspring of a man nearing sixty, one afflicted with rheumatic fever and a heart condition. As for his letter, it was a recognition of their tryst and of her condition, and of his generosity and nothing more. My mother did indeed return, with her son, to Llanwern, in the spring of 1916.

By December that year D.A. Thomas was President of the Local Government Board and in Lloyd George's cabinet, and absent, by and large, from Llanwern thereafter until his final ill health and lingering death in the summer of 1918. She said that she believed relations between her father and the parlourmaid had ceased long before. Margaret, for so I will insist on calling my half-sister, said she "vaguely" remembered me and "vividly" recalled my being discovered in a high chair, "in an almighty mess", the day after my mother absconded, at the age of twenty, without "so much as a by your leave" and only a note to the effect that her sister in Aberdare be contacted to come to fetch me. And where indeed I did live until life and strength and war conspired to take me away. But that's another story, for another time.

I could have argued with her. I did demur. I said the letters seemed proof enough. That I had only wanted to meet her. I was ready to leave, when she softly, very softly, said she was indeed sorry. Perhaps there was more to it than she had wanted to know or believe. She had found it so difficult when her father, stricken with angina, sat in the semi-wild garden at Llanwern, amongst the spring flowers with his gramophone playing his favourite tunes from musical shows, my mother sat at his feet or dancing in front of him, whilst I tottered across the lawn. On the morning he died, Margaret forbade my mother directly from going to his cremation and to the subsequent burial of his ashes, which she planned to place beneath the ancient yew tree in the churchyard. My mother did not wait for any change of heart. She left the house forever, and me of course, on 4th July – did she know it was Independence Day? Why not? He, who wished to be an American would surely have told her that – the day after he died. Margaret said – and these were her very last words as I stood to go – "I do not expect you to forgive me, David. I do not even expect you to understand. But I loved him. And him alone. And I wanted you, of all people, to know that before I, too, die." You know me well enough, Billy, to know I neither wanted nor asked for nor received anything else. Besides she had shown no interest in my life, not Cassino or the pits or anything, not in Mona or in you. Why didn't that surprise me, I wonder. So sod her, I thought. And all that the foul air around her brought with her. We had no need of it. Then or now. My half-sister died in Westminster Hospital just a few weeks after we had met for the first and only time.

I have mulled it over, and over, of course, again and again the past few years since your mother died. And I decided to let it all go, for me at least. But I determined that one day you should, if the occasion arises, know the connections for yourself. That they are significant I do not doubt. What it means as we go on I don't know. Will you? I suppose that he was ours as much as we are his, but I certainly do not think by any meaningful ties of blood or personal relationship. Only the unbreakable, inexorable, irredeemable bonds of a society which has been as little as it has been so much and as hopeful as it has been wretched.

Love (of course)

From Dad

* * * * *

I lay back on the bed amongst the rubble of my old man's literary excavations. I had been spun back to a beginning I had not suspected. In the early years of a new century I was being told the false dawns had all come and gone, and the one that might have been was, in changed ways and circumstances now of course, the only one from the early years of the last century which had offered a glimpse of the actually possible. A final wake-up call. I was not remote from that. I was a living part of it. It was, then, pure sentiment to dream of any way other than through the order and gradation and acceptance of discipline that leadership and vision offered. Ceri had discovered the hard truth of this for himself, just as the old man had once invested it in the Party, and his own lost and found father had secured it in the management of the affairs of men and women whose lot was to labour, but not, he would say, in vain. All this I weighed up and now understood in a detail and with a specificity I had not possessed before. Ceri would have his answer. I'd phone him in the morning. He could do what he liked after that.

Friday

Haf picked me up, as arranged, at nine in the morning outside the hotel. She was leaning against her car. She was parked in a taxi rank but effortlessly protected from their professional wrath. The rain had stopped. She raised her right hand in a wave and dropped the cigarette in her left. There were no half measures about the smile. I liked that smile. I could grow to like someone who could smile like that at nine in the morning. She looked as if she'd just stepped out of the shower, shaken her hair, tied together a tight cardigan, dark green, over a tight T-shirt, a white one, pulled on jeans, blue, and boots, black, and was ready to go. She'd more than do. She was an energy burst to cancel my sombre mood and grey suit, which was ageing me despite an open-necked magenta sports shirt. I gave her a paternal hug and a kiss on her cheek. I had told her what I had done and what I intended to do if other things did not happen that morning. She smiled.

She drove carefully and skilfully out of the traffic dodgem-ride that was the city centre. We were going east through avenues full of lofty semi-detached villas that gave way to retail warehouses and elongated superstores, until we finally made it to the motorway. She pushed the Clio as much as was possible and the needle flickered gallantly around seventy in the slow lane. We exited to the north, through the overspill estates that marked the city's boundaries, and up into a switchback succession of interlocking valleys, seeking out the new bypass roads that kept the narrow terraced streets well away from us.

The roads cut across the slopes instead of following contours. They seemed the latest way to ignore all these settled places. In Haf's car, window-gazing was easy. She couldn't go quickly enough to cause any blurred vision. So I caught the salute of a thousand satellite dishes above or below, whichever way the road *is this a joke or a mistake?*

swooped or rose, and felt the sinister ranks of stuka pines – the biggest forestry plantation in an industrial area of Europe, Haf had told me – bristle above the topmost terraces like a buzz of crew-cut hair. I wondered if anyone could now recall these valleys as once properly industrial. They certainly weren't really post-industrial. More like shagged-out-and-thrown-back formerly industrial. Her own politics were young politics, green shoots and all that, but not cosily environmental, more angrily mental. She said she worked with groups who were out to occupy the husks of institutes with a virtual and alternative culture based around community time-sharing. I must have looked blank. It was people, she said, who mattered for her, who "made" a place. I let that one pass. It was why she'd told me she'd been so bothered by the book of my *Crazy Horse* exhibition. I had, she'd felt, blotted out the people, the good with the bad. I told her I didn't do those categories, even then. But Haf was too intense to let that pass. Blotting out human faces was denying them their humanity. I had disassembled them into machine-like pieces. I was not seeing anything beyond fragments. I had to put them together again. I said I'd hoped I was acknowledging a spirit that could not be seen or captured, only remembered. She said that now she didn't understand. That there was no sense in having memories that did not serve life.

We left it there for a while, though we weren't seeing much life ourselves as we climbed higher and further until we came on the eastern rim of the former coalfield to one of the old iron and coal townships almost at a valley's end, and even then we didn't stop but left behind its great clefts of re-planted landscape and the concrete silos and sheds of the dead steelworks, on whose re-claimed acreage the windows in clusters of executive houses now winked hopefully in the fitful sunlight. We followed the signs that proclaimed, in stylish blue-and-gold Euroscript, *Canolfan Cymoedd Dyfodol* : Future Valleys Centre. The road took us through a gothic arch, a stone gateway, down a drive through a thickly wooded deciduous copse with ornamental ponds and lichened statuary hidden behind glossy evergreen shrubbery bushes. The square coalowner's house that had long ago become council offices waited at the end of a rutted and potholed drive, but to its right a newer strip of road led us on to a glass and chrome cube, the *Canolfan*. The car park was to the side and the back and already full of cars more recent and gleaming than Haf's French banger. She lined it up between a black Saab convertible and a steel-grey Golf.

The short walk back to the *Canolfan* gave us the 360° perspective on the higher hills of an escarpment above us and the wooded slopes, screening any unsightly human habitation, below us. At the entrance to the *Canolfan* I waved an embossed press card and steered Haf, with a knowing smile at the doorkeepers, into the downstairs atrium. A couple of hundred people were either queuing up for coffee at long linen-covered tables or clutching their cups and moving thoughtfully in the very centre of the space around a glass-covered dome in which a model of the proposed development sat. Haf and I skipped the coffee and went straight for a gawk. The modelled development ascended in pentagon-like building pods from the lower wooded slopes above the valley townships until they scattered, seed-like, around the *Canolfan* on this flatter ground and then climbed again, built into the walls of the escarpment, nestling in abandoned quarries, colonising mountain pools and rivulets as in the trajectory of a waterfall going in reverse. The model's landscape had been sculpted with an eye for the detail of the terrain, down to tinted pathways and the painted-in re-planting, a colour scheme of sage green and eggshell blue hinting at an outdoor/indoor Georgian idyll. But the pods, the capsules, were the thing. They were individual pentagons of glass-fronted rooms, set above a car port with carousel elevators, each one three tiers high and capped by roofs of weathered pine that were pitched at 20° angles so they almost appeared flat. The pods were interlinked by tubular glass and steel passageways leading from their second tiers. What made their uniformity somehow organic was the support structure each one had. Their skeletal frames of matt-burnished steel were legs which stood at different angles and heights depending on the lie of the land. They looked as if they were adjusting their weight and stance to embrace the earth on which they squatted. Here and there the architect had dotted a few expensive-looking cars, a number of tanned and suited men and women who even in their mannequin form seemed cheerfully at ease, powerful. And, positioned at car doors, in front of elevators, in the shrubbery there were other figures, more bowed and in attendance, a platoon or two of servants.

All around us was a murmur of approval. You could tell which particular man-and-womankind these spectators envisaged as themselves. Haf was giving wall maps and diagrams a scholarly look that told me she knew the topography by heart. I guessed that Maldwyn had sectioned this moonscape of iron and coal patches into a forensically planned mapping of further ownership and later availability that would have given the Domesday Book compilers a run for their money. Or his money. It wasn't a scam, of course. It was a strategy. A magnet. Be attractive if you want to attract. Silly me, as Ceri had told me. Haf had displaced any emotional revenge she might have wanted to feel into what she saw as a more acceptable vengeance against these predatory exploiters, these fat cats, establishment bigwigs, land speculators, people movers, and here in this sanitised sanctum a whole ragbag of green and environmental and humane instincts flooded her cheeks, and made her blush with righteousness. Me, I couldn't see anything wrong with personal revenge, the quicker the better. Outside, Sir Ceri's black, chauffeur-driven Audi had pulled up. I saw Gwilym simultaneously emerge from a shoal of notables like an oil slick in search of a better beach. That would be Ceri, then. I'd forgotten how gestures had changed. The European creep, even here. In the old days, between old friends, a nod of the head and a grip of a handshake. But, here, now, Gwil actually embraced Ceri, who, in turn, did not stiffen. They were almost kissing. Ceri turned, smile at the ready, and then the wince did come, in the shape of a frown directed my way. I had been standing to make sure that I was in his eyeline. I positively beamed. My mouth cracked open so wide that it could have accommodated the San Andreas fault line. He looked hard at Haf. He would have read the letter. This was my counterstrategy. And I could tell it had disturbed him. Then things got even better.

Maldwyn's nose was squashed into a wrap-around bandage. His eyes were two small blood oranges, peeled, and the cuts and abrasions to his cheeks were a homage to the memory of Tommy Farr's seventh round against Joe Louis in 1937, as told to me by the old man. I don't recall Tommy having a broken arm after his slugfest with Joe, but my Tommy had given Mal one, for sure, if that sling was anything more than a fashion accoutrement. The conspirators huddled together. Ceri had changed colour when he saw Mal up close and personal, from ruddy to off-white. Gwilym had coloured in the contrary fashion, the real sign of amateur embarrassment in public that Ceri had long sloughed off. And Mal just stood there, his facial tints way off the chromatic scale of any palette used since Matisse completed a painting of his wife in green and crimson. I wondered about his teeth since his full, oh-so-kissable lips were split and scabbed. He opened them, with some difficulty, to spit something out. I muttered an "Oh" out loud with a soft purr of appreciation since there were at least two teeth missing, and his smart-arse tongue was swollen into inarticulacy.

Sir Ceri could see that standing about was no good, that action was needed. He moved forward and onwards, the smile back in place, whilst Maldwyn hung back, consigned to his wake, with just Gwilym bobbing along beside him into the hall. Haf and I were swept along as the crowd moved in. We were close enough now to see Bran on Ceri's other side, where his bulk had protected her from view. Mal, flanked by Wheelie who had pushed open the double-doors for him, limped down the aisle to sit in the front row. There were about two hundred chairs in the inner auditorium, rows of gilt-framed red plushed seats for the expectant backsides of councillors, estate agents, businessmen, journalists, accountants, politicians, academics and developers. A panoply of the professionally purposeful. We sat near the back and watched as the stage party assembled. The backdrop was a screen displaying the words:

Canolfan Cymoedd Dyfodol
Future Valleys Centre

And to the bottom right:

Tir y Werin : *Bywyd y Werin*
A People's Land : A People's Life

To the side and behind the stage party were ten foot-high pop-ups with pictures of past, present and glorious future. There was a podium with a microphone to the left, and shiny metal boxes with pinprick blue lights. The local Mayor thanked everyone, introduced Dr Gwilym Jones, and quickly sat down. Gwilym puffed himself up like a pouter pigeon, made a few stirring remarks about historical oxygen levels, social adrenalin, and the valleys heritage – all just broken and breached ramparts apparently – before switching to a PowerPoint presentation that hailed the foresight of civic leaders, business entrepreneurs and academic creativity, all of which was set to propel us from this very base camp to the Himalayan heights we would need to ascend, socially and culturally, from the foothills of entrepreneurial endeavour where we were now stranded by our past. It was, all in all, to be a quick two-step into the future. Gwilym gushed a little more about the combination of architectural genius and locality which we had beheld in the model in the atrium, a sure-fire Gold Medal winner when built, in his opinion, and how it was making use of the sole real attribute that was left to "our people" – I liked that "our" – namely, the landscape, blighted or pristine, contaminated once, now cleared for use, an "Alpine Echo" which we, in our inane yodelling up and down the streets of a defunct past had failed to register as our true legacy. But here it was at last, caroming off the higher slopes of the foresight of our truly visionary leaders, to invigorate those below who could now look up, and hear the call. Gwilym's speechifying flourished, on and on, for ten minutes, with more and more exotic blooms pulled from behind his back, out of his sleeves and out of his mouth, as the screen behind him dispensed with its headlines, slogans and logos, to flash images, from black and white and grey miserabilism to the cool, sharp pictography of the architectural present, and on to the fully imagined and animated hub that was our "only hope", our very own patch of kryptonite, the super-messiah of a Future we must embrace, otherwise we perish. He ended with an introductory paean of over-the-top praise to Ceri which relished the great, self-made, articulator of the best we had been and the better we could be, in the person of the man who had, at this late stage in his distinguished career, agreed to head up the consortium that would deliver the *Canolfan* from concept to full reality in the next five years. Sir. To a ripple. Ceri. To a wave. Evans. To a crash. Applause. And Ceri diffidently rising, but at last on his feet. Alert, as ever, to the mood. Aware, instinctively that Gwilym had lost the audience, minutes ago, with his burbled boosterism and digital flash cards. Ceri walked slowly from his reserved seat in the front row to the podium. He paused. He began,

"Thank you. All. And thank you, Dr Gwilym Jones. Friends, I'm afraid I can't, this morning, match the informative flow of all that eloquence. And, as for pretty pictures, well, as you know, I don't do those. Technically incompetent, me. I fear I am, in my own person, my very own PowerPoint presentation!"

Laughter. A self-deprecating smile. And he leaned forward into the audience. Somehow, no longer speaking at them or to them but being, at one, in speech, with them. A conversation in all senses except for the fact that it was only him doing the speaking. I felt that I had come only to learn that, sink or swim, Ceri would not drown. I just still wasn't absolutely sure which shore he would strike out to reach.

"Where flattery is so shameless, Mr Chairman, blushing thanks are always inadequate – I must remember to come back sooner and stay longer. Does wonders for my self-esteem: political Viagra never felt better. And all this vigour on my home patch. For here, of course, I really am at home. Amongst friends, some very old friends. With comrades, unfashionable word for what we thought ourselves to be once. In the justest of causes.

Home ground. As I said. Names and places I carry with me wherever I now go. And sometimes, nowadays, there *are* only names to remember for some places long gone. Names, my friends, which are, still, for some of us like a roll call of battle honours. Battles fought. Some won, and most lost. Always with honour.

I drove here, up the valley, to this green and hopeful place this morning on our new bypass roads. Naturally I therefore passed around or looked down on townships and villages and streets upon whose very formation more clichés have been bestowed than we might hear in a bishop's Easter sermon. The sentiment is put there, precisely, like the roads themselves to avoid the close-up look. In every sense, we have been by-passed.

Even perhaps betrayed. Yes, I think so. A betrayal. But, as ever, of what, by whom? Betrayed by successive governments – whatever their political hue – fobbed off with the empty promises of empty warehouses, empty factory spaces, empty industrial estates. Betrayed by local government, too, in my very own vineyard of endeavour, where too often a want of imagination has been in cahoots, too many times, with a lack of faith. And betrayed from within. Betrayed by the feral, the anti-social, the resentful, the feckless who betray themselves by betraying the generation to come, and the memory of those who have been! And, for the rest, we close our doors. We blank our minds. We are atoms without fission. The chain of reaction amongst us is a mere flicker of yesteryear. And betrayed too by me. By people like me. Maybe, most of all because we have ceased to be the advocates. We speak, too often now, like the dummy on the ventriloquist's knee.

Why? *Because* we still cling to a learnt mantra. One which declares that however much is changed, all around us, materially for the better if spiritually for the worse, that, still, our values, our core sense of communities and cohesion remains one to cherish. Bollocks! It's all bollocks, and you know it, because the whole edifice was built on a concatenation of forces that cannot be repeated, or even sustained. It is arrant nonsense to suggest we can regenerate all that has withered on the vine with buckets of social manure, vials of economic potassium and dollops of cultural bio-energy.

And that is why we are here today, is it not? Able at last to speak out truthfully because of the ark of this stunning project which we are able to float amidst the deluge, even in our wreckage. You have seen the plans. You have seen the scale models. You have noted how the architects of this spaceship of hope explain and illustrate their vision. Let me remind you of it. Only the landscape can be our salvation now, and only if it is returned from the depredation of industry and restored with care and expert attention. At the tops of all our valleys. Attention paid to that detail of waterfall, rock screes, copses with real trees, not the suffocating blanket of pine trees sown for profit. Only then will we truly attract new blood, new energy, new money, new owners. Friends, the fantasy of a cultural tourist trade, buoyed up by industrial museums and heritage trails, is the chimera of a 1980s dream that was always fantasy. A jerky reaction to a History vanished. Instead they tell us now, our expert carers, that at the mouths of our fabled gulches, near cities and motorways, we can indeed gather and commute to work but that, *here*, we must see that landscape is all. Not mean streets. Not meaner people. But a beauty of natural shape or form that can entice others, provided we ensure that entry in and exit from the mothership, is pleasurable and painless. The Valleys, our valleys, to find their final destiny as … a national park. The newest. The latest. The best.

The Vision, this new dream, by-passes the detritus of our past, by shutting it out. At last a future that is made afresh, clean and whole, not one regenerated piecemeal and messily. This future will open up, properly, at veritable gates – gates through whose portals we will funnel the work done for the spaceship – the cooks and chefs, the cleaners, the gardeners, the drivers, the bar staff and waitresses, the electricians and plumbers and carpenters, the brickies, security men and receptionists and telephonists, to all who will ensure that the new, and perhaps, why not passing-through inhabitants? are protected to think, secured to relax and gated to be special. That army of workers will, naturally, come and go every day, their pockets clinking with the gold with which their labour has been bought."

* * * * *

He paused to let a burst of clapping punctuate his speech. He had moved effortlessly to the shore I did not have in mind. Then he continued, his tone imperceptibly sharper, his blend of demotic speech and oratory mixed for the occasion as ever. Ceri had not lost it. I had underestimated him.

"You're right to applaud! What else have we been trained now to do? How else can we think? What, after all, can be wrong with turning our people into peons? What's amiss with losing the haphazard hits of cultural tourism by replacing it with colonial settlements? We once made an art out of our very selves – in politics and in our common culture – why not become the artefacts necessary for the greater lives of others? I have, my friends, been giving this a great deal of thought. My conclusions are neither comfortable nor easy for me to state in front of the partners with whom I have worked on this enterprise, an enterprise that could, of course, work. But I have concluded, only at the cost of being an even greater betrayal than any we have yet experienced.

It would betray the one thing we still uniquely possess

– our collective DNA, our sense of ourselves – and that is: our own history. We can never re-live it. We shouldn't want to, but we cannot be ourselves without it. It cradles the essence of what once gave us purpose. And you know what? That isn't heart and soul and sentiment. It isn't nostalgia. It's intellect. We thought once not just of what would improve some lives, but how to make it happen for all. In education, in and out of school, in the ambitions of our parents and the aspirations we had for each other at work and play. We created institutions that were indeed collective and voluntary, from trades unions to brass bands, from choirs to rugby teams, a committee not as a tired joke but as a director of purposefulness. Our people came together initially for the purpose of work and wages, but out of mere aggregations of people they created – one way or the other – communities of purpose. Are we to let all that achievement drift? Are we to spurn our potential to make our heritage a creative one again?

We must, even at this late stage, think with our imaginations not our slide rules. I propose in place of this gated commune for visitors, a new city on the hill for ourselves. On this land, in this place, let us create galleries to show our art, and wipe away the cataract of clichés that make us blind and others myopic. All landscape and no mindscape, my friends, makes Dai a dull boy. Let us create here space for studios and performance where our young musicians and film-makers and writers and dancers can come, on generous bursaries for residence, mentored by the best international talents we can muster. Let us remember that the miners' institutes and welfare halls were, with their book-crammed libraries and lecture halls, once the brains of the coalfield, and let us find space here for Institutes of Learning that can envision, not just administer or tinker with, a future. Let there be conferences, and debates, seminars and festivals, of music and theatre and science and sport and video and film, a sculpture park and a garden setting for the best of contemporary public art. Let it be open, let it be young, and let it be ours. A centre that both radiates out and connects inwards.

You know we have the tools and the means for it. But what we must have, here today, now in this place at this time, is the will. We must resist the cry that there is no alternative. You know who said that first, don't you? If we resist its lie we can create a future that comes from us and for us. Will you help me?

I am formally proposing this morning that we establish a new charitable trust, endowed by the funds hitherto received by Tir Werin who will, I know, freely give up prior claim to all the land they own, and the cash flow. The new trust – the Haf Trust, for this will be our summer of content – will elect members from communities across the Valleys to serve with elected and nominated members of the arts and sports community, backed by university expertise, even supplemented, perhaps, by a politician or two! I will be happy, if asked, to serve as an interim founding chair and drive this idea into a shape that makes it an international beacon of excellence. Have no fear that Europe will not support us on this. They will welcome the initiative. They will applaud a brave experiment. Will you? Will we? We must.

It is time, my friends, to become comrades once again, if only in an endeavour of this kind. The only gate to the present we ever need is that symbolised by Janus, who looks both backward and forwards in order to progress.

I expect to be accused of idealism. I have been accused of worse. I expect to be pilloried for impracticality. I have learned little in a long life of anything that benefits us at all by following the narrow lines of rigid practice. I only wonder that we have not done this before. We have been atrophied, as I have been, by the shrivelling social veins of the culturally timid. If I seem, here today, to return to the political roots some claim I have spurned, think again! I am re-freshed not restrained by that past. Political life, we once understood, was what made us, together, free, because it made us, individually, engage with what we had in common. Our very humanity. Then, we did not hide away in the fearful corners of our spluttering, individual lives. We had so little we made the sacred flame of our values immense. We possessed nothing so we owned everything. And the chosen life of a man or woman in public life was the valued gift of a people which wished to make its voice heard wherever the silence of submission still held sway. Those voices were from the chorus, and it is time to hear that chorus sing out their music again, so that, together, we may drown out the siren calls of despair and helplessness.

I read academic papers that tell me that we have been cursed by the twinned poverty of deprivation and the poverty of aspiration. But I know now that these were mere descriptions of the despond into which we sank, buoyed up by occasional sweetmeats and fair promises. I know now, with all the fibre of my being, that we have misplaced our proper weapons and must pick them up again if we are to end our poverty of intellect through fresh imagination, and replace our poverty of purpose with the dream of a city on the hill, one whose name and spreading presence will become legion."

* * * * *

I'd like to say that when he finally sat down next to an ashen Maldwyn and a bewildered Gwilym that the ripple of applause near the platform turned into the bravos and cheers I felt in my heart. Instead there was an uneasy silence. The hacks, who had no handouts for this, could scarcely have kept up with the outpouring, and the rhetoric was as unexpected as it was strictly retro. I caught Ceri's ever-alert eye. He winked. He actually winked. He was off the hook, at least with me, and he knew it. If the thing he outlined lived, then all praise was his. If it stumbled and fell at any hurdle, then he was blameless for the failing of others. The money had passed hands, sure, but that would not be a story to reveal now. Gwilym would play the broker role that had always suited him. The business plan would be re-written, and Maldwyn would seek revenge. Sometime, somewhere. Bran would shrug and turn it into a PR triumph which, she'd claim, she'd been hatching all along. A committee would indeed form. But it would need Haf as well as Ceri to drive it. They would make, maybe, a suitable kind of father and daughter. Perhaps they were already. I saw Haf applauding and smiling. Ceri smiled warmly back. I felt a deep sadness. It was all starting again. All wrong. Nothing had changed. Nothing would alter. Energy would gravitate to the darkness we could not escape.

* * * * *

I left Haf to find her way through the press huddle to Ceri. They would have lots to do together. And lots to learn about each other. Outside I found Bran waiting for me.

"Did you think I'd disappear, slink off with my tail between my legs?"

"Or whatever," I said.

294

"That's cheap, even for you."

I agreed. "So what now?" I asked.

"The truth, of course."

"I know too much of that."

"Not all, you don't."

I had had a bellyful of her poised ambiguities. It was over. I wanted it dead. I wanted to hurt. So I just said it as it was for me.

"Look, Bran, I know you – not even you would try to arrange it so that Maldwyn, for whatever sick purpose, would sleep with Haf, not even you would do that. But I also know you told him he wasn't the father to hurt and humiliate. And telling Haf it was, perhaps, me, to make for confusion and longing, and what you did fucked her up more than was bearable, didn't it? And I think she still is. I'm assuming it really wasn't me. You'd have used that if it had been. I hope to God, for your sake as much as hers, that it really isn't Mal. So who? Home comforts for Tommy, a bit of rough? Or, and my best guess, if Ceri later why not then?"

She surprised me one last time.

"You poor bloody fool," she said. "Is that what you think? Really think?"

"Could be, couldn't it?"

"Could have been but wasn't. And as I told you it wasn't you. By a whisper, but not."

"Then who?"

"Your old man," she said.

I flinched. I wanted to hit her. I nearly did.

"You're a bloody liar," I said, but I knew it was not a lie. She would not have said it as a lie. Not like that. So she told me the truth. In detail. How when I had left, after the exhibition, she had gone to see him, not with anything in mind, just to talk, about me and her and how so many things beyond both of us had gone wrong. How he'd cried. I'd never seen him cry. How she'd held him and stroked his hands. I hadn't held him close since I was a boy. How a hug had led to an embrace, that she kissed him, and he sighed. That they'd made love, and it had been only once but she'd timed it back after Haf was born, and she was certain. It could have been me. It happened to be him. Haf was my half-sister. Bran said she never saw my old man after that. He had died within a couple of months. Pneumonia and his wrecked lungs killed him. She'd gone, with Ceri, to the funeral. Mal had moved in before then. When Haf was born, he thought it was just a slightly premature birth. She looked to see if I was shaken. I was.

* * * * *

In the car park a taxi from the city was waiting for me. I walked towards it. From behind a hand touched my shoulder. Haf.

"Are you going? Don't go. Stay," she said.

"It's done. You can turn this around," I said, not truly believing it, but hoping for her sake. "Use the trust. Use the money. Use Ceri. You don't need me, Haf."

She grasped my hand and spoke softly to me, as if to a child.

"Do you think I really believe him? It has to be done differently. Slowly. With no let-up. You need to be here."

I looked closely at her. Not quite able to trust myself to take in what she was saying.

"You need us, Billy," she said.

* * * * *

The dream through which he had been drifting had ended, even if the tangle within it had not been resolved. He would have to tell his sister who she was. That would define who he was as well. A camera would still be as hard to pick up and use to any purpose, as would untangling those threads. He knew the two acts would be connected. He knew that he would need to try again to look at faces, with and without a viewfinder, and with a perception more raw than his skills had once allowed him. He would settle for less if it meant more than just being an observer, a recorder, a cheerleader, an exile. There were some dreams which stayed with us. If only we could recall them. If only we could see. If only we made their reality integral to life. At least, he thought, his old man, in homage and echo, would have said that it was pretty to think so.

"FOR IN THE LAST ANALYSIS IT IS HUMAN CONSCIOUSNESS WHICH IS THE SUBJECT MATTER OF HISTORY."

MARC BLOCH *THE HISTORIAN'S CRAFT* (1949)

Birth Certificate(s)

He didn't have one. As he told the boy, this had occasionally made for problems in his life, but mostly with whichever authorities he was confronting at the time. So the Army had been one such, and the worst as such. Mostly he had just managed, uncertified so to speak, he'd say, to live, and then love, without one. He had been born, that was clear but not, for whatever reason and by whichever sleight of a powerful hand, ever registered. This made him, and he grinned whenever he said it, a real, legitimate bastard.

By extension, he claimed that the world, his very particular and specific part of it, was a mongrel one. Which suited him, he said. Gave him a kind of natural-born ease of entry into such a haphazard breeding ground. The boy, intermittently bombarded with all this, was never sure, not then at least, how much he was meant to understand, or even believe.

What mattered more to the boy, at least then, was the man more than his words. He would wait after school until a summery dusk dropped, at the bottom of the steep hill at whose top they lived, until he heard the distinct light tenor of the BSA's engine thrum in the air before the bike, with its stocky and darkened driver hunched over its jet black frame, came into sight. His father would cut back the engine to an idling putter so that he could reach out with his one free, muscled arm to hoist his son, wordlessly and instinctively, onto the pillion seat behind him. The boy would clutch his father around the stomach as they took off, in a rough perpendicular hurry, up the hill to home.

He had never learned to drive. In these years, twenty or more after the war had ended, cars had finally proliferated and had begun to crowd onto the space once used for games and talk in narrow streets. He kept to his motorbike, and rode it, as he'd done in the Army, as if he was fleeing something, never arriving, always leaving. So the boy would hold him as tight as he could, his hands clasped together, with fingers intertwined to a whitened pressure, feeling his father's body tense beneath a billowing shirt, and they would scramble up and across the intercutting ledges of streets until they turned into the top street beneath the mountain's edge. The boy only wanted to grasp at his father's fleeting presence. Neither exits nor entrances interested him in those hold-fast days.

Yet, they obsessed his father even as, all around him, a kind of settling was being accepted by others. Sometimes he'd say to the boy, and it would be more in exasperation than resentment, you'd think that with all we, they, us, have been through – and a sweep of a cigarette-wielding hand would take in the life histories of a generation more scarred than cosseted – that memory would never dwindle, that brains would remain fluid for action, not scrunch up like dessicated walnuts only fit for someone else's nutcracker of indifference. For a time, he'd insist, there had been a chance, just a chance, for quivering change. Now, he'd say, to capture again the textured moment of that you had to admit, and it was a defeated confession, that you had to be able to feel it, there and then, as it was. To express it you would need to show it, all of it, so that its restless shapes could be understood to have once mattered even as they flattened and subsided. Later, in his view, when those pregnant, few post-war years had been dismissed as a false, ectopic issue, he'd say the time for showing was over, that it would only be a nostalgia trip of social cowardice designed so that the willingly immobile could stay mired in the sweet shit that dribbled down their legs, and stuck them fast. To tell was to be conscious, he said; just to show was to sleepwalk through a life deprived of dreams. Yet, once, he had lived in both ways and he refused to let its pastness be inert. So, he would try to tell the boy by showing him, too.

* * * * *

At almost the very end of the war, in mid-February, 1945 to be exact, he'd caught a troop train dockside in Dover and stood in its steam-fugged corridor for hours, along with hundreds of other temporary escapees on a long weekend's leave from the British Army, then paused at the Rhine before its last thrust. He'd had to change trains twice to cross through the west of England and into Wales. All so eerily familiar and quiescent. He would remember how, when he left the train at the general station the sudden cold stung his cheeks. Soldiers, tough and young as they were, pulled up the collars of their greatcoats, their kitbags and slung rifles nestling closer to their shoulderblades as they hunched up inside their uniforms.

It was towards the end of a Saturday afternoon. The sky was a deep purple, low and livid in the retreating light. He pushed and was jostled in a crowd of civilians and soldiers milling out of the station towards the parked bull-nosed buses, separately liveried out in the metallic colours of their various urban district councils: cobalt blue and clotted cream, coffee and white, emerald green and ochre, and the blocked-in red of his own valley's fleet. Queues, dressed in the wartime drab of worn cloth and darned wool, stood and stamped, and grew anxious. It felt, he said, as if something more than a storm was about to break over them. The intense cold, the temperature dropping minute by minute, actually seemed a shield against the coming storm. Too cold to snow was what he heard muttered all around as the buses opened their doors and filled up. And so it was. But not too cold for the

305

hail which instantly rattled onto the roof of the departing bus as a sudden downpour of rain turned to ice and fell as spherical rocks. Beyond the canopied shelter of the bus stops the roads were carpeted in white grit by the downfall, and the gutters were alternatively clogged with hailstones and a-swirl with twists of running water.

At the outskirts of the city, where the hopeful suburbs of the 1930s had begun and then halted, the sky, darker still now, was riven with the jag of forked lightning which followed, metronomically insistent, on the drumbeats of thunder rolling down from the hills to the north. It was still an hour away from official blackout time when all lights had to be dimmed for the wartime evening, but the home patch to which he had returned was already shrouded by a lowering pall of inky black clouds which scudded across the horizon now that the hailstorm had passed. The clouds were never still for an instant, whether bunched or in skeins, and the darkness they brought was too deep for night itself.

What traffic there was – a few private cars and a bus or two – thinned after a few miles as the road moved into the bottom of the valley. His bus edged forwards with just a pencil line of light from a slit in its headlamps to show the centre line of the meandering road. Nothing was coming down the valley. No people walked on the streets. Shops had closed. After the jokers had exhausted their banter about frogs and locusts, the passengers had fallen silent, one or two leaving at the deserted bus stops in the emptied townships through which they were passing. Then the wind rose again and seemed to rush through and around them and the sky, swept clear of cloud, lightened again, but with the sudden alarm of a flashbulb, a glare that lit every corner, and the rain and the hail spluttered in one last gout as if it had been caught and then dropped from an awning before, as if by a magician's unseen trick on a fully illuminated stage, all was driven away by snow. This snow fell on them not as a soft, downy flutter of flakes but as an avalanche of unstoppable whiteness in a blizzard which, in an instant again, blanked everything out so that the bus, blind and isolated in its road, had to stop, its windows, front, back and sides, caked over in thick inches of ice particles which froze in granulated sheets on the panes and the door.

The bus had been halted in the centre of the small, second settlement in the one, long continuous street that was the valley. The storm of snow and ice and howling wind that made it pile and drift lasted more than half of a bitingly cold hour before it stopped with the unexpected suddenness with which it had begun. Two or three together had to push and shove at the door of the single-decker motor coach before it would open sufficiently against its wall of white. The bus could not move on, and as it turned out no traffic would be on the move again until Monday morning had come and gone. People considered where they might stay, who knew of friends, whether they could walk, and how far. He did not, however, ask or wait. He stepped down from the bus, sinking into the snow, adjusting his kitbag over his left shoulder and pulling his beret tight over his forehead, checking the weighted heft of his weapon by pulling its sling of canvas webbing tighter, and setting off, in a wet stumble over the clumps and crevasses which hid and transformed the world he had known.

No one followed him. He picked his way along the road, choosing lines of least resistance, or on the pavements wherever the snow had blown into mounds in shop doorways or into side alleys. It was a slow march, scarcely a progress, more a crouched inching forward to sideways steps. His heavy woollen trousers were soon soaked to the thigh, and chafed his legs with their scratchy, sodden fibres. The snow melted to ice water where it seeped into his nailed and toe-capped boots, and stayed frozen in the thickness of his socks. He wore no gloves, so switched one numbed hand then the other into the sidepockets of his coat. His face turned a glacial pink in a hissing wind and icy splinters crystallised amongst his eyelashes and pricked his eyebrows when he blinked. He tried not to think, just to move on.

He knew he was trudging past remembered places and the familiar markers of his growing up, and that beneath his feet were coal seams he had once worked, and the main headings that had led him to the coal face. He knew this by a trace of memory and by a sense of what should be there, for under their ghastly burial mounds of snow they might never have existed in any previous form. It was as if all had been made anew, or at least that was the illusion as his boots dinted the virginal white world with their hobnailed tread. Even as he walked a lesser, finer snow filled in the footprints he was leaving behind him through a night as pitch dark as any day he had ever spent underground.

With nothing to see as distinguishing marks he felt as empty as the snow-filled streets. He found thoughts of the war from which he had come, and to which he would yet return, impossible to deny. He thought of it involuntarily. It came in instances and images, and through unexpected lurches of fear in the pit of his stomach and the dryness of his throat. It was of Italy mostly, where the winters had been wet, billeting under canvas bone-chilling, and living was a daily passage through mud and blood. In Sicily, months before all that and the halting of the army at the Cassino bottleneck, there had been sunshine and quick advances, and lemons amongst the olive groves. And in the oak trees there were hidden killers, left behind to pick them off as the Nazis crossed the straits to the mainland, sharp shooting snipers whose deadliness came from nowhere more threatening than thick-leaved branches bending in the breeze that blew off the sea to cool them. He thought of how the anger had built because of a perception, absurd but tellingly so, of the unfairness of such individualised killing. He thought of what they had done to a sniper they had isolated in a small copse to the side of the road on which they had recently marched. The German had shot two of them before they doubled back and surrounded him. He threw down his rifle and half-stood, half-crouched, on a broad branch. He held up both hands, and said something they chose to ignore. They lined him up in the sights of their own guns until Tommy Cross, the battalion's flame-thrower, came to the front. No one spoke. Tommy began at the bottom of the trunk and sent his liquid flames up it, like a molten river running the wrong way, until he burned to a charred cinder the treetop assassin. He'd cheered Tommy on along with the rest of them. The thought of it now was not of regret but of disgust. There was bile rising into the back of his mouth. He stooped to pick up a mouthful of snow and felt its coldness rinse his gums. He spat it out.

Tiredness dulled him again. He forced one foot to lift in front of the other. He did not want to stop. To rest. To knock at any door whose pulled curtains hinted at a light, at a coal fire banked up in a back kitchen. He brushed the fallen, heaped snow off a signpost. Two miles more to go, and three hours gone already since he'd left the bus. At the post he turned left and more steeply up the cwm which would take him to the house and terrace at its cul-de-sac end. He walked in the middle of the road, leaning his body into a high snow bank, and stumbled at its crest against some kind of barrier. He reached out to feel it. Planks of wood, a few barrels, an old chest of drawers, all yanked together in a line, hidden by snow and nightfall. Behind the barricade he glimpsed a pinprick of torchlight. He heard a voice, at once sonorous and officious:

"Halt! Who goes there?"

He told the boy he had recognised the voice. Baritone in the choir and bombastic everywhere else. It was Ikey Isaacs, self-appointed Home Guard for this patch of ground and inveterate reminiscer of his service in the previous war.

"Halt!" said Ikey. "Halt, or I'll shoot!"

His father said – wondrous for which farce or tragedy had brought him and Ikey, colliery official, chapel deacon and local councillor, to this – that he croaked back, "Ikey, boy. It's me. Dai Maddox. From Number 10 Top Row."

"Password", Ikey replied. "Password. Say the Password."

He could see Ikey's bulky figure, his hands fiddling with some sort of outmoded gun, and his moonface, reddened by the cold and wrapped up in a homemade woollen balaclava helmet, looming up above him behind the makeshift wall. He was very tired now.

"I don't know the fuckin' password."

"Password or stay where you are."

"Christ! Ikey. I'm on leave. On foot, see. No buses, right. I fuckin' don't know no fuckin' password but I fuckin' know you, you fuckin' arsehole. Now get out of my fuckin' way."

"No need to be insolent, or foul-mouthed. Rules are rules. The enemy can take advantage in conditions like this. Password comes first."

At which point, his father told the boy, he unslung his own oiled and ready rifle, slid the bolt back with a loud click and jumped up, minus discarded kitbag and all friendly inhibitions, onto the middle plank of the barricade. From there he nestled the rifle's stock into his shoulder and levelled the barrel point blank into the round and incredulous moonface of Ikey Isaacs, Protector of the Rules, and said, "Now move out of the fuckin' way or I'll blow you and your fuckin' password to kingdom fuckin' come."

Ikey sat down with an abrupt and unwanted suddenness, and the stain spread underneath him on the snow. Not the bright crimson stain of shed blood but the tobacco yellow acidity of urine. Ikey had pissed himself. His father shouldered his rifle, retrieved his kitbag and walked on.

* * * * *

The point is, he'd tell the boy when their laughter stopped, that was what he thought then some of it had been about. Home, yes. But a kingdom yet to come. Or if not, what had been the point of lives that were otherwise mere existence, and may as well write the obituary on it all from the off. Yes? No. The boy had learned that all the questions asked were rhetorical. The point was, and in the end it was the only point, to keep asking them. Nothing worth having was worth repeating but passing through was not the same as passing over. You could not answer by default. What was singular, as experience, still had to be connected if meaning was to be derived. Or else life itself was just a discard, so throw the bloody thing away. He said that on Monday, after that freak weather weekend, you could see snowdrops rising up beneath the remaining snow.

His father clung to connection. The boy avoided it as much as he could. Not easy when it was laid before him in such a bewildering variety of ways. The boy had put to one disbelieving side his father's claims to the wartime friendship, via Italy, of the US Army circus entertainer, Burton Lancaster. The movie star's backlist of films was catalogued by his father's memory in days before video recordings. And recounted endlessly to the boredom of the boy who'd scarcely seen them. Then, in 1968 when the boy was ten, his father took him to the new comic Western, *Scalphunters*, in which Lancaster is fur-trapper Joe Bass and Ossie Davis, through capers and hokum, his erstwhile black slave Joseph Lee, educated and mature to Bass's "noble savage". It finished, clumsily but movingly, in a symbolic unity of master and slave, black-and-white, when Lancaster and Davis fist-fight to exhaustion in a mud-hole which cakes their skins to a similarity. They are one. Joe Bass now mounts the horse he has ridden through the movie whilst Joseph Lee has walked behind him, tethered or pulled; but this last time, without looking down, Bass reaches out an arm and pulls Lee, his doppelgänger, up and into the saddle behind him. If it was corny, it was wonderful too. If only for the way his father, in the cool dark of the picture house, gently nudged the boy's ribs, and said:

"See. That's not acting, boy. That's for real. That's what I've been telling you. That's to come. That's Burt, pure Burt. See."

And he did. It was registered with him. How to live a life. Or try. From birth. With or without a certificate.

Dai Smith was born in 1945 in the Rhondda. He was educated in South Wales before reading Modern History at Balliol College, Oxford and Comparative Literature at Columbia University, New York. He has been a lecturer at the Universities of Lancaster, Swansea and at Cardiff, where he was awarded a Personal Chair in 1986, and was subsequently a Pro-Vice Chancellor at the University of Glamorgan. In addition to his academic career, he has also been a broadcaster on radio and television since the 1970s, and he became Head of Programmes (English language) in the 1990s at BBC Wales where he commissioned, presented and scripted a number of award winning documentary programmes and other series. His many publications - books, - articles, journalism - have centred on the dynamics - culture and society, politics and literature of his native South Wales, and most recently have expanded into the form of biography *Raymond Williams: A Warrior's Tale*, memoir *In The Frame: Memory in Society* and the novel *Dream On*.

Dai Smith was the founding Editor of the Library of Wales Series. He has led Arts Council Wales as its Chair since 2006. He holds a part-time Research Chair in the Cultural History of Wales at Swansea University. He lives on Barry Island where he is writing more fiction.

Publications

History
The Fed: A History of the South Wales Miners in the Twentieth
Century
(with Hywel Francis)
Fields of Praise: The Official History of the Welsh Rugby Union
(with Gareth Williams)
Wales! Wales?
Aneurin Bevan and the World of South Wales
Wales: A Question for History

Biography
Lewis Jones
Raymond Williams: A Warrior's Tale

Memoir\Essays
In The Frame: Memory in Society,1910 to 2010

As Editor
A People and a Proletariat: Essays in the History of Wales 1780
to 1980
Writer's World: Gwyn Thomas 1913-1981
The People of Wales: A Millennium History
(with Gareth Elwyn Jones)
A University and its Community: The University of Glamorgan
(with Meic Stephens)
Story 1 & Story 2 The Library of Wales short story anthologies

Fiction
Dream On

Awakening
Stevie Davies

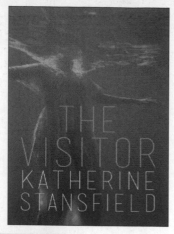

THE VISITOR
KATHERINE STANSFIELD

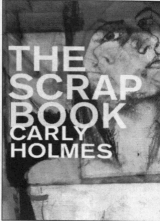

THE SCRAP BOOK
CARLY HOLMES

PARTHIAN

NEW FICTION

'Carries an impressive deal of intensive research lightly ... the portraiture throughout is graphic, richly detailed and subtly shaded'
New Welsh Review

Dream On
Dai Smith

WHILE NO ONE WAS WATCHING

DEBZ HOBBS-WYATT